# THE
# SHEPHERD'S
# WIFE

# THE
# SHEPHERD'S WIFE

## ANGELA HUNT

**BETHANYHOUSE**
*a division of Baker Publishing Group*
Minneapolis, Minnesota

© 2020 by Angela Hunt Communications, Inc.

Published by Bethany House Publishers
11400 Hampshire Avenue South
Bloomington, Minnesota 55438
www.bethanyhouse.com

Bethany House Publishers is a division of
Baker Publishing Group, Grand Rapids, Michigan

Printed in the United States of America

ISBN 978-0-7642-3385-2 (trade paper)
ISBN 978-0-7642-3779-9 (casebound)

Scripture taken from the Tree of Life Version. © 2015 by the Messianic Jewish Family Bible Society. Used by permission of the Messianic Jewish Family Bible Society.

This is a work of historical reconstruction; the appearances of certain historical figures are therefore inevitable. All other characters, however, are products of the author's imagination, and any resemblance to actual persons, living or dead, is coincidental.

Maps are copyright © Baker Publishing Group.

Cover design by LOOK Design Studio
Cover photography by Aimee Christenson

Author is represented by Browne & Miller Literary Associates.

22  23  24  25  26      7  6  5  4

*The Old and New Testaments are filled with stories of daring men and noticeably few courageous women. This is not surprising, for the inspired writers could not recount every story of each man, woman, and child who encountered God. But even though few women's stories are recorded, they are still worthy of consideration. The JERUSALEM ROAD novels are fictional accounts of real women who met Jesus, were part of His family, or whose lives were entwined with the men who followed Him.*

N
W E
S

*Mediterranean Sea*

PHOENICIA

GAULANITIS

UPPER
GALILEE

Chorazin ●          ● Bethsaida
Capernaum ●
Gennesaret ●
● Ptolemais          LOWER    ● Cana    Magdala ●    Sea of    ● Gergesa
                     GALILEE                         Galilee
                                       Tiberias ●              ● Hippos

                     ● Sepphoris

△ Mt. Carmel        Nazareth ●
                              △ Mt. Tabor
                     Nain ●                          ● Gadara

                                          Jordan R.
                                                     DECAPOLIS

● Caesarea          SAMARIA

0        5        10 mi
0    5    10 km

But you, watchtower of the flock,
are the hill of the Daughter of Zion.
To you she will come.

Even the former dominion will come,
the kingdom of the Daughter of Jerusalem.

Micah 4:8

# CHAPTER ONE

# Pheodora

I did not feel like celebrating.

Surrounded by the aroma of roasted chicken and herbs, I looked around the table and tried not to care that the people most precious to me—my eldest brother, my husband, and my mother—were missing. Everyone else had gathered at our childhood home—James, Joses, and Simeon; Jude and his betrothed, Tasmin; Damaris and her five oldest daughters; me and my four little girls. Damaris's youngest, a two-year-old, had remained at home with her grandmother.

"It doesn't seem like Pesach without Ima," Damaris said, passing the bread basket to her husband. "How many Passover dinners has she missed now?"

"Three," Jude answered, glancing at his future wife. "Perhaps next year she will join us."

"Perhaps next year Yeshua will be weary of wandering." From across the table, Simeon met my gaze. "Speaking of wanderers, will we see Chiram anytime soon or will he insist on remaining in Bethlehem?"

I drew a deep breath to suppress a rise of irritation. "You know he cannot leave during Pesach. He has to take the lambs to the Temple."

"But surely there are other shepherds who can do the work. If he cannot come for Passover, why not come to Nazareth for a Sabbath? We do not see enough of you."

Damaris pinned our brother with a stern look. "Leave her alone. The shepherd is with his family often enough— Pheodora has four children to prove it."

"Four daughters." Joses, our youngest brother, flashed an infectious grin. "If he came home more often, he might have had a son by now."

As my other brothers snickered, I lifted my chin. "A shepherd who does not spend his days and nights with the flock is not doing his job. I did not choose my husband's profession, but neither do I fault him for it."

I lowered my head and cast around for a topic to divert attention from Chiram. I could easily turn the conversation toward our missing brother whose activities were a frequent focus of our conversations.

I forced a smile. "Earlier, I was minding my own business at the market—"

"Bethlehem has a market?" Damaris interrupted. "I did not think it big enough."

"It does. But I was in Nazareth, if you must know. And if you will let me finish—"

"Sorry." Damaris inclined her head in a regal nod. "Go on."

I blew out a breath, then began again. "A man came over to me and asked why Yeshua hated the Temple. I said he did not hate the Temple, but the man insisted that Yeshua had said the Temple would be torn down with not one stone left atop another. According to this man, news of Yeshua's prophecy has spread throughout Jerusalem like a plague."

From the head of the table—the place where Yeshua should have been seated—James frowned. "Surely he heard a false report."

"I said the same, but he insisted it was true. The people of Nazareth already think Yeshua is a blasphemer; now they will hate him even more."

Joses nudged me, then nodded at the platter of roasted chicken. I passed it to him, then glanced at my daughters to make sure they were eating. The girls were often too excited to eat when we visited my family, and I did not want them to go to bed with empty stomachs.

Judit had eaten well, while Eden had not taken any vegetables. No surprise, for she had never liked them. Jordan had eaten three of the flat loaves we served in honor of Passover, but Shiri, my youngest, seemed to think the chicken was some sort of plaything. She had tipped her head back and was dangling a scrawny wing above her open mouth as if she were a baby bird waiting to be fed.

"*Shiri.*" I underscored her name with reproach. "We do not play at dinner."

She dropped the chicken wing onto the floor, eliciting a chuckle from my sister. "Leave it," Damaris said, shaking her head. "She is only doing what must come naturally for the daughter of a shepherd. Out in the fields, I would imagine that few men practice proper etiquette."

I stared at my sister, amazed at her audacity, crossed my arms and turned to James. He was now head of the house, so if he was going to lead us in a blessing for the meal we had enjoyed, he had better do it before these young girls—and my sister—completely forgot their manners.

Joses waited downstairs with a lamp, eager to show me the donkey he had borrowed for my trip back to Bethlehem, but Damaris pulled me aside before I could join him.

"Sister," she said, giving me an unusually sweet smile, "I am not sure how to ask this, so forgive me if I seem too forward."

I lifted a brow. "You have never before felt the need to ask forgiveness before speaking your mind."

Damaris shrugged, then her pleasant expression shifted to a look of concern. "I couldn't help noticing that your girls are much thinner than my daughters. Are you sure they are getting enough to eat?"

I drew myself up to my full height, which still left me a handbreadth short of Damaris's. "My girls are slender because they take after their father."

My sister lifted her hands. "I know, and I don't mean to intrude. But if you lack anything—food, clothing, anything at all—you have only to come to me. Write to me, if you must. Shimon will let me give you anything you need. I know it must be difficult to provide for your children when your husband is poor. And he is away from home so often—"

"We are fine, sister." I spoke firmly, because the last thing I wanted from her was pity.

"I know you are. But since we rarely see each other, why don't you spend tonight at my house? The girls can eat sweet cakes and tell stories while we talk all night, just as we did when we were children."

I glanced toward the front door, remembering that Joses waited in the courtyard, then looked at my daughters, all of whom were watching me, their eyes alight. They had been

12

to Damaris's house before and were awed by how different it was from our humble home.

"Surely, Shimon does not want his house filled with giggling girls—"

"Shimon and his father went to Jerusalem for Passover. I do not expect them home for another week, which will give us plenty of time to catch up. Please, Pheodora Aiya, come home with me tonight."

Her use of my full name—an effort she exerted only when she wanted to be especially charming—tugged at my heart. Why not go? After all, I had not seen my sister in months, and my girls always enjoyed playing with their cousins. Her girls were a happy lot, all of them plump and rosy-cheeked from indulging at their prosperous grandfather's table.

"All right." I gestured toward the door. "But I promised Joses I would look at the donkey he borrowed. He seems to think Chiram's knowledge of livestock has rubbed off on me."

"As if you would want it to." Damaris released a charming three-noted laugh, then flashed a quick smile. "I will join you as soon as I have said farewell to everyone else."

I sighed as she went off in search of James and the others.

◈

Damaris and Shimon lived in the elevated section of the city, where homes stood a dignified distance from one another and were festooned with architectural details never seen in the lower part of town. Torches gleamed at both sides of the wide entrance to Damaris's house, and when we reached it she led the way into the courtyard, holding the ornate gate open while our daughters swarmed in and scrambled up the stone steps to the living quarters. Jeremias, Damaris's father-in-law, had enjoyed great success as a merchant, and his house commanded the best view in the city.

After climbing the steps, I took a moment to turn and look east—all of Nazareth spread before me like a sea of buildings settling into the depths of night.

Judit, my oldest, turned as well and caught her breath at the sight of dozens of torches flickering against the gathering darkness. "How beautiful!" she whispered, bringing her hands together. "The little lights below and the stars above . . . do you think Abba can see this from where he is?"

"Your father can certainly see the stars," I assured her, "but if he has left the Holy City, tonight he sleeps in a field, with soft grass for a pillow and the trickling of a brook for music. When he closes his eyes, he will dream of coming home to his beautiful girls."

Judit grinned, and yet I found myself missing Bethlehem. Chiram had been born in the City of David so he loved the little town, and I had come to love it, too. No one in Bethlehem knew my siblings; no one compared me to my beautiful older sister. In Nazareth, with its steep roads and stubborn people, I always felt overlooked and inadequate.

"Come in, all of you." Damaris opened the door, then stood back and smiled as we stepped inside and removed our shoes. Almost reverently we tiptoed into a vestibule that opened to an inner courtyard. To my left lay a wide hallway that led to Jeremias's grand house, and to the right stood the smaller structure Shimon had built for my sister. One day Shimon would inherit the larger home, though Damaris seemed content with her more modest living arrangements. My siblings and I were the children of poor, hardworking parents, so we had never expected to live in luxury.

We moved into the wide, open space of Damaris's living area, and the girls—hers and mine—gathered around her. "Ima, we are hungry," her oldest girl whined. "Can we have something to eat?"

"We just had dinner," Damaris answered, her face twisting in mock amazement. "How can you be hungry?"

Amarisa patted her belly. "I don't know, but I am."

Damaris lifted her empty hands. "I have nothing for you. But if you ask Safta for some honeyed dates, I am sure she can find some for you."

My girls looked at me with pleading eyes.

"Um . . ." I hesitated. "Would your mother-in-law mind—"

"Of course not." Damaris smiled at my daughters. "Follow your cousins and mind your manners. There will be honeyed dates for you, too. Perhaps even a sweet cake."

Judit stopped by Damaris's side. "Is Uncle Shimon home?" she asked, giving my sister a shy smile.

"She likes him," I said. "Probably because he gave the girls copper coins the last time they saw him."

Damaris tugged on Judit's braid. "I am sorry, sweetheart, but your Uncle Shimon is traveling tonight. I am sure he will be sorry he didn't get to see you."

When all the older children had gone, Damaris walked over to a basket where her youngest, a little girl of two, had been sleeping. She picked up the drowsy toddler and moved to a chair, then opened her tunic to let the child nurse.

She looked at me. "Sit," she commanded in her best older sister tone. "The children will eat and play for a while, and then we will put them to bed. But first I want to hear all about life in Bethlehem. How is your husband?"

I sank onto a cushioned bench and tried to relax—in Damaris's house I was always fearful of soiling a pillow or breaking some expensive bibelot. "As far as I know, Chiram is well. He does not get to come home during the weeks before Pesach. He is always out in the fields with the livestock, and then he must herd the animals to the Temple."

Damaris nodded as she shifted her nursing child to a more comfortable position. "I understand what shepherds do, but I will never understand why you agreed to marry one. Even more puzzling is why a shepherd would seek a bride in Nazareth. Were there no virgins in Bethlehem?"

I sighed, not wanting to repeat the answers I had been reciting for ten years. Damaris knew the history of my marriage, so why did she keep harping on it?

"Chiram is a good man," I told her, firming my voice. "And he is wonderful with animals."

"But"—she shuddered slightly—"a *shepherd*! I cannot believe you would marry the lowest of the low, the sort of man who is unable to testify before a judge because everyone knows shepherds are untrustworthy and unable to worship in the Temple because they are consistently unclean, smelling of dung and grass and animals." She closed her eyes. "I would rather remain a virgin than marry such a man. I cannot imagine those odors in my bed."

I was about to argue that Chiram did not smell like a beast, but in truth, sometimes he did. Still, I loved the warm scents that clung to him—the tang of grass and the earthy aroma of his skin and clothing. The natural scent was much more pleasing than the perfume that practically dripped from my sister, particularly when she was trying to impress me.

"Speaking of smells"—I felt a smile curve my lips—"I noticed an unusual aroma when you came into the house tonight. Are you wearing a new perfume?"

"Oh." A dimple appeared in her suddenly rosy cheek. "Not perfume. You were smelling my shoes."

My gaze lowered to her bare feet. "Your sandals?"

"No, I wore slippers to dinner. They are the latest accessory, and the fabric soles are lined with herbs. Every time I take a step, the aroma scents the air. They are very popular in Rome."

"Ah." I lifted my chin. "Your father-in-law."

"Who else? Would you like me to get you some slippers? You would have to wait, because Jeremias will not be going back to Rome right away, but I could always ask him to bring me another pair."

I shook my head. "I would feel silly in those shoes. I will be more comfortable in sandals or bare feet."

"I suppose scented slippers on a shepherd's wife would make as much sense as perfume on a cow."

I bit my lip to stifle a retort, but Damaris didn't seem to notice my reaction. Since marrying Shimon, my sister had enjoyed a sizable promotion in social status, and sometimes I wondered if she forgot we had been raised by a simple carpenter and his wife. Our family home still stood on a crowded street with a dozen others just like it, and on the ground floor my brothers still kept chickens and cats to keep the rats at bay . . .

If Jeremias kept livestock on his property, the beasts must be hidden in the back. I could not smell, hear, or see anything resembling a domestic animal.

Damaris shifted her toddler to her shoulder and patted the girl's back, then looked up as the older children rushed into the room. Her soft-bellied daughters wore tunics of fine linen, their stubby toes peeking out from the hems like rows of stout fence posts. Standing beside their cousins, my girls looked like linen-wrapped twigs.

"To bed now, all of you." Damaris stood and handed me the toddler, then lifted her hands and shooed the other girls toward the chamber where they would sleep on proper wooden beds and mattresses, not straw-stuffed pallets. "We must say our evening prayers, and then I want everyone to sleep. Your aunt Pheodora and I still have to catch up on all the news."

I shifted on the bench, bracing for the inquisition yet to come.

---

By the time the sun rose, I was more than ready to return to my little house in Bethlehem. I tried to leave right after morning prayers, but Damaris insisted on feeding us bread, cheese, honeyed almonds, and fruit, stuffing my children until I thought little Shiri might be sick.

I knew I should be grateful. We rarely had fruit at home; we usually broke our fast with a small dab of goat cheese on bread. My children would not enjoy a meal like this for a long while.

When we finally emerged from my sister's house, I looked up, surprised to see Joses standing outside her gate. "*Shalom aleichem*," he called, waving. "You are looking well, my sisters and nieces."

The girls grinned, and Joses cracked a smile as I came through the gate. "I thought you might be ready to return to Bethlehem. Do you need to go back to the house first?"

I squeezed his arm in a silent expression of gratitude. "Yes, I think the girls might have left a few things. And you are right—I am ready to go home. And I'm grateful you are willing to go with us."

"What else is a brother for?"

I laughed. "I can think of lots of things, but accompanying your sister and her children on a four-day journey isn't one of them."

He grinned. Once we had said good-bye to Damaris and moved down the street, he lowered his voice and winked at me. "I thought you might be ready to talk to someone else. A night of sitting through Damaris's questions would weary even the strongest soul."

"How right you are, brother."

I matched my pace to his and tried to keep my children from straggling behind. "I love my sister, but she kept asking about Chiram. When I said he was fine, she pressed me to say more, almost as if she wanted me to complain about him."

"She has a hard time understanding why you married a shepherd."

"She has made that abundantly clear. But Abba approved of Chiram, and I trusted Abba."

"And you have no complaints about marriage to a man who is rarely home?"

"I knew he lived with sheep and goats when I married him." I gave my youngest brother a teasing smile. "Perhaps that was part of his appeal. After living so long with five brothers, the thought of having a house to myself was attractive. Well, almost to myself. Chiram's father was still living when we married, though he was never any trouble."

"The old man was feebleminded, wasn't he?"

"Yes, but he was kind, never rough or hateful. I don't think he ever realized who I was. He would smile at me and then look out the window. He was always looking out the window."

"Looking for someone in particular?"

"I don't know. He had stopped speaking by the time I

married Chiram, but even when Chiram was home, Eleazar wanted to sit in his special chair so he could watch at the window."

Joses squeezed my shoulder. "You were kind to care for him. Not every new wife would be so gracious."

I lowered my head, embarrassed by the compliment. "I kept remembering what Abba used to tell us—'Even as the broken tablets of the Law were kept in the ark, so old age should be venerated and cherished.'"

Joses smiled as he reached out to stop Jordan, who had been about to run after a kitten. "Stay with us, girl," he said, releasing her braid. "We'd hate to lose you before we start for Bethlehem." Jordan threw him a pouting look, then settled down to walking with her sisters again. Joses grinned at me. "Did you ever dream you'd have a house filled with girls?"

"That was HaShem's doing, not mine."

Joses's eyes gentled. "Though I have not spent much time with Chiram, I like him. Abba wouldn't have approved your betrothal to a man who wouldn't love you."

"He didn't. Chiram does love me." To avoid slipping on the slanting street, I linked my arm loosely through my brother's. "Sometimes, though, especially when the girls are unruly, I wish he would spend more time at home. I would be happy to let him settle our daughters' arguments."

"You can always call on your brothers." Joses patted my hand. "Any of us would be happy to help."

"If you lived in Bethlehem, I would call on you all the time! But honestly, I would feel like a failure if I had to ask for help. None of the other shepherds' wives seem to grow weary or lonely. I see them at the market, their children lined up behind them, and wonder what I am doing wrong. Sometimes I wonder if Adonai meant for me to be a mother."

"If He had not wanted you to have children, He wouldn't have sent them." Joses nodded as if he had settled the question. "Doesn't the Scripture say, 'Blessed is the man who has his quiver full of them'?"

"The man . . . but it's the *woman* who wears herself out." I glanced up at my brother. "I don't want to complain because I love my children. I love my husband and know he is a good man. Yet it is not easy being a shepherd's wife. When Pharisees pass through Bethlehem—something that does not happen often, since none of them would want to live in Bethlehem—they move away when I approach, as if dust from my sandals might get between their toes and defile them."

Joses patted my hand again and made quiet sounds of sympathy.

"That reminds me," I said, catching a fleeting thought. "Is Jude ever going to marry Tasmin? They have been betrothed more than a year. Why have we not celebrated a wedding?"

"Yeshua." Joses bit his lip, as if embarrassed he had answered so quickly. "It's not anything Yeshua has done, but he is attracting too much attention, and Jude doesn't want trouble at his wedding. Sometimes I think James and Jude are sick of all the notoriety, but what can we do? Yeshua is the firstborn of the family, so he can do whatever he wants."

"Ima certainly believes in him," I said, thinking of our mother. "I cannot believe she has stayed away from Nazareth so long."

"She would follow Yeshua anywhere."

I bit my lip when I heard a sharp tone—was it jealousy?—in Joses's voice.

"She will not stay away forever," I promised. "When you and the others are ready to marry and have families, she'll come back. She will want to help with your children and give advice to your brides."

"She hasn't been around to help with *your* children," Joses pointed out. "Like your husband, she seems content to let you handle them alone."

I silently acknowledged his point. But I was accustomed to being overlooked and overshadowed.

I studied my parents' house as we approached. The courtyard gate hung askew, a solitary, tattered grapevine clung to the arbor, and a sad-looking chicken sat on the courtyard wall. Clearly, the woman of the house had been away for some time.

Joses stopped before the gate and turned to me. "You never said why you married Chiram. Did you agree only to please Abba?"

I opened the gate while I considered my response. Why did I marry Chiram? I wasn't sure I could answer in a way Joses would understand.

"I never imagined I would marry a shepherd," I began, idly watching my girls enter the courtyard. "Nor did I ever think I would marry a man who would take me away from Nazareth and my family. I am not sure why Abba brought him to the house, or why he agreed to read Chiram's betrothal contract. All I know is when I saw Chiram, I knew he was meant to be my husband. Abba's agreement to the betrothal confirmed what I felt when I first saw the shepherd."

Joses's eyes crinkled as he looked down at me. "Did you . . . would you say you heard the voice of HaShem? Did the Spirit of Adonai speak to you?"

"Does HaShem speak to sixteen-year-old girls?" I gave him an uncertain smile. "I don't know. But I agreed to marry him, and though marriage to a shepherd has not always been pleasant, I have not regretted it."

Joses sighed and stared out at the horizon. "I have no plans to marry soon," he said, "but when I do, I will need more assurance than a feeling."

"Silly boy," I teased, following my daughters. "When it is first born, love *is* a feeling."

# CHAPTER TWO

# *Damaris*

I had just settled the children in their bedchamber when I heard voices outside the house. I flew to the door and peered out, then hurried down the steps to greet my husband and father-in-law.

"Shimon!" I rose on tiptoes to embrace him, then smiled at Jeremias, my father-in-law. "Blessed be Adonai for bringing you home safely. How was the Holy City? Did you have a joyous Passover?"

"Indeed we did," Shimon answered, slipping his arm around my shoulders. "And where are my beautiful daughters?"

"Sleeping—and I hope you will not wake them. I had trouble getting them to sleep. Amarisa and Bettina kept saying, 'It's been two weeks since Passover, so when is Abba coming home?'"

"HaShem was good enough to give us a safe and speedy journey." Shimon turned to murmur something to his father, then he led me toward our door. "I have news," he said, lowering his voice. "News only for your ears, not the neighbors'. Adonai has truly smiled on us."

The undercurrent in his voice sent a thrill shivering through my senses. With difficulty I bit back a hundred questions and let him escort me into the house.

Once inside, Shimon took my hands and pulled me to sit beside him on the couch, his dark eyes snapping above his black beard. "I met many important people when we were in Jerusalem. We ate the Passover with a family Abba knew—they are also in the business of exporting wine."

I lifted a brow. "Are they your father's competition?"

Shimon laughed. "There is so much demand for good wine that even our competitors are friendly to us. After the meal, we talked about the future, and Abba's friend, Lavan—who also lives in Nazareth—said I would be a good candidate for the *chaburah*."

My mind whirled at his response. Nazareth had several chaburahs, groups of men who met regularly for dinner and religious discussion, though Shimon had never expressed interest in joining any of them.

"Why—what?" I shook my head. "What sort of chaburah is he—?"

"The Pharisees." Shimon breathed the name with holy reverence. "Lavan is a member of that exalted group and thinks I would be a credit to the fraternity. He is willing to speak for me at their next meeting so that I may join them."

I blinked as words and images tumbled in my head. "The Pharisees—here? Or in Jerusalem?"

"Both." His grin flashed, dazzling against his tanned skin. "I already go to Jerusalem several times a year on my father's behalf. I can combine my purposes, attending cha-burah meetings and selling wine. On the journey I can tour vineyards, examine fruit, and oversee the workers. While in Jerusalem I can attend meetings and sit under Torah teachers at the Temple."

I caught my breath. "You . . . a Pharisee? Me, a Pharisee's wife?"

Shimon chuckled. "And our girls, a Pharisee's daughters." He squeezed my hand. "You would benefit richly from this, my love. You would be given respect from people in Nazareth as well as Jerusalem. Our sons, should we have any, would be allowed to join the chaburah as soon as they came of age. They would study under the most respected Torah teachers in Jerusalem, and they would marry daughters of Pharisees. Our daughters would find respected husbands, devout men who follow the Law like no others."

"Would we have to move to Jerusalem?"

"No, we would remain in Nazareth. Once I have been admitted to the chaburah, I will be a brother to all Pharisees, no matter where they live. Do we not all follow the same Law?"

I pressed my hand to my chest, trying to imagine my precious daughters as respected, exalted women. We would all rise in social standing . . . "Your parents would also benefit."

Shimon nodded. "My father wants this for me. Because HaShem has blessed us with wealth, I will never need to labor at commerce. I will be free to study the Law wholeheartedly. The vineyards will provide an income when he is in the grave, and our lives will be established in holiness."

My husband took my hands and gently held them between his own. "Our lives are about to change, Damaris. Judeans will no longer consider us ignorant Galileans; we will be Hebrews of the Hebrews. We will be among the elite, the set apart."

Caught up in my husband's enthusiasm, I blew out a breath. "I am with you in this, as always."

"Good—because you will need to teach the children more stringently. They must not only know the Law but also the teachings of the rabbis and all the oral traditions."

I hesitated, blinking in bafflement. "I teach the girls everything they need to know. We say our prayers three times a day, we recite the Shema—"

"That is all good, but you must begin to stress what is clean and unclean, pure and impure. We can no longer enter a heathen city, for it is unclean to us. You must not speak to a Gentile, nor enter a Gentile home. If, for instance, a Gentile woman comes to ask for a bag of grain, you cannot offer it or let her into the house. She is unclean, as is her entire household. You must not speak to her."

I pressed my lips together, silently absorbing my husband's directive. We had no Gentile neighbors, but Nazareth lay on a great highway that traversed Galilee. People of all sorts entered our town to draw from our well or buy goods at our marketplace. Nazareth was also a priestly center, where off-duty Levites throughout the land came to spend a week in fasting and prayer for their brethren working at the Temple. What if I mistook a Gentile woman for one of the priests' wives? To be safe, would I have to refrain from speaking to any stranger?

And what about Capernaum? When he was not traveling, Yeshua lived in Capernaum, and I was fond of the Galilean city. Though it had been a largely Jewish community, Gentiles also lived within its walls—a Roman centurion had built the city's synagogue. And what about Magdala, famous for its market, and Tiberias, home to Herod Antipas? They were Gentile communities—were we never to visit those cities again?

Despite the fire in my husband's eyes, I slumped in disappointment. "I will miss shopping in Magdala," I whispered. "The fabrics and salted fish at that market are far better than what we find here."

"I will bring you salted fish," Shimon replied, bending to peer into my eyes, "by the bucketful. I will search for the finest fabrics and bring them home for you. You will lack for nothing, Damaris, and you will gain more than you can realize. So, say your prayers and hope that all goes well with me. Lavan is coming for dinner tomorrow, and he will tell us everything we need to know."

# CHAPTER THREE

# Pheodora

I had just set a hot loaf of bread on the table in my cozy Bethlehem house when I heard a shout from the street. Peering out the doorway, I saw a man standing outside the courtyard gate. He wore a ragged tunic, a linen head covering, and carried a shepherd's staff.

I hurried into the courtyard, covering my head with my shawl as a married woman should. "Yes?"

"Pheodora, wife of Chiram?"

"I am."

"This is for you."

Grinning, the man handed me a flat rock, which I seized with trembling fingers. *Beloved wife*, a rough hand had written, *I am coming home.*

I looked up, my heart overflowing, and realized I should offer the shepherd some refreshment. "Wait!" I called. "Would you like some water? Bread?"

He moved away, waving as he went. "No need."

"But where is Chiram, and when should we expect him?"

The man stopped, his smile disappearing. "He set out with me from Jerusalem but was detained by a tax collector. He should be no more than an hour behind me."

*A tax collector?* My heart sank, for no one wanted to be stopped by one of the men hired to collect taxes on everything we bought and earned. The *tributum capitis*, or poll tax, did not exist before Roman troops stormed into our land, but was levied annually on all persons, bond or free, until the age of sixty-five. The Romans imposed another odious tax on everything we produced—one-tenth of all the grain and one-fifth of the wine and fruit. A man could not transport his harvested crops without being stopped by a tax collector.

But Chiram would not have been carrying produce. He must have been halted by a publican, a slave or foreigner employed to stop travelers and arbitrarily assign an amount due for a bridge toll, road toll, or tax on whatever goods the traveler possessed. His donkey, if he traveled with one, would have been unloaded, his pack searched, his purse emptied. Not only would the publican have applied the tax required by his Roman master, the publican would have added an additional fee to defray his costs in collecting the tax.

I clenched the scrawled stone and stared at the departing shepherd. No wonder the fellow traveled with so little. He had probably passed through the collection point with no trouble, but . . .

I closed my eyes and hoped my husband had traveled lightly.

# CHAPTER FOUR

# Damaris

With a small square of linen, I blotted perspiration from my chest and the back of my neck, then nodded at the servants Shimon had hired for the evening. We had never had a Pharisee join us for dinner, and my nerves jangled at the thought of making a mistake before such an august personage. What if I tracked dust from a Gentile's footprint into the house? I would have to be certain we had plenty of water jars and basins in the vestibule.

I mentally walked the path our guest would take as he joined us. As he approached the house, the rows of ornate pillars would surely catch his eye, so my handmaid had already cleared them of cobwebs and dust. Our home was one of the largest in Nazareth, though surely it would seem small in comparison to the palaces of Jerusalem. If this Lavan spent much time in the Holy City, he probably considered Nazareth a provincial village.

A wide staircase would lead my husband's friend from the street to the flat roof where the guest chamber awaited him. A whitewashed balustrade, built to the required height of two cubits, would easily sustain his weight if he wished to sit on it to enjoy the evening breeze or lift his thoughts in prayer.

When he chose to come downstairs, by another staircase he would descend to the courtyard where a fountain provided soothing sounds and a terebinth tree offered shade in the hottest part of the day. Passing through the open area, he would reach our living quarters, furnished with the best tables, couches, candlesticks, and lamps we could provide. My generous father-in-law, who had an eye for beauty and an appreciation for fine furnishings, frequently bought new cushions, adornments, and carved cabinets for his home and ours.

But surely Lavan the Pharisee would not be overly concerned about physical surroundings. As one of the truly separated, he would look for signs of our commitment to purity. Since the time before the Maccabees, when Greek thought, practice, and religion permeated Judea, the Pharisees set themselves apart from the common culture and committed themselves to following the Law. None of them would ever be found wearing a foolish Greek hat, entering a gymnasium, or allowing his son to avoid circumcision.

With this in mind, I had arranged for pitchers and bowls to be placed on stands at the front door, in the dining room, and in the guest room. No graven image would be found in our home, no sketch or drawing of any living thing.

I wiped my hands on my linen square and took a last look around, then hurried to my chamber to dress for dinner. My new handmaid waited there—a gift from Shimon, who wanted me to make a particularly good impression on our guest. The young slave bowed as I sat before the oval looking brass in which my worried face wavered back at me.

"I will let you apply the cosmetics," I said, watching as the girl carefully opened the alabaster boxes containing my perfumes, salves, and ointments. Her hands trembled, so I reached out and caught her wrist. "Do not be anxious," I said, taking care to keep my voice calm. "I am a fair woman and will not be harsh with you. What is your name?"

She swallowed hard, then found her voice. "Yuta."

"How old are you?"

"Fourteen years."

I smiled, realizing that my husband had been unusually frugal, since the price of a girl under twenty was only ten shekels. "Are you Jewish?"

She nodded.

We did not often buy Jewish slaves because after six years they had to be freed. Something—most likely poverty or death—had forced this girl into slavery, yet HaShem had led her to us.

"Yuta"—I forced a smile—"I would like my hair plaited and curled, then adorned with these." I opened a carved wooden box filled with gold clips and combs. "Can you plait and curl hair?"

The girl nodded. "I believe so."

"We shall see, then. And I will need you to help me into my tunic."

"Which one?"

"The silk one on the bed, with the matching girdle. I believe it will make me look more slender." I caught her eye in the looking brass. "After six children, a girdle is critically important."

Satisfied that I had done all I could do, I sat back and watched as the girl painted my face for a type of battle my husband would never understand.

# CHAPTER FIVE

# Pheodora

The sun had already slipped behind the horizon when I heard the creak of our courtyard gate. A moment later the door opened and my weary husband appeared. "Shalom," he said, his dusty face brightening when he saw us.

The girls leapt up from the floor and ran to him, each of them jostling for the best position to hug his lanky body. I waited, because even though we had been married ten years, I preferred to wait until I did not have to compete to hold him in my arms. How long had he been away this time? I was about to count the weeks, then stopped when I looked out and saw a donkey standing in the twilight.

"What . . . ?" My voice trembled as I remembered the tax collector. "What is that?"

Chiram gave me a crooked smile. "Gifts." He walked into the courtyard, opened the pack saddle, and lifted out a water jar and a leather bag. As he came back into the house, a smile shined through his unruly beard. "I brought gifts for all the girls. For you, Judit, a stylus and ink so you can practice your writing."

Judit accepted the gift with quiet dignity, then hurried to the table.

"For you, Eden, a flower from Jerusalem." Chiram unfolded a delicate sheet of parchment, revealing a pressed and dried rose, likely one of the first blossoms of spring. Eden gasped when she lifted it, and Chiram smiled. "You are *my* little rose."

Jordan danced in anticipation. "For me, Abba? Anything for me?"

"Ah, Jordan." Chiram reached into a bag and pulled out a carved block of wood. He gave it to Jordan, who turned it over and looked up at her father. "What does it do?"

Smiling, Chiram took the block and ran his hand over it. The block opened, revealing an inner compartment. "It's a secret box," Chiram explained. "You press here, and here"—he touched two opposite corners—"and it opens to reveal whatever is inside."

Jordan took the two pieces in her hands and set about trying to put the box back together.

Chiram looked at little Shiri, who stood with her thumb in her mouth. "And for you, my baby girl," he said, pulling a package from the pack saddle, "there is this."

Chiram pulled away the fabric wrapper, and there lay a ball of raw wool. Yet this ball had four twig legs affixed to it, along with two eyes, two ears, and a mouth. A lamb.

Shiri popped the thumb out of her mouth and took the lamb, then hugged it tightly.

I stepped toward my generous husband. "You shouldn't have gone to so much trouble. You will spoil them."

"I enjoy spoiling my daughters. And I am not finished—I

have something for you, my dear wife." Chiram rummaged through the pack again, pulling out a square of folded fabric. With a snap of his wrist, he unfurled a tunic in the most beautiful shade I had ever seen—the color of the Galilee sea at dawn, a rich turquoise.

"It's lovely," I whispered, fingering the fluid fabric. "But you should not have spent your wages on such things."

"If I cannot be here with you," he said, watching the girls enjoying their gifts, "at least I can give you something to remind you that I am always thinking of you."

"We don't need reminders. You are always in our hearts." I dropped the tunic and went to him, slipping my arms around his waist and pressing my cheek to his chest. I breathed in the warm scents of wool and grass and felt his arms enfold me.

"It is good to be home."

"I heard," I said, not daring to lift my head, "you were stopped by a tax collector."

"Yes." His voice roughened. "The man insisted on taxing me for everything in my pack *and* the donkey. When I protested that the donkey was only borrowed, he substituted a road tax for the livestock tax."

I lifted my head. "Did you have enough to pay him?"

His cheeks went red beneath his beard. "I did not, nor did anyone with me. The amount was far too much, but what could I do? Yet the tax collector had a friend, a Greek, sitting at a table beside him. He offered to loan me the money, and I had no choice but to accept."

My throat tightened. "How much . . . do we owe?"

"The tax was a single denarius. But when the moneylender stops me again, I will owe him four."

"Four denarii—" My voice broke. A denarius was a day's wage, enough to buy a sheep or a goat. Four denarii! Chiram might as well owe the value of our home. We had not seen four denarii in all the years we had been married, and we were not likely to see that amount anytime soon. Every coin Chiram brought home went to buy food, clothing, and a little grain for the two hens who gave us eggs. What I could not afford to buy I obtained through barter.

A thrill of fear shot through me at the thought of owing so much money, but I wanted to trust my husband. I looked up at him and resolved to remain calm. "What will we do? We have nothing to sell unless—wait. We can sell the things you brought us. I do not need a new tunic, and the girls do not need toys."

"You are not to worry about this." Chiram kissed me, then sank to a stool, his eyes intent on our daughters. "I will take care of it. And if I cannot, we will trust Adonai to provide for us."

"Trust Adonai." I moved to the bench opposite him as joy ebbed from my heart like wine from an old wineskin.

# CHAPTER SIX

# Damaris

If I had not known our guest was a Pharisee, I would have realized it as soon as he crossed our threshold. After removing his sandals outside the door, he paused to pray, drawing his feet together, smoothing his clothes, and bending so low I could see every bone in his back through the fabric of his tunic. As Shimon and I waited in the doorway, Lavan offered two benedictions, one after the other as if the blessing would be increased by the number of words pouring out of his mouth.

When Shimon looked at me, I lifted a brow, silently sending a message: Did all Pharisees suffer from an overabundance of words?

Finally, Lavan straightened and dipped his head in a bow. "Shalom aleichem," he said, stepping into our home. "Peace be to all who dwell in this house."

"Aleichem shalom." Shimon genuflected and gestured toward the inner courtyard. "We are honored by your presence. Please come in."

I waited until our esteemed guest had passed before closing the door, then I turned to greet him. "We have prepared the upper floor if you would care to relax before dinner. Would you like to enjoy the guest chamber?"

Lavan frowned, and I realized I had violated some rule about speaking directly to a man who was not my husband. "Shall we proceed to dinner?" he asked Shimon.

Shimon motioned to the dining chamber, while I, thoroughly embarrassed, followed the men.

The Pharisee was dressed in a white undergarment, heavily embroidered at the hem, with a shorter upper tunic of fine linen. He did not wear the Grecian hat so popular in Jerusalem, but a turban, the ends of which hung gracefully over his back. His neatly trimmed beard gleamed with perfumed oil that scented the air in his wake. As he reached out to grip my husband's arm, ivory bracelets clacked together on his arm, and I saw he had chosen a gold ring to adorn his spotless hand.

Noting his fondness for jewelry, I was glad I had worn my earrings and nose ring, as well as two necklaces, one fitted close to the neck, the other dangling over my chest. Perhaps he would make note of my anklets, which made tiny tinkling sounds above my bare feet. I did not want him to notice me as a man notices a woman; in fact, I did not believe such a devout man could be capable of coveting another man's wife. Yet if he approved of me, he might be more inclined to favor my husband.

We made our way into the dining chamber, where the servants stood ready to serve the meal. The three-sided table had been laid with spoons, knives, and silver plates, the best we had to offer. Shimon gestured to the largest couch, abundantly decorated with pillows, and our guest stood before it.

But before sitting, he offered to bless the bread. We waited while he bowed again, curving his back into an ostentatiously uncomfortable position while he offered the blessing. This prayer went on longer than the benedictions at our door, and I shot Shimon a questioning glance. Were we to pray all night? Shimon shook his head in silent rebuke, and we waited until our esteemed guest finished and took his seat on the couch.

As the servants brought trays of roast lamb, chicken, salad with lentils and beans, bread, and pears boiled in wine, Lavan talked about his teachers in Jerusalem and how he had studied the Holy Scriptures since childhood. "I have come to realize," he said, ignoring the food, "that it is more punishable to act against the words of the scribes than against those of Scripture. If a man were to say, 'There is no such thing as tefillin' in order to act contrary to the words of Scripture, he should not be treated as a rebel. But if he should say, 'There are five divisions in the prayer fillets' in order to add to the words of the scribes, he would be guilty of rebellion. Everyone knows there are only four divisions in the prayer fillets worn on the forehead."

I coughed, the only way I could voice my disagreement without being impertinent. How could it be worse to contradict a scribe than holy Scripture? My father would not have agreed with Lavan's assertion, but surely the Pharisees with all their learning knew more about such things than a simple carpenter.

Lavan looked up at Shimon, then turned his attention to me. "I noticed there is no *mezuzah* on your door," he said. "Surely this is something you will want to correct."

"My family never had a mezuzah on the door," I replied, since he seemed to be speaking to me. "My father always said it was more important to hide the Word of HaShem in our hearts than to put bits of it on the doorpost."

"How can anyone see the piety in your heart?" The man gave me the smile he would have given an ignorant child. "Was your father a rabbi?"

"No," I answered, my cheeks burning. "He was a carpenter who loved HaShem with all his heart, mind, and soul."

The Pharisee ignored my comment. "The brothers in my chaburah are descended from those who clung to righteousness at a time when many in Israel followed the Greeks and set aside their obedience to the Law. They were the *Hasidim* who joined the Maccabees to fight for Israel's freedom. And when the Maccabees followed the Greeks into debauchery, our people remained true to the divine Law—not only the laws given to Moses on Mount Sinai but also the secret ordinances that HaShem shared verbally with Moses. We are bound by vows and obligations of the strictest kind, and if you join us"—he shifted his gaze to Shimon—"you must swear to follow and obey the written and the oral Law. If you agree, and if I judge you worthy, I will present your name to the chaburah. You will undergo a time of testing and observation, and if after one year you do not fail in your obedience, you will become one of us and will no longer be among the *am ha'aretz*."

*The am ha'aretz?* I caught Shimon's eye and silently begged for an explanation.

"I have long wanted to rise above the common, ignorant people who do not fully obey the Law." Shimon bowed his head. "I would count it an honor to join you. I will not disappoint you."

"We are committed to separation," Lavan went on. "We must be *nivdalim*, separated from the filthiness of the pagans around us."

Shimon shifted on his couch and leaned toward our guest. "How, exactly, does one do that?"

"We observe purity in two areas." Lavan paused to sip his wine, then lowered his glass. "The first is a rigorous submission to all the laws of Levitical purity. You must never buy from or sell anything, liquid or dry, to anyone outside the chaburah. You must never eat at an outsider's table because you might partake of something that was not properly tithed. You must never invite anyone outside the chaburah to dine at your table unless he has put on the garments of our chaburah. You must not enter any burial ground, nor give tithes to any priest who is not a member of the chaburah. In short, you are never to do anything of consequence in the presence of a non-member."

I looked at Shimon, who was drinking in the rules as if they were water and he a parched soul.

"As regarding the tithes," Lavan went on, "we know the people gladly give the *therumah*, or priestly heave offering, but neither the Levitical tithe nor the tithe of the poor is regularly paid. Such a serious transgression cannot be overlooked, because a man who does not pay these tithes is personally using what belongs to HaShem. So we consider anything sold by people outside the chaburah as *demai*, or untithed goods. In such cases the buyer has to regard the tithe on whatever he has purchased as a payment still due.

"But we have vowed to pay these tithes before use or sale, so you may buy from a member of the chaburah without incurring any additional debt. Still, anyone who purchases from you must pay the tithe on everything he purchases."

I stared at my plate as my head spun with talk of tithes and payments. I had always been taught that every man owed a tithe on any goods he earned or produced, no matter what happened to them once they left his hands. But after hearing Lavan speak, I began to think the Pharisees had invented a system for avoiding tithes. If Lavan grew grapes and sold them to Shimon, who sold them to Jude, wasn't Shimon responsible for tithing his income? Not, apparently, if Jude belonged to the chaburah.

Shimon nodded at Lavan. "I will not have a problem following the laws of tithing and purity. My wife, my daughters, my servants—we will all commit to obeying the Law."

"Good." Lavan pressed his hands together. "There is one other thing we must discuss before I can take your name before the council."

Shimon leaned forward, his hands clasped. "Speak, please."

Lavan glanced at me, then leaned closer to my husband. "Your wife has a brother, Yeshua ben Joseph. We have heard of his activities in Galilee and Judea, even in Jerusalem. On several occasions he has agitated the crowds, even going so far as to rouse pilgrims in the Holy City."

A flicker of apprehension ran through me as Shimon lowered his gaze. But then he lifted his chin, determination shining in his eyes. "Yeshua has nothing to do with us. We are not among his followers, and we have not seen him in . . ." He turned to me. "How long has it been?"

"Months," I said quickly. "Years. The last time Yeshua and I were together was at a wedding in Cana—and Shimon was not with me."

"So you see, we are not at all connected with him." Shimon spread his hands. "I hope you will carry our assurance back to the council in Jerusalem. Yeshua is not associated with us, nor we with him."

"Good." Lavan leaned forward and fingered a curl in his beard. "He has caused quite a bit of concern among my brothers. We have tried to speak with him, to question his intentions and ascertain his authority, but he has never given us a satisfactory answer. Perhaps you, Shimon, will be able to help us. I know you are not one of his followers, but are you close to him? Close enough that he would trust you?"

I stared as Shimon took a wincing little breath. "He is my brother-in-law," my husband finally answered. "So, yes, I believe he would trust me. I have no quarrel with him, but I am not blind to the trouble he has caused. If put to a choice, you can be sure I will side with HaShem and the Law, not with one who casts doubt on the religious authorities."

"Exactly what I needed to hear." Lavan stood and lifted his hands. "And now, if you will allow me, I would like to offer a benediction upon this household."

I shifted my weight, making myself more comfortable on my couch. If Lavan's threshold-crossing prayer was any indication, Shimon and I would be sitting here for some time to come.

Not until the long prayer concluded did I realize why our guest had not eaten a single bite of the dinner I had painstakingly planned. Because we were not Pharisees, Lavan could not be certain we had properly prepared and tithed the food we offered him. Because we were not members of his chaburah, he had decided we were *am ha'aretz*—ordinary, impure, common people.

That understanding did not comfort me.

⎯⎯⎯⎯⎯ • ⎯⎯⎯⎯⎯

The next day I wandered around the house and tried to force my confused emotions into order. What had we done, Shimon and I, to merit this sort of attention from a Pharisee? We had tried to live a righteous life and follow the Law, but I never expected my husband to be approached by so exalted a group as the Pharisees.

The Pharisees had their detractors—my brother Yeshua among them—but they supported the Maccabees when nearly everyone else in Israel adopted the pagan Greek lifestyle of the Seleucids. Like all Jewish parents in Judea, my parents had taught me about how the Pharisees, whose forerunners were known as *the faithful ones*, resisted the laws forbidding Jews to observe the Sabbath, honor the Temple, and abstain from eating pork. Some of them sacrificed their lives after enduring horrendous torture by those who would eradicate Jews and our religion from the face of the earth.

But Judah Maccabees and his brothers won the war against the Seleucids. The Hasidim supported Judah's family, the Hasmoneans, until those who became high priests merged the holy office with kingship. The Hasidim could not support the notion of a combined high priest and king, and many were so vocal in their condemnation that they forfeited their lives. Alexander Jannaeus, who reigned before the Romans entered Judea, once crucified eight hundred of their number on a single day because they opposed his reign.

For a while the Pharisees remained quiet as many fled Judea, but when Alexander Jannaeus died and left his throne to his wife, the pious Salome Alexandra, the Pharisees had rebounded and gained control of the Temple and the Sanhedrin.

My thoughts shifted to the present as I climbed the stairs to the rooftop where I could sit and ponder the life-changing choice Lavan presented to my husband. A brilliant white blur of sun stood fixed in the spring sky and bathed the air in golden sunshine. I walked to a bench—the one Lavan had not visited—and sat down to enjoy the morning.

I had been chagrined to realize our dining chamber wasn't suitable for our guest, but wasn't such piety a mark of the Pharisees' utter devotion to HaShem? If the chaburah accepted Shimon, would he ever be able to join me at a dinner with my brothers? I didn't think so. And I didn't think my brothers would appreciate being told they weren't holy enough to dine with my husband.

Joining the chaburah would be wonderful for Shimon, of course, but my daughters stood to benefit the most. I stood and looked down into the paved courtyard, where they were playing on the smooth stones. I loved each of them more than I ever imagined loving anyone, and I could not help but feel a bold confidence about their futures. Every woman worried about her daughters, but with one decision Shimon had banished my anxiety about my girls' futures.

As a child, I had no assurance of a good match. My father had been a good man, a righteous man, and my mother had been a devout believer in HaShem. But though they had both sprung from the royal tribe of Judah, not a whiff of royalty remained about them. As David was born in poverty, so were the children of my family. Our parents were so poor that when Ima went to the Temple for her purification offering after each of our births, she could only afford to purchase turtledoves for the sacrifice.

Words from the prophet Isaiah echoed in some dim recess of my mind:

> "Then a shoot will come forth out of the stem of
>     Jesse,
> and a branch will bear fruit out of His roots.
> The Ruach of Adonai will rest upon Him,
> the Spirit of wisdom and insight,

the Spirit of counsel and might,
the Spirit of knowledge
and of the fear of Adonai."

Recently I heard a Torah teacher expound on that prophecy at synagogue. "As a sapling grows out of lowly roots," he had said, lowering his scroll, "even so Messiah will not be born until the house of David has once again returned to the poverty it knew during the days of David's father, Jesse. Messiah will be born into a house of lowliness. Yet Messiah will have the sevenfold fulness of the Holy Spirit of God."

If the Torah teacher spoke truly, the time was right for our Messiah. Those who sprang from the house of David now were as poor as field mice.

Even so, my daughters would not have to marry poor and humble men. I had been unusually fortunate—something about me had caught Shimon's eye, but whether it was my wit, my confidence, or my beauty, I could not say. Thanks be to HaShem and Shimon, I had managed to escape poverty, and my daughters would do the same. Their grandfather, Jeremias, had elevated them, and their father would lift them from the am ha'aretz, the uneducated, lowly people who only halfheartedly followed the Law.

Shimon would soon join the ranks of the devout, the pious, the highly esteemed. And he would take his family with him.

# CHAPTER SEVEN

# Pheodora

I rose early, wrapped my shawl around my shoulders, and went to the window that opened into our small courtyard. Our two hens—red layers who rarely failed to produce an egg every morning—were busy scratching in the dirt, hoping to find some tidbit or a worm in the compacted earth. I leaned on the windowsill and looked up at the brightening sky. Was HaShem looking down at me? The Torah teacher who led our synagogue said HaShem spent all His time looking after Israel, safeguarding His chosen people in a treacherous world. "Did David not write," he frequently reminded us, "'Behold, the Keeper of Israel neither slumbers nor sleeps'?"

The rabbi urged us to fix our hopes on the promised Messiah, so we mentioned him in our daily prayers: "Speedily cause the Branch of David, your servant, to shoot forth, and exalt his horn through your victorious salvation; for your salvation we are hoping every day. Blessed be You, O Lord, who causes the horn of salvation to sprout forth."

So where was the horn of salvation? We had been praying for so long . . .

My parents also prayed morning, noon, and evening, and their thoughts were focused on the salvation of Israel, as well. Everything in our lives centered around our nation, and I did not regret praying for my people. If HaShem had not guarded us, we would have been destroyed countless times, wiped from the earth by Pharaoh in Egypt, the Amalekites of Canaan, Haman of Persia, and others. Of all the nations in the world, Israel alone had Adonai, Creator of the Universe, as her Defender, her Light, and her Salvation.

But sometimes, in the stillness of a Sabbath afternoon, I lifted my eyes to the heavens and wondered if HaShem cared about *me*. About a woman with four children and an often-absent husband, a woman who would rather sit and think than gossip at the well or bake bread for her family. A woman who was the least talented, least likable, least attractive of her parents' children. Surely you had to stand out if you wanted HaShem to notice you . . .

Was I a terrible person because I yearned to know if Adonai cared for me? Or in HaShem's eyes, was I but one grain of sand on a vast shore, one point of light in an endless constellation?

David, they said, was a man after God's own heart. I read his psalms, I knew he spoke to HaShem, and the Almighty listened to David's prayers. I had been born into David's house, but was my lineage enough to merit attention from a busy God? Or was His heart expansive enough to care about every man, woman, and child who chanted their morning prayers?

I turned at the sound of a yawn, thinking one of the children had awakened, and saw Chiram standing behind me.

Giving me a sleepy smile, he stepped forward and wrapped his arms around my shoulders, then bent and breathed a "good morning" into my ear.

I sighed and leaned into him. "Why are you up so early? The sun has barely risen."

"I wanted to spend time with you alone. Once the girls awaken, you never stop moving."

As his lips brushed my hair, I turned to look up at him. "How long can you stay this time?"

"Not long. We are supposed to pick up some animals outside Caesarea. It is time to begin preparations for *Shavuot*."

I sighed, knowing I should be grateful for the endless cycle of festivals and sacrifices that provided my husband with work. Because land was too valuable to use for anything but planting crops, no one pastured livestock in Israel. Only the animals used for Temple sacrifices were allowed to live off the land, and they were kept at Migdal-eder, where an ancient tower allowed shepherds to keep watch over the goats, sheep, and cattle. Like his father and his grandfather before him, Chiram was one of the shepherds entrusted with keeping the flocks safe.

"Before the girls wake," Chiram said with an urgent tone, "I need to tell you how I plan to pay off the debt I owe Barauch the moneylender. It involves the goats of Yom Kippur."

"Did you say *goats*?"

He nodded. "The Temple priests always select a certain kind of goat for the Day of Atonement—identical he-goats without blemish. Every year they ask for white goats, but *pure* white goats are rare. Yet I have found two pure she-goats and have already made arrangements to breed them to a white buck. An old friend breeds goats on the plain of Sharon and keeps them through the rutting season. I have to pick up the she-goats in Caesarea. If the breeding was successful, the does should produce pure white kids for Yom Kippur—not this year's festival, but the next. The sacrificial animals must be yearlings."

I frowned, thinking of the dozens of animals who grazed the fields around Migdal-eder. "How will you keep your goats separated from the others? You cannot brand them."

A smile lifted his tanned cheeks. "My she-goats will not mingle with the others. I am going to bring them here where you can keep an eye on them. You can keep them in the courtyard—and if any of the neighbors complain, bring them into the house. They will be too valuable to lose and too important to risk being taken to the Temple by another shepherd."

Speechless, I stared at my husband. "You want me to raise goats in our small house. With our children."

"Goats are no trouble." He shrugged. "And the price they will fetch will be worth any inconvenience. Trust me, Pheodora—I did not think I would be using the profit to pay a moneylender, but we may still earn a little extra. Enough to buy more chickens, perhaps."

I snorted softly, then turned back to the window overlooking our small courtyard. "You will bring these goats here. Will you also take care of them?"

"If you insist," he said, wrapping his arms around me again. "I will find a way to come home more often to check on them—and on you. Because I am well aware I am asking you to take on more work."

"Goats." I shook my head. "Why not lambs? They are gentle and sweet."

"Wait until you see the kids," he said, smiling. "You will fall in love with them, I promise. You can trust me on this."

"I probably will," I said, tilting my head back to better see him. "Did I not fall in love with you?"

# CHAPTER EIGHT

# *Damaris*

My heart fairly leapt in my chest when Shimon came home at the end of the day. I hurried to him and knelt to remove his sandals. "Did you have a good day at the synagogue? A good discussion with the rabbi?"

Shimon sighed as he sank to the bench by the washbasin. "Our rabbi does not appreciate the art of study and debate." He rubbed the back of his neck. "I had hoped to increase my knowledge by studying with him, but apparently he is content to remain as simple as the tradesmen around him. For the kind of learning the chaburah expects of me, I shall have to go to Jerusalem."

I looked up, aghast at the idea of being left alone for a protracted length of time. "Surely you will not leave me here?"

"Never, my love." He gave me a quick smile, then leaned against the wall. "I would leave you for only a week or so, then I would return. I will not shirk my responsibilities to my father and our children."

What about his responsibility to his wife? I frowned, not

understanding why I should remain behind. If I could spend a week in Jerusalem, a week to shop and mingle with wealthy and powerful people, I could come home and show Nazareth how life was meant to be lived.

"I could go to Jerusalem with you—"

"What would you do while I studied? You would be more comfortable here at home. You have a busy life in Nazareth."

I made a face. "A child could do what I do here. I would much rather be with you, husband. While you study, I could get to know a few well-connected women. I could visit Herod's palace or ask for an audience with the procurator's wife."

Shimon chuckled. "Do you think she would see you?"

"Why not? My husband is on his way to becoming one of the most important and learned men in Judea."

"*Galilee,*" he corrected, the light in his eyes dimming. "I could become one of the most learned men in Galilee. Those who live in Judea have had access to great Torah teachers all their lives. Even after I become a Pharisee, most of the men in Judea will consider me as backward and brutish as a fisherman who makes his living by the sea."

"Then you shall prove them wrong." I put my hand on his shoulder and smiled. "If you are ever inclined to take me to Jerusalem with you, I promise to do my part. I will dress like Herodias, if you think that would help, and I will remain silent except to smile and flatter important men. And"—I ran my fingertips over his chest—"if I befriend the wives of those important men, I might prove to be a valuable asset to your cause."

"You are always an asset." Shimon caught my hand and pressed it to his lips. "Perhaps one day I will take you with me to Jerusalem, but not now. My next trip is too important, and I have too many other things to consider. I would rather not be distracted by concerns about your welfare."

I put on a pouting expression that had proved persuasive before, but Shimon did not even notice my puckered lips. "What is for dinner?" He stood. "I hope it will be better than the tasteless flatbread I ate this morning."

By the time I rose the next day, Shimon had already ordered the servants to carry his trunk to the courtyard. I pulled on a robe and went downstairs to bid him farewell. I found him in the vestibule, adjusting the head covering that would protect him from the blistering sun. "Were you planning to leave without saying good-bye?"

He greeted me with a surprised smile. "My love! Of course not. But I wanted to have things in order by the time Lavan arrives."

I gestured toward the trunk. "Is he bringing a wagon, or do you plan to have a mule drag that all the way to Jerusalem?"

He laughed. "I adore your sense of humor." He bent to kiss my cheek, then lifted his head at the sound of horses' hooves. "Here he comes now. Have you seen Lavan's horses? I must admit, I am glad he will not have an opportunity to see my mule. My beast would seem pitiful compared to his."

As Shimon hurried outside, I followed, wrapping my arms around myself as I studied the approaching caravan. Lavan did not travel lightly, for not only did he ride a magnificent horse, but another pair pulled a wagon of polished wood. There were three trunks and several baskets on the wagon's flat bed, and soon my husband's trunk would be added to the load.

I looked behind the wagon, where two other men rode

black mules—fine animals, despite Shimon's disparaging comment. I recognized the men but did not know their names. From their attire I could see they were Pharisees and part of Lavan's chaburah.

"Shalom!" Lavan called. "Are you ready to travel, Shimon?"

"Absolutely." Shimon opened the courtyard gate and waved over the servant driving the wagon. "Stop here and let my servants help you with my trunk."

The driver halted while two of my husband's slaves hurried forward to lift the trunk and put it with the others in the wagon. When they had finished, Lavan's servant pulled a heavy cloth over the cargo.

Lavan dismounted and approached Shimon, then paused to nod at me. "Shalom. Might we trouble you for some refreshment before we leave the city? We have already been at work for over an hour and the sun is hot."

My cheeks burned beneath his subtle rebuke. I should have had refreshments waiting, perhaps even a water jug. But what could a Pharisee eat at my house? I did not often send my husband off with Pharisees.

"I will return in a moment," I said, bowing. "Please excuse me."

I ran up the stairs and into the house where I found my handmaid in the kitchen. "Quickly, Yuta, take a pitcher of lemon water outside. Do we have any dried dates? Yes. Good. And the bread? Yes. I will arrange the tray; you see to the water. Oh! And fill a basin with water. Bring it outside with a clean linen cloth."

While the maid hurried to do my bidding, I uncovered a clay pot and pulled out several dried figs and some date bread. The bread was still soft with no signs of mold, so I put it in a basket along with the figs. I found a small bag of nuts and grabbed a handful of shelled almonds, adding them to the basket. If Lavan and his friends could not eat it, at least Shimon could. He was not a sworn Pharisee yet.

With the basket in my arms, I drew a deep breath and made my way toward the stairs. But as I stepped onto the landing, Lavan's voice rose up to meet me.

"The leaders in Jerusalem are quite unhappy," he was saying, loud enough for everyone in the courtyard to hear. "Everywhere he goes, the crowds eagerly follow. The authorities are considering various ways to stop his teaching before he goes too far."

Without being told, I knew he was speaking of Yeshua. Who else could it be?

"Surely the leaders have pointed out his heresies," Shimon said, crossing his arms. "After all, everyone knows it would be impossible for any man to destroy the Temple and rebuild it in three days."

"The am ha'aretz are easily deceived." Lavan shook his head. "You would think the common people would see through him, but he tickles their ears with what they want to hear—the poor will inherit the earth, those who suffer will be comforted, the sick will be made well. His teaching overflows with promises of peace and prosperity, and the people drink of it as eagerly as a cat laps up spilled milk."

He turned and saw me on the stairs. "Ah, Damaris. Whatever you have brought us is much appreciated."

I walked downstairs on legs that felt like stumps of wood, not daring to look at my husband. Though I could not argue with what Lavan said, surely he knew he had spoken of my beloved elder brother. I could not agree with everything Yeshua was doing, but my brother was a righteous, guileless man and I loved him.

I stopped at the bottom of the stairs and held my basket, watching as Lavan and the other men peered at the figs and bread I had brought to break their fast. But before Lavan would touch anything, he lifted his eyes to heaven and offered a blessing: *"Barukh ata Adonai Eloheinu melekh ha'olam borei p'ri ha'eitz." Blessed are You, Lord our God, Ruler of the universe, who creates the fruit of the tree. "Barukh ata Adonai Eloheinu melekh ha'olam hamotzi lehem min ha'aretz." Blessed are You, Lord our God, Ruler of the universe, who brings forth bread from the earth. "Barukh ata Adonai Eloheinu melekh ha'olam shehakol niyah bidvaro." Blessed are You, Lord our God, Ruler of the universe, at whose word all came to be.*

When he had finished blessing every variety of food within my basket, he looked at me. "Is there water to wash?"

I glanced rapidly from left to right, wondering what had delayed my maidservant, but Shimon was faster than I. He clapped, and one of his men came running forward, a basin of water in his hands and a towel draped over his shoulder.

Nodding, Lavan dipped his hands in the water, shook them off and wiped them on the towel. I stood silently as Shimon and the other men did the same. Then each man took fruit from my basket and ate.

A wry smile curved my mouth. Lavan must have decided that a Pharisee-in-training's food was acceptable. Either that, or today the man was granting his hunger a higher priority than his scruples.

While they ate, my gaze drifted over the horses, the wagon, and the piled luggage. I thought about my brother, whose name still seemed to hang in the air, and knew he and his men traveled in a very different manner.

⸻•⸻

With Shimon gone to Jerusalem and nothing pressing to do, I thought I would take the girls to see my brothers. Our house seemed empty and altogether too quiet when Shimon was away, but my brothers' house buzzed with banter and activity whenever they were home. I dressed the girls in simple tunics—no need to impress my brothers, who wouldn't know fine linen from common—and chose to forgo the litter, opting for a walk instead. I smiled as the girls giggled their way down the street, the younger ones striving to keep up with their older sisters. At twelve, Amarisa moved with the self-conscious awareness of a girl on the brink of womanhood, and ten-year-old Bettina trailed in her shadow. Eight-year-old Jemina was still much a child, overflowing with energy and enthusiasm, while Jerusha, at six, struggled to keep up with her. Lilah, four, and Zarah, barely two, walked with me, holding my hands.

My heart twisted when I looked down at my little ones. My womb had remained empty since Zarah, and though my brothers teased me about having a full quiver, I longed to give Shimon a son. I was still young, not yet thirty, and earnestly desired to bear him a son who would follow him into the chaburah. My girls might become wives of important men, but Shimon would be far happier to know his son would follow him or become a respected Torah teacher, perhaps even in Jerusalem . . .

Every Shabbat, after we had finished our meal, Shimon placed his hands on our daughters' heads and prayed, *"Ye'simech Elohim ke-Sarah, Rivka, Ra-chel ve-Lay'ah." May HaShem make you like Sarah, Rebecca, Rachel, and Leah.* Now that Shimon was on his way to becoming a chaber, perhaps HaShem would bless us with a son so that Shimon could pray, *"Ye'simcha Elohim ke-Ephraim ve'chi-Menashe."* *May HaShem make you like Ephraim and Manassah.*

My thoughts turned toward my first family when we turned the corner and saw my parents' house. The mud-brick building had endured years without alteration—an unusual situation, considering that the house had been occupied by a family of carpenters. But Abba had always used his tools for others, and his sons did the same.

Even when my brothers were small, Abba taught them as he worked, reminding them that the first man to be filled with the Holy Spirit was a craftsman. "Then Adonai spoke to Moses," he frequently quoted, "saying, 'See, I have called by name Bezalel son of Uri son of Hur, of the tribe of Judah, and I have filled him with the Spirit of God, with wisdom, understanding and knowledge in all kinds of craftsmanship, to make ingenious designs, to forge with gold, silver and bronze, as well as cutting stones for setting and carving wood, to work in all manner of craftsmanship.' So, my sons, whether you use a hammer or a chisel, when you create something, you are using a gift from HaShem. He is a maker of things, and so are we."

Our brothers made cabinets, beds, and pergolas, but Pheodora and I made daughters.

Amarisa and Bettina reached the gate before I did. They turned and waited, the wind blowing the hair away from their youthful faces. I watched them with an appraising eye—Amarisa could well be married in three or four years, and Bettina in four or five. They were fresh-faced and pretty, but Nazareth abounded with pretty girls. To ensure they would find wealthy and important husbands, they would need their father's connections.

And now, thanks be to HaShem, Shimon was working hard to pave their way.

"Hello, down there!"

I looked up and saw Joses on the rooftop, standing near the balustrade. He grinned down at us. "Are you coming to see us or are you out for a walk?"

"What do you think?" I teased, shading my eyes from the sun. "Come down, please, and bring some water. We are about to melt in this sun."

Joses disappeared for a moment, then reappeared on the front stairs. He trotted down the steps and opened the gate, leading us into the house.

I picked up Zarah and carried her into the front room. The thick walls kept the space in deep shade, and the resulting coolness was a blessed relief. Beyond the entry stood another staircase that led down to the interior of the courtyard, where shimmering dust motes swirled in honey-thick sunlight.

I set Zarah on the floor and sank to a bench where I kicked off my sandals and gestured for the girls to do the same. "Where are the others?"

Joses set several cups on a table and poured water into each. "James and Simeon are at the well. They left some time ago, so they must have been detained. Jude is out talking to a man about building a house."

"For his betrothed?"

Joses shook his head. "Jude has not yet begun his house."

"Poor Tasmin. At this rate, they will never be married."

"Jude doesn't seem to worry about it." Joses gave cups to each of my daughters, then offered one to me. "What brings you down the hill?"

Shrugging, I took the cup and stretched out my legs. "I

felt like taking a walk. And since Shimon has gone to Jerusalem—"

"For business?"

I hesitated, then decided my brothers might as well know the truth. "He has been invited to join the chaburah of Pharisees. He has a local sponsor but needs to be approved by those in Jerusalem . . . or something. I'm not exactly sure of the process."

A warning look settled over Joses's features. "Best not tell James."

"Why not?"

"Just last week, James became angry with a Pharisee who came late to the synagogue and made a poor man move from the front row. James was about to rebuke him, but then he got up and left."

"Well . . ." I cast about for some excuse for the Pharisee's behavior. "Isn't it right that the learned men sit up front? Should not we respect those who have devoted their lives to the study of the Law?"

Joses scowled in answer, and at that moment James and Simeon entered the house. My girls ran over and clamored for their attention, deafening my brothers with their enthusiastic greetings.

"This is a surprise," Simeon said, greeting the girls as he removed his sandals. He shifted his gaze to me. "Shalom, sister. What brings you here?"

I drew a breath to reply, but Joses answered for me. "Shimon has gone to Jerusalem to meet with some Pharisees. Apparently, he will soon be joining their esteemed company."

James's face darkened with unreadable emotions. Then he smiled at Jemina and Jerusha and asked if they wanted to go downstairs and look for the rooster.

"Ah. Well." Simeon patted his bulging belly and went to the table. "Would you like something to eat, sister? We haven't much in the house, but we might be able to find a bit of salted meat or flatbread."

"No, thank you," I said, resisting a shudder. I stood and grabbed the hands of my youngest girls. "We only came by to see how you were doing. As I see it, you are all barely getting by."

"We are fine." Joses gave me a distracted smile. "When we get hungry, we go to the market. Or the woman next door brings us food."

"Old Bethel?" I blinked. "She is still living?"

"She has taken us under her wing," Simeon said. "She is the reason we still have meat on our bones."

"Then may HaShem bless her." I moved toward the door. "And if you need anything else, let me know."

I waited for them to say something about Shimon—to pass along a greeting or wish him shalom—but none of them said anything. My brothers seemed to have entered an immediate and tacit conspiracy to never again speak my husband's name.

I blew out a breath and went downstairs to look for Amarisa, Bettina, Jemina, and Jerusha.

## CHAPTER NINE

# *Pheodora*

Girls! Come say good-bye to your father."
From every corner of our small house, the girls left their activities and ran to Chiram, who gave each of them a hug and kiss. His eyes were wet when they lifted to meet mine, and my heart grieved as I stepped forward for my embrace. After ten years of marriage, I should have been accustomed to saying farewell, but when it came time to do so, I found it easier to pretend Chiram was an acquaintance or a stranger I barely knew. If I looked up and saw him as my husband, my lover, and the father of our precious daughters, a knot formed in my throat and choked off the words I wanted to say.

"Travel safely," I managed, awkwardly pulling myself from his arms. "Write to me once you have returned from Caesarea. I worry about your traveling so far."

"Do not worry. We have traveled that road many times. And you will see me before I go back to Migdal-eder, remember? I have to bring the goats to you."

"Oh." I smiled. "How could I forget?"

He smiled at the girls again, ruffled Shiri's hair, then picked up his bag and staff. Judit opened the door, her chin quivering with a repressed sob, and we moved into the courtyard to watch him leave. When the gate closed, the girls ran to it, where the older ones waved over the top and the youngsters peered through the slats as their father strode away.

As the tallest, nine-year-old Judit had the best view of her departing father. She lingered longest at the gate, then turned to me. "When will we see Abba again?"

I placed my hands on her shoulders. "I am not sure. When he returns with his goats, I suppose. Or, if the goats aren't suitable, after Yom Kippur."

Five-year-old Shiri was sucking her thumb, a sure sign of distress. "Where did Abba go?"

I leaned forward and popped the thumb out of her rosebud mouth. "Abba is going to get some goats. They are far away from Bethlehem." I lifted her into my arms and gave her a squeeze. "Abba takes care of the animals needed at the Temple, remember? He's a very important man."

Eden crinkled her nose. "He doesn't take care of the animals by himself, does he?"

"No, he has helpers who take turns staying with the flocks. But since only very special men want to be shepherds, we should be happy your father is able to come home when he can."

I herded my little flock inside the house and set them to work. Judit went to the table where she was learning how to knead dough. At seven, Eden's job was to sweep the house, so I gave her the broom and asked her to pay particular attention to the corners. Jordan, the six-year-old, took a bag of grain and fed the chickens, while Shiri curled up in the center of a straw-stuffed mattress and sucked her thumb until she fell asleep.

I watched her, envious of her innocence. I would love to go to bed and fall into a carefree sleep, but I had dinner to prepare, children to care for, and a husband to miss until he returned home again.

If HaShem was merciful, I would not miss him for long.

# CHAPTER TEN

# Pheodora

A week later, we had heard nothing from Chiram. I told myself all was well—why should he write while he was traveling home? He would likely arrive before any messenger.

While the girls worked at their morning chores, I washed a few vegetables I had picked up at the market, then cut them into pieces for a stew. We had no meat, but plenty of lentils and a small pat of goat cheese from our neighbor. It might not be the richest dinner, yet it would serve to fill our bellies.

After setting my stewpot on the fire, I clapped for my daughters' attention. "Come, girls, gather around. Time for midday prayers."

They sat on the bench by the table, and I stood opposite them. "All right. Judit, begin by saying your Scripture verse."

From the time they could talk, I had followed the example of my mother and taught my girls a verse that began with the same letter as their Hebrew name. My verse—since my Hebrew name was Aiya—was always the first thing I thought of when I began to pray: *Adonai our Lord, how excellent is Your Name over all the earth!*

Judit drew a deep breath. "Joshua said to all the people, 'Behold, this stone will be a witness to us. For it has heard all the words of Adonai which He has spoken to us. So it will be a witness to you, lest you deny your God.'"

"Very good. Eden?"

Eden closed her eyes and began to recite, "Esther had not disclosed her people or her lineage, because Mordecai had commanded her not to make them known."

"Excellent. Jordan?"

Jordan, who seemed to have trouble memorizing, counted on her fingers to help her remember. "Justice is turned back, and righteousness stands far off. For truth has stumbled in the street, and uprightness cannot enter."

I smiled at Shiri. "Do you remember your verse, little one?"

Shiri nodded, then looked at her sisters as if hoping to find help. "Sssss——"

"Salvation," Judit whispered.

Shiri began again. "Salvation is far from the wicked, for . . ." She looked at Eden. "Do you know?"

Eden nodded. "For they do not seek—"

"I remember now." Shiri took a deep breath. "Salvation is far from the wicked, for they do not seek after Your big knees."

"Decrees," I said. "They do not seek after Your decrees. *Decrees* means *laws*."

Shiri smiled. "De-crees."

I led them in the midday prayers, then pulled my stewpot from the fire and served dinner.

I was washing hands and faces when I heard a knock on the door. Alarmed by the unexpected sound, I dried my hands, told Judit to keep the girls with her, and hurried to the front of the house. I opened the door a crack, then smiled at the sight of my brother James.

He gave me a quick nod, looked past me and grinned at the girls. "You are well, my pretty nieces?" he asked, stepping into the house. They answered him in an enthusiastic chorus, but when I saw that his smile did not reach his eyes, I bade the girls lie down and rest.

I pulled James into the courtyard and closed the door. "What has happened?" I asked, facing him. "Is there trouble in Nazareth?" If something had happened to one of my brothers or Damaris, it happened several days ago, because James would have needed four days to travel to Bethlehem . . .

James lowered his voice. "A traveler stopped at the well and asked for me. When I came out to meet with him, he said Chiram had been imprisoned at Arimathea."

My heart nearly stopped beating. The world seemed to swirl as I stared at James, then it abruptly righted itself as I pulled back my hand and slapped my brother's face.

"I am ashamed of you, James. Did Joses put you up to this? I would expect a sick joke from the youngest brother, but not from you. You are the responsible one."

He lifted his hand, his eyes wide as his fingertips grazed the red spot on his cheekbone. He gaped at me and shook his head. "A man *did* come to the well with news of Chiram—"

"Then the man must have confused someone else with my Chiram. My husband has done nothing—would never do *anything*—to merit prison."

James lowered his hand, his eyes filling with distress. "Pheodora, you must listen to me. Apparently a moneylender stopped Chiram on the road and demanded payment for a debt. Chiram said he did not have the money, so the man ordered a guard to take Chiram to prison. Chiram resisted, which only made matters worse. The man who told me these things said Chiram was badly beaten before being taken away."

Swallowing a sob, I looked away and tried to sort through what I knew to be true. Chiram had told me about a debt, but how could anyone demand payment for money loaned only a few days before?

"This report cannot be right," I insisted, staring at James. "Chiram told me he'd been stopped by a tax collector on his way home, but a moneylender—his name was Barauch—gave him a loan. He has not had time to earn enough for repayment because he was home only a few days. Then he left to pick up some livestock in Caesarea—"

"They stopped him outside Arimathea," James interrupted. "On the way to Caesarea. I will go see him and ascertain the truth of the matter."

I pressed a hand to my forehead as new thoughts pounded for my attention. Chiram had been stopped by the tax collector outside Bethlehem, so what were the odds he'd meet his moneylender outside Arimathea?

"I still don't understand." I shook my head. "Do these moneylenders not understand that a man needs time to pay a debt of four denarii? If you're going to see him, I should go with you. I will have to take the girls. If you stayed with us tonight, we could leave early with the dawn. I don't know what we could do to help, but at least the girls might be able to cheer him—"

"Something is not right. The tax collectors have never been reasonable, but never have I heard of a situation like this. Someone must have something against your husband."

I barked a laugh. "Who would be offended by my simple shepherd? He does not move in important circles; he does not know important men. I will go at once and see what can be done about—"

James put his hand on my shoulder. "I would not advise you to go, sister. The moneylender is undoubtedly a publican."

I blinked. "So?"

"So he works for a Roman, one of the Publicani. They make their own rules, and they expect to earn a great profit from the money they invest in hiring other Gentiles to charge us taxes and fees. If the publican sees that Chiram has a wife and children . . ." He blew out a breath. "Stay away from the prison, Pheodora. In his current state, Chiram looks like a poor man."

"He *is* a poor man. Wait." I clutched at a sudden ray of hope. "Did he have goats with him? From what I understand, they were valuable animals."

"I heard nothing about any goats."

"Then couldn't they see he is not wealthy? Where are we supposed to get four denarii within a week's time? We have no riches, no treasure stored away—"

"Pheodora, think a moment. Chiram has a wife and four daughters. If the publican knew this—" James caught his breath, then met my gaze head-on. "I do not think you will want this publican to know how blessed you are. Four daughters are worth a great deal at the slave market."

I took a half step back, staggered by James's statement. A creditor had rights—he could demand anything the debtor owned, anything at all. A piece of furniture, a trunk of clothing, a house.

Even a child.

James was right. Better that this moneylender know nothing about our family.

I sank to a bench as my knees gave way. I had been thinking Arimathea was not too far to visit, but perhaps it would be better if we stayed away, at least for a while. Tax collectors and moneylenders traveled a circuit, so after several days this Barauch would move to another location, and then we could visit Chiram. Of course, if the debt persisted and we were unable to pay, the moneylender might inquire about us, and in his travels he would eventually learn that Chiram had a home and family . . .

My brother's image blurred as my eyes filled with tears. "James, what am I to do?"

"You should pray." He squeezed my shoulder. "At sunrise I will set out for Arimathea. I will find Chiram and speak to him. I will learn what happened and discover how large his debt is—"

"Four denarii," I mumbled.

James sighed. "The debt *was* four denarii. But the moneylender will charge interest, so the longer it goes unpaid, the greater the amount will be."

"But the Torah forbids us to charge interest on a loan."

"We are not to charge interest on loans to *our brothers*. But the moneylender is a Gentile, and so is his Roman master."

I closed my eyes, imagining four silver denarii that split in half, becoming eight, then sixteen, then thirty-two . . . When would it end?

"Goats." The word leapt off my tongue.

"What goats?"

"Chiram was on his way to pick up a pair of she-goats." I met my brother's questioning gaze. "He said he had made arrangements to buy a pair of goats because he wanted to breed pure white animals for the Yom Kippur sacrifice. He said the goats he had in mind were perfect."

James nodded. "I will ask him about the goats. But quietly, lest the publican hear about them and demand them as payment."

"Oh, James . . ." On the verge of weeping, I covered my face with my hands. "Can you forgive me? You walked all the way to Bethlehem to give me this news, and what did I do? I slapped you."

His mouth quirked. "You hit me harder when we were children." He sat beside me and leaned forward, folding his hands. "I am going to visit Chiram, then I will travel back to Nazareth and talk with our brothers. We'll try to figure out the best thing to do, then we'll send word to you. Do not worry. We are going to help you."

I sniffed and gave him a wavering smile. James had not been able to solve my problem, but at least he had given me hope.

"My girls and I are in your hands," I told him. "Whatever you think we should do, we will do it."

———◆———

I could not sleep. My daughters, who seemed puzzled by my frayed smile, went to their beds and slept like innocents while I lay on my mattress staring at the ceiling. What could I do? Chiram's plan for the goats now seemed a colossal folly. I knew nothing about raising goats, and the beasts were in Arimathea, not Bethlehem, so how was I supposed to get them? I had no pasture for livestock—indeed, the only pasture near Bethlehem was around Migdal-eder, and Chiram did not want the goats taken where they might be mistaken for goats of the herd . . .

But why was I fretting about goats when I would not have a husband to support us? How was I to feed my children? I could sell eggs if I parted with those our hens gave us nearly every day, but my girls would suffer because we could not afford meat.

If I could get another half-dozen hens, I might have enough to feed my girls and sell surplus eggs at the market. Perhaps I could work out an exchange with one of the women who had admired my sewing. With six hens, I would average four or five eggs a day, which meant I would have about a dozen to sell every week. Everyone loved eggs, but since nearly every household in Bethlehem kept a chicken or two, I would have to rely on sales to travelers or wealthy visitors who did not keep poultry.

What else could I do to support my family? I would sell my new tunic immediately, of course. I would ask the girls if any of them wanted to part with the gifts Chiram had brought . . .

Unbidden, the image of a white goat floated before my eyes, but how was I supposed to achieve the impossible? This house barely had enough room for the six of us, so how could we add two goats? Chiram must have been daydreaming when he imagined I could keep goats. From what I understood, goats attempted to eat anything within their reach, so I could definitely *not* keep a goat in the house.

I sat up and pounded the lumpy mattress in frustration, then lay back down. In that instant, the answer crept into my head as if an angel had dropped the idea on my pillow. Why was I feeling so desperate? I had a sister whose husband had money to spare. Had Damaris not offered to help us in any way possible? Had she not assured me of her love? Had she not expressed her concern about my children's health?

All I would have to do is explain what had happened to Chiram and she would understand. She knew how unjust and greedy the tax collectors were. She cared little for politics or world affairs, but she knew moneylenders could be ruthless. She would ask Shimon for whatever amount Chiram owed, and we would ransom him, paying off his debt and freeing him from prison. Chiram would be too proud to accept the payment as a gift, so he would promise to pay it back in installments. And Shimon, thank heaven, would not charge us interest.

I smiled and closed my eyes, grateful I had a sister who had married well. Damaris had always made me feel inferior, never more than when we were girls and she offered to share her belongings with me. I never accepted because I knew she offered this out of pity, but for Chiram, I would even beg from my sister.

She would share this time, too. She would save Chiram from debtors' prison and prevent me from losing my home. As soon as I found out exactly how much Chiram owed, she would finally have her opportunity.

---

I spent the next day in a state of agitation. I rose shortly after sunrise, recited the morning prayers, and stepped into the courtyard, expecting to find my brother asleep on the bench. But James was gone, a folded blanket and a clucking chicken resting in the place where he'd slept. I picked up the blanket and shooed the hen away, then found a warm egg on the blanket. At least my girls would have a bite or two to break their fast.

As the day went on, I tried to remain calm in front of my girls, but I snapped at them when I didn't want to and wept when I thought they weren't looking. I tried to pray, but rarely got beyond, *Blessed are You, oh Lord our God, King of the universe, who hears us in our hour of need.* I wanted to believe Adonai would hear my prayer, but would He hear a woman who had nothing to offer Him?

My thoughts kept returning to the psalms in which David begged God to deliver him from his enemies. I no longer saw my enemies as faceless foreign oppressors, but as a sour-faced tax collector and smirking Gentile moneylender. Though they might not be conspiring against my life, they were conspiring against my family. And if they learned that Chiram had a house and a family, they might well demand the unthinkable.

I couldn't forget about the goats. Chiram had hoped to provide for us by selling spotless goats, and I admired his initiative. Unusually valuable goats might be enough to get him released from prison. Right now, however, they were merely specks in their mamas' bellies, if they existed at all. No moneylender would accept the *promise* of valuable goats as payment, so what good were they?

Sitting by the window, I stared into my courtyard and released a choked, desperate laugh. I hoped James had the foresight to purchase food for Chiram. I had never been inside a prison, but my parents had always prepared food and drink for their visits to the prison in Nazareth. Only one man guarded the squat little building near the city gate, and the prison rarely held more than one or two prisoners. But whether the unfortunates inside were friends or strangers, my parents visited them on the first day of every week.

Once I asked Abba and Ima why they knew so many people in prison. They looked at me in surprise, then laughed. "We do not always know the people we go to visit," Abba told me, "but prisoners need friends more than anyone. So we go to them and offer food, clean water, and friendship."

"Especially food," Ima had added. "The jailers give them only gruel and stale bread. Prisoners rely on friends and the kindness of strangers to stay alive."

Oh, how I wished I had thought to send something—even flatbread—to Chiram! If I could not soon pay his debt, I would take food to Arimathea myself.

While I tried to keep busy with my chores, the hours crawled by, even though I knew I would not hear from James for several days, perhaps a week. More than once I wished I could set out for Arimathea myself, yet I had daughters to care for and a household to run. I was anything but a free woman.

Throughout the day, I stepped out of the house, looked up and down the street, then went inside and closed the shutters against the glare of the hot sun. Who else had heard about Chiram? Since James brought the news from Nazareth, surely my other brothers and my friends from home had heard about his imprisonment. I had welcomed James but did not want to see Damaris yet. I needed time to think about how to approach her. One thing I knew for certain: when I told her about Chiram's situation, she would chide me again for agreeing to marry a shepherd.

No matter, for I had followed my heart, even as she had followed hers.

By the time I put the girls to bed, I had decided to leave Bethlehem and travel to Nazareth straightaway.

———————— • ————————

"We are going on a journey?" Judit's eyes widened. "But we just came from Nazareth."

"We are going to Nazareth *again*," I said, forcing a smile. "Don't you want to see your uncles? We will also see Aunt Damaris and your cousins."

Eden tugged on my tunic. "How long will we stay? Until Shabbat?"

"I don't know . . . maybe longer. We might be there awhile."

"Why?"

"Because, dear one. Now stop asking so many questions and pack a bag with whatever you want to bring. Judit, bring your second tunic and your scrolls. Eden, pack your sewing supplies. But do not pack anything you cannot carry."

I looked around, realizing I needed to gather food for the journey. Once we arrived, we would be fine. My parents' home was fully furnished and currently occupied by James, Joses, Jude, and Simeon. They would welcome me and my girls, especially since they knew about Chiram's situation. I would stay with them until we could arrange his release, and while there I could help by preparing meals and taking care of the house.

In return, my brothers would make sure my daughters and I didn't starve. Without their help, I didn't see how we could survive.

I picked up a woven bag and dropped in an extra pair of sandals, as well as a comb so I could do the girls' hair. My brothers weren't likely to have many tools for hair styling around the house, especially since Ima had been traveling with Yeshua for two years. Damaris would have anything I might need to borrow, but I did not want to approach her with outstretched hands. The request I had to make of her and Shimon was large enough; I would not bother her with little things like combs and headscarves.

I put a few of the girls' belongings into my bag and filled a basket with all the food I had in the house—a sack of dried figs, flatbread, lentils, and a block of cheese. I added a bag of dried beef, an expensive treat I had picked up at the market in exchange for my new turquoise tunic.

We would drink water from the wells and creeks we passed on the journey. We might suffer thirst when water was not available, but we had no donkey and none of my daughters was strong enough to carry a water jug.

I slipped my arms into the basket straps, settled it on my back, and turned to see my girls lined up beside the door. Each of them was carrying her gift from Chiram. Judit clutched her stylus and bottle of ink, Eden held her pressed rose, Jordan carried her secret box, and Shiri had her woolen lamb close to her chest.

I swallowed hard and struggled to find my voice. "Girls, we should leave those things here."

When they raised a chorus of protest, I shook my head. "You will grow tired on the road and will not want to carry anything. Or you might set those things down and leave them somewhere, never to see them again." I looked at my girls' woebegone faces and tried to muster a smile. "Let's leave them, shall we? So when we return with your father, he can give them to you again."

Little Shiri began to cry, but she followed her sisters' example and placed her lamb in the center of her mattress. Then each of my daughters picked up their cloth bags.

I lifted my own bag. "We're going to leave town and walk out to the road," I said. "We'll wait until we meet a friendly group traveling north and then we'll join them. In a few days, we'll be in Nazareth with your uncles."

"I get tired of walking," Shiri said. "Will there be a wagon?"

"I don't know, but we'll hope for the best. Maybe someone will have a donkey or a mule."

I nodded toward the small cage I had fashioned from twigs and twine. My two red hens sat inside, anxiously peering out at me. "Judit, you carry the chickens. When you get tired, Eden can carry them for a while. We'll take turns carrying the birds as we walk."

"Where will we sleep?" Eden asked, slipping into her sandals.

"With everyone else from our group," I answered. "Think of it as another adventure."

I herded the girls out the door, then took one last look around and silently said good-bye to our Bethlehem home.

---

We were fortunate. We joined a group traveling from Jerusalem to Cana, many of whom knew Tasmin, Jude's betrothed. Though thoughts of Chiram constantly troubled my mind, I was able to relax a little by talking to the women about Tasmin, Jude, and their upcoming wedding. One of the families had a wagon, so my girls were able to ride when they grew weary.

After discussing our common acquaintances, we talked about the latest scandal in Jerusalem. A leading Pharisee had invited a wealthy Roman exporter to be his guest for the evening. Though he housed the Gentile in another building and did not break bread with the man, he did allow his slaves to serve him.

The man telling the story would say no more in mixed company, but I learned the rest of the story from an older woman.

"Apparently," she told three of us who walked with her, "the Pharisee had a virgin slave, a young girl who was quite beautiful. The Roman bade her come into his room, and when she refused, he forced her to lie with him. Once he had finished, he told the weeping girl to leave. When she protested that she had been ruined, he threw her out of the guesthouse." The woman lowered her voice, forcing us to draw closer. "The girl was so distraught she opened her veins in the garden. When the Pharisee's daughter found her dead the next morning, the Pharisee confronted the Roman. The Gentile could not understand why his host was upset, but he gave the man thirty shekels to cover the expense. The Pharisee threw the money on the ground, refusing to touch it."

We responded with a collective gasp, and the older woman nodded. "The Romans have many gods, and those gods are as licentious as the men who worship them. Only HaShem, blessed be He, gives His people a holy Law to guide our lives."

"Amen," we murmured. We walked for a time in silence, pondering the lawless ways of heathens and the mercy of our God.

Five days later, my girls and I bade farewell to our traveling companions and entered through Nazareth's city gate. I had never been so relieved to see familiar surroundings—the marketplace humming with activity, the workshops of the tanner and the potter, and the city elders, sitting on their benches to observe the comings and goings of visitors and neighbors.

The elders fingered their beards and murmured to each other as my daughters and I passed. I doubted any of them recognized me—after all, none of them had spoken to me when we visited at Passover. As the youngest daughter of Joseph's family, I had never received much attention. Damaris had always been the beauty, Yeshua the scholar, and James the diplomat. Jude was the negotiator, the most outgoing of my brothers and the best at selling Abba's handmade furniture. Simeon was the dreamy one, the short one, and Joses the jokester. I had always been the looking brass that reflected my more remarkable siblings.

I led my daughters down my childhood street, through the gate of my parents' house, and up the front steps. Without knocking, I opened the door. Jude was seated at the table and looked up when the door creaked. His eyes widened and his jaw dropped as he rushed over to us, his arms extended. "Here you are," he said, giving me a squeeze before bending to embrace the girls. "And you've come such a long way!"

The girls hugged my brother, then Judit dropped onto a bench and let out a long sigh. "I'm thirsty."

"Water for all of you." Jude turned to a pitcher and basin. He slanted a look at the chickens in my basket. "I take it you will be staying awhile?"

"Only until Chiram is released." I dropped into a chair and wiped perspiration from my forehead. "Has James returned from Arimathea?"

"Not yet, but I expect him sometime today or on the morrow. He sent word that he was going to Arimathea so we would know when to expect him." Jude brought over several cups of water and set them on the table.

I watched as my girls gulped down the water. Turning to Jude, I asked, "How is your betrothed?"

He grinned. "Tasmin is well. Her boy is growing like a weed."

I nodded my approval. Tasmin, the twin sister of one of Yeshua's disciples, had found an abandoned boy while she and Jude were searching for her brother. She had originally intended to find a home for the boy, but she fell in love with the little lad.

"So you already have a son."

"Apparently so."

With difficulty, I stifled a yawn. "I'm sorry, Jude, but would you mind if the girls and I took some time to rest? We are worn out from the journey and the heat."

"Of course." Jude gestured toward a room off the dining area. "Take your old bedchamber—no one uses it now. It is yours for as long as you want to stay."

I thanked him with a smile, then stood and urged my daughters to follow me. I had taken only a few steps when I turned and caught Jude's eye. "One thing I need to ask—does Damaris know about Chiram?"

Jude frowned, then tugged at his beard. "I doubt it. We have not seen her, and she never goes to the well, so I doubt she hears the town gossip. But she might have heard whispers at synagogue."

I nodded. "Thank you. I will tell her everything when I see her."

I hurried after the girls, ready to put this day behind me. We would sleep and wake refreshed, and soon we would hear from James. We had begun the work of freeing Chiram, and surely the worst was behind us.

---

For two days we waited for James. Because busy hands are happy hands, the girls and I cleaned the house, baked bread, and made our hens comfortable in the courtyard. The resident rooster, a scrawny bird that had not yet recovered his feathers from the fall molt, was not happy to share his space.

"Give him time," Jude said, grinning. "He'll figure out soon enough that he's just been blessed with a harem."

Finally, on the third day, the front door opened and James came into the house, his face weary and somber. His brows lifted when he saw me, and a twitch at the side of his mouth told me he had news he dreaded to share.

I pulled him inside and placed my finger across my lips—the girls were napping.

"I didn't expect to see you here," he said, slipping a pack from his shoulder. "When did you arrive?"

"We left the day after you did," I said, desperate to learn his news. "Please, sit. I will get you some water and something to eat, but first, tell me—how is my husband?"

James sank to a bench, resting his arms on the table as his head hung low. "Remind me never to borrow money from a Gentile."

I caught my breath. "Is it so bad?"

"The news is not all bad." He lifted his head and took a deep breath. "Chiram is well, considering that he was soundly beaten when they took him to prison. His eye and cheek are swollen, but he says he is not in much pain. He is more concerned about your well-being than his own."

I waved his comment away. "What did he tell you? Has his debt increased?"

James lifted his gaze to meet mine. "The amount owed was four denarii, but because Chiram resisted the arresting guards, the jailer assessed another fee. The total debt could go as high as twenty denarii or even more, depending on how long the debt remains unpaid."

I gasped. How could a tax on a few trinkets result in such a large amount?

"Here." James pulled something from his tunic and gave it to me. "Chiram wrote this for you."

He handed me a shard of pottery, scrawled with ink that

barely left a legible mark. "They couldn't give him parchment or leather?"

"He had to use what we could find in his cell. The ink is from berries on a plant I found outside. I prayed it would still be readable by the time the message reached you."

I moved the jagged piece of pottery into a stream of sunlight and began to read.

> *Forgive me, wife. I will not waste space with news James could share for me.*
>
> *If you would free me from this place, you must get the two she-goats I have in Caesarea. Nathan ben Abram, a friend, is keeping them for me at his home outside the city. The two females should be pregnant. You must take them home with you and protect them as best you can. I know the task will not be easy, but in late spring they will bear kids, and those kids must be raised with care. Try to keep them away from other animals lest they be afflicted with disease. And next year, when they are yearlings, take them to Asher ben Yakov at Migdal-eder. He will be the one who procures animals for the Temple. Let him see the yearlings and tell him I have bred them especially for Yom Kippur. Then pray he will buy them and be generous with you.*

I stared at the words, then looked at my open hand as if I could see the names of the months written on my fingers. Born in late spring? Yearlings? He wanted me to raise goats *for more than a year?*

I closed my eyes and tried to imagine an entire year without Chiram. Though he rarely spent more than a few days of every month at home, we depended on his wages. While we had never been wealthy—no shepherd was—without him, we would be destitute. The girls and I would have to depend on the kindness of family and strangers for our needs, and I would have to start gleaning the fields to feed my family. And how could I raise four girls alone? Though much of the responsibility for our daughters fell on my shoulders, I had never felt alone because Chiram was always present and attentive when he was home with us. He listened to our daughters' stories, he led them in prayer and Torah study, and every night he placed his hands on their heads and blessed them: *"Y'simeich Elohim k'Sarah, k'Rivkah, k'Rachel, ooch'Leah."* May God make you like Sarah, Rebecca, Rachel, and Leah.

How could I raise four girls by myself? I did not have Chiram's patience or his love. I was too tired, too anxious, and too quick to lose my temper . . .

But wait. I drew a deep breath to calm myself. I would not have to wait a year. Damaris and Shimon would help us, and we would free Chiram within the month, if not sooner.

When I looked up again, James was watching with compassion in his eyes. "I am glad you came home," he said. "We will help you. Joses, Simeon, Jude, and I are working, so we will share everything with you and your girls. I will also send word to Yeshua, so perhaps he will be able to do something."

"I don't expect you to—"

"Nonsense. Abba and Ima would want us to pull together."

Unbidden tears sprang to my eyes, and I quickly blinked them away. My parents had worked hard to feed their children and never depended on the generosity of others. We were not wealthy and yet we did not go hungry because we worked together. My brothers would support me and the girls, but what about my husband? He would waste away to skin and bones unless someone cared for him.

"What about Chiram?" I whispered. "He is alone in Arimathea; he does not have friends or family there. He is far from his people in Bethlehem, and far enough from me that I will not be able to visit often, perhaps not even every month—"

"Do not worry, little sister." James leaned forward and placed his hand on the back of my neck, drawing me forward until my forehead rested against his. "You have a family, and we will help you through this, no matter how long it takes. HaShem is faithful, and He will give you the strength you need. HaShem will care for Chiram, too."

I believed in God, truly I did, but what care would the Master of the universe have for a simple woman? I was not a king like David, or a mother of nations like Sarah or Hagar. I was a simple woman raising four daughters . . . but at least I had brothers and a sister who loved me.

# CHAPTER ELEVEN

# Pheodora

The next morning I rose early, washed my face and hands, and made certain my daughters' tunics were clean. I braided each girl's hair and asked Judit to see if any flowers were blooming on the hillside behind the house. She returned with four wild roses, so I wove a blossom into each girl's braid.

When I was certain we looked presentable, I took Shiri's hand and herded the others through the doorway. Damaris lived on the far side of town, at the highest point in the city, and our walk carried us through winding streets and up steep stone steps. I nodded politely to several neighbors watching from their doorways and arranged my face into pleasant lines. They had to be curious about why I had come home, and soon all of Nazareth would know the story.

Finally we stood outside Damaris's gate, and there we called out a greeting. A servant let us in and bade us wait in the entry until Damaris was ready to receive guests.

The slave who welcomed us was unfamiliar to me and

seemed young for such an important position. As my girls marveled at the beauty of the furnishings, I smiled at the girl and attempted to make conversation. "I don't recall seeing you before. Are you new here?"

She lifted her head and nodded.

"Do you enjoy working in this household?" I asked.

She glanced toward the hallway, as if afraid to be caught speaking to me.

"Do not worry—Damaris is my sister. I will not let you get in any trouble. You seem terribly young for a house servant."

"I am fourteen," the girl said, keeping her voice low. She glanced at Judit. "I have not been here long."

"I hope my sister treats you well," I said, catching Shiri before she escaped down the hallway. "Shalom."

As the girl hurried away, I moved to a luxurious couch and tried to organize my thoughts. I had lain awake for a good while the night before, rehearsing my words and trying to decide on the best approach. Should I approach Damaris with a casual air, as if our predicament were but a light and momentary nuisance? Or should I approach her with a sad face and stooped shoulders, so she would realize the severity of our situation? Should I tell her the entire truth, or should I omit any mention of the moneylender? The Scriptures were filled with warnings about the dangers of usury and cosigning loans, but Chiram had not cosigned anything and was taking full responsibility for his actions. As far as I could see, he had done nothing wrong.

The room seemed to brighten when Damaris swept in and held out her arms, giving the girls a gracious smile. "Come give your aunt a hug," she called, stooping to embrace them. "Judit, I believe you have grown since I last saw you! Eden, how do you make your eyes sparkle like that? They are most attractive. Jordan, you are as lovely as the river, and Shiri, have you a kiss for your aunt? Thank you, precious."

Damaris seemed genuinely surprised to see us, leading me to suspect that she hadn't heard anything about Chiram's plight.

She straightened and pointed to a long corridor. "Go there, girls, and you will find your cousins. Play with them while your mother and I talk. Run along now—I will have one of the servants bring you honey water."

Judit took Shiri's hand and led the way, Jordan and Eden following close behind.

When they had gone, Damaris dropped to the couch next to me. "Why have you returned to Nazareth?" she asked, her smile vanishing. "What is wrong, little sister?"

I blinked, surprised by her greeting. "How did you know something was wrong?"

"You are wearing your worried look. Not only that, but I cannot remember the last time you put flowers in the girls' hair when it wasn't a feast day. So, tell me why you have returned to Nazareth and come to visit before the sun is halfway up the sky."

Casting off my carefully planned approach, I spoke plainly. "Chiram is in prison," I began, spewing words in a flood of emotion. "The tax collector took every lepton he had on his way home to Bethlehem, and the publican who loaned him money demanded payment days later when Chiram encountered him on the way to Caesarea. Since he could not repay the loan, they beat him and threw him in prison."

Damaris folded her arms. "Where?"

"Arimathea." I swiped at my runny nose, but already I felt comforted by my older sister's demeanor. Damaris always seemed unflappable; I could not recall her ever being frantic with worry. Then again, she had married a wealthy man, and the rich seemed to have fewer problems than common people. My sister appeared to study the carpet as she searched her thoughts. "Of course I will help you," she said, her voice flat as she considered the problem. She looked up at me. "How much does your husband owe his creditor?"

"Four denarii," I told her. "But the amount will increase with time. The moneylender is a Gentile, so he is charging interest."

She winced. "That is not good."

"It is outrageous, considering how little he owed in the beginning. But you know the moneylenders—they charge a high rate of usury because they serve greedy men."

Damaris gave a firm nod. "Do not worry. I will have to ask Shimon, but I am sure he will agree to repay whatever Chiram owes."

"It must be considered a loan, not a gift," I hurried to assure her. "Please tell your husband we do not expect him to forgive the debt. We will pay him back, little by little, no matter how long it takes."

"You know we could never leave a family member in prison. Not after all Abba and Ima taught us about helping the less fortunate." Damaris patted my hand. "Fear not, little sister, I will do everything I can to help you. How long will you be staying in Nazareth?"

"As long as it takes to free my husband." I wiped my damp hands on my tunic and smiled with an overflow of gratitude to know Chiram would soon be redeemed. "James brought me the horrible news, then went to visit him in Arimathea. While he was away, I thought I might as well come home. At least I could stay with family while I waited for my husband's release."

Damaris made a *tsk*ing sound. "You should not have worried, yet I am glad you are here. Our girls will enjoy playing together while we wait."

"Damaris . . ." I caught her gaze and held it, hoping she could see how truly grateful I was. "I cannot thank you and Shimon enough. I had envisioned months of hardship ahead. A shepherd does not earn a lot, but Chiram earns enough to keep us fed and safe—"

"Think nothing of it." She placed her hand on my cheek, then sighed and stood. "I will send you back to our brothers with what I have on hand—bread and wine and a large cheese fresh from the market. I will gather some fruit and send it with a servant. What else do you need? Knowing our brothers, I doubt there is much food in the house."

"I need nothing." I sighed as a burden rolled off my shoulders. "The food will suffice until the debt is paid. Once Chiram is free, he will return home and go back to his work." I gave her a small smile. "He has plans to earn additional money, so we will be fine."

"Good." She crossed her arms, her silk tunic rustling, and smiled down at me. "Are you sure you need nothing else?"

I stood, too, and gave her a hug. "I knew I could count on you," I whispered in her ear. "You are a blessing to me and my girls. If you had not been able to help, I don't know what we would have done."

"What sort of person does not take care of family?" Damaris took my arm and led me toward the room where the children were playing. "Your girls are more lovely each time I see them. And while I don't understand why you chose to marry a shepherd, I will say this—your husband certainly sired beautiful daughters."

# CHAPTER TWELVE

# Damaris

Pheodora and her children left before midday, but they burdened my thoughts for hours afterward. How many times had I told my sister not to marry the shepherd from Bethlehem? Everyone knew shepherds were flighty and untrustworthy, and now a shepherd had brought trouble into Pheodora's life. If only she had listened to me . . .

I had been aghast when I heard that a shepherd—from tiny Bethlehem, no less—had given our father a betrothal contract, and I was stunned when Abba considered it.

*A shepherd?* Though our father had been a humble tradesman, he was honest and good and devout. Abba never aspired to power in Galilee, let alone Judea, yet he had a sterling reputation for righteousness. As his children, we shared in his reputation, so I fully expected Pheodora to receive at least three or four offers of marriage from the sons of rabbis, merchants, or scribes.

Instead, she accepted the first man to approach our father, the shepherd from Bethlehem, a man ten years her senior.

The match made no sense to me, especially since the standard marriage contract specified that the husband would not force his wife to leave her hometown if she did not wish to do so. I was certain Pheodora agreed to marry the shepherd because she would rarely see him, until I learned she had agreed to move to Bethlehem. Whatever for? Despite being the place of David's birth, Bethlehem was an insignificant village, home to fewer than three hundred shepherds and farmers, a place where the men smelled like manure and the women had dirt under their nails.

Why did Pheodora think she could ever feel at home in a village like that?

When the sound of my husband's voice interrupted my musings, I checked my reflection in my looking brass, pushed a stray strand of hair back into place, and bit my lips to make them redder. Then I pasted on a smile and went downstairs to greet Shimon.

I found him in the center chamber, a small scroll in his hand. He had removed his shoes at the door and was reading, his brow furrowed. But his countenance brightened when I approached and kissed his cheek. "Would you like me to wash your feet, husband?"

He gave me a quick smile and returned to his reading. "The servant already did," he said, his thoughts clearly on the letter in his hand. "Thank you all the same."

I sat on a nearby sofa and waited for him to finish. Speaking to him now would be a waste of time, for his thoughts were clearly occupied. I had learned to judge his moods before asking for anything. An ill-timed request would almost certainly be refused, while a request at the appropriate time would result in pleasant agreement.

Shimon enjoyed being known as a generous man. When he

made a sizable contribution to our synagogue, he requested his gift be acknowledged by a carved monument near the door. "My example may spur others to give," he told the rabbi. "Everyone will benefit by such a notice."

I did not think Pheodora would want everyone to know that Shimon's generosity had saved her husband from prison, but my husband certainly wouldn't mind.

Finally, Shimon lowered his scroll, rolled it up, and slipped it inside his tunic. Then he sat beside me and slapped his thighs. "And what is happening in the household?" He arched a brow. "You have news, I see it in your eyes."

I tilted my head and smiled, acknowledging his observation. "My sister and her children visited me this morning. She was embarrassed, but she made a request—her husband, Chiram, could not pay the tax collector a few days ago, so he accepted a loan from a moneylender. As he was traveling to Arimathea a few days later, he met the same moneylender, who demanded payment. Chiram could not pay, of course, so he is being held at the debtors' prison in Arimathea."

Shimon braced his hands on his knees. "Do we know which tax collector stopped him?"

"Pheodora didn't say."

"And the moneylender—do we know who employs him?"

"No, but it must be a Gentile, because he is charging interest."

"Do we at least know the amount owed?"

I repeated what Pheodora had told me.

Shimon made a sound deep in his throat and studied the floor.

"Well?" I said. "May I tell my sister we will pay his debt? Pheodora has promised they will repay you. It may take a while, but she says Chiram has a plan to earn—"

"I cannot promise . . . yet." Shimon cut a look at me, then went back to staring at the floor. "Lavan, my mentor, has relationships with several of the Publicani. I do not know details, but I know they often do business together. How would Lavan feel if one of his associates employed the man who put Chiram in prison and I paid the debt before the creditor could realize a solid profit?"

I blinked, confused by the revelation, and Shimon softened his tone. "Do we know what happened when the shepherd was arrested? Was he insolent? Violent?"

My throat tightened. "Pheodora did say he was beaten. James has seen the bruises."

"Ah." Shimon swung his head in disbelief. "Lavan would not appreciate my role in releasing a man who could be dangerous, perhaps even set on vengeance. I can do nothing, wife, until I have investigated the matter further. I must proceed carefully and take care not to offend Lavan. He has powerful friends in both Jerusalem and Rome."

I sat back, exceedingly disappointed. Pheodora had left our home believing everything would soon be settled. How could I tell her she would have to wait for her husband's release . . . perhaps indefinitely?

"If you cannot help her, what is my sister to do?"

Shimon shrugged. "The debt could easily be paid. How many children does your sister have?"

"She has four daughters," I whispered, thinking of sweet little Shiri. "The youngest is only five."

"Old enough to be sold," Shimon said. "If she is sold now, she would be free by the time she is of marriageable age. She might learn a trade, so her time of service would be well spent."

I stared at him. "You want Pheodora to *sell* her child?"

Shimon quoted from the Torah. "'If your fellow Hebrew—a man or woman—is sold to you and serves you six years, then in the seventh year you are to set him free. When you set him free, you are not to send him away empty-handed. You are to provide for him from your flock and threshing floor and winepress. As Adonai your God has blessed you, you are to give to him.'"

He looked at me, a small smile curving his mouth. "The answer is simple. Sell the child—any of them—and put the girl to work. A female child will bring ten shekels, more than enough to pay the shepherd's debt. Then Chiram can return to his flocks and the family can go back to Bethlehem."

I looked away, my field of vision clouding with a gray mist. Could I sell one of those sweet girls into slavery? Could I sell one of my own daughters? My father would have given his life before allowing such a thing to happen to one of his children, and Pheodora would undoubtedly feel the same way. My brothers would never permit it, but if selling one child could free Chiram . . .

Pheodora would not do it, and I could not blame her.

"Please do what you can to help them," I told Shimon, placing my hand on his arm. "As part of my family, they are also part of yours. Their misfortune is your misfortune, and it will not be good for you to have a brother in debtors' prison. If you help them, people would praise you for your generosity."

Shimon tilted his head, probably imagining how his reputation would be enhanced by such a charitable act. He looked at me and nodded. "I will make inquiries about the moneylender and tax collector," he said, a light flickering in his dark eyes. "Then I will give you my answer. Until then, do not mention this matter to me again."

## CHAPTER THIRTEEN

# *Pheodora*

Three days passed and still Damaris had not come to me, neither had she sent word by letter or servant. At first I remained confident, supposing she was busy with household affairs, but as the days slipped by and we devoured the food she had given us, I wondered if she had encountered an unexpected difficulty. Had Shimon gone away? Had he fallen ill? Perhaps he had gone to Jerusalem on business or was traveling with his father . . .

On the fourth day, Damaris appeared at the courtyard gate carrying a large basket. I watched from the rooftop as she lifted her tunic so her hem would not touch the dirt in the courtyard. I saw her repulsed expression as she sidestepped chicken droppings on the steps leading up to the door.

She knocked, and I hurried downstairs to answer.

"Pheodora." She tried to smile, but I saw distress behind her eyes. "How are you?"

I embraced her and led her into the house, then gestured

for her to sit at the table, where the girls were eating bread and the last of the cheese.

"I have brought food." She took a bag of salted fish from her basket. "You will find dried figs in there, pomegranates, and more bread."

"Thank you," I said, "we are truly grateful. We have been waiting to hear from you—I had hoped to hear from you before today."

"I know." She sank onto the bench and gave Judit a weary smile. "I spoke to Shimon the day you visited. He is reluctant to commit to helping your husband. He has a mentor, the man who sponsored him for the Pharisees' chaburah, and that man has dealings that might involve the moneylender. I do not understand all the relationships involved, but I do know this—Shimon wants to be certain he will not be interfering with his mentor's business affairs."

I stared at her in astonishment. "He regards the feelings of a Pharisee more highly than those of his brother-in-law?"

"Things become complicated when you are involved with important men," Damaris explained, spreading her hands. "When you are wealthy, you can find yourself entangled in the interests of powerful people. Shimon must be careful, because his future depends on his relationships with these men. Our lives, the lives of our children, and our children's children—"

"What of *my* husband and children?" More hurt than angry, I stared at her across the table. "Honestly, Damaris, I cannot believe what I am hearing. What would Abba say if he could hear you now? What would James and Yeshua think?"

She tilted her head. "James might understand. Abba, too, if he knew my family's future was at stake. But Yeshua . . ." She shook her head. "Truly, I would rather he not know, because he would condemn Shimon. These days Yeshua seems determined to make an enemy of every Pharisee he meets. Things will be difficult enough for Shimon when people realize Yeshua is my brother, so how can I add the burden of a brother in debtors' prison to Shimon's situation?"

I propped my elbows on the table and felt my shoulders slump. Clearly, Damaris was not going to help us. My plans for a joyful journey to Arimathea vanished like dew on a hot summer morning. I would not be leaving Nazareth soon; I would be staying for months, depending on my brothers for food, shelter, and help with my daughters.

Now I had no choice but to pursue Chiram's goats. I would have to travel to Caesarea, find the she-goats, and bring them back to Nazareth.

I closed my eyes as a sardonic smile twisted my lips. I hope my brothers did not mind goats, because they were about to have a pair living in the center of their house.

"Shimon did have one suggestion," Damaris said, her eyes downcast. "You will not like it, yet it might be of help."

Desperate, I lifted a brow. "What suggestion?"

Damaris drew a deep breath, then leaned across the table and lowered her voice. "A child sold into slavery can bring ten shekels. If one of your daughters . . ."

I stared, tongue-tied, as she swallowed hard and continued.

"It would only be for six years. If you sold Shiri, she would be free by the time she is ready for betrothal. And she could learn a trade while she is away—"

"Get out." Anger heated my blood to boiling as I rose and stumbled away. "Leave this house now."

Damaris stood. "I am sorry I cannot do more. If I was able to help, of course I would. At least you will not have to worry about food for a while."

Tart words crowded the tip of my tongue, but, mindful of my watching children, I swallowed them and jerked my chin in an abrupt nod. "I appreciate what you have brought," I said. "Judit, you and Eden may put those things away."

As my daughters unpacked the basket, I walked Damaris to the door. I had a strong feeling I would not see much of her in the days ahead. "Thank you," I said again, wiping my damp hands on my tunic. "And shalom to your household."

"And to yours," she echoed. She took a half step forward as if to embrace me, then seemed to think the better of it and turned away. I watched from the doorway as she held her head high and walked down the stairs, but her shoulders sagged as she reached the street and began the uphill trek home.

That was when I realized she regretted having to give me such horrible news. Still, she valued her husband's ambition more than her sister's family.

---

I must confess, after Damaris left, the shock of defeat left me immobile for the rest of the day. My daughters sensed my black mood and tiptoed around me while I fretted at the table and stared at the wall.

I should have known that victory would not come easily; nothing ever came as easily to me as it did to my sister. Life had always led Damaris over a smooth road, while life had pointed me toward a steep and jagged mountain.

After a sleepless night, I rose with new determination. I should never have counted on Damaris. She had her own life, I had mine, and I needed to live it. Chiram still had she-goats and I had chickens. My plan was neither complicated nor quick, and the rewards might be small, but at least I would be able to feed my daughters and eventually free my husband.

I rose from my bed, dressed, and went downstairs to the courtyard, which occupied the first floor and the center of the house. My mother's clay oven stood in the corner, and several smaller chambers opened off the courtyard and provided room for storage and a cistern.

My two hens were happily scratching around with the solitary rooster my brothers kept. In truth, I didn't know if the rooster was well and truly *kept*—I think he might have flown into their courtyard and decided to remain. After a few days of chest bumping, chasing, and picking at each other, the three birds seemed to have settled their pecking order and decided to cooperate.

My girls took one look at the rooster's bedraggled feathers and fell in love with him. Judit named him Asher, *happy*, and when I commented on the unsuitability of the name, Judit corrected me. "He may not be happy now, Ima," she said, sounding far older than her nine years, "but after some loving care, he will be the happiest chicken of all."

What could I say? I sighed, realizing that if we were starving, we would have to eat shoe leather before the girls would let me cook Asher.

My hens, who had managed to remain nameless, laid one egg a day, except for when they observed a chicken Shabbat. Since I had never had a rooster, their eggs had never been fertile. But with Asher around, I could hatch chicks if I let the eggs remain under the hens. And if I hatched chicks, I would soon have more eggs to eat and a surplus to sell at the market. Chicks did not lay eggs, however, until they were five or six months old, and we had to eat every day. So if I wanted to add a few laying hens, I would need to barter for them. But what could I trade?

I looked around the house where I had grown up. Our

family had owned few valuable possessions, but over the years Damaris had given my brothers gifts that could be traded for a hen. In the dining room I spotted an inlaid tray too fine for everyday use, and I was certain my brothers cared nothing for it. The polished stones in the decorative pattern were whole and unscratched, so if none of my brothers minded, I would take it to the market on the first day of the week.

The memory of the turquoise tunic filled my head. It was gone forever. Yet Damaris had given Judit a nice linen tunic. My daughter had never worn the tunic and would never miss it. As for me, I had a necklace made of Roman bronze coins—not particularly valuable, but when Damaris gave it to me, she said the necklaces were popular throughout the Empire. With the tray, the linen tunic, and the necklace, I ought to be able to trade for three or four hens.

No one would miss the tray or the necklace, but the tunic . . . I closed my eyes, imagining Judit wearing it in a few years, the soft linen clinging to her slender form, her long hair flowing like a dark river over her back. My eldest daughter deserved a beautiful garment. Damaris's daughters would wear lovely tunics once they came of age, and I wanted Judit to feel as special as her cousins.

I decided to let the tunic remain at the bottom of Judit's bag. I would keep it for her and Eden, Jordan, and Shiri. And someday, years from now, I would gather my daughters and granddaughters around me and tell them of the day I nearly sold that bit of linen so we could survive one of the darkest periods of our lives . . .

But I could not bear to let it go.

I cleaned the girls' faces, braided their hair, and told them to stay close to me in the marketplace. In Bethlehem, I visited the market only occasionally, quietly exchanging coins for things we needed, but today I would have to bargain like a shopkeeper.

Fortunately, my hens laid their eggs early that morning, so I steamed the eggs over the fire, peeled them, cut them in two, and let the girls break their fasts with half an egg and a chunk of goat cheese. Afterward we fed the chickens, locked the courtyard gate, and walked to the marketplace.

The sun was nearly at its zenith by the time we entered the row of booths where farmers and craftsmen offered their wares. The sun warmed our faces, and I realized summer would soon be upon us. Had Chiram's she-goats conceived yet? I would have to ask my brothers if one of them could go with me to Caesarea. But first I had to find a way to feed my family. I couldn't ask my brothers to take full responsibility for feeding five extra people.

James had given me permission to sell anything in the dining room, so I carried the inlaid tray under my arm, wrapped in rough fabric. The necklace jangled on my chest, an odd sensation because I had never worn it apart from the day Damaris hung it around my neck. How could one wear money as jewelry? The bronze leptons were almost worthless—one hundred twenty-eight of them were required to buy one sheep. Even so, the idea of wearing money seemed foolish to me.

Moving through the crowd, I felt uncomfortably self-conscious. I was a stranger to most of the people I saw, and so were my daughters. I had been away ten years, yet here I was, jangling in a gaudy necklace with a package beneath my arm and four young girls in tow. How should I go about letting people know I had items to sell? I had no booth, and no one to offer me space in theirs.

So I stopped, removed the wrapping from the tray, and asked Judit to carry it with the design tilted toward the men and women working the booths. I pushed my hair back, exposing the necklace, and walked slowly in front of the booths, boldly meeting the gaze of anyone who looked in my direction.

I blushed when I realized how foolish—or how wanton—I must have appeared. My awkward approach to selling *did* draw attention, though, because several people stared at me with interest. Finally I saw a woman studying the tray. She elbowed her husband, who then engaged me with a smile.

"Lovely workmanship. Are you selling?"

"Of course." I took the tray from Judit and held it out with both hands. "I believe this came from Rome."

The man nodded as his wife's smile broadened. "The pattern is beautiful."

The woman seemed to take my measure in one head-to-toe glance. "How much?" she asked.

I swallowed. "What—what would you offer?"

She gestured to the table in front of her, where she had displayed several items: hair combs, lengths of linen, several wigs, and a set of false teeth.

I cleared my throat. "I was hoping to buy some hens."

"Hens?" The man laughed. "We do not sell chickens."

"But that is what I need." I lifted my chin. "If you want the tray, you will meet my price."

"My dear girl," the woman said, laughing, "we have not yet heard what your price is."

"My price is six laying hens." Aware that my daughters

were watching, I folded my arms and tried to appear resolute. "Or enough coin to buy six hens."

The woman looked at her husband, and he jerked his head toward the back of their booth. She called for a servant, who thrust his head through an opening in a curtain, then darted away at her command.

"Four hens," the woman replied, narrowing her gaze. "I will give you four of my own hens and not a feather more. But you will also give me that necklace."

I glanced down, having momentarily forgotten about the necklace. I had hoped to entice another buyer with it and go home with bread or vegetables as well as hens, but what if no one wanted to buy Roman jewelry?

I turned to Judit—the girl was watching with wide eyes— and wished one of my brothers had come along. I was woefully inexperienced at bartering such useless items, and every merchant in this row of booths likely realized it.

"I know you," the woman said, her sagging cheeks lifting as she smiled. "You are one of Joseph and Mary's daughters."

I nodded.

"But you moved away. I heard . . ." She hesitated.

"What did you hear?"

She showed her teeth in an expression that was not a smile. "I heard you married beneath yourself and moved to Bethlehem. And the other day I heard that your husband has landed in prison."

"I did move to Bethlehem, but I married a fine man who should not be in prison at all. I will give you the tray and the necklace for six hens."

The woman glanced at her husband, then lowered her head and sighed. "We always liked your parents. Wait here, and our servant will get the hens for you."

"Thank you."

I handed the tray to the husband, then pulled the necklace over my head and gave it to the woman. She held it up, examining it in the bright sunlight, then called again through the curtain. A moment later, the servant appeared with a covered basket.

I lifted the lid and counted six white hens of a decent size. "Are they laying yet?" I asked.

The woman raised one shoulder in a shrug. "If they're not, they soon will be."

I replaced the lid and took the basket from the servant. The startled birds did not appreciate the transition from light to darkness. Regardless, I was pleased with what we had accomplished.

While the girls chattered about the new chickens, I carried the basket with both hands and led my daughters home, my heart lighter than it had been in days.

---

The new chickens were not exactly what I had hoped for. After getting them home, clipping their wing feathers, and examining their red combs and wattles, I discovered that three of the six were too young to lay eggs. The red wattles assured me they would lay soon, but they were still young and skittish, not nearly as settled as mature hens.

"How can you tell?" Judit asked. "They look big to me."

"Laying hens will stand still when you walk up behind them." I walked to a spot behind one of my red layers. The chicken promptly squatted and flattened her back. "They are easy to pick up. Young hens are flighty."

Judit grinned and walked over to our second red hen. It

squatted and squawked when my daughter lifted her. "Squatting makes it easier to catch them."

"Well, at least our new hens aren't old," I said, watching the new hens eye their counterparts with suspicion. "There's no sense in keeping a hen who is too old to lay eggs."

"What about that one?" Eden pointed to a young chicken that seemed unwilling to part from two larger hens.

I peered more closely at the chicken as it walked with an erect posture and a jaunty tilt to the head. The comb and wattle were bright red, more vibrant than the others. "I think that may be a rooster. We'll get no eggs from him, but we might get some baby chicks."

Jordan and Eden clapped at this news. Shiri brought her hands together as well, though she probably didn't understand why her sisters were so delighted. I herded the girls through the doorway that led from the outer courtyard to the center of the house and gave them grain to toss on the packed ground for the new birds. My flock would spend the next couple of days sorting out the pecking order, although the new rooster would eventually assert his dominance and keep the females in order.

As for the old rooster, he would make a fine Shabbat stew.

Once we finished our chores, we went upstairs. I had just settled Shiri and Eden for an afternoon nap when I heard a commotion coming from the front of the house. I opened the door to find James carefully making his way through the chickens, dust and feathers flying as he made his way toward the stairs.

He squinted up at me. "What have you done, sister?"

"I've been busy." I bade him enter with a smile, then closed the door behind him and gestured to the bench, where a basin and pitcher waited. "Wash the dust from your feet while I explain. But first, what brings you home in the middle of the day?"

"You, of course." He glanced down the hallway and saw Shiri and Jordan on a mattress, then lowered his voice. "How are you doing?"

I sighed and sat next to him. "I traded some things at the market this morning and I bought chickens so we could have more eggs. If the three pullets don't start laying soon, we'll be having them for Shabbat dinner."

"The crops will be ready for harvest soon. You will be able to glean the fields after the reapers have gone through."

"I'm counting on it, and the girls will be able to help."

"Have you heard from Damaris?"

I winced. "Yes—and no. Yes, she came to see me, and no, Shimon will not be able to pay Chiram's debt. Apparently the moneylender is associated with the man who is sponsoring Shimon for the chaburah. My husband was imprisoned at an inconvenient time."

The corner of James's mouth drooped. "I cannot say I'm surprised Shimon let you down. I am sorry."

"As am I. But all is not lost. I am glad you are here—I need to ask you a favor."

"Ask."

I drew a deep breath. "I need you to go with me to find a man who lives outside Caesarea."

James grunted. "Why do we need to find this man?"

"According to my husband, he owes us a pair of pregnant goats."

# CHAPTER FOURTEEN

# Pheodora

I woke to the persistent thump of someone pounding on the door. I groaned, hoping one of my brothers would investigate the source of the sound, but they were either already up and gone or still abed and in a deep sleep.

I pulled a headscarf over my shoulders, crept to the door, and peered out. An old woman, short and wrinkled, stood on the stair landing, and for a moment I didn't recognize her. Then her name came rushing back on a tide of memory: Bethel, the woman who lived next door with her husband, Seth. She had aged in the ten years since I had left this house, and the scowl on her face only aged her further.

"Shalom," I croaked, my voice crusty from sleep.

"There is no *shalom* to be had, not since you arrived," she said, crossing her arms. "How many chickens do you have? I hear them early, before the sun has risen, and I hear them when I am going to bed. My husband hears them when he says his prayers. You must get rid of them or we will never sleep!"

I blinked the sleep haze from my field of vision. "My chickens? They are not so loud."

"When you are accustomed to sleeping in silence, they certainly are. What do you have, a dozen roosters cock-a-doodling at the crack of dawn?"

I cleared my throat. "I have one little rooster that has not even begun to crow, and an old one that was here long before I arrived. The hens are not noisy unless they are frightened. Perhaps you did something to upset them?"

"Why—" She shook her fist at me. "I used to keep chickens, and I know not to disturb them."

"What's the problem?" I turned to see James approaching, his hair tousled and his eyelids heavy. He stepped behind me and smiled at his neighbor. "Bethel, shalom to you. How are you today?"

The woman's countenance shifted, the sourness melting away like butter in the hot sun. "James. Shalom. How are you and your brothers?"

"We are well." He leaned against the doorframe and squinted at our visitor. "You are up early this morning. Are you having trouble sleeping?"

"Well . . . yes. My husband and I cannot sleep because this woman's chickens are so noisy. The rooster crows day and night."

"Ah, that." James gave her a lazy smile. "The rooster you hear lives across the street. Our roosters are quiet."

"Across—" She blinked. "Across the street, you say?"

He nodded. "A most handsome fellow. You will probably see him strutting around if you look for him. He guards his hens with great enthusiasm."

"Ah. Well." She narrowed her gaze at me. "And what of this woman's chickens? How many are there?"

James dropped his hands onto my shoulders. "Bethel, surely you remember our sister Pheodora? She and her daughters have come to stay with us while Ima is away."

The woman's face went blank with astonishment, then her lined mouth curved. "Pheodora . . . can it really be you?"

I dipped my head in a bow. "It is good to see you again."

"Yes . . . good to see you, too." The lines on her face lifted as she smiled. "And how is your husband?"

I decided to spare her the unpleasant details. "He is well. Thank you for inquiring after him."

Bethel looked as if she wanted to know more, but somehow she managed to rein in her curiosity. She looked at James. "Please give my love to your mother, if you see her. Is she still traveling with Yeshua?"

James nodded. "We hope to see her soon. Shalom, Bethel."

Gently but firmly he closed the door, then propped his arm against it and grinned. "You have to know how to handle her."

"She was furious," I said, still irritated by her manner. "I thought she was going to demand I get rid of my hens. But her attitude quickly changed when you appeared."

James shrugged. "She likes me. She probably thought you were threatening her claim to the charming brothers she has taken under her wing." James yawned and moved toward the kitchen. "Any bread left from last night?"

"On the table." As he walked away, I opened the door and peered out. Bethel was standing in the street, surreptitiously tossing bits of bread to a dog I had seen lurking in the shadows. Odd that she would feed a wild dog—which would bark at almost any provocation—yet complain about the chickens. Or maybe James was right, and the arrival of an unfamiliar woman had upset her. Perhaps she resented me for encroaching on what she felt was her God-ordained responsibility . . .

Everyone, even a difficult older woman, wanted to be useful.

I made a mental note to take the girls to Bethel's house for a visit.

---

Though my brothers frequently overshadowed me in my younger days, I had to admit, they had never let me down. If they were married, their responsibilities to their own families would take precedence over mine. As it was, James and Simeon volunteered to travel with me to claim our she-goats. Yeshua, of course, was teaching somewhere, while Jude was occupied with a carpentry job. So that James, Simeon, and I would make better time, Joses agreed to stay home and take care of my daughters and my feathered flock.

We planned to leave for Caesarea on the first day of the week, right after Shabbat. James had arranged to borrow a donkey to carry our water jugs, blankets, and food for the journey. The trip to Caesarea should take three or four days, yet I wasn't sure how long it would take us to return. Were pregnant she-goats good travelers?

As soon as the first stars came out to signal the end of Shabbat, I walked over to the house that adjoined ours. The man and woman who lived there, Bethel and Seth, had built the house when we were children but had never been overly friendly. I thought things might be different now that we were no longer noisy children, so I went to see them before we departed.

The old woman's eyes narrowed when she opened her door and saw me standing outside her gate in the twilight.

"Shalom," she croaked, her eyes implying anything but neighborly peace. "What do you want?"

"Shalom." Forcing a smile, I wondered if I had made a mistake in coming. "I hate to disturb you, but my brothers and I will be traveling tomorrow. Joses will remain here to take care of my daughters—"

"What was your name again?"

I swallowed hard. "I'm Pheodora, the youngest daughter of Mary and Joseph."

She stared at me, clearly trying to recall where we'd met, then her feathery brows shot up to her hairline. "The one who went away," she cried. "The one who came back with chickens."

"I did not desert my family," I said, striving to be gentle. "I went with my husband, who lived in Bethlehem. But now I am staying with my brothers and I need to go to Caesarea. I'm leaving my daughters with Joses—"

"I know Joses," she said, her voice rough. "I know all the sons of Joseph. I take them stew and bread every Shabbat."

"Do you?" I nodded. "Well, Joses will have his hands full while we are away. I wondered if you might keep an eye on my chickens. I would ask Joses, but he is likely to forget. You may keep any eggs they lay, of course. I don't want any of them to be eaten by dogs or foxes."

Her dark eyes flashed a warning. "I hear those infernal birds at all hours of the day and night. And now you have a rooster!"

"And you feed the dogs." I smiled and folded my arms. "I know there is goodness in your heart because you take pity on the wild dogs roaming the streets. That is why I thought of you. If you would scatter some grain on the ground for my birds—you will find the grain in a clay jar by the gate—

113

they can take care of themselves. My daughters will help, but I'm not sure how dependable they will be. Please take the eggs for yourself. We should return within two weeks' time."

For a moment I thought she would refuse, but either the casual compliment or the promise of eggs must have persuaded her. She stared at me for a moment, then jerked her chin in a nod and closed her door.

I found Judit waiting for me on the street, and she took my hand as we walked home. "Do you think she will do it, Ima? That woman did not look happy."

"Her name is Bethel," I reminded her. "And she said she would, so now we have to trust her."

"But what if she doesn't? What if our chickens starve? What if she *eats* them?"

"She would not do that," I replied, responding with a conviction I did not feel.

# CHAPTER FIFTEEN

# Pheodora

In the end, Simeon could not travel with us to Caesarea. An unexpected client appeared at our door, and because Simeon knew he needed to help support the growing number of people in the house, he decided to remain in Nazareth and build a cradle for an anxious first-time father.

James, however, would not abandon me. So, on the first day of the week, we rose early, packed the donkey, and left the house while the others slept. Though travel was often fraught with risks because of thieves, Romans, and tax collectors, James and I joined a group heading west and set out on our journey.

I found walking and the quiet a welcome change from my daily routine. Our group traveled at a sedate pace, for an elderly couple traveled with us and we did not want to tire them. The change of scenery allowed me to set aside my concerns about Chiram and my daughters. Most of my travels had been from north to south, from Nazareth to Bethlehem or Jerusalem. Yet on this trip we walked westward through the fertile Esdraelon Valley, covered with plots of tilled and planted land. Descending the hills of Nazareth, the green landscape stretched westward, dissected by the River Kishon, which, James told me, emptied into the Great Sea near the base of Mount Carmel. Finally, after several days, we reached that storied mountain, the place where Elijah defeated the four hundred prophets of Baal.

"Look." James stopped on the road and turned. From the elevation of Mount Carmel we looked southward and beheld the Plain of Sharon, where the land slanted toward the Great Sea. I had never seen any body of water larger than the Galilee, and the sight of so much shimmering blue snatched my breath away.

"This man we seek," James said, "does he live north or south of Caesarea?"

"His name is Nathan ben Abram," I replied. "I don't know where he lives—we will have to ask."

James pointed at a distant settlement on the southern horizon. "That is Caesarea. Herod developed the city into an outstanding port, so it is truly grand. But it is filled with Gentiles."

"The man we are seeking is neither grand nor Gentile," I said. "Chiram said he lives outside the city. The sooner we find him, the sooner we can take the goats home."

Several in our caravan left us at Mount Carmel, so we said our farewells and then the rest of us headed toward the southern highway that led to Caesarea.

The donkey James had borrowed was a good beast, as far as donkeys go, neither recalcitrant nor overeager. "Do you remember," I reminded my brother as we descended Mount Carmel, "the time we all went to Jerusalem and the donkey wouldn't budge until Yeshua spoke to it? We were among the last to return to Nazareth, and Abba suffered so much teasing over that stubborn animal."

"I remember," James said, grinning. "Yeshua has always had a way with animals."

At midday we stopped to rest beneath the shade of a terebinth tree. While I spread a blanket and James took food and water out of the pack saddle, our traveling companions spread out on their blankets or lay on their backs in the grass. After about an hour of rest, we pulled our things together and continued walking, a contented party . . . until our leader spied a tax collector's booth on the road ahead.

James halted. "Is this the spot?" He forced the words through clenched teeth. "Is this the place where they levied that outrageous fine against your husband?"

"Not here," I whispered. "They taxed him outside Bethlehem and imprisoned him near Arimathea."

"Accosted twice," James muttered. "As if once wasn't enough."

We walked on, but an undercurrent of grumbling went with us, and from the corner of my eye I saw furtive movements as our companions sought to hide belongings that might draw the tax collector's attention.

The tax man who halted us—a short, balding fellow in an expensive tunic—sat at a table beneath a tent of blue fabric. A papyrus scroll lay open before the man, along with the tools of his trade: a purse, stylus, and a bottle of ink. A heavily muscled man with a sword at his belt stood at the tax collector's right hand, his arms crossed and his face set in a scowl.

Less than ten paces away another man sat at his own table, and without being told I surmised he was a creditor who made loans to anyone who could not pay their tax. Judging from the moneylender's oiled hair, expensive tunic, and fine horse, he had done well for himself. Noting the man's clean-shaven face, I wondered if he was Greek . . .

Was this tax collector the man who taxed my husband? And was this Barauch, the Greek moneylender who had him thrown in prison? I tugged on my brother's sleeve. "What if it is the same men?" I whispered. "I want to know if these are the men who stopped Chiram."

"What if they are?" James lifted one eyebrow and pitched his voice for my ears alone. "If they are the same men, what difference does it make?"

"If I knew for certain, I could look them in the eyes and tell them how terrible they are, how unjust!"

"And you would risk being taxed for the tunic you are wearing and the sandals on your feet." My brother's expression darkened, and he shook his head. "Better to remain quiet, sister."

"What they did to Chiram is not right!"

"True, but consider their arrangement. The first man charges more than a traveler can possibly pay, and the second gives the traveler a loan to pay the debt—but with unreasonable interest."

"What can a common man do about it?" I asked, studying the pair. "The tax collector is a Jew—"

"Who cheats his own people." James's voice dripped with contempt.

"And the moneylender works for Romans."

Our group halted short of the tax collector's table. The little man at the first table stood and waved us forward, smiling as though he was eager to offer us a gift. "Come," he called, his voice as bright as the sun overhead. "I will not keep you long."

118

"There's no way out," James muttered. "Might as well get it over with."

He strode forward, leading the way for the others, and I hurried to keep up.

"James ben Joseph of Nazareth," James said, giving his name and town. "I am traveling with my sister."

The tax man glanced behind James to see if anyone else would step forward as part of our family, then shifted his attention to the donkey. "Is your beast carrying goods for sale?"

James shook his head. "Only food and water for our journey, and the beast is not ours. It is borrowed."

"I see blankets."

"If we are not near a village, we stop and sleep on the road."

The man squinted at James, as if he could discern truth from falsehood by narrowing his eyes. "If you are not carrying goods, then why are you traveling?"

"We are going to pick up some livestock."

"Ah. So you will have taxable property on your return journey."

James's jaw tightened. "If HaShem wills."

"Of course." The tax man waved James away. "Off with you, then. Shalom. Next!"

James released an exasperated sigh as we walked past the moneylender and moved to the side of the road to wait for the others. "We should pray those goats of yours don't give birth before we reach Nazareth," he said, his voice heavy with sarcasm. "We do not want to owe that man any more than necessary."

We were approaching Caesarea when we stopped at a well to inquire about Nathan ben Abram. I watched from the shade of a sprawling oak while James spoke to a man, who nodded and pointed to a hilly area to the east. James thanked him, then came toward me, a smile gleaming through his beard.

"I have found your goat man," he said, his eyes snapping. "Nathan ben Abram lives down that road"—he pointed to a path leading into the wilderness—"on this side of the city."

He pulled the donkey's lead from the branch he'd looped it around, but I caught his arm. "Wait," I said, my throat clotting. "I am not ready to get the goats . . . yet."

James cocked an eyebrow at me. "Speak, sister. What is on your mind?"

I swallowed hard, knowing I had no right to ask what I was about to ask. James had been kind enough to come with me this far, so perhaps he would be kind enough to indulge my heart. He was not married, so I did not expect him to fully understand, yet he was my brother, and he knew at least a little about love . . .

"We are not so far from Arimathea," I said, my voice wavering. "I know I am asking a lot, but I need to see my husband. I need to be sure he is well and assure him I am doing all I can for him. I need to tell him how much we miss him. Please, James . . . can we continue on to see Chiram? We can pick up the goats on the way back."

If James had not wanted to go to Arimathea, I would not have objected. But he was a son of Joseph and Mary, and every week my parents had visited the prison outside Nazareth. With such an example before us, how could either of us neglect my husband's welfare?

James looked southward as if he could see Arimathea

from where we stood, but that city was another two-day journey. Then he nodded. "We will go." He wrapped the donkey's lead around his fist. "We will pick up your goats on our return. I'm sure you are right—prison is lonely, and Chiram needs to see his family. So let us fill the water jars and get started."

Grateful for an agreeable and unselfish brother, I squeezed his arm and helped him with the water.

Mixed feelings surged within me as we approached Arimathea. I desperately wanted to see Chiram, to encourage and assure him I would do everything I could to secure his release, and yet I dreaded seeing him in prison. I had heard horrible things about such places, and what if he did not want me to see him in such horrible conditions?

One thought gave me comfort—at least the girls were not with me. If something happened to Chiram during his confinement, I did not want my daughters' last memory of their father's face to be shadowed by iron bars.

Finally reaching our destination, James led the way through the city gate, then paused to ask one of the elders about the prison. The man pointed to a stony ridge outside the city wall. "There," he said. "That is where you will find our unfortunates."

After thanking the man, James came back to me. "Are you sure you want to do this?"

"I am."

He nodded. "Bring whatever food we have in the pack saddle—Chiram will be grateful for it."

From the leather pouch I pulled out bread, cheese, and boiled eggs, then walked with James toward a cave guarded by a single man. The guard did not wear a Roman uniform, so he must have been an ordinary citizen, armed only with a dagger and a spear. I had a feeling this prison held no truly dangerous criminals, only debtors who had fallen on hard times.

James spoke for me when we reached the guard. "We have come to see one of your prisoners, a man called Chiram, from Bethlehem."

The man looked us over, then frowned at the bundle in my hands. "What's that you're carrying?"

"We have come a long way," I said quickly. "I have not packed much, but I did want to bring food for my husband."

The man gestured toward the linen in my hand, so I held it out. He lifted the folded flap, grunted at the contents, took one of the boiled eggs, and waved us away. "Take care you do not give him food in front of the others. Hungry prisoners have been known to inflict damage over a scrap of bread."

I wrapped the remaining egg, bread, and cheese, and followed James into the cavern. As we entered, I heard a faint trickle of water—condensation dripping off the stone walls, or perhaps someone had tapped into an underground stream? I took another step into the cave and recoiled at the stench. The odors of unwashed bodies, human refuse, vomit, and decay assaulted my nostrils so violently I had to turn and cover my face.

"Easy," James said, gripping my arm. "Think of the men inside—they have to live here."

I pressed a hand to my mouth, fighting the involuntary rise of my gorge. "How could anyone—?"

"Breathe through your mouth," James commanded, his hand tight around my arm. "Think of Abba and Ima, who thought nothing of visiting afflicted souls in places like this.

This is true religion, Pheodora, no matter what the Pharisees would tell you."

With difficulty I parted my lips and lifted my head, determined to follow my brother's example. If my husband could endure this unpleasantness for weeks, surely I could bear it for an hour.

We moved farther into the cavern, walking toward the barred chamber at the end of the tunnel. The people of Arimathea had done their best to build a prison without incurring great expense. Inside the natural cavern, they had fashioned a holding cell large enough to hold half a dozen men. Someone had wedged metal bars into the stone and cut a hole in the ceiling to allow light into the space. Three shadowy figures lounged on the earth beneath the opening, but as I drew near, one of them stood and approached the rusted bars. "Pheodora? Can that be you?"

"Chiram?"

James halted, allowing me to hurry to my husband. My hand slipped through the bars and found Chiram's. In that moment I was unspeakably grateful James had agreed to travel the extra distance to Arimathea. I would probably go out of my mind with grief and loneliness if I had to spend more than a day in such a place, and Chiram had been imprisoned for over a month.

"I brought you something," I said, using my free hand to press the wrapped food into his palm. "It is not much, but you must eat it quickly. I do not want you to lose it to the others here."

Chiram took the bundle and held it to his chest while he studied my face. His skin—what I could see of it beneath his tangled hair and unruly beard—had darkened with grime. His eyes shone from crevices of bone, shadowed by his protruding brow. I stepped back to look him over and felt my heart squeeze when I saw how gaunt he had become in such a short time.

"Do they not feed you anything? You are so thin!"

A small smile glimmered in his beard. "They give us old bread and water—the 'bread of affliction,' they call it."

"Then you must eat now. I cannot leave, knowing you have not had at least a little decent food."

He gave me an apologetic smile, then opened the cloth and held its contents toward the other men. "My wife has brought us something," he said, his voice vibrating with warmth. "Come, share my bounty."

I watched in disbelief as the other two men—both of whom were even thinner than Chiram—pulled themselves up from the floor and teetered toward him on skeletal legs. I was certain they would grab the choicest bits, leaving nothing for my husband. Instead, they waited beside him until he broke off parts of the cheese, bread, and egg, then placed pieces in each man's palm. His division of the food was accurate, even generous, and left but a third of my scant offering for himself.

"Chiram!" I hissed, keeping my voice low. "I brought that for you!"

He placed part of the egg into his mouth, chewed, and swallowed. "When I arrived, I realized I could make these men friends or enemies. We are much more content as friends."

I turned my head, unwilling for him to see the tears rising in my eyes. And Damaris could not understand why I had married this man . . .

He ate the rest of my offering, then gave me a trembling smile. "I am so sorry to bring such trouble on you, and I know you traveled many days to get here. How are the girls?"

I swallowed the lump in my throat and struggled to speak normally. "They are well. They are staying with my brothers in Nazareth—we are all staying there until you are free." Tears spilled over my cheeks despite my resolve to remain strong. "When we leave this place, James and I are going to Caesarea to find Nathan ben Abram, as you directed me."

Chiram glanced at James and nodded. "Thank you, brother."

James dipped his chin but remained behind me, giving me and my husband as much privacy as possible. "Do you understand what you need to do?" Chiram asked. "If the mating was successful, the she-goats should be pregnant."

"Do not worry, husband. I will get the goats, and James will help me take them to Nazareth. The courtyard at my mother's house is larger than at our home in Bethlehem, so all will be well—"

"Be careful . . ." Chiram glanced toward the opening of the cave and lowered his voice. "Be careful who you speak to outside Caesarea. It is a Gentile city, and not everyone you meet will be trustworthy. These are exceptional goats, and someone might be tempted to steal them. When you arrive at the city gates, ask for Nathan ben Abram—you will know him by his white beard. He was a friend of my father and is my friend, as well. He will surrender the she-goats into your hands."

"We will do as you say." I tried to give my husband a reassuring smile. "I miss you. I cannot imagine how you are enduring this . . ."

Chiram's fingers curled around the iron bars. "Do not think of this place at all. I spend my time here praying for the day I will walk out and join my family. Whether that is tomorrow or next year, I pray HaShem will work His will."

"It will not be tomorrow." With a heavy heart, I told him about Damaris and Shimon's unwillingness to pay his debt. "I had hoped Shimon would put an end to all of this, but he is unable or unwilling to help."

My husband's countenance fell. Then he lifted his chin and held me firmly in his gaze. "So let it be a year from now, or a year and a half. Find the she-goats and take them back to Nazareth. Watch over them vigilantly—they should bear kids by early summer. Raise the young ones carefully and make certain they are kept safe from wild animals. They must have no blemishes, no marks or scars. After Passover, when they are a year old, take them to Migdal-eder and present them to the shepherd who purchases for the Levites. Show him the kids and tell him I arranged this breeding for Yom Kippur. If he is not interested, tell him if there are better goats to be found, he is welcome to try to find them. But"— even in the gloom, I saw confidence in Chiram's smile—"he will find no better animals. I selected the sire and she-goats carefully, and these two females should bear perfect offspring for the Day of Atonement."

I wrapped my hands over his. "May HaShem help me do all I can to bring you home again."

"Home." His voice brimmed with wistfulness, and his eyes shone with tears. "I am beginning to think I should give up shepherding and find work in Nazareth. It is not right that my daughters should grow up without having their father close by."

"You would do that?"

"Considering what you are about to do for me, how could I do less? If you want a full-time husband, Pheodora, you have but to ask."

I did not ask in that moment because I could not see the

future. Would he feel the same way if I failed in my task? What if something happened to the goats? What if the Levites preferred other goats for the Yom Kippur sacrifice?

Silence stretched between us, then Chiram lowered his head and pulled his hands away. "I know the journey to Nazareth is a long one. Do not feel you have to visit this place again . . . unless you *need* to see me. We can always write each other."

"I wonder . . . should I try to bring the girls? They miss you so."

"No. Do not bring them here, ever. It is enough for me to know they are well, and with you and your brothers."

He took a half step back as if reluctant to touch me again. "Shalom, wife. May HaShem guard you on your journey and bless your efforts on my behalf."

I wanted to respond with a blessing of my own, but my tight throat would only allow me to speak in a small whisper. "Farewell, my beloved."

## CHAPTER SIXTEEN

# Pheodora

Because Caesarea was a Gentile city, built by the first Herod in honor of Rome's Caesar Augustus, we walked around it until we reached the well where we had stopped before. We knew Nathan ben Abram lived down the road that led away from the well, so we turned toward the rising sun and followed the trail.

We had not gone far when we spotted a middle-aged man, cutting hay in a field.

"Shalom," James called as we drew closer. "We are seeking Nathan ben Abram."

"I know Nathan," the man said. "We all know him."

"Good." James smiled. "We have come to discuss some business with Nathan."

The man acknowledged us with a nod, then plucked a long stalk of uncut grass and stuck it in his mouth. "What sort of business would Nathan have with strangers?"

My brother's smile tightened. "Do you know where we can find him? We have come a great distance."

The man lowered his gaze and rubbed the back of his

neck. "Nathan is an old man, and I haven't seen him in days. He might be ill."

Though a warning bell had begun to chime in my head, James ignored the man's lack of hospitality. "Then perhaps we should visit him to cheer his spirit. Where does he live?"

The man shrugged. "I would be happy to take you to him, but I cannot leave my work. I am sure you understand—I am responsible for getting the hay cut before sunset."

"Then shalom to you." James held the man in a smiling gaze, then turned and led me from the field.

I waited until we had moved away before erupting in frustration. "What are you doing?" I asked, not bothering to hide my irritation. "That man knows where Nathan lives."

"And so do we," James said. "That man did not want us to visit Nathan, but he carefully chose his words so he would not speak falsely. I wouldn't be surprised if he were related to the old man."

"A son, perhaps?"

James nodded. "That is what I'm thinking."

"Why wouldn't he want us to visit his father?"

"Perhaps he was being protective . . . or maybe he has a reason we know nothing about. But one thing is clear—someone lives at the end of this trail, and it is likely Nathan ben Abram. These fields aren't suitable for farming, but they'd be perfect for grazing goats."

"Or sheep," I added. "You don't know what we'll find ahead."

"I do not," James admitted. "Still, if we do not find Nathan, I'm hopeful we will find someone who knows where he lives."

After following the worn path until the sun stood directly overhead, we crested a hill and stopped at the highest point. Before us lay a valley in which sat a small house with a shelter attached to its side. Even from where we stood, I could see several pens churning with sheep and goats.

I glanced at James. "I think we found Nathan ben Abram."

"I agree," he said, tugging the donkey forward.

We made our way down the hill, and as soon as we were within shouting distance, James called out, "Nathan ben Abram!"

Almost at once, a man with a long white beard stepped out of the shelter. He lifted a hand to shade his eyes and raised his head like a dog parsing the wind. A woman came out of the house and stood in the courtyard, wiping her hands on a piece of linen as she studied us.

"Shalom aleichem! I am James, son of Joseph of Nazareth, and this is my sister, Pheodora. She is the wife of Chiram, a shepherd in Bethlehem."

"I know Chiram," Nathan said, a smile gathering up the wrinkles by his eyes. "I once watched the flocks with his father at Migdal-eder. Please"—he gestured toward the house—"I was expecting Chiram, but if he sent you . . ."

"Chiram is in debtors' prison," James said. "He sent us to bring home the goats he bought from you."

Nathan stood silent for a moment, absorbing the news, then he nodded. "I have them." He indicated that we should follow him. "Come inside and join us for dinner and prayers. We will talk, you will rest, then you may take the goats and be on your way. But first I want to hear about my friend."

Nathan and his wife, Miriam, not only invited us to their midday meal, but after hearing we had come all the way from Nazareth, Miriam insisted we spend the night. "Traveling with livestock is not easy," she said as she set a savory pot of stew on the table, "especially when the animals outnumber the people. I am sure you can manage, but the journey to Nazareth will not be easy."

"We will do whatever we must," James assured her, sitting on the bench at the table. "These goats are important to Chiram and Pheodora."

Nathan chuckled. "They are important to a great many people. My own son keeps asking what we will do if Chiram does not show up to claim his she-goats. I think he may be guilty of coveting those unborn kids."

"Your son." James shot me a knowing glance. "I think we met him on the road."

Nathan nodded. "I will be happy to tell him that Chiram's goats will soon be on their way home." He released a heavy sigh. "I am so sorry to hear he has been imprisoned. Prison is not the place for a man like him."

"We have just come from visiting him," I said. "It is truly a horrible situation. I cannot believe he may have to spend months there."

"Let us pray he does not." Nathan took his place at the head of the table, which had been set with spoons and clay dishes. When his wife took her seat, he lifted his eyes to heaven. *"Barukh ata Adonai Eloheinu, Melekh ha'olam, bo're minei m'zonot." Blessed are You, Lord our God, King of the universe, who creates varieties of nourishment.*

Miriam passed me a loaf of bread. "We have been eagerly waiting to hear from Chiram. The mating was successful, and the she-goats are carrying babies. We were beginning to think they would give birth here."

"I am sorry we were delayed," I said. "Chiram is grateful you were willing to sell him the she-goats. He has high hopes for the kids."

"Your husband has a good eye for animals." Nathan plucked a chunk of meat out of the stewpot with a palm leaf, then popped it into his mouth. "He chose the does and the buck. If the kids are as good as we expect, he is to be commended for his knowledge and ability."

"So." James broke a loaf of bread. "You used to live in Bethlehem?"

Miriam nodded. "We did, until Nathan reached fifty years. Then he decided to come here where he could enjoy the open space of the wilderness and breed his own animals. Chiram helped us move our belongings."

"He did?" I smiled, surprised by this news. My husband could have easily made the trip during one of his weeks away; I was only surprised he never mentioned it.

Miriam chuckled. "You didn't know, did you? I understand, because my father was a shepherd and often away from home. He did things during the week and forgot to tell us about his adventures. Once he killed a lion. Another time he saved part of the flock from a band of thieves. Other people looked down on us because of my father's trade, but what would they do without us?"

I nodded, understanding exactly. Those who were devoutly religious shunned tradesmen like shepherds and tanners because such work left a man ritually unclean. But how could you care for animals without occasionally touching a carcass? Chiram said you could not work with livestock without encountering dead stock. His work did not allow him to remain ritually pure for long, so he rarely attended Temple services. "I still worship," he once told me. "I worship HaShem under a canopy of clouds, with music provided by a choir of birds accompanied by the whispering wind."

"My father—" Nathan paused to swallow—"often said there is none whose trade HaShem does not adorn with beauty."

James nodded. "My father would agree."

I turned back to Miriam. "Your father was a shepherd? Did he know Chiram's father?"

"He certainly did." She tilted her head and gave me a mysterious smile. "Has your husband ever mentioned—it would have happened more than thirty years ago, but my father never forgot it. He died in peace because of what happened that night."

Mystified, I stopped eating. "What happened?"

She shook her head. "The story would make no sense if I told it. Better to hear it from your father-in-law."

"But Chiram's father is dead."

"Then surely your husband can tell you."

"I . . . don't know if he knows. He has never mentioned anything unusual. Then again, he didn't tell me about moving you and your husband up here, either."

"You must ask him." Miriam's eyes danced as she smiled. "I am sure he knows, and I am sure you will be astounded by the story."

I looked at Nathan, hoping for some sort of clue, but he looked as secretive as his wife and made no effort to enlighten me.

"I will try to remember," I told her. "But right now, I am more interested in meeting my husband's special goats."

After helping Miriam clean away the remains of our dinner, I followed Nathan and James outside. A few goats stood on the rocky hillside, munching on weeds and scrub, but Nathan kept his breeding stock in pens. Looking across the fenced area, I realized I never knew goats came in so many varieties—large and small, horned and hornless. I saw goats with tan sides, goats with black forequarters and tan hindquarters, goats with dark bellies and white bodies, goats with stripes down their spines, goats with dark bodies and pale legs, goats with black bodies and tan faces . . .

"Over here," Nathan called.

A moment later, I found myself eye to eye with a large white goat. A doe, Nathan said. A pregnant she-goat, due to deliver her kid in two months. Another doe of roughly the same size stood in the pen next to her. On the other side of the barn, a larger goat, the buck, watched us with interest in his odd, wary eyes.

"At least we will not have to travel with the male," James remarked, crossing his arms. "I have heard they are difficult."

"They can be," Nathan agreed. "You wouldn't want to travel with a buck. The males are protective of their females, and you wouldn't be able to get near these girls if he was nearby. So, yes, take the girls to Nazareth, but walk them gently, don't hurry them, and stop for greens and fresh water every hour or so. I saw you have a donkey—keep the does away from him, because if they don't like his looks, they may not walk at all."

James blinked. "Why wouldn't they like his looks?"

"If there's a creature more stubborn and cantankerous than a donkey, it's a pregnant female of any kind," Nathan said. "Let them walk in front; that will keep the donkey out of their sight. But mind my words—don't walk them too hard, too far, or too fast."

I stifled a groan. I had been hoping to reach Nazareth in another four or five days, but if we had to match the pace of these swollen mothers-to-be . . .

"And tempt them," Nathan added. "If you want them to walk for you, dangle something they like to eat in front of their noses. That is all it takes to motivate a goat."

James stared at the goats as if he had never seen one before. "What do they like to eat?"

"Almost anything," Nathan said, "including whatever you're having for dinner."

I walked slowly around the beasts, wondering if I could handle the task of caring for these animals. Ima had a goat when we were small, though I never paid much attention to it. I looked up at Nathan. "What if a goat gets sick? How will I know, and who should I ask for help?"

The old shepherd grinned. "All you have to do is describe the ailment to anyone who knows goats."

"How do I do that? I don't know anything about goats."

He walked to the pregnant goat's side and placed his hand on the juncture of her shoulder blades. "The withers," he said. "The stifle joint is the place above the knee on the back leg. The pastern is the place where the hoof joins the leg. The bone at the front of the foreleg is the cannon bone. The pin bone is a bony protrusion at the back, right above the tail. The escutcheon is the arch between the legs, which should be high and wide, allowing room for the udder—"

"Thank you." I lifted my hands and backed away, my head spinning with the shepherd's strange words. "Maybe I should find a goat expert near home."

"I don't understand why these goats are so unique," James said, gingerly running his hand over a goat's back. "They're white, but so are lots of others."

Nathan chuckled. "Lots of goats are white, along with other colors in their coat. These two females—and yonder buck—were born almost completely white, with not a single brown or black hair. They grew a few brown hairs later, yet we hope their offspring will be perfectly white, even after they are a year old."

"And if they grow dark hairs?" I asked.

Nathan shrugged. "They will be like any other mostly white goat. Still acceptable for the sacrifice, but you know the Levites—they place great importance on purity."

James turned to Nathan. "I thought pure white animals were sometimes sickly, or blind and deaf."

"You are thinking about albinos." Nathan nodded. "And you are right. A white goat with pink eyes will tend to be sickly, but these she-goats have brown eyes, as does the sire. Their kids should be healthy."

I studied the she-goats again. Both were white, or mostly so, with only a few light brown hairs sprinkled across their backs. Long ears hung on each side of their narrow faces and brown eyes. The goats were bigger than I expected, with long necks and thin legs. Having never examined a goat so closely, I wasn't sure how to tell if the goat was pregnant or only big-bellied. "These goats *will* have babies?" I asked.

"I witnessed the mating myself," Nathan replied.

"And you're sure they're pregnant."

His smile widened. "Trust me, these goats will have kids. Would you like to feel them?"

I blinked. "Feel—what?"

"Come here." He moved to the first she-goat and gestured

to me. I walked to his side, then watched as he placed his hand on the goat's belly. He held his palm against the skin for a moment. "The baby is kicking now. You can feel it, too." As James looked on, I placed my hand against the goat's side. At first all was still, and then I felt a faint stirring within her, the same motion I recognized from when I carried my daughters in my own belly. "Amazing." Feeling embarrassed, I pulled my hand away and smiled at our host. "I believe you." I bent to glance beneath the goats. The udders still looked relatively small, which was probably normal for a goat who had not yet given birth.

"Look here." The shepherd squatted and tapped the skin in front of the udder. "At two weeks after mating, the skin here becomes tight. At two months, the belly gets bigger. At three months and onward, you can put your hands on the belly and feel the kid kicking. Soon the udder will fill with milk. After that, if the belly gets big, she'll have one baby. If the belly gets *very* big, there are two or more babies inside."

"Just like a woman," I muttered, and the goat breeder chuckled.

"Do not worry. Chiram trusted me with his goats, he selected a beautiful buck, and he has watched these does since they were newborns. They are his hope for a better life for his family. So now I am pleased to surrender his goats, and his dreams, to you."

I slumped as the heavy mantle of responsibility fell on my shoulders. I who knew nothing about goats or midwifery, would have to care for these creatures, help bring their babies into the world, and guard those kids with my life. If I failed, my husband would probably die in debtors' prison, and if he died with the debt outstanding, one of my daughters would likely be sold to satisfy the creditor.

I staggered at the thought, and James stepped forward, slipping his arm under mine. "Easy there," he said, holding me steady. "Watch your step."

He thanked Nathan, then watched carefully as the goat breeder demonstrated how to tie a lead around a goat's neck. My mouth quirked—what, no gold-adorned bridle for these precious creatures? No scented slippers for their dainty hooves?

As we walked back toward the house, James asked Nathan, "What do we feed them? We have to convince the goats to keep up the pace. We don't want to rush them, but we must get home as soon as we can. So, if you can tell us something they like to eat—"

"Anything," Nathan said, grinning.

# CHAPTER SEVENTEEN

# Pheodora

Apparently anything colorful and edible kept the goats moving forward. We fed them vegetables from the market until the goats ate everything in our pack saddle. Then James snatched handfuls of grass from the roadside and found that holding the grass behind his back worked just as well. I cautioned him, however, to keep an eye out for any plant life he didn't recognize. I wouldn't want to poison the goats before we made it back to Nazareth.

Fortunately, a paved road led from Caesarea through Samaria and Galilee. We would sleep under the stars each night, for we did not want to leave the goats unguarded and we were unsure of our welcome in Samaritan territory. Easier to stop at sunset, secure the donkey and goats, and sleep under the nearest tree.

The walk home was hot, tiresome, and dull, and only travelers like us were desperate enough to journey during the hottest part of the day. Even tax collectors packed up and moved on to shady spots at midday. I worried about the sweltering heat harming the goats and their developing babies, so I insisted we stop every hour or so and allow the goats to rest in whatever shade we could find. We led them to water when we found it, and when water was not to be found, we let them drink from our water jugs, choosing to thirst rather than let the goats suffer. The goats needed water, while James and I could endure a little discomfort.

As we walked, I thought of my parents, who, to my knowledge, had never traveled this road. What business would they have had in Caesarea? Like most Galileans, they probably could have walked blindfolded to Jerusalem, having made the annual pilgrimages—Passover, Pentecost, and Tabernacles—as often as possible.

My heart always warmed when I remembered our family pilgrimages. Passover was a precious, holy time when we shared the Seder with Jews from around the world. Tabernacles, *Sukkot*, was perhaps the happiest festival, when we slept in temporary shelters and watched the priests do summersaults in the Temple.

Yom Kippur, on the other hand, was a different sort of festival. We did not travel to Jerusalem to witness it, though one time we happened to be in the Holy City for that most holy day.

I looked over at James, who had been walking in a thoughtful silence for some time. "Do you recall the time we were in Jerusalem during the High Holy Days?"

His brow furrowed, then he nodded. "You were small. I'm surprised you remember."

"I remember bits and pieces. Probably because I had never before seen the ceremony of atonement."

He threw me a sidelong glance. "How much do you remember?"

"I remember staying with a butcher and his wife. I remember the high priest performing the daily offering in a special golden tunic."

James nodded. "Yes. He only wears the gold tunic on that day."

"I remember him sitting in a special mikvah in the Temple courtyard. As a child, I thought it strange to see him taking a bath."

"The cohen gadol must be clean when he stands before HaShem in the Holy of Holies. He is atoning for everyone's sin—his own, his family's, and the people's."

"I remember the goats, too, but only vaguely. They were in the courtyard while the high priest drew lots from a box. One goat won."

"He didn't *win*," James corrected. "One goat was selected for Adonai, the other for Azazel."

"He tied a red scarf around the horns of the second goat. I felt sorry for the beast, though I had no idea what Azazel meant."

"It means *wilderness*," James said and gestured to the arid land around us. "Like this."

I tipped my face toward the sun. "I find it odd to think my family's future depends on the goats of Yom Kippur. I wonder if Chiram is right about their wanting pure white goats. What if the Levites don't care what the goats look like? What if *any* goat will suit their purposes?"

James made a *tsk*ing sound. "You must not worry about that. The priests are particular about animals, especially at Yom Kippur. Seven days prior to *the* day, the high priest is sprinkled with spring water that has been mixed with the ashes of a red heifer. A red heifer is a rare animal, and if the priests find even two black hairs on a red animal, it is disqualified. The animal must never have borne a yoke. The men who search for red heifers would certainly be interested in a pure white goat. Trust your husband. I believe he is right."

"But do the Scriptures say the goat must be white?"

"No, but I would not be surprised if having found pure white goats, the rabbis require it from this time forward. They are fond of adding to the Law." His voice soured. "They are eager to make our service to Adonai even more difficult."

I glanced at the goats behind me, then checked to see whether our donkey, walking on an extra-long rope, did not mind being the last beast in our little caravan. For some reason, he seemed content to walk behind the she-goats. Perhaps he was fascinated by their scent or by their dainty steps. I didn't know, yet I was glad he had not decided to be stubborn on this journey.

The steady sound of the animals' hooves carried me back to my childhood, when my family and I had stood in the crowd and watched the Azazel goat stand before the high priest. With both hands on the goat, he confessed the sins of Israel, and we prostrated ourselves on the pavement when the priest pronounced the holy name of God. While he prayed for Israel, I could hear the people murmuring, confessing their sins. When the priest finished, he stepped back as a handler took the goat's rope and walked it through the streets, leading it outside the city. My family and I followed for a little while, then we stopped and waited until we heard the crowd cheer.

"What happened?" I asked.

Abba looked down at me. "The goat has reached the wilderness."

"And now what happens?"

Abba picked me up and held me on his bony hip. "Inside

the Temple, the high priest is preparing to slaughter two rams as an offering."

"Why does he kill them, Abba?"

"Because payment for sin requires the shedding of blood, little one. That is what HaShem told Moses: 'For the life of the creature is in the blood, and I have given it to you on the altar to make atonement for your lives—for it is the blood that makes atonement because of the life.'" Abba had looked at me then, his eyes shining with tender concern. "You are young to be asking so many questions."

I was still asking questions, but James and I had little else to talk about as we walked past the barley fields teeming with harvesters.

When James and I heard the sound of hooves behind us, together we looked over our shoulders. A uniformed Roman was rapidly approaching, his black horse gleaming with perspiration.

In the hollow of my back, a drop of sweat traced the course of my backbone. What sort of trouble was this? Though he was no tax collector, in the name of Rome he could coerce us to do anything he wanted . . .

Wordlessly, James lifted his chin, directing me to move off the pavement. I pulled the goats with me while James handled the donkey. We stood silently with our heads down, hoping the Roman would not take notice of us as he passed.

Instead, the Roman reined in his horse and halted only a few steps away.

"Shalom," he said, nodding in what he probably thought was a pleasant expression. "You have animals, so I assume you have water?"

I glanced at James, who stepped forward to answer. "We do."

"Then water my horse," the man said, easing his grip on the reins. "We have been riding hard under a cursed sun."

James did not say a word as he moved to the pack saddle and lifted out one of the heavy water jugs. He pulled out a shallow trough and poured water into it, then set the trough on the road. When the horse did not immediately nuzzle at the water, James picked the trough up and held it directly in front of the animal's mouth.

The Roman—guard or centurion or whatever he was—gave the animal its head, and the grateful beast slurped at the liquid. The water disappeared almost immediately, spittle flew over James's chest and face, and the Roman jerked his chin at my brother. "More."

Again without a word, James refilled the trough, pouring until the last of the water dribbled into the shallow container. The horse drank it in, then whickered, nosing around for more.

"More," the Roman commanded.

James pointed to the jug, now lying on its side in the road. "We have no more water."

The Roman cursed in a foreign tongue and looked around, but the area was as dry as a desert. Then he pulled up his reins and snapped them across the horse's withers. The horse charged ahead, compelled by the bronze spurs on the rider's heels.

As relief and irritation warred in my heart, I gritted my teeth and watched them go. After the Roman had disappeared, James and I pulled our animals back onto the road.

"HaShem has just blessed us," James said. "That man could have commanded us to go find water for his beast. I suppose he realized he'd be more likely to find it on his own."

"But now we have none for the goats." I looked back at the she-goats and saw that they had slowed their step. "HaShem will protect them," James said, his voice firm. "We will walk slowly if necessary. The goats will be fine." I pointed at a group of travelers, who had stopped on a hillside up ahead. "Perhaps," I said, lifting a brow, "we will run into Yeshua and his followers. It would be nice to see our brother and mother."

A melancholy frown flitted across James's features, but he said nothing as he studied the group resting on the hillside.

After Yeshua's first few months as a traveling teacher, my brothers—particularly Jude—tried to persuade him to return home and take his place as the head of the family. Yeshua only smiled and said he had other work to do. Oddly enough, Ima did not disagree but remained with him, which left James responsible for handling the family carpentry business.

As we drew closer, I spotted several women and children among the group. What were they doing away from their homes? Were they traveling to a wedding or funeral? Or were they moving somewhere?

When we passed the group, we smiled and greeted them but did not stop because we did not recognize anyone. Most of the people wore the garb and headdresses of Samaritans, and we were not certain we would be welcome. Better to keep walking than to face an unpleasant situation and risk losing the goats and the donkey.

I had hoped we would find our mother and Yeshua. That hope magnified the longing I had felt ever since returning to Nazareth, and suddenly I wanted to see Ima and Yeshua more than I wanted water. I longed to sit on the ground with my head in my mother's lap, to feel her stroke my hair and tell me everything would be all right, that HaShem would not let me fail my husband, and Chiram would be freed.

I yearned to see Yeshua, as well. I loved all my brothers, but Yeshua had always been different. Though we were only six years apart, he always seemed much older. Whenever I had a problem or something on my mind, he was the first to come and sit beside me, bending his head to look into my eyes. "What is on your mind, Pheodora Aiya?" he would ask, the faint beginning of a smile on his mouth. "Tell me about it."

And I would tell him. Whether my problem was with Damaris or Jude or Simeon or the girl down the street, Yeshua would listen. And when I had finished, he would take my hand, cradle it, and say, "Love the Lord with all your heart, Pheodora. And love"—Damaris or Jude or Simeon or the girl down the street—"as you love yourself. Now, what do you think you should do?"

At that point, I always knew how to respond. Always.

James nudged me, a brotherly gesture to get my attention. "What are you thinking about? You seem preoccupied."

I laughed, warmed by the realization that he had filled Yeshua's place in many ways. "I was thinking about Ima and Yeshua. I wish they would come home, if only for a visit."

James sighed. "I would love to see them, but they are busy. Ima is a good traveler. She and Abba journeyed from Nazareth to Bethlehem when she was heavy with child. Yeshua was born in the City of David, just like your husband."

I gave James a sidelong glance of utter disbelief. "You are surely mistaken. We were all born in Nazareth."

James shook his head. "No, Damaris and I were born in Egypt."

"*Egypt?*"

He laughed. "You should pull your head out of the clouds

more often, little sister. Yes, Abba and Ima lived in Egypt for a while, then they returned to Nazareth."

"Why would they go to Egypt? Unless there was a famine . . ."

"There was no famine. I asked Abba about it, and he said HaShem told him to go to Egypt, so he went."

I stared at my brother as if he had just sprouted an extra pair of ears. How had I not known this part of our family history? I had never paid much attention to Abba's rambling stories, but since everyone I knew had been born in Nazareth, including Ima and Abba, I assumed we all had. But just like Chiram, Yeshua had been born in the City of David . . .

The words elicited a feeling of déjà vu, and after a moment I realized why. I grabbed James's arm. "Is that why Yeshua thinks he is the Messiah? Because he was born in Bethlehem? Is that why people say he's our promised king?"

James snorted. "I do not believe Yeshua would ever claim to be king. If he did, Herod Antipas would not allow him to live. That man guards his position even more jealously than his father did."

I pressed my lips together as a stream of new and troubling thoughts filled my head. I had paid little attention to Yeshua's activities over the last three years. I knew he spent time with our kinsman John, called "the Immerser," then I heard Yeshua moved to Capernaum. I cared about my older brother, yet how could I keep up with him when I had four little daughters and a husband to support?

The last time I saw Yeshua was at a wedding in Cana. Our entire family attended, and Yeshua invited some of his followers, who seemed like pleasant men. Like us, they were from Galilee, and they seemed to hang on every word that came out of Yeshua's mouth. On the last day of the wedding, we heard rumors about the host running out of wine. Then suddenly there was plenty for everyone, so much that the servants filled even the foot-washing jars with the delicious vintage.

That day would live forever in my memory for other reasons, as well. That was the day Jude met Tasmin, and the only time Chiram had been able to join us for a family event. Chiram and I had gone to Nazareth for a visit when Yeshua told us about the wedding. I had been surprised when Chiram agreed to travel to Cana, but I think he realized how desperately I missed my family . . .

I closed the curtain on my memories when we spotted the Samaritan village of Lebonah. Since the goats needed water, we headed toward the city gates. Heads turned as we entered the town with the animals, probably because we were Jews. Still, no one bothered us as we made our way to the well. Once we arrived, I pulled up the water bucket while James hauled our water jugs from the pack saddle.

"Shalom." A well-dressed man, a merchant perhaps, halted a few feet away. "A fine pair of goats you have there."

James grunted in reply.

"May I ask what you are doing here? If one of those animals is sick, you will render our water supply unclean—"

"They are not sick," James interrupted, setting the trough on the ground. "And they will not drink from your water bucket. Put your mind at rest, friend."

The man drew back as if affronted, but remained quiet as I poured water into the troughs. As the animals drank, I drew water for the jars and filled them. While James sat in the shade and waited, I drank from a clay cup and could not help but overhear another man in the village square. He had a donkey with him, so he was likely another traveler.

"I heard him preaching in Galilee," the man said, and I startled at the word *preaching.* Yeshua?

I clucked my tongue to catch James's attention, then nodded toward the man. James leaned forward to listen.

"He said he had not come to bring shalom, but division. He said households would be divided—father against son, and son against father; mother against daughter, and daughter against mother."

"That is not what I heard him say," another man argued. "He spoke of loving our enemies and blessing those who curse us."

The traveler lifted a fist. "When I heard Yeshua, he said he had come to pour fire on the earth. 'How I wish,' he said, 'it were already ablaze!' Are those not the words of a man who would kindle our spirits to fight the Romans?"

"He sounds like a king!" another man called.

"Would a king tell us to be compassionate to our enemies? Would he tell us to lend and expect nothing in return?"

The voices blurred into confused bickering, and James came toward me, his face a mask of exasperation. "I don't know what Yeshua is doing," he said, pitching his voice for my ears alone. "But if he meant to stir up the people, he has certainly accomplished his goal." He looked toward our animals, which had finished drinking. "We should get them away from here before these people grow even more agitated. Let us be on our way."

I did not think the goats had rested sufficiently, yet James made a good point. All of us—people and beasts—would be safer away from this unruly crowd.

# CHAPTER EIGHTEEN

# *Pheodora*

We spotted the watchtower of Nazareth on the sixth day of our journey home. We had traveled more swiftly than expected, and I was relieved to know I would soon be sleeping under my brothers' roof. My girls would be excited to see the new goats, though Shiri and Jordan were sure to be disappointed they couldn't make pets of them.

"I am glad you have come to stay in Nazareth," James said. "Your courtyard in Bethlehem would not be large enough to house these animals."

"No, it wouldn't." I bit my lip. "I suppose HaShem approves of the arrangements I have made. If only He would also approve of our plan to free Chiram from prison."

"How do you know He doesn't?"

"If He wanted Chiram to be free, why did He allow Chiram to be arrested? And why didn't He lead Damaris and Shimon to pay his debt?"

James tugged at his beard. "I don't know. But I do know HaShem acts in His own time and for His own reasons."

"What I have observed," I went on, "is that HaShem acts

for Israel, for prophets and kings and wealthy men. For women like me, He remains silent."

James lifted a brow at this, but he did not argue. "In any case," he said, "I am glad you will be living with us for a while. We have room, and we have space downstairs for the animals. Since Ima has been away, the house has missed having a woman beneath its roof."

I opened my mouth to reply—*you mean you've missed having someone to cook and clean*—then realized how I had already benefited from living with my brothers. I would not have to fear for my safety as I would if I were living alone. My girls would enjoy spending time with their uncles, and my brothers would undoubtedly spoil the girls whenever possible. My daughters had not spent much time with their father, so it would be good for them to have a man lead them in their prayers and Torah studies.

"It will be nice having a woman in the house," James said, a spark of merriment lighting his eyes. "And if you felt like cooking, we would not complain."

"Hmmpf." I crossed my arms. "In return, I suppose you wouldn't mind helping me with the girls?"

"Not at all." He grinned. "I like hearing the laughter of children in the house."

I smiled as relief flooded my heart. "Thank you. I know nothing about goats, so it will be good to have my brothers to call on when the she-goats give birth. I am terrified I will fail Chiram."

"Why worry? Goats have been birthing other goats since the creation of the world. Once we get settled, I will get Simeon and Joses to help me build a pen and a birthing stall."

"Do goats need a birthing stall?"

He shrugged. "Don't know. But we may as well find out."

Buoyed by a newfound sense of confidence, with a lighter step I followed my brother home.

———•———

Two days later, Joses and Simeon had constructed two lovely pens in the center of the ground floor. When we were young, Ima had kept a goat for milk and cheese in that central space, but it had been years since any animal larger than a chicken had lived in the area that opened to the outside. My chickens happily wandered in and out of the goat pens, and my daughters enjoyed checking on the goats and bringing them treats.

Naturally, my girls wanted to name the goats. I told them it was a bad idea to give them names, but Judit and Jordan would not be dissuaded. "We understand, Ima," Judit said. "We know the goats will be sold one day. But can we not give them names until then?"

"It will help you know which goat we're talking about," Jordan added. "What if we want to tell you one of them is sick. You will say, 'Which goat?' and if we say, 'The white one,' you would not know which goat is sick, would you?"

Who could resist such logic? So we named the larger one Delilah and the smaller one Hannah. "Now," I told my girls, "if one of them is sick, you must be sure to give me the right name."

As we all settled into a normal routine, I felt as though I had stepped back in time. Once again I found myself waking my brothers, preparing their food, and packing lunches for them to eat wherever they were working. Once again, we sat around the dinner table at sunset and laughed and talked and complained about life under the Romans, tax collectors, and publicans.

"I don't know how you all have survived without Ima to

clean up after you," I groused one evening as I wiped the table. "I'm surprised the grease on this tabletop isn't thicker than it is."

"We've had some help," Joses admitted. "Bethel comes over now and then to make sure we are not drowning in dirt. She also bakes for us on occasion. Her honey cakes are amazing."

"I can make honey cakes," I said. "And if my bread is good enough for my husband, it is good enough for you."

James grinned. "You will break Bethel's heart."

"That reminds me—she took care of my chickens while I was away. Did she take the eggs?"

"No." Jude pointed to a corner of the room. "She left them for us."

"Oh." I stopped cleaning and spotted the basket of eggs on a windowsill. I had wanted her to keep them; now I would have to thank her again. "She was kind," I said, humbled by her generosity. "I will have to stop over and see her."

I asked my brothers if they remembered Ima doing anything special for the she-goat we kept years ago. "Fresh water and food," Joses replied. "That is all I remember. Ima gave her fresh water every morning and made sure she had plenty to eat. Wait . . ." He grinned. "I do recall a he-goat coming around every year so our goat would produce milk. He used to butt me with his horns."

The thought of having to temporarily house a male goat made me wince. Then I consoled myself with the knowledge that Chiram had already taken care of that difficulty. Since our goats were already pregnant, they would soon produce milk. If they produced a lot of milk, my girls would benefit as well as the kids. I might even have enough to make cheese for the market.

Fortunately, Jude's memory was better than my other brothers'—or he had paid more attention to Ima's goat. "I remember a lot about the wee beast," he told me. "I know she ate almost anything, but we had to be careful not to give her wolfsbane. Ima said wolfsbane would kill a goat quicker than anything."

"Wolfsbane?"

"Not much of it growing around here. It has a purple flower. Avoid those and you will be fine."

That night, after washing the clay dishes, leading my daughters in evening prayer, and putting the girls to bed, I lay down on my stuffed mattress and asked HaShem to bless Israel and speedily send our promised Messiah.

Then, in case He was inclined to listen to the prayer of the least of the least, I prayed for my animals. I prayed the hens would continue to lay, their eggs would be large and well-shaped, and they would not get sick. I prayed for the goats, that their babies would be healthy and strong and perfectly white. I prayed the Levites would be so impressed by the beauty of those yearling kids that they would not consider any others but would purchase Chiram's kids so I could pay off his debt.

Then I prayed, perhaps selfishly, that my husband would be willing to move to Nazareth, where he could begin a new life with his wife and his daughters. That he would find another trade and learn to be happy living in a house instead of under the stars.

And that I would never again have to tend a pair of goats.

# CHAPTER NINETEEN

# Damaris

A nd what else?" I popped a grape into my mouth and smiled at Yuta, who had just returned from the city square.

Yuta shrugged. "Your sister and the goats are doing well. I walked by the house, just as you asked, and could hear bleating sounds coming from the inner courtyard. The little girls were laughing while your brother poured water into the trough."

"My sister didn't see you, did she?"

"No, my lady. I covered my face in case she watched from the rooftop."

"Good thinking." I straightened in my chair. "Finish my hair, please. I think I will take my daughters to the market, so the arrangement should not be complicated. I do not wish to spend all day in this chair."

Yuta picked up the comb and began to work it through the tangled lengths of my hair. I closed my eyes, enjoying the relaxing sensation of having my hair combed. If only

Pheodora had a maid! She might find it easier to relax if she experienced even the tiniest bit of pampering every now and then. But no, Pheodora wanted to work, to care for chickens and goats and whatever else she was raising in our brothers' courtyard.

Yuta brought me reports every morning. Though my guilty conscience would not allow me to visit my sister, I was not unfeeling or unaware of her struggles. I would have given anything to persuade Shimon to pay Chiram's debt, but a woman could not disobey her husband, especially when he had expressly commanded her not to take a certain action.

So I listened to Yuta's daily reports, reassuring myself that Pheodora was, as always, resilient and resourceful. She had left Nazareth with James and returned with a pair of goats, and Yuta said she seemed in no hurry to sell them. Perhaps she was going to make and sell cheese? Yuta did not know, and truth be told, I didn't care what Pheodora had planned for them. I was content to know she and her daughters were not homeless or starving.

Once Yuta had finished my hair and helped me don an elegantly simple tunic, I went downstairs and summoned my daughters. I gave each of them a lepton and told them we were going to the market. "Don't spend your coin on anything foolish," I reminded them. "Some sweetbreads, perhaps, or ribbons for your hair. But be polite and always remember—your father will soon be a respected Pharisee, and you must never forget that people are watching you."

Because a gentle breeze stirred the warm air outside, I sent the litter bearers away and told the girls we would walk. Amarisa groaned—she despised walking—but followed me with a determined step, her anticipation of procuring a new trinket stronger than her aversion to physical effort. Bettina,

Jemina, and Jerusha followed, while Yuta and another servant carried Lilah and Zarah, the little ones.

The market filled the center of town, the various booths
brimming with vegetables, fruits, and goods of all sorts. My
daughters spent their coins carefully—ribbons for Amarisa
and Bettina, honeyed dates and sweetbreads for Jemina,
Jerusha, and Lilah. I bought a stick of hard bread for two-
year-old Zarah, knowing she would chew on it throughout
the morning.

I fingered colorful fabrics from Magdala, tested lemons
for ripeness, and tasted a sample of olive oil from a grove
outside Jerusalem. I waggled two fingers at Yuta, my signal
for granting her permission to purchase a vial, then moved on
to the cheesemaker's booth. After sampling several flavored
cheeses, we stopped at a cobbler's stall, where the girls had
their feet measured for new sandals. "Something simple,"
I told the shoemaker. "They need something for when they
visit their cousins."

While the man fussed and made various remarks designed to flatter me and my girls, a distant flurry of move-
ment caught my eye. The salted-fish booth was operated by
a man and his wife, Gentiles from Tiberias. I did not buy
from them, of course, but over the months I had noticed
that the wife was expecting a child. Of late her pregnancy
had been painfully obvious, and last week I had remarked
to Yuta that the woman had better stay home or she would
have her baby in the open.

My words must have been prophetic, for she was leaning
hard on the table in her booth, breathing heavily while her
frantic husband attempted to fan her with a palm frond.
"My love," he said, perspiration pouring from his forehead,
"all will be well. I will find a midwife."

He looked up, his brown eyes wide and bulging. "Can anyone help?" he called, his voice rising to a shrill note. "Anyone know a midwife?"

No one answered. The men at the neighboring booths recoiled from the sight of his anguished wife, and the other women retreated behind curtains or pretended to be occupied with arranging their wares. The beardless man rushed out of his booth and looked left and right, his face flushed, droplets of sweat running down his jaw.

The laboring woman curled her hands into fists and screamed as a contraction ripped through her. I knew that pain, having borne six children of my own, and my body contracted in sympathy. She needed a quiet corner to rest, a place where she could grip someone and squat, allowing gravity to pull the child from her womb . . .

I looked down and saw Amarisa, Bettina, Jemina, and Jerusha watching me, confidence and pride in their eyes. "You can help her, Ima," Amarisa said. "You know all about having babies."

I drew a breath, about to rise, when Shimon's words came back to me on a wave of memory. *"You must not speak to a Gentile, nor enter a Gentile home. If, for instance, a Gentile woman comes to ask for a bag of grain, you cannot offer it. She is unclean, as is her entire household. You must not speak to her."*

I exhaled in a rush, knowing I could do nothing for the woman or her husband, for they were unclean, and I was . . . set apart for holiness.

But in that moment I did not feel holy.

I turned away, unable to look in the woman's direction, and caught Yuta's eye. "We must go," I said, rising as my pulse pounded thickly in my ears. "We must leave this place at once."

# CHAPTER TWENTY

# Pheodora

One afternoon, a stranger and his wife stopped by our front gate. I stepped out of the courtyard and offered a tentative smile, wondering if I had met this couple before.

"Shalom," the man called. "We are looking for Pheodora, wife of Chiram, who is said to be living with James ben Joseph."

"I am Pheodora." I wiped my hands on a towel and stepped forward to meet them. "How can I help you?"

"We have something for you," the woman said. She pulled a small scroll from their donkey's pack saddle and handed it to me. "We picked it up at a well near Arimathea. A letter for you."

My breath caught in my lungs. Only one person in that part of the world would have reason to write me. I thanked the couple, then carried the scroll into the goat pens, looking for solitude. The girls were upstairs, studying their Hebrew lessons with Joses, so I would have a few moments to myself.

I untied the scroll, unfurled the crisp parchment—where did Chiram get parchment?—and saw bold ink strokes on the inner side.

*My dear wife,*
  *I hope this letter finds you in good health and sha-lom. I am well because I carry your memory in my heart. Though I did not want you to ever think of me in a place like this, I am glad you came because now I cannot look at the bench behind the bars without seeing you there. You were kind to come.*
  *And we are no longer forgotten. We have our regular guards, of course, but of late we have had another visitor. The man reminds me of your father, he of blessed memory, and like your father he visits us regularly, engaging us in conversation and offering a bit of hope. His name is Uriah, and he is a farmer, yet he has a brother who is a Pharisee. I do not know how a man as simple as Uriah could possibly have a brother on the Great Sanhedrin, but I am a man of limited imagination. After all, who would ever have imagined that a daughter of the esteemed Joseph of Nazareth would agree to marry a simple shepherd from Bethlehem?*
  *This Uriah comes to visit us on the first day of the week, without fail. I asked our jailer if he has always done this, and the jailer said Uriah had only been visiting for a few weeks. So one afternoon, after Uriah listened to our complaints, prayed with us, and tended our little wounds, I asked why he came to the prison. "I would be surprised if most of the people in Arimathea even knew a prison stood outside their city walls," I told him. "So why do you come?"*

*He looked at me as if wondering why I would ask such a question, then a smile overtook his features. "I come because of Yeshua," he said.*

*I was so stunned by his answer that I sat up and moved closer, eager to hear more. "Yeshua?" I asked. "Which Yeshua?"*

*"You might not know him, being from Bethlehem, for he is from Nazareth, though of late he lived in Capernaum."*

*He stared, amazed, when I told him Yeshua was brother to my wife. He asked your name and whereabouts and how you were faring with a husband in prison. When I told him about our daughters, he smiled. "So Yeshua has nieces. I should have known. He is good with children."*

*As the hour grew late and the light faded, I asked how it was that Yeshua had made him come. "Did he challenge you to visit prisons?" I asked. "Did he command you?"*

*Uriah closed his eyes and quoted, "'Then the King will say to those on His right, "Come, you who are blessed by my Father, inherit the kingdom prepared for you from the foundation of the world. For I was hungry and you gave me something to eat; I was thirsty and you gave me something to drink; I was a stranger and you invited me in; I was naked and you clothed me; I was sick and you visited me; I was in prison and you came to me."'"*

*By the time he looked at me again, I was weeping.*

*"So you see," Uriah went on, his own eyes filling with tears, "I may not be able to feed and shelter and clothe HaShem, whom I love, but I can do those things for you."*

*Whatever your brother Yeshua is doing, I now know it is good. He is pointing men to HaShem in a way the Law and the Pharisees have not.*

*My heart is full, dear wife, and I know I have written a long letter, but there is little else to do in this place. Uriah has begun to bring me parchment and ink, so I will continue to write and hope these letters find their way to you. I miss you and our daughters. I pray HaShem will keep and protect you and watch over you until we are together again.*

*Chiram*

———•———

The goats proved to be the least of my worries. A few days after our return with the goats, Abigail, one of my original laying hens, did not come running out to greet me, and she had not produced an egg the day before. When I mentioned something about her to Jude, he joked about her honoring the Sabbath, but I was in no mood for humor. Abigail always produced the biggest and most beautiful eggs, and her eggs sold immediately at the market.

I needed eggs to trade for grain and hay to feed the goats. My brothers were providing me with a home and food, and I did not want them to support my goats, as well.

So I went back into the courtyard, where Joses had built a row of nesting boxes for the hens. Abigail was sitting on a pile of hay, her feathers fluffed. I tried to coax her off the nest by offering a handful of weeds, but she would not budge. Judit brought me a worm she had found in the mud, and not even that tasty treat convinced Abigail to get up. Not knowing what else to do, I left the courtyard and walked to Bethel's house.

The old woman's eyes narrowed when she saw me on her doorstep. "Shalom," I said, though I felt anything but peaceful. "I have a sick hen. You said you used to keep chickens, so I wondered if you might be able to tell me what's wrong with her."

Bethel's chin rose, and for a moment I thought she would slam the door. Instead, she grabbed her headscarf, wrapped it over her gray hair, and pointed down the stairs. Together we went to my courtyard. She did not hesitate but walked through the gate, strode toward Abigail, and picked up the hen. Abigail squawked as Bethel set her on the ground. The chicken waddled with an erect posture, her body stick straight, as though she were balancing on her tail feathers.

"Egg bound," Bethel announced, scooping up the bird again. "Warm some water and pour it in a foot basin."

I frowned—*a foot basin?*—but decided not to argue. I set a pot on the fire and waited until it began to steam, then poured the heated water into the basin we used for washing feet.

Bethel eyed the water. "Too hot. Add cold water until it is warm to your fingers. You wouldn't want to cook the bird."

After adding the cool water, I looked up at the stairs and saw all four of my daughters watching with wide eyes. I was afraid Bethel would scold them, but she seemed not to notice her audience as she soothed Abigail and set the bird in the water.

"Now we let her soak," she said, smiling at the girls. I stepped back and watched, mystified as Abigail sat perfectly still, content to sit without complaining for the grumpiest woman in Nazareth.

"The egg comes down through the hen, you see," Bethel said, speaking to my daughters, "and sometimes, especially with a young or very old hen, the egg gets stuck inside. A warm bath relaxes the bird and helps her push it out. It is the same when a woman has a baby. It's HaShem's way of bringing life into the world."

I looked at my youngest daughters, both of whom seemed bewildered by the juxtaposition of chicken eggs and babies. Judit and Eden remained intently focused on the hen.

After a few moments, Bethel reached into the water, lifted the hen slightly, and pressed two spots on opposite sides of the hen's vent. I stood behind her to watch as the tip of an egg appeared through the opening, which stretched as the egg protruded. Then, with an ease that belied Abigail's distress, the egg slid into Bethel's hand.

She handed the wet egg to me, lifted Abigail out of the water, and set her on the ground. "Keep her warm," she directed as Abigail waddled away, "and if it happens again, do exactly what I did. Be careful not to press too hard—if you break the egg inside the hen, she will be cut up by the eggshell and likely die."

Admiration shone in Judit's eyes as she looked up at the older woman. "How did you learn how to do that?"

Bethel smiled back with no trace of her former animosity. "My mother taught me. The hens tell us when they're not well, just as Abigail told your mother. But you have to watch them—chickens know the weak get killed, so they like to pretend they are healthy. So when they finally tell you they are sick, you have to act right away."

"Should we call on you whenever they get sick?" Jordan asked.

Bethel cackled a laugh. "You can call on me anytime, sweet child. Anytime at all."

Later that afternoon, I stepped outside and found Bethel peering over the top of the wall that separated our courtyards. Her eyes were focused on my she-goats, which had moved into the sunshine. "You didn't tell me your goats were pregnant," she said.

"Did I not mention it?" I walked over to her and studied them from her perspective—not an easy task, considering how short she was.

"You didn't need to. They are as round as melons." She gave me the look one would give an ignorant child. "How much do you know about goats?"

I leaned against the courtyard wall. "Not much. But Chiram, my husband, said they are easy to care for. And Ima always kept a goat when we were small."

"Sure, your mother kept one for the milk. But it's been a while since this house has seen a goat, and now you have two. Things are different when you keep two goats."

I stared at the animals, wondering what I had missed. "How so?"

"When you have more than one goat, one will be the queen. From what I've seen, this one is your royal lady." She pointed to Delilah, who was slowly chewing some straw.

"How can you tell?"

"She ate first. She will want to be milked first, and her baby will eat before the other's kid. Wait and see. You should not have any trouble as long as you tend to the queen first each time you step into the courtyard. Make sure the other goat observes the rules."

I bit my lip, hoping I would always be able to tell them apart. Delilah was larger now, but what if Hannah grew?

"How are they handling the move?" Bethel asked. "A goat can lose her kid if she doesn't take to her new surroundings.

They don't like being out in the rain or being crowded. You and your brothers should walk them every afternoon."

"The goats?"

"Who else? Those goats need to exercise. Just remember to let the queen go through the gate first."

I looked down our crowded street, which was nothing but sand and stone. "Where should I walk them?"

"Outside the city. Walk them along the road or through an empty field. Just let them walk. Not too far, but enough to keep them from being bored."

I tilted my head, suddenly aware of how much I didn't know about goats. "Anything else I need to know?"

Bethel lifted her finger like a scolding Torah teacher. "You should put a collar on the goats. A goat needs regular handling or they can become wild—even pregnant she-goats. Always let the goat know you are in charge. Keep her head up and don't let her lower it or she may buck. If a goat gets away from you, grab her back leg. Don't grab the foreleg or you could break it. If you cannot grab her back leg, let her go until she stops running. Chasing a goat is bad for the animal, especially if she's pregnant."

"And for the goat herder, I would assume."

Bethel's lined face split into a grin. "You will learn most things the hard way, I expect. When your baby goats are ready to be born, come fetch me. That will be a new chapter for you, but I will help you through it."

"I cannot thank you enough." I had never been more sincere.

And as she walked away, shaking her head and muttering under her breath, I realized HaShem had supplied a need I did not even know I had.

After dinner, I addressed my goat problem with Joses, Simeon, Jude, and James. "My goats need to graze," I told them bluntly. "And Bethel says they need exercise. Since we have no pasture in the city, I need someone to walk them outside the walls so they can eat greens. Who can help me with that?"

My brothers looked at each other, then Jude cleared his throat. "Could Judit and Eden walk the goats for you? We want to help, but we also must work. I have been working on furniture for a house in Nain, and I need all the hands I can get."

I crossed my arms. "Do you think I would send my daughters outside the walls alone? To walk on a road traveled by Gentiles and Romans and bandits?"

A flush darkened Jude's cheeks. "Sorry. I wasn't thinking."

"I would be happy to send the girls," I said. "It is good for them to work. Yet I cannot send them unescorted. They need exercise, too, and they enjoy the goats, but—"

"I will go," Joses said. "On the first day of every week."

James nodded. "A brilliant plan. I will take them every second day."

"I will go with them on the third," Simeon said. "Jude can go on the fourth day, and you, Pheodora, the fifth and sixth. That way none of us will spend too much time away from work."

I smiled, thrilled by this small but satisfying victory. "The goats will be healthier for it," I added, "and it will be good for my daughters to spend time with their uncles."

"And on the seventh day," James said, lifting his cup, "goats and people will observe Shabbat. Agreed?"

We lifted our cups together. "Agreed."

# CHAPTER TWENTY-ONE

# *Damaris*

Our days of waiting passed slowly, testing my patience and my husband's temper. After rushing from the market and the laboring Gentile woman, I decided I would be safer and far more serene if I went out as little as possible. I could keep my heart, mind, and soul undefiled if I remained in the safe sanctuary of my home, surrounded by my loved ones, the writings of the scribes and rabbis, and the words of HaShem. Once Shimon became a Pharisee, I would not feel as though everyone in the city were watching and measuring me.

Shimon, who had been indulged since childhood, was not accustomed to waiting on others. He had won Lavan's approval and had met with several Pharisees of the chaburah in Jerusalem. He had even begun to study with a learned rabbi, though he had not been formally accepted into the chaburah's probationary period. He was still waiting on that news, which had not yet arrived.

"How do I know they have not already approved me?" he

would ask every night, pacing in our bedchamber. "Perhaps they voted last week but have forgotten to send a message. Or perhaps they will send someone to deliver the news in person? We should consider moving to Jerusalem. We can inquire about building a house the next time we go to the Holy City."

"If we lived in Jerusalem, you would worry about being away from your father," I reminded him. "You would not be able to oversee his business dealings and would become out of touch with the people of this area. Didn't Lavan say the Pharisees had a particular appreciation for your understanding of the people of Galilee?"

"I could understand those people just as well if we lived in Jerusalem." Shimon thrust his hands behind his back. "The Judeans don't trust Galileans. They cannot forget Rehoboam and the rebellious northern tribes who left HaShem and fell into idol worship. Even though this is a different time, with different people, they will forever look at us northern folk as if we are more likely to fall away than the people who live in the south."

"The scribes have long memories," I said. "But if you are concerned about being overlooked or forgotten, why not visit Lavan? Talk to him and put your mind at ease. Then I may relax, as well."

Shimon took my advice. The next morning he visited Lavan, then came home and told me to prepare for the evening. We had been invited to dine with Lavan and his wife.

I immediately sent for my handmaid, knowing I would have to look my best before that couple's appraising gaze.

When my hair had been curled and arranged, my skin anointed with perfume, my eyebrows blackened with antimony and oil, and my sandals strapped on, I was nearly ready. My maid still had to help with my nose ring and necklaces, but when we were finished, no one would be able to look at me and say I did not honor my husband with my appearance.

On the other side of the bedchamber, Shimon stood at his jewelry chest, fumbling with rings and bracelets. No one would ever convince me that women were more vain than men. As he slipped a large gold ring onto his finger, I decided to put him out of his misery.

"There, husband. Perfect." I smiled with approval. "With the matching bracelet and cuff, you will look quite prosperous."

Finally he slipped into his outer robe and ran a hand over his curled hair, smoothing the frizzled ends. When he was satisfied with his reflection in the looking brass, he turned to me. "Are we ready?"

"We could not be better prepared."

Lavan and his wife kept a house on the north side of Nazareth, not far from ours. While we could easily have walked, Shimon sent for the litter, which soon arrived with its contingent of panting slaves. With both of us as passengers, four men were required to carry the sedan chair, and from their stony expressions I could tell our servants were not pleased at the thought of conveying us through the heat.

At least they would not have to travel far.

When we alighted at Lavan's house, a slave in a spotless white tunic led us inside, then bade us sit and wait in the anteroom. We sat on high-backed chairs while another slave offered us a cup of wine. Aware that the servants were listening, Shimon said a proper blessing over the wine, then we drank. A moment later, another slave appeared with a tray of appetizers—olives seasoned with a spice I did not recognize. Again, Shimon said a blessing, this time for the olives. Once we had eaten everything on the tray, another servant brought a basin of water for washing our hands. Then the first servant poured additional cups of wine. Again Shimon blessed the wine. As we lifted our cups, I could not help admiring the gold paint on the arches and the ornamental details in the room. I hoped Lavan would be as impressed by Shimon's frequent and appropriate prayers.

Just as I was beginning to wonder if we would ever see our hosts, Lavan and his wife entered together, extending their hands in welcome.

"We have been looking forward to this," Lavan said, taking Shimon's arm. "Come, let us go into the triclinium where dinner will be served."

Lavan's wife, Eritha, took my arm and led me to a couch next to hers. After making sure I had been comfortably seated, she reclined on her couch, leaning her head toward mine. I took advantage of the moment to compliment her appearance and her home. "You have spread such a lovely table," I added. "Such beautiful gold plates! HaShem has obviously blessed you."

Eritha thanked me, then folded her hands and smiled. "Lavan esteems your husband highly. He looks forward to— well, I should not speak of such things yet. I will let him share the news."

My eyes widened in pretend surprise, though I had not doubted Shimon's acceptance into the chaburah.

While the men kept their heads together and conversed in low whispers, Eritha and I talked of the weather and our favorite jewelers. But when the food arrived—peacock on one platter, pheasant on another, bowls of nut cakes, honey-baked figs, and stuffed dates in honey—Lavan opened the conversation to us women, as well.

"One thing has given me concern about you, Shimon." Lavan paused to pull a leg off the peacock, then held it aloft as he pinned Shimon with a look. "And that is your wife's relationship to this would-be messiah." He lifted a brow in my direction. "You say you are not supporters, but you cannot escape from your relationship with Yeshua, can you?"

I forced a smile. "If you are asking if I would deny or renounce my brother, no, I would not. No man loves HaShem more than Yeshua."

"Yet he is critical of the Pharisees and has openly insulted some of my brothers." He tossed a sharp glance at Shimon. "Can you see why this would cause some in my chaburah to hesitate regarding your nomination? How can they know you will not publicly criticize us like Yeshua has?"

Shimon released a hollow laugh. "He is my wife's brother. And though she loves him, I bear no loyalty to the man and know him only a little. Anyone will tell you that we are not among his followers. We have not gone to hear him speak. None of my wife's other brothers support him, either."

"No one in the family?"

"Well . . . his mother does. She has been with him since the beginning of his public work."

"So I have heard." Lavan wiped his fingers on a linen square. "Mothers are always blind when it comes to their children." He took a bite of the peacock, then swallowed and looked at me. "Do you love your brother, Damaris?"

I blinked, as surprised by his direct approach as by the question. "Of course."

"How can you say that when you do not support him?"

My throat tightened. Though I wanted to look at Shimon

for direction, I knew I could not. Lavan had spoken directly to me because he wanted my answer, not my husband's.

"I can assure you," I said, dismayed to hear a tremor in my voice, "that our family, apart from our mother, considers Yeshua sincere but misguided. We are not certain what his intentions are, but every day we pray he will come home and take his rightful place in the family business."

A smile lifted the corner of Lavan's mouth. "You want the prophet to be a carpenter?"

"That is what our father taught him to be. That is what my brothers expect him to be."

Lavan shifted and fixed Shimon in a piercing gaze. "If the men of the Jerusalem chaburah approve your nomination, can you swear before HaShem that you will not support your brother-in-law?"

Shimon gave a firm nod. "I can."

"Good." Lavan dipped his fingers in a small bowl of water. "I am relieved. I did not feel comfortable bringing your name before the council because of these apprehensions, but now that I have your word, I will do it at my first opportunity. Rest well, my friend—your future is assured."

Shimon broke into an open, relieved smile, and Eritha patted my hand. I blew out a breath, grateful to know we need not worry any longer. Now, surely, we could relax as friends and enjoy the evening.

"Here, have some meat." Lavan gestured to a servant, who carried the largest platter to Shimon. "Have you ever had peacock? Truly the most delicious meat in the world. A bird fit for kings."

Shimon used his knife to spear a hunk of the meat, then tasted it and smiled. "Very good."

Lavan took a palm leaf and casually scooped up a fig from

another platter. "If you are ever at a family gathering where this Yeshua is present—"

"I would leave immediately," Shimon finished. "I would not want to be thought of as one of his—"

"No, you misunderstand. Of course you should remain at a family gathering. People would expect you to remain for your wife's sake. But if you are there and you overhear Yeshua's plans . . ."

"What sort of plans?" Shimon's brow arched. "As I have said, I barely know the man."

Lavan shrugged. "Any kind of plans. Plans to raise an army or rouse the people to action—or stir them to anger. If you are ever in such a position, can we count on you to send word at once? You can send a message to me or one of the elders in Jerusalem. We must be kept informed at all times; we must always consider our duty to guard the people from those who would draw them away from the Law, from true worship."

A look of discomfort crossed Shimon's face and faded almost immediately. "If I hear Yeshua planning revolution, I will certainly tell you," he promised. "But I can assure you, I am not likely to hear any such thing. From what I have seen, Yeshua is a gentle soul."

"Would a gentle soul overturn the money changers' tables in the courtyard of the holy Temple?" Lavan's mouth thinned with displeasure. "Would a gentle soul rise up and confront a leading Torah teacher, calling him a whitewashed tomb? He said we Pharisees were hypocrites, beautiful on the outside, but full of dead men's bones and all kinds of filthiness." Lavan shuddered. "As if we would *ever* touch anything unclean. We are focused on holiness, so how could we ever be less than pure?"

Shimon pressed his hand to his throat. "I am sorry. I was not present. I do not know what Yeshua meant or said—"

"He is a madman," Lavan snapped. "Intent on revolution. Therefore, it would be wise for us to have a man who could be admitted into his inner circle without suspicion. That man, Shimon, is you."

I looked at my husband, pity and shock mingling in my breast as I watched emotions flicker across his face. Were the Pharisees only interested in Shimon because he could spy on Yeshua and then report back to them?

Shimon would never admit such a possibility, of course. He would never believe a group as righteous as the Pharisees would want him for any reason other than his piety. After all, few men had the luxury of devoting their entire lives to the study of Torah and the Law, but because his father was wealthy, Shimon was such a man.

"I am so glad you will be joining us," Lavan said, toying with the curls of his beard. "There remains only one other concern. You asked if I had any association with the publicans who work in this region—yes, I do. I also happen to know that another of your relatives, a man from Bethlehem, is currently in debtors' prison. I believe his name is Chiram."

A knot tightened in my stomach at the mention of my brother-in-law. The man was a lowly shepherd—what threat could he possibly be to the Pharisees?

Shimon flushed. "Though I would not want to interfere with any of your business dealings, Chiram is a poor shepherd, and the amount he owes is small—"

"I know. I also know that to a man like you, his debt is a mere pittance, something you could easily pay."

"Then I shall." Shimon smiled in what looked like relief. "And with pleasure, if the money will help your friend."

"You misunderstand." Lavan's eyes flashed. "This Chiram deserves to be in prison. I have my reasons, and if you trust me, you must trust my reasons. He has deeply offended and deserves his fate."

A faint line appeared between Shimon's brows as he felt his way through the conversation. "Chiram is a simple man. Whatever he did or did not do, perhaps he was simply ignorant of—"

"You should not make excuses for him." Lavan's brows rose, eloquent wings of scorn. "My friend Glaucus, a member of the Publicani, does not care about losing a few denarii. But my brothers of the chaburah believe it is far more important to set an example for the am ha'aretz. We are princes of the Law, and as such we deserve respect. So do you, which is why you must not pay his debt. If the common people heard that a Pharisee paid the debt of a simple shepherd, they would expect us to wipe out the debts of *all* the poor. How could we then be free to study the Law? We would have to put aside our study in order to work because the poor expected all their debts and taxes to be paid by the righteous. That would not honor HaShem."

I could hold my tongue no longer. "But he is only one man—"

Shimon sent me a sharp look that effectively bridled my tongue. An instant later, he lifted his hands. "You need not worry about this matter, my friend. I have not offered to pay Chiram's debt, and I will not."

"Good." Lavan rose from his dining couch and extended his hand. "Let me walk you to the door, Shimon. You should soon be hearing from my brothers in Jerusalem. They are most anxious to welcome you into the fraternity of the chaburah."

Shimon stood, smiling, and waited for me to say my farewells to Lavan's wife. I did so, offering perfunctory thanks for a lovely evening, then followed Shimon to the door as a cloud of misgivings swirled in my heart.

-------◆-------

Our litter bearers leapt to attention when they saw us leaving the house, but for once I wished we had walked to our destination. I wanted to speak privately with my husband, and I could not do so in the company of four servants.

Still, after we climbed in the litter and drew the curtains, I could almost believe we were alone. The sound of the men's steps crunching the gravel would surely drown out our voices if we spoke in whispers.

"Husband, when we married, you said I should always speak my mind and never hold back my true thoughts."

"Indeed I did." Shimon placed his hand upon mine. "Have you something on your mind—something other than great satisfaction that will be ours when I am inducted into the brotherhood of Pharisees?"

I ignored his comment. "I am not happy with what we heard tonight. First, Lavan asked you to spy on my brother. How could you even consider such a thing? And how could a man devoted to the Law ask one of his brothers to spy for him? If the Pharisees trust HaShem to work His will, why do they look at Yeshua with such distrust? He has done nothing but preach the kingdom of God and heal the sick—"

"They believe he is subversive." Shimon's face darkened. "You must admit he causes the people to question everything they have been taught. I have heard some of the things he says, and I do not blame the Pharisees for questioning his motives."

"*What* motives? I am his sister, yet I am not clear on what his motives are. He teaches the people about God while encouraging them to love one another and be content with what they have. What law is he violating? What harm has he done?"

"None . . . yet." Shimon shifted, turning his face to the curtains and peering out at the street. "But the Pharisees want to be prepared in case trouble erupts. Surely you cannot find fault with that."

I folded my arms and stared at my husband's back. I could never believe Yeshua would cause trouble of any sort, but neither could I disagree with my husband. If they had asked him to spy on some other would-be messiah, some revolutionary who encouraged men to pick up swords and challenge the authorities, I could easily agree with Shimon. But Yeshua was not that sort of man. Shimon should have said as much to Lavan.

"And what about Chiram?" I pinched Shimon's arm so he would have to look at me. "What harm would it do if we paid his debt? We could do it anonymously. No one need know who paid the creditor."

He turned, rubbing his arm, and frowned at me. "I promised I would not pay it."

"How is Chiram supposed to earn money when he cannot work? He cannot draw wages where he is, and Pheodora barely earns enough to feed her children. You cannot allow my sister's husband to sit in prison for the rest of his life—"

"Your sister has already moved in with your brothers," Shimon said. "She will not starve, nor will her daughters be harmed. And Chiram's situation is not hopeless. If he truly wants freedom, he has assets. He has a house in Bethlehem. He has four daughters, any one of whom could be sold and the proceeds given to his creditor. He has the means to earn his freedom."

"You would have him sell Pheodora's home?" I stiffened, surprised that he considered this a solution to my sister's problem. "Would you sell one of *our* children to pay your debts? Would you sell our home?"

"HaShem has blessed me . . . and because He has blessed me, I will never find myself in Chiram's situation. I do not know what Chiram did to offend, but I would never do such a thing."

How could he be so sure? I stared at him, then sighed and turned away. Shimon always replied with a logical answer, only this time his words did not ring true. Had HaShem not blessed Chiram? He had given him a good wife, four lovely daughters, and a pure heart—or at least it had always seemed pure to me. Then again, I did not know Chiram well. But I knew Pheodora, and though I had often questioned her sanity in marrying a shepherd, I knew she would not have married a man who did not honor God. Our father would never have agreed to let Chiram have Pheodora unless he approved of the man and the marriage.

And I did not know Pheodora had returned to Nazareth until Yuta brought me the news. Why had Pheodora not told me? Did she feel such a distance between us that she would not visit when we lived only a short walk from each other?

I pressed my lips together and stared at the swaying walls of our conveyance. Perhaps she did not visit because the matter of Chiram's debt stood between us. But Shimon would brook no argument in this matter, and I would gain nothing if I tried to press him. He had given his word to Lavan, and Lavan and the Pharisees were more important to Shimon than anything—and anyone—else.

———●———

The next morning I rose early, made sure the children were fed and dressed, then set out to visit Pheodora, determined to set things right between us. I did not take the litter, preferring to walk. After the events of the previous evening, taking a litter to see my poor sister would feel . . . pretentious.

Fortunately, the walk to my childhood home was not a great distance. The sun warmed my face, and I glimpsed several women watching my progress from their courtyards. I was better dressed than the women who lived in the lower part of town, and they must have wondered what I was doing in their neighborhood. They might have recognized me as Mary's daughter, if they looked beyond the jewelry and makeup and fine clothing . . .

I turned onto the winding street that led to my brothers' house, strolling through the courtyard gate and climbing the front steps. I was halfway up the stone staircase when a squawking sound startled me. I looked down and saw several chickens scratching at the dirt in the courtyard. My mother had kept chickens, but my brothers never expressed much interest in poultry.

The door opened, and Pheodora peered at me from the doorway, her youngest child clinging to her tunic. "Damaris?" Surprise echoed in her voice as she stepped aside to let me enter.

"My servant told me you had returned to Nazareth," I said. "If *you* had told me, I would have visited sooner."

Pheodora shrugged as she closed the door. "You have much on your mind, and I have been busy." She moved to the table, cut a slice of cheese for her youngest daughter, and gave it to the little girl. "Why have you come?"

I went into the living area and dropped onto the carved bench our father had made, making myself comfortable on the cushions. "I must admit, you have made the place look more like home. Ima would approve."

"Thank you." Pheodora glanced around. "I expected the house to be in worse shape, but the brothers have done well."

"Are they keeping busy with work?"

"Yes, but they are also a big help to me. Joses is at the market now, selling my eggs. And Simeon has taken the older girls and goats for a walk."

I leaned back, pretending to be surprised. "Goats?"

Pheodora sat on a stool across from me. "Before he was imprisoned, Chiram invested in a pair of goats. James and I went to Caesarea to get them."

"Why did you go so far? Dozens of people around here have goats—"

"Chiram bred these goats. They should deliver their kids in a few weeks."

I gaped at her, as astonished as if she'd told me she would soon give birth. "What do you know about raising goats?"

"More than I used to." Pheodora's smile deepened, and she made a vague gesture to her left. "The woman next door—remember Bethel? She used to have goats and chickens, so she has been a big help. She helps me with the girls, too. At first she didn't seem happy about my living here, but now I think she enjoys my company."

"She was probably jealous. She's had the brothers to herself since Ima left."

Pheodora chuckled. "She's welcome to them. Between the girls and the goats, I have my hands full."

We fell silent, and I didn't know what else to say. An odd sensation stirred within me, a resentful feeling that swam up through the years and brought with it a wave of nostalgia. I used to feel that sort of jealousy when I had to help Ima, but Pheodora got to stay outside and play with Joses and Jude . . .

"I am glad you are here," I said, running my hand over the arm of Abba's bench. "Things have been busy at our house. Shimon thinks of little but his studies these days—his desk is cluttered with scrolls, writings of this rabbi and that scribe—I cannot keep track of all of them. Lately he has been studying Gematria."

"What is that?" Pheodora drew her lips into a tight smile. "I have never heard of such a thing."

I blew out a breath. "As far as I can tell, it involves learning the numerical value of each of the letters in a word. Shimon explained it like this—the Torah says Moses married a Cushite woman. The numbers in the word *Cushite* add up to 736. So, because some scholars object to the idea that Moses married a black woman, they substitute the words *of fair appearance*, because the numbers of those words also add up to 736. Does that make sense?"

Either Pheodora did not understand or she did not like the idea. "But if the Torah says he married a woman from Cush, then he married a woman from Cush, whether or not she was fair." Pheodora stared into the space above the courtyard, her features hardening in a look of disapproval. "No matter how the numbers add up."

"Let us leave it to the scholars to decide." Unwilling to argue, I waved the matter away. "Such things are not for women to interpret or worry about."

Pheodora shifted her gaze to me. "My husband is in prison, so I have to worry about all kinds of things. Until I find a way to pay his debt, I will worry about anything that concerns my family."

I looked away, stinging from the dart in her words. She was not asking me to pay her husband's debt, but reminding me that she knew I could.

Yet I couldn't. Any more than I could help that poor woman in the throes of labor at the market.

I stood and brushed the wrinkles from my tunic. "I am afraid I must go now. It was good to see you, sister. If you need anything for the girls or our brothers, please let me know."

She had to notice I did not add *or Chiram*.

"Shalom," Pheodora said, her voice as cool as a winter wind. "I will tell our brothers you came by."

I moved to the door and lifted my hand in farewell, but I did not—could not—turn to look at her.

# CHAPTER TWENTY-TWO

# *Pheodora*

I had just set a platter of bread, fruit, dried fish, and figs on the table when I heard a terrible ruckus coming from outside. I flew down the stairs and saw two feral dogs racing through our courtyard, chasing my chickens.

"Out!" I cried, flapping the cloth I had just used to dry my hands. "Get out! Go!"

The thinnest dog, a mangy creature with a long snout and black fur, fled through the open gate, while the larger one stopped and snarled at me, one of my best hens in his mouth.

I should have retreated, but the sight of Abigail's limp body sparked something in me. I ran toward the beast, flapping my cloth with all my strength. The dog dropped the hen and charged at me. I was certain he would veer away and flee, and he did—but not before biting my leg and nearly knocking me off my feet.

I screamed, and an instant later my brothers rushed down the stairs. By the time they arrived, the dog had disappeared, leaving me to hobble around the courtyard in search of my frightened hen. I found Abigail beside her nest, a little dazed but apparently no worse for wear. I saw no signs of bleeding, so I picked her up, smoothed her feathers, and tried to calm her trembling body.

"You're bleeding." Joses pointed to my leg, which I had not yet examined.

"I will be okay." I gently set the hen back in her nest. "I just need to clean the wound."

Joses and James insisted on helping me up the stairs, where I sank to the floor, lying at my startled brothers' feet as my heart began to pound as if it would come out of my chest.

"Pheodora?" Joses peered down at me. "Are you—?"

"I'm all right," I gasped. "Just—let me catch my breath."

I closed my eyes, ignoring the sounds around me as my blood beat a rhythm in my ears. What if the dog had killed all the hens? He easily could have. What if he had reached the goats? A wild dog could rip open a goat's throat in mere seconds. I could have lost everything . . .

When my heart finally resumed its normal rhythm, I lifted my head. Simeon bade me sit on a bench while Joses poured water into a bowl. I examined my torn leg. While the bite wasn't deep, the dog's teeth had ripped the skin halfway down my calf. Joses winced as he poured water over the wound.

"Should I fetch a doctor?" Simeon asked.

I shook my head, but Joses told him to go at once. Simeon left, and after the door slammed behind him, another voice mingled with my brothers'.

"I heard screaming—is everyone okay?"

Bethel had slipped into the house. She took one glance at my leg and burst into tears. "I heard the barking," she said, dabbing her eyes with her headscarf. "It is all my fault. I should not have fed those dogs. They've become too bold, and with your chickens so close—"

"My chickens are fine," I assured her. "And this is not so bad. A little water, maybe a bandage to keep it clean."

"Let me do that." Bethel nudged Joses out of the way and took the blood-streaked cloth from his hand. "I have repaired many a wound in my day. I nursed the wounded during Herod's war over Jerusalem, then my husband decided we should move to Nazareth in search of peace. I keep waiting for it, but I've begun to believe I may not see peace in my lifetime." She turned to James. "Recently I heard people talking about Yeshua. He seems to arouse strong feelings wherever he goes."

James's expression remained sober as he nodded. "We have heard the same."

"What think you of your brother? Could he actually be the promised Messiah?"

James sighed. "He has never claimed to be—not in my hearing."

"Nor mine," Simeon added. "We do not know what to make of all these rumors and reports."

"But your mother . . ."

"Our mother loves her firstborn," I whispered, knowing it would pain my brothers to admit that Ima seemed to love Yeshua more than her other children. I knew how they felt—as a child, Yeshua came first, then James, then Damaris, Jude, Simeon, and Joses. Whether Ima was doling out bread or blessings, I always seemed to get whatever was left over.

Bethel folded a clean cloth and used string to secure it around my wound, then leaned back to check her work.

I stood and placed my weight on the injured limb. "Thank you, Bethel."

"How does it feel?"

"Fine, I think. Now I should see to my poor hen."

"I will come with you."

We went downstairs and into the courtyard, where most of the hens were hiding behind the nest boxes. Speaking softly, I found Abigail and lifted her into my arms. She barely acknowledged me and was uncharacteristically still.

"I don't see any wounds," I told Bethel, lifting the chicken up to examine her belly. "Surely she will be okay."

"Has she laid yet today?"

"None of them have. It's still early."

Bethel shook her head. "I hate to give you bad news, but she may not survive."

I froze, stunned by Bethel's pronouncement. "Why not? She's not hurt."

"Some wounds, dear girl, cannot be seen with our eyes."

Bethel took the hen from me, set her on a bench, and pressed two of her fingers to the hen's rear. "Some hens die from shock." She gently slid the tip of one finger into the hen's vent. "And others . . ." She pulled out her forefinger, coated now in yellow yolk. "I'm sorry, dear. The dog must have crushed the egg inside her. She will pass it, but the shell may cut her inside, and the spilled yolk will cause putrefaction. I do not think she will survive the day."

I gasped in disappointment, scooped Abigail into my arms, and tried to comfort her. A chicken might be one of HaShem's smallest creatures, but ever since we moved to Nazareth, this one had faithfully given me an egg a day. Her eggs had helped me feed my girls. Her eggs had helped us survive. Abigail had been more helpful than my own sister.

I looked at the other hens, still cowering in a corner. "Will they be all right?"

Bethel nodded. "Yes, but take care to keep your gate locked. I will no longer feed those dogs—they can go to the next village for food. Or someone can take them in and keep them contained. But we must keep this sort of trouble away from your house."

At the top of the stairs, the door opened and Judit appeared, trailed by Eden, Jordan, and Shiri. "Ima, what happened?"

"Come on down, sweet girls," Bethel said before I could answer. "Your mother and the chickens had a little scare, but everyone is all right. We must be careful to always lock the gate from now on."

Down they came, my lovely daughters, and while I cuddled Abigail they ran to Bethel, who opened her arms and hugged them. I watched, bemused, as Bethel placed kisses on each girl's head, then helped them feed the chickens.

James came and stood beside me, his gaze locked on Bethel and the girls. "You have been a blessing," he said.

I barked a laugh. "By getting bitten by a dog?"

"By allowing your girls to love our neighbor. She and Seth had no children, but you are sharing yours."

I watched Judit take Bethel's hand and lead her through the doorway that led to the inner courtyard, where the she-goats waited for their daily dose of loving attention.

Maybe James was right. If so, I hoped someone in Arimathea was showing the same kind of love to my husband.

---

*My dear Chiram,*

*Your letter made me so happy! I am grateful Uriah has begun to visit you. Oh, that I were an angel on his shoulder, so I could sit and talk to you as easily as he does. But he has made it possible for us to exchange our thoughts while we are apart, and that is a great gift. Please tell him your wife thanks him and is glad that Yeshua influenced him to do what he is doing.*

*Our daughters are growing like weeds. My brothers spoil them, of course, and I am glad they have strong men around to encourage them while you are away. My brothers and I have come to a mutually beneficial arrangement. I keep the house for them, preparing dinner each day and keeping the dust off the floor and the furnishings. In return, they take my eggs to the market and bring home food for all of us.*

*They have even offered to pool their resources in the hope of paying your debt. But despite their generous nature, they do not earn enough to pay your debt and keep food on the table. HaShem could always send an unexpected blessing, I suppose, but that has not yet happened. Every day HaShem provides what we need, no more and no less. Still, we are grateful for His goodness.*

*Damaris's husband is planning to join a chaburah and is studying to become a Pharisee. I think he and Damaris thought this would please us, yet my brothers seem offended by the idea of Shimon wearing a Pharisee's blue-bordered prayer shawl. James says he might as well wear a sign proclaiming his holiness. "Why do the Pharisees walk around declaring their purity?" he asked at dinner recently. "I think the man in humble circumstances should boast in his lofty position, and the rich person in his low position, for the rich man's possessions will pass away like the flowers of the grass.*

*But the poor man who has learned to depend upon HaShem is rich indeed."*

*He may have been thinking of you, dear husband, because we all think of you day and night. The girls ask about you and mention you in their prayers, as do I.*

*The she-goats are well. Both are big-bellied and calm, which Bethel says is a good sign. Have I told you about Bethel? She is the woman who lives next door, and she has proven to be a great help with many things, including the animals. Our girls love her, and so do I.*

*Now I must go, dear husband, so I leave you with this Sabbath blessing:*

*"Mi ha-ish, he-hafetz hayim, ohev yamim lir'ot tov? N'tzor l'shon'kha mei'ra, u'sfotecha mi-daber mirma. Sur mei'ra va'aseh tov, bakesh shalom v'rod'feihu."*

*Who is the man who is eager for life, who hopes for long days of good fortune? He guards his tongue from speaking deceit, he turns from evil and does good, he desires peace and pursues it.*

*You are such a man, husband.*

> *Your loving wife,*
> *Pheodora Aiya*

# CHAPTER TWENTY-THREE

# *Pheodora*

My leg had barely healed when Delilah became ill. At first I didn't realize she was sick. When her left side began to bulge, I thought the kid in her belly had simply shifted its position—after all, the time of labor was approaching. But when Delilah wouldn't eat and began grinding her teeth as if she were in torment, I ran next door to fetch Bethel.

She came back with me and immediately strode into the goat's stall. She eased in beside Delilah, pressed her ear to the goat's swollen side, and looked at me. "Where did you walk her today?"

"Off the main road," I said, struggling to recall where we had gone. "In a harvested barley field."

"Did you see flowers?"

"Yes."

"Purple flowers?"

She was thinking of wolfsbane. "No, no purple flowers. She didn't eat any flowers."

*The Shepherd's Wife*

"Did she eat grass?"

"Yes. Lots of it."

"Hmm . . ." Bethel thumped Delilah's side with her finger, patted the animal, and then jerked her chin at me. "Bring me a cup of oil and a hollow reed. And have one of your brothers fetch a log or a stool, something I can stand on. We'll need fresh straw, young branches, or berry leaves for her to eat once she regains her appetite."

I went upstairs to get the oil and call for help. Moments later, James, Joses, and I gathered around Delilah. The poor goat looked at us with wild eyes. Judit and Jordan came downstairs, too, but I told them to remain outside with the chickens.

"Put the reed in her mouth," Bethel commanded. "I'm going to stand on the stool and pour the oil into the reed. Once we get the oil inside her, we'll massage her swollen belly."

Fear blew down the back of my neck. After all our hard work, what if I lost Delilah now? Would I lose everything, including my husband?

"What is causing this?" I asked. "Is it the baby? She cannot lose the baby. We have to do whatever we can, even if we have to cut the baby out—"

"It's not the baby giving her trouble," Bethel said. "She's bloated."

"What?"

"Too much gas is trapped in her stomach. For some reason—probably all the grass she ate this afternoon—she cannot belch, so she cannot release the gas. We're going to help her belch, then she will be well again."

Judit, who had been listening outside, giggled at Bethel's pronouncement, yet Jordan remained silent, as if she

192

understood the seriousness of the goat's condition. I had never imagined a goat could suffer from an overabundance of stomach gas. Clearly, Bethel knew much more than I did.

With an agility that belied her years, Bethel took a broad leaf, rolled it into a funnel and climbed onto the stool, which Joses had placed at the goat's head. James handed her a cup of oil. She poured the oil down the reed I held in the goat's mouth, flat against her tongue. Standing beside Bethel, James held Delilah's chin high, forcing the oil downward while Joses massaged the goat's belly. With the last drop of oil gone into the reed, Bethel waited a moment before stepping off the stool. "Now," she said, looking at James, "carefully pull the queen forward until her front legs are on the stool. Joses, keep kneading her belly like you would a lump of dough."

Delilah, growing more bewildered by the moment, did not want to stand on a stool, but James and I gave her no choice. Pulling and lifting, we maneuvered her front legs onto the stool. Once she was in position, I held her in position by enticing her with handfuls of fresh straw and berry leaves.

"How long do I have to do this?" Joses asked as he pressed and prodded Delilah's belly. "My hands are getting tired."

Bethel waited a moment more, then nodded. "Now we walk her."

James and I pulled Delilah off the stool and led her into the courtyard. We walked the goat in a circle, around and around until the sun drew down and the stars came out to watch. Finally, just as I was about to fall asleep in mid-step, we heard the distinct sound of a goat passing gas . . . and we erupted in hysterical relief.

Bethel straightened her shoulders and pushed damp hair away from her forehead. "Good work, everyone. Now you may go to bed. I will check on the wee beast in the morning."

I thanked and hugged her, said good-night, and led my exhausted goat queen back into her stall.

———————◆———————

As our she-goats entered the last month of their pregnancy, Bethel became my best friend. Not only did she help take care of my daughters and my brothers, but she also brought in the eggs and prepared them for the market, arranging them in palm baskets she had woven herself.

Whenever I couldn't find her, I knew she would be downstairs with the goats. One day, a week before we expected the kids to arrive, I found her trimming the fur around the she-goats' udders. I watched, fascinated, and finally had to ask, "Why are you doing that?"

"So the babies can find the teat." She glanced up at me. "A few weeks after kidding, the mama will have a bloody discharge that can build up around this area. A little trim will help keep things clean."

We had stopped milking the goats so they would have enough energy to prepare their bodies for birthing. Neither Delilah nor Hannah seemed to eat as much as usual, but stood silently in their stalls, their tails twitching as their swollen bellies moved of their own accord.

My daughters, who loved watching the kids play beneath their mamas' skin, spent hours peering through the railings of the goat stalls. Judit, Eden, and Jordan had a good grasp on the situation, while Shiri overflowed with questions. She would point to the bulging belly and ask, "Is that the baby? How does it get out? How did it get in there?"

I gave her as much information as she needed. "Yes, that is the kid. Soon it will come out, and we can watch it eat. How does it get out? You will soon see."

Bethel helped me prepare for the births. Since we didn't know which doe would give birth first, Bethel said they might as well have their own birthing areas. So we cleared out two separate spaces, scrubbed the walls with hot water, and covered the ground with a thick layer of straw. We cleaned buckets and clay pots and stacked them nearby.

Bethel collected the items we would need and spread them on a bench: an oil lamp, in case the kids came at night; a sharp blade to cut the cords; string for tying the cords; cloths for wrapping the kids; oil, in case we needed lubricant; honey, in case of bleeding; and feed sacks to place under the mama goat.

After I put the girls to bed one night, Bethel called from the courtyard. I joined her downstairs and saw that the she-goat's rump had changed. Her tailbone had risen, and the muscles connecting the tailbone to her hip bones had stretched. I could see hollows on both sides of her tail and noticed her udder had gone tight and shiny.

"She's bagged up," Bethel said, pointing to the udder. "She's close to giving birth now. Be alert and watchful—you might want to sleep down here tonight."

"Will I have to . . ." I fumbled for words. "Will I have to *do* anything?"

Bethel cracked a smile. "Most goats give birth without help. But every once in a while one of them will have trouble, and that is when you will be needed. In the first stage, the she-goat will stand and bear the pain for several hours, maybe all day. After that, her breathing will change and she will make noise as she pushes the baby out. She will get up and lie down; she will try to lick herself. She will want to be left alone, so keep the children and the chickens away. Or she may want you near, especially since she's seen a lot of you lately. Once she starts pushing, she should not take more than an hour to get the kid out. Get a water clock and keep an eye on it. If the baby takes longer than an hour to come out, your mama goat is in trouble."

I wiped my sweaty palms on my tunic. Both Delilah and Hannah appeared calm, so I figured neither of them was in labor yet.

"Should I come get you when the time comes?" I asked. "Do you want to watch?"

Bethel chuckled. "If it's daylight, come fetch me. But don't wake me up in the middle of the night."

"Anything else I should know?"

Bethel thought a moment, then held up a finger. "If the baby comes breech—tail or hind legs first—you might have to swing the kid to clear its lungs. Better have some extra cloth handy, because the baby will be slippery."

I stared at her. "*Swing* the kid?"

"Wrap the kid in a cloth, then stand in the middle of the room so you will not hit his head on the wall. Use one hand to hold his back legs and the other to grip the skin behind his neck. Swing him back and forth several times with his head facing out. Then check the kid's breathing—if he's breathing, you've done your job. If he's not, you need to swing him again because he probably inhaled fluid from the caul."

I drew a deep breath and hoped my she-goats would give birth in daylight. I could not imagine doing this without Bethel.

———✦———

Two days later, as I was putting my youngest daughters to bed, I heard Simeon and Judit talking downstairs. "Better go get your mother," Simeon said. "Something's wrong with this goat."

I gave Shiri and Jordan a quick kiss, then hurried down to the courtyard, passing Judit on the stairs. Simeon and Joses were standing beside Delilah's stall, where the goat was pacing and breathing hard. She looked up at me and bleated, turned and knelt on the straw, front end first.

Of course she would give birth first—she was the queen.

"I think she's ready to have her baby." I opened the gate and led her into the birthing room, then placed my hand on her swollen side. I could see contractions tightening her belly, so this had to be the most active stage of labor. "Um . . ." I glanced up to be sure Simeon and Joses and Judit were still with me. "I think I have everything I need. Will you fill the bucket for me, Judit?"

"We're out of water," she said.

Naturally, because it was the end of the day.

"I will go to the well." Simeon grabbed the bucket. "Anything else?"

"Better take both buckets." I gestured to an empty container by the doorway. "Judit, bring me the folded cloths I left upstairs on the table. All we can do now is watch and wait."

When Simeon returned with the water, I poured a cup into the water clock and sat back to watch it drip. The bowl was designed to release water over a one-hour period, so when it had emptied, Delilah's baby should be born.

The water in the bowl was almost half gone when I noticed the first sign of imminent birth. Just below the tail, a bubble appeared. I leaned forward to have a closer look, and saw two little hooves and a nose inside the bubble.

I heard Judit squeal as she came in with Simeon. The three of us watched in awe and wonder as Delilah groaned and pushed, bursting the bubble. Our tired she-goat twisted, trying to lick the emerging baby, but couldn't quite reach it. Then she bleated, gave another push, and two hooves emerged from her body. Next came the nose, the head, and more of the legs. I watched silently, grateful that Judit was receiving an unforced lesson about the way HaShem designed childbirth.

Within a few more minutes, a perfectly white newborn kid slid onto the straw. I bent beside him, checked to be sure he was breathing, and sighed when he lifted his head. Delilah began to nuzzle him, and I nearly melted in delight and relief.

"He's beautiful!" Judit squealed.

"Is it a he-goat?" Simeon asked.

I reached out and turned the little one over. "Yes," I said, smiling. "It is a male."

I closed my eyes, wishing I had some way to share this good news with Chiram. His first white goat had arrived safely, and it was male. Though female animals could be used for goodwill offerings, only male animals could be used for sin offerings. The goats for Yom Kippur had to be male.

"Ima," Judit said, studying Delilah, "why is she still making that noise?"

I glanced at our queen, who had stopped nuzzling her baby and was attempting to stand. "I don't know. Perhaps she's trying to push out the afterbirth."

Delilah strained and groaned, yet no afterbirth appeared. I was about to run for Bethel when a second bubble appeared, with another set of hooves inside.

"Two babies!" Judit exclaimed, understanding before I did. "Delilah is having twins!"

I felt a warm glow flow through me as I leaned against the wall. Not only would we have two babies to sell to the

Levites, but with Hannah's baby we had an unexpected blessing. We could always use more milk and cheese, or we could sell the extra goat to another family.

Delilah's second baby dropped onto the straw, but remained encased in the caul. I knelt and leaned forward, trying to remember what Bethel had said about the birth sac. One thing was obvious—the sac would have to be broken so the baby could breathe. I fumbled with the slippery substance for a moment, finally splitting it and pulling it away from the baby's nose. I wiped the kid's nostrils with a cloth, and my pulse quickened as I realized the little animal was not breathing.

*Swing the kid.* My heart began to thump against my breastbone.

"Stand back," I called, and everyone stepped away. I wrapped the cloth around the kid's back legs so I could get a sure grip, then stood. As my breath came in gasps, I swung the kid back and forth, left and right, praying I wasn't doing more harm than good.

"Have you lost your mind?" Joses shouted.

I lowered the kid to the straw, then used my fingers to open its mouth and swipe at its nostrils. When it still did not breathe, I choked back a frantic sob, rose to my feet, and swung the kid again. Simeon and Judit watched, openmouthed, as I lowered the kid and knelt, trembling, to check his breathing.

Somehow he managed a tremulous bleat.

I slumped in relief. "It's alive."

Simeon grinned and looped his arms around Judit's neck. "Congratulations. What now?"

"I need a bucket of honey water for Delilah." I struggled to remember all the things that should be done for the mother and her kids. "And give her some grain while I take care of the babies."

While Judit and Simeon fetched the honey water, I cleaned the babies' bodies with a cloth and tended their umbilical cords. I tied the ends with string, cutting them a knuckle's length from the kids' bodies. I then covered the end of the cords in honey, stood the babies under Delilah, and watched as they nosed about. Soon they found the teats and latched on.

Fortunately, Delilah had two teats and two babies. I don't know what we would have done if she'd had a third kid in her belly.

"Um, Pheodora . . ." Simeon, who had wandered over to Hannah's stall, waved for my attention. "I know you're tired, but I think something is happening over here."

I snapped out of my exhausted reverie and stumbled over to the second stall. Hannah was panting, and I spied a line of foamy white mucus beneath her tail. I swallowed hard. "I will need more water," I told Simeon, my voice cracking. "And clean cloths. If you're too tired to help with this one, wake James—"

"I would not miss this," Joses said with a grin. "I know what this means to you and Chiram. And now I have a fair idea about what to do."

He ran off to get what I needed while Judit and I walked Hannah to the second birthing area and prepared to help bring another kid into the world.

# CHAPTER TWENTY-FOUR

# Pheodora

We were waiting to deliver Hannah's second baby when I realized the water clock had run dry. The first kid had arrived with no trouble, though the baby was smaller than Delilah's offspring. Bethel had warned me that a small kid probably meant the mother carried more than one, so I suspected another was on its way. But after several minutes of watching the goat's rump, I did not see another nose, but what looked like the top of a head. Was the kid in the wrong position, or was I dizzy with exhaustion?

"Where are the hooves?" Judit asked, and I did not know what to say.

"I'm sure they're coming," I said, speaking with a confidence I did not feel. I glanced over at Simeon. "I know Bethel said she didn't want to be awakened in the middle of the night, but I don't know what to do if the hooves don't appear. I'm going to need her."

Simeon turned and left the courtyard. I placed my hands

on Hannah's rump and wondered if the rabbis had a prayer for goat birthing.

I lifted the oil lamp to better examine my patient. A bubble of birth sac protruded from Hannah's rear, and I could see white fur beneath the shiny caul. Was it the baby's head or his side? If the latter, could a kid be born side-first?

A few moments later, I heard Bethel shuffling through the gate. She had come in her night tunic, not even taking the time to grab a head covering.

"I'm sorry we had to wake you," I began, but she brushed away my apology.

"I was teasing. I would be upset if you didn't send for me." She stepped up and studied the goat, her face alight with interest. "I would not miss this."

Her pleasant expression faded when she saw one kid in the straw and the other still in the mother. She blew out a breath. "I need to push the baby back into the womb and see if I can feel my way around. I will need oil and honey. And water. Lots of water."

"We have both." Simeon turned to fetch the honey and oil.

Bethel poured some of both into a dish, stirred them with her finger, and slathered the mixture onto her right hand and arm. While Judit and I moved to the side to watch, Bethel eased her hand into the goat's birth canal and pushed the baby back inside. Then she pushed her arm in farther, up to the elbow, and grimaced.

"I can feel an eye socket," she said, giving me a wry smile. "That is good. I was afraid we were looking at the kid's side, and I cannot turn a kid who is sideways. But if I can get this kid's chin up, we can tilt the head back and bring it forward."

She struggled, compressing her lips as perspiration pearled on her forehead. From the next room I could hear the sweet, high-pitched sounds of newborns' bleating, but from Hannah we heard only panicked groans.

Finally, Bethel pulled her hand out of the animal and gave me a defeated look. "The baby is too big, and I know of only one thing to do. So tell me again—the kids are the most important thing, correct? Your husband bred these goats for the kids?"

Dread enveloped my heart as I nodded.

She sighed. "I can cut the kid out of the mother. There will be no way to save the she-goat, but we can ease her pain."

I looked at Judit, whose eyes had widened with horror. "You should go upstairs," I told her, gentling my voice. "You've had a long day. You've been a big help, but Bethel and I can take care of this."

"Can't I tell Hannah good-bye?"

"Hannah is suffering, daughter. Go on now. I will see you in the morning."

Judit hesitated, then ran up the stairs, choking back a sob.

A cold panic prickled down my spine as I wiped my hands on my tunic and looked to Bethel for direction. "Do whatever you must, and tell me how to help."

She nodded. "Stand behind the goat in case the baby starts to come out again. Tell me if you see anything."

While I moved into position, Bethel took the blade from the bench, walked over to Hannah's head and cut the goat's throat with an ease any priest would have envied. Immediately after the goat fell to its knees, she ran the blade firmly over the goat's belly, exposing the pink womb. After another quick cut, I saw the kid, its head lowered and its legs pointed toward the mother's head. Grabbing it by all four legs, Bethel lifted the kid out of the steaming body and handed it to me. While I pulled the gelatinous sac away from its head, Bethel wiped the nostrils and mouth. "We need to swing him."

"I know."

She stepped away as I stood with the baby and swung him with all the strength in my broken heart. A moment later, the baby released a tiny bleat, and I lowered him to the straw beside his sibling.

Then, overcome by weariness and emotion, I burst into tears.

<hr />

Raising orphan goats, Bethel assured me later, would not be a problem but would be far easier if I could rent a she-goat and have her nurse the orphaned twins. So James went to the town center, where he searched until he found a family willing to lend us a goat for two months. After that, Bethel assured us, our kids would no longer need to nurse.

The rented goat was called Jezebel, and her name suited her temperament. She adopted Hannah's babies without hesitation and threatened to butt anyone who came near them. More than once she tried to bite me when I entered the stall to give her fresh water, and I found myself counting the days until we could send her back to her own family.

My girls, of course, wanted to name the kids. I cautioned them about becoming too attached to the animals, but since I had allowed them to name Delilah and Hannah, my argument crumbled before their persistent pleas. Finally I agreed, mostly because we needed a way to tell the perfectly white kids apart.

I thought the names might be prophetic—at least, I hoped they were. The girls named Delilah's firstborn Tikvah, for *hope*, which was what I felt every time I looked at him. The second kid they called Simcha, for *joy*, and that lively little male seemed to embody the word. The third kid they named Hupsah, for *freedom*, and I wondered if my girls realized the kids were the key to their father's release from prison. The little female they called Ora, which meant *her light*. Considering that Chiram remained locked in a dark and awful prison, I thought her name especially appropriate.

Joses carved little wooden circles and inscribed them with the goats' names. Judit and Jordan attached the circles to woven collars and tied them around the kids' necks. Every time I looked at the lively little creatures, I wanted to go to Arimathea and tell Chiram his dream was being fulfilled before my eyes. The breeding had produced four spotless white kids, three males and one female.

As we moved into late summer, I yearned to see Chiram for other reasons, too. I needed to know he was well, his health good, and that he had not lost heart. I had not received a letter in several weeks, so I did not know what he had been thinking or if he'd become discouraged. I had not suffered much in our difficult situation, because I had the help of family and friends. Who besides Uriah was lifting Chiram's spirits? What comfort did he have, apart from his faith in HaShem?

And though I would admit this to no one, I worried because the bond between us seemed to stretch thin during our time apart. Sometimes, as I lay on my single mattress and reached for him in the darkness, I tried to imagine him sleeping next to me and couldn't. His hair had always had a reddish tinge, but was it still red now that he was not in the sun? His face had always been narrow, but when I tried to envision it across from me at dinner, I saw my brothers' faces instead. I would close my eyes and try to hear Chiram's voice, and my ears filled instead with the masculine voices around my dinner table.

When the kids were two months old and eating solid food, I took Jezebel back to her owners and thanked them with several baskets of eggs. Returning home, I stood in the courtyard and watched all four kids frolic around Delilah, who seemed not to care that her little family had doubled. The kids appeared healthy and strong, another proof that Chiram knew more about breeding goats than anyone had supposed.

One night after dinner, I sent the girls outside so I could talk to my brothers. "I need your help," I said, looking from James to Joses to Jude and Simeon. "If you are willing, I would like one of you to travel with me to Arimathea. The rest of you must stay here and take care of my children and the animals."

"Only one of us needs to remain behind," Simeon said. "And you should have at least two of us with you. The stronger the traveling party, the less likely you are to attract trouble."

I laughed. "Do any of you think you can handle the girls and the animals alone? The work isn't easy."

"I will stay," Jude said, leaning back in his chair. "Because Bethel will help me if something goes wrong."

James rapped the tabletop with his knuckles. "It's settled, then. Give us a couple of days to finish up the project we have under way, then the rest of us will go with you. Jude will stay and mind the household, and we will all pray for him."

My brothers nodded, and tears filled my eyes as I looked around the circle. In my younger years, I would never have imagined that my brothers would make this kind of sacrifice for me, but none of them had denied my request. I had not spent much time with my brothers since my marriage, yet this season of adversity had reminded me that they were good men. Abba and Ima might not have had much in the way of material possessions, but they had taught us to love each other. And with love, what else did we need?

Two days later, James told me we were ready to depart for Arimathea.

---

We set out on the first day of the week, knowing we would be traveling three days each way, plus stopping to observe Shabbat on the return. I kissed my daughters and told them I would see them in about ten days, Adonai willing. I urged them to be on their best behavior and to help their uncle Jude. I told Judit she would be in charge of collecting eggs for the market and warned Eden that the goats would need fresh water and plenty of food. "And if you have any trouble," I reminded all of them, "Bethel is willing to help you. All you have to do is ask."

James, Simeon, Joses, and I joined a group of travelers not far outside Nazareth. They were going to Emmaus and welcomed our company since they planned to go through Samaria. We were also planning to pass through that region, knowing we would be less likely to face harassment if we traveled in a large group.

My brothers walked with the men and talked of crops, government, and religion. Never, at least not in my hearing, did they mention Yeshua. I knew why—after three years of traveling through the land, his name alone was enough to divide a company, to incite fierce loyalty or hatred among any group of Judeans or Galileans.

We women also guarded our tongues. We talked of children,

of shopping and fashions, and the challenges of keeping a
ritually pure household. I told my new friends about my
adventures in goat birthing. Another woman spoke of her
travail in giving birth to twin boys. We lowered our voices
and giggled about our husbands, thanking HaShem for the
things our mothers did—and did not—teach us about men
in general and husbands in particular. "If I had known," one
woman said, "that my husband would belch and make other
impious noises in our bed, I would never have married him."

The trip passed more quickly than I thought it would, and
we regretfully bade farewell to our traveling companions as
we turned toward Arimathea. Approaching the city and its
prison, I tried to put its horrors out of my mind. I had come
to bring Chiram good news, to cheer and encourage him. I
would not dwell on the awful aspects of imprisonment or
mention the difficulties I had faced, but would do my best
to be a light shining in darkness.

The prison seemed less daunting this time, and my heart
did not leap into my throat as we neared the entrance. The
man who guarded the place looked as bored as ever, and he
did not say anything when Joses said we had come to visit
Chiram. This time I did not come empty-handed but carried
a basket filled with bread, dried fish, figs, and pomegranates. I had brought as much food as our pack saddle would
hold, knowing Chiram would freely share with his fellow
prisoners.

My eyes required a few moments to adjust to the dim light
of the cavern, but soon I recognized shapes in the shadowed
interior. I spied the bench for visitors, the iron bars, the
stone walls. Against those walls, farther back, I discerned
the outlines of four men, one of whom had risen and was
moving toward the iron bars.

"Chiram?" My voice trembled as I quickened my steps. The approaching man straightened and stood in the light streaming through the opening in the cavern. I would not have recognized my husband if I had passed him on the road. White threads shone in his dark beard, now shapeless and untrimmed. His hair lay limp against his shoulders, and a layer of grime covered his skin in irregular blotches. The hands gripping the bars were bony and covered in filth, with dirt encrusted beneath overgrown fingernails. His eyes were sunken, with only dim sparks of light to bear witness to the life glowing within the skeletal frame.

"Chiram . . ." I forced a note of happiness into my voice. "It is good to see you."

"Pheodora." The hands on the bars trembled, as did the voice. "I cannot believe you came."

"We have brought food." I gestured to Simeon, who stepped forward with the basket, then knelt and pushed it through an opening at the bottom of the bars. Chiram did not bend to examine it, but one of the other men scrambled forward and took it, then withdrew to the back of the cave as if afraid we would demand our basket back.

"Are you not going to eat?" I asked in a whisper.

The suggestion of a smile touched his lips. "They will save some for me. We have decided sharing is better than watching one another starve."

Suffering from a sudden lack of words, I reached out and touched his hand. "We come with good news, husband. The goats have given birth—we now have four beautiful white kids in our courtyard. Delilah is proving to be a good mother to them all."

His eyes brightened, then quickly dimmed. "And the second she-goat?"

I shook my head. "The second baby was not positioned correctly, so Bethel—the woman who lives next door—had to open the goat's belly. She said the female would not have survived otherwise. This way, at least the baby lived."

Chiram nodded slowly, then a small smile appeared in the tangles of his beard. "You are blessed to have such an experienced neighbor. Few men would have attempted what she did."

"She has raised goats before. I don't know what I would do without her."

Chiram lifted a hand and rubbed mine as best he could. "How are our daughters? Growing like the summer grass, I would imagine."

I did not feel like laughing in such a horrible place, but I knew my husband needed to hear the cheerful sound. He and the others needed to know that one day they would laugh again, too.

So I forced laughter up from my throat. "The girls are getting so big. Judit is quite grown up now—she actually helped me birth the kids. I let her observe everything, right until the time when Bethel had to cut the second she-goat. I think Judit could help with any goat now."

"Perhaps one day she will be a shepherdess. And the other girls?"

"Eden and Jordan are learning something new every day. Shiri is growing ever more independent. She doesn't say much but follows her sisters around and observes. She seems especially fond of Bethel, who would spoil the child if I let her. Oh—and she has stopped sucking her thumb. Bethel told her it would ruin the shape of her mouth, and Shiri stopped almost immediately."

Chiram smiled, and in the silence that followed I realized

the men behind him were listening intently. Were they so desperate for news they would hang on every word about another man's daughters?

"Anything else?" Chiram shifted his weight, still clutching the bars. "Any news from your family?"

I glanced behind me, where my brothers waited on the bench. "Have I forgotten anything, brothers?"

Simeon folded his arms. "Yeshua is still preaching in Galilee. And every day the religious rulers grow more agitated on his account."

"True." I looked at Chiram again. "Nearly every day I hear people talking about Yeshua at the well. Though he grew up among them, some believe he has been overtaken by the spirits of dead prophets. Some say he is John the Immerser, others that he is Elijah. A few say he must be the Messiah, but that opinion is unpopular in Nazareth."

Chiram's eyes softened. "What do you think?"

I snorted, while Joses and Simeon chuckled behind me. "I think—*we* think—Yeshua is the son of Mary and Joseph of Nazareth. Who else would he be? He is a good teacher, certainly, and like other scholars he seems to have dedicated his life to studying Torah and following HaShem. Which is fine—if he'd rather study than marry and raise a family, there is precedent for it. But it is hard to imagine him as anything other than our brother."

Chiram shifted his weight again, and for the first time I realized his feet seemed to be bothering him. Like the others, he was barefoot, and a layer of dirt covered his feet. With an apologetic grimace, he lowered himself to the floor.

"Are you all right?" I asked, kneeling. "Do you need a physician? Your feet—"

"I am fine. I am simply not used to standing." He bent his

legs and rested his elbows on his bony knees. "I don't expect you to be uncomfortable. You should sit with your brothers."

"And be so far from you?" Without hesitating, I lowered myself to the floor and tucked my tunic around my legs. "I want to look at you while we talk."

He smiled, and his eyes shone moist in the faint light. "Every time I close my eyes I see your face, but it is better to behold you in the flesh." He slipped his hand through the bars and I held it between both of my own, glad to feel his skin, still warm, still alive.

Silence stretched between us as we held each other. I heard the far-off cry of a bird of prey, the distant sound of passing voices, and the rattling breaths of a prisoner against the back wall. Searching for a light topic of conversation, I recalled an event from our journey to Caesarea.

"When we went to pick up the she-goats," I said, smiling, "Nathan's wife told me a story about something her father saw when he watched the flocks at Migdal-eder. She thought your father might have seen it, as well."

Chiram tilted his brow, then nodded slowly. "My father did speak of that night."

"And you never told me?" I squeezed his hand. "I thought a husband and wife were meant to share everything."

He drew a deep breath, then met my gaze. "I have learned to be careful with that story. People who hear it tend to think I am either lying or mad."

"But I am your wife. I know you are not mad and do not lie."

"All right." He paused, licked his cracked lips, and continued speaking in the low tone he reserved for our quiet times together. "I was just a boy, so I wasn't with Abba at the time. But one night, while my father and a few other shepherds watched the spring lambs in the fields outside Migdal-eder, an angel of Adonai appeared to them. The glory of the Lord shone all around them, so bright it completely lit the place where they had been resting; so bright, my father said, that the sleeping flowers awakened and turned toward the source of the light. Abba and the other shepherds were terrified, but the angel told them not to fear because he brought good news of great joy to all the people." Chiram's eyes came up to study my face.

"Go on." I tightened my hands around his. "I am with you."

Chiram looked to his right, as if he were seeing the animals his father had guarded. "'Today,' the angel told them, 'in the City of David, a Savior has been born to you; he is Messiah the Lord. You will find the baby wrapped in strips of cloth and lying in a manger.'"

My mind began to whirl. "In Bethlehem?"

Chiram nodded without looking at me. "Suddenly a multitude of heavenly armies appeared behind the angel, praising God and saying, 'Glory to God in the highest, and on earth shalom to men of good will.' The sound was so overwhelming, my father said the trees trembled and the grass shivered. He looked at the animals, certain the lambs would be so terrified they'd run, but none of them did. They simply stood there, Abba said, as if they were accustomed to seeing and hearing incredible things.

"When the angels finally departed, my father and the other shepherds decided to go into the city and see the thing Adonai had made known to them. So they left a young lad with the lambs and went into Bethlehem, where they found the baby in a cattle stall. The child's parents were astonished to have visitors, so my father told them about everything the angel had said. Then they were relieved, and all of them were filled with great joy."

"Who were the parents?" I interrupted. "And what were they doing in a barn?"

Chiram shrugged. "My father did not ask their names. They were in a barn because they could find no other place to rest. The woman gave birth in that humble shelter and laid her baby in the only bed she could find, a manger."

From the bench behind me, Joses cleared his throat. "And what did your father do with this amazing news?"

Chiram met Joses's gaze and smiled. "They went back to guard the sheep, of course. And the next day, when they went to Jerusalem to deliver the lambs for the morning sacrifices, they stood in the outer courtyard and told the story to anyone who would listen. Not everyone believed them, because why would Adonai send a holy angel to speak to a group of unclean shepherds? But an old man named Simeon and an elderly prophetess named Anna were ministering in the Temple, and they came out and listened with great interest. Afterward, they questioned my father privately. After he recounted all he had seen and heard, Simeon and Anna rejoiced to know the Messiah had been born. They confirmed the date of the child's birth with the shepherds and said they would be looking for him when his mother came with her purification offering."

I took a deep breath as a half-dozen questions rose in my head. Clearly, Chiram believed this story, but if our Messiah was alive and in Israel, why was he waiting to reveal himself? And what did he think about Yeshua?

My thoughts flitted back to the memory of Chiram's father, who lived with us in the first five years of our marriage. Though he barely remembered who we were, he used to sit and look out the window for hours. I always wondered who he was looking for . . . could he have been watching for the man he first met as a baby in a manger?

"Chiram"—I gripped his fingers—"I must know. Did Anna and Simeon find him?"

Chiram's shoulders drooped. "I do not know. On later visits, my father, being unclean, could not go inside the Temple and did not have an opportunity to look for the old man or the woman. He did not hear anything else about the child, but he said I should keep my eyes open, for the Messiah was living among us. For years I have searched and waited. But I have heard nothing, unless—"

"Many have claimed to be the Messiah," James interrupted, his tone clipped. "Men who are now dead because of their presumption."

"I hope our brother corrects those who refer to *him* as the Messiah," I added. "If this baby is alive in Judea, I would not want him to see Yeshua as a threat."

"The baby is now a man," Chiram said. "I remember the night my father came home with the story. I was seven. I am now forty. The baby would be thirty-three now."

"Wait." Simeon leaned forward and focused intently on Chiram. "You cannot think Yeshua is this baby your father saw. Our brother is no messiah."

Chiram gave Simeon a look of patient amusement.

"Chiram is not saying that." I whirled to face my brother. "He simply told a story." I forced a laugh. "The idea that Yeshua—it's ridiculous. If he were the Messiah . . ." I found the idea so incongruous I laughed aloud, unable to finish my thought.

Joses snorted. "The answer is obvious. Crowds filled Bethlehem in those days, and many of those people were pregnant women. Yeshua was born around the same time and near the same place. A coincidence."

"Your father told you a lovely story," I told my husband. "But perhaps you have confused the dates. If the Messiah had come, the chief priests at the Temple would have welcomed Him and announced His coming."

Chiram offered me a distracted nod, then slowly returned my smile. "Perhaps you are right. Yet if Adonai could choose a young shepherd from Bethlehem to be King of Israel, could He not choose the infant son of a carpenter to be our Messiah?"

I had no answer for that, and neither did my brothers.

"That is a question for HaShem alone," I said, gripping his hand again. "For now, the sun sets and we must find shelter for the night. I hope you remain well, husband, and the food strengthens your body and soul. Until we meet again, be assured I have dedicated myself to freeing you from this awful place. Next year at this time, I will be preparing to sell those goats for money to pay your debt."

"Bless my daughters for me," Chiram said. He slipped his hand through the bars and placed it on my forehead. *"Eishet Chayil mi yimtza, v'rakhok mi'pninim michrah. Batakh bah lev ba'alah, v'shalal lo yekhsar. Piha pat'cha v'chochmah, v'torat chesed al l'shonah. Kamu vaneha v'ya'ashruhah, ba'alah vay'hal'lah. 'Rabot banot asu chayil, v'at alit al kulanah!'"*

*A woman of valor, who can find? Her worth is far beyond rubies. Her husband trusts in her, and lacks for nothing. Her lips are full of wisdom, her mouth with loving-kindness. Her children rise and bless her, her husband sings her praises. "Many women have done well, but you surpass them all!"*

I stood and stumbled out of the prison, Joses guiding me, because my eyes had been blinded by tears.

# CHAPTER TWENTY-FIVE

# Pheodora

My brothers and I did not talk much during the walk home. I could not tell what thoughts occupied James, Joses, and Simeon, but I suspected they were pondering Chiram's story about the child born in Bethlehem. Surely, Yeshua was not the only thirty-three-year-old who had been born in Bethlehem. But how many others were there?

The answer occurred to me almost immediately: not many. Because around that time, King Herod ordered the massacre of all baby boys in Bethlehem age two and under, just one of many atrocities our former king committed. Herod had been insanely cruel, executing his favorite wife and at least three of his own children . . .

There it was, the missing piece.

"I have found the answer," I told my brothers. "Yeshua cannot be the baby Chiram's father went to see."

Joses lifted a brow. "And you know this because . . . ?"

"Because Herod executed all the baby boys in Bethlehem. The baby in the manger would have been killed."

Joses thought a moment, then looked at James. "Where were you born?"

James's mouth quirked. "Egypt."

"Why were you born there?"

"Because that is where Ima and Abba were living."

Joses turned back to me. "Yeshua and James are two years apart."

I was not as quick as Joses, but I finally realized the implication: our parents had left Bethlehem and gone to Egypt. Messiah or not, my brother—perhaps both Yeshua and James—might have been killed if not for my parents' decision to sojourn in the Black Land.

I blew out a breath. "Then it is all coincidence."

"I agree with you," Joses said, "but others will not. They are desperate for a Messiah, so they pin the prophecy on anyone who might help them throw off the yoke of Rome. If they hear about a baby announced by angels and then learn Yeshua was born in Bethlehem—"

"Yeshua does not talk about resisting Rome. In fact, he does the opposite," I said. "He is not a rabble-rouser. He is a scholar, more devoted to HaShem than to politics. I would not argue with anyone who called him a prophet, for he is very wise. He has spent years studying the Scriptures."

James nodded. "Agreed."

"So what *is* he telling the people?"

James looked at Joses, who shrugged. "You should talk to Jude. Two years ago, he and Tasmin spent several days listening to Yeshua."

"What does Jude say?"

"Talk to him," Joses urged. "From what he told me, Yeshua

preaches against only those ones who would twist the words of the Torah to suit their own purposes."

My thoughts shifted to what Damaris had told me about Shimon's study of Gematria—how the Pharisees changed the meaning of the Scriptures from "Moses married a woman from Cush" to "Moses married a woman of fair appearance." A perfect example, it seemed to me, of twisting the Torah's meaning.

I frowned, not sure which would be more dangerous— Yeshua inciting revolution against Rome, or against the Temple authorities.

As the sun set, we stopped at Sepphoris to observe Shabbat. We unpacked the donkey's saddle in the courtyard of the inn, then took advantage of the innkeeper's hospitality and joined his family for their Sabbath meal.

After the blessing of the food and the lighting of the candles, we began to eat. The innkeeper, called Boas, asked from whence we had come, and Simeon told him we'd been to Arimathea. Lest the man ask too many questions about our business there, I spoke up and said we were on our way home to Nazareth.

"Then your journey is nearly complete," he said, a smile lighting his round, jovial face. "You are nearly there."

"Yes," Joses answered, helping himself to bread. "But we know Sepphoris well. My brothers and I spent many days here when Antipas commenced his building program."

Boas clapped his hands. "Wonderful! Some of our people complain about the Romans and all they have done, but Sepphoris greatly benefited from their projects. Thanks to Antipas, we now have a strong wall, a theater, an upper and lower market, and a palace. My wife and I are happy to live in one of the most beautiful cities in all of Galilee."

My brothers smiled politely while I kept my gaze lowered. I remembered the days of Herod Antipas's construction. He began to build not long after his father's death, and my brothers had gone off to work in Sepphoris as soon as they were old enough to be trusted with a hammer and chisel. Our father worked in Sepphoris, too, and died in this city when a beam fell from a rooftop and crushed his chest. Ten years ago . . .

I blinked tears away and hoped none of my brothers glanced in my direction. To look at any of them, to know they were thinking of Abba, would destroy my fragile self-control.

"I am told," James said, his voice rough, "that you have several fine synagogues in the city."

"Oh, yes," our host said, brightening. "Not long ago, one of our Torah teachers, Ezra ben Gershom, he of blessed memory, called his students around his bedside as he prepared to die. They expected him to be calm and gentle, but to their astonishment he burst into tears when they arrived. They asked what was wrong, and he replied, 'If I were now to be brought before an earthly king, who lives today and dies tomorrow, whose wrath and bonds are not everlasting, and who can be assuaged or bought off by money—I should tremble and weep, so how much more reason have I for tears when I am about to be led before the King of kings, the Holy One, blessed be He, Who lives and abides forever, whose chains are chains forever, and whose sentence of death kills forever, whom I cannot assuage with words nor bribe by money—in light of Him, shall I not shed tears?'"

Boas paused, clearly expecting some comment from us, yet I had no idea what he expected us to say.

"Is this not an example of piety?" Boas pressed. "That even a great Torah teacher can weep with trepidation when he is about to meet HaShem?"

I looked to James, who cleared his throat and nodded slowly. "It is a remarkable example of . . . fear."

"We have another synagogue," Boas continued, "whose Torah teacher died last year. On his deathbed, as his students gathered around, he lifted up both hands and proclaimed that none of his ten fingers had broken the Law of God. Is that not an example of holiness?"

James sent Simeon a sharp glance, then managed a smile. "The latter is an example of confidence," he said, "but one has to wonder if any man can live without breaking the Law of God even once. When does such confidence become pride? Because Scripture tells us that pride goes before destruction."

Though our host maintained his gallant smile, his face stiffened and his hands clenched. Suspecting my brothers were about to destroy the peace of Shabbat, I drew a breath and dared to speak.

"I was present at my father-in-law's deathbed," I said, smiling around the table. "He was no Torah teacher, but he loved HaShem with all his heart, mind, and soul. As he lay on his bed, preparing to meet the Holy One, he opened his eyes and stared as if he were looking into heaven. His face, which had been lined with pain, suddenly brightened, and his lips curved in a smile. Then, though he had not spoken in days, he lifted his voice and said, 'Deliver me, Adonai!' After that, he breathed his last and departed this life."

Silence wrapped itself around us, then James nodded. "That was surely the death of a righteous man. As Job said,

'Even after my skin has been destroyed, yet in my flesh I will see God.' Like Abraham, your father-in-law approached HaShem in simple faith, believing, and HaShem reckoned it to him as righteousness."

Boas would not argue with Scripture, so he straightened and gave us a lopsided smile. "More lentils?" he asked, offering the bowl.

———•———

When we arrived home, I hugged my girls, thanked Bethel for helping with my daughters and my animals, and went downstairs to check on the newborn kids. Delilah had slimmed down, though her udder was still shiny and full, which meant we'd have plenty of milk for making cheese, since the kids had been weaned.

"Are you sure they're healthy?" I asked Bethel as I watched the young goats. "I'm not sure I could tell if they were sick."

Bethel clicked her tongue. "Study their demeanor and their droppings," she said, pointing to a pile of dark pellets on the straw. "Those are normal droppings, so if they look proper, all is well. But if the droppings appear runny or a different color or blood-streaked, your kid is sick. In the same way, a sick kid will not be leaping and playing like these. It would be standing alone with its head down or perhaps lying on the straw. Trust me, you will know if you have a sick kid in the same way you know if one of your daughters is ill."

I patted Bethel's arm and smiled at the little goats, who seemed to delight in leaping on the bales of straw, onto the bench, and onto each other. "If I only had their energy," I said, sighing. "It was good to see my husband, but I'm ready to rest."

"How is he?" Bethel's squint tightened as she looked up. "I have never met him."

I leaned on the railing of the goat pen. "He is as well as can be expected, I suppose. He looks terrible, but he wasn't coughing and I don't think he had a fever. He was thrilled to hear we had two sets of twins, and he said we were blessed to have you nearby and available for help. He was sorry we lost the smaller she-goat, but those kids are our future—and his freedom. Without them, he could be in prison for years."

Bethel's broad smile assured me that Chiram's gratitude meant a great deal to her. As a child, I had never taken the time to know her, but now I realized that an older woman might think her life finished unless she served some useful purpose. With my family, Bethel had no reason to worry—I seemed to need her more every day.

I thanked her again and went upstairs to prepare something for dinner. My brothers usually came home to eat around midday, then went back to work. I had just pulled out a crock of ground grain when Jude came through the door.

"Welcome back," he said, kicking off his sandals. "How was your trip?"

"I'm glad you're here," I said, forgetting about the loaf I had been about to bake. "Chiram told me a story while we were there, a story I cannot forget."

He walked over to the pitcher and poured water into the basin. "Must have been a good one."

"It was. Apparently, years ago an angel appeared to his father and some other shepherds in the fields outside Migdal-eder. The angel said the Messiah had been born in the City of David, and they could find him lying in a manger."

Jude paused, his hands dripping, and looked at me. "Truly?"

I nodded. "Chiram seemed to think Yeshua might be the Messiah. I told him it was impossible, but I don't think I convinced him."

Jude chuckled as he reached for a linen towel. "He's like so many others—desperate enough to see messiahs on every street corner. And why wouldn't he when we pray for His coming in our morning prayers?"

"I wanted to ask you about Yeshua's teaching. I've never heard him speak except at the synagogue. You're the only one who has actually heard him interact with a crowd, so I would like to know what you think."

Jude wiped his hands, then sat on the bench near the table. "What does Yeshua preach? He encourages the people. He tells stories about things they understand—farmers, fathers, sons and daughters. He tells the poor they are blessed because they are humble. He tells the rich to sell all they have and give it to the poor. He tells everyone to love their enemies and do good to those who would curse them." Jude shrugged. "I have never heard him say anything about revolution or fighting the Romans, but I did hear him say that if a Roman commands us to carry his load for one furlong, we should carry it for two."

I made a face. "That is not what I expected to hear."

"You have to understand, little sister—not everyone who hears Yeshua decides to follow him. Some go away angry. Some go away grieved, especially those who are rich. I haven't yet met a rich man who rejoiced to hear he should give his wealth away if he wants to prosper in eternity." He laughed. "Yeshua said it was easier for a camel to go through a needle's eye than for a rich man to enter heaven."

"He talks about the afterlife? The Pharisees must love that, since the Sadducees don't believe in one."

"I've seen Pharisees in the crowds around Yeshua, but I've seen none among his close followers. I believe they seek him out only because they are curious. They would feel it is their duty to report him if he says anything blasphemous."

"Has he?"

"What?"

"Has he said anything blasphemous?"

Jude shrugged. "Not in my hearing. But I'm not a Pharisee. I don't tithe the salt I sprinkle on my meat."

"What about Abba?"

Jude's forehead wrinkled. "Abba?"

"He was devoted to HaShem. What would he say about Yeshua's lessons?"

Jude tugged on his beard for a moment, then dipped his chin in a firm nod. "I do not think he would find any fault with Yeshua's teachings. Abba was always practical. Remember the time a dog fell in the village well on Shabbat? Many said it would be wrong to pull the dog out, but Abba insisted the dog's life be preserved. Yeshua would agree."

"So perhaps Yeshua is preaching what our father taught— that we should visit the debtors in prison, comfort the sick, and help the helpless."

"You are right." Jude smiled, his eyes crinkling at the corners. "If only Damaris would understand."

I crossed my arms, confused by the reference to our sister. "Have you seen Damaris lately?"

"Yesterday—she came to the house."

"Did she want anything in particular?"

"I think she wanted to see you. When I told her you were away, she stayed only a few minutes and then left."

I sighed and looked at the table where I had not yet begun to make bread. "Perhaps I should go see her."

"In all your free time?" Jude came over and gripped my shoulder. "I don't know how you manage to do all you do, but if you can find the time to visit our sister, be my guest. Someone needs to remind her that Abba did not care much for Pharisees. She seems to have forgotten that."

"Do you think it would make a difference?" I stood there, blinking, as Jude shook his head and walked away.

# CHAPTER TWENTY-SIX

# Damaris

I leaned forward and checked my reflection in the oval looking brass. My new handmaid had done a good job with my hair, but the makeup seemed a bit understated. "I need more color in my cheeks." I pointed to the pot of ground red ochre. "And more kohl for my eyes."

"Yes, my lady." The girl dipped her fingertips in the paint pot and applied a dab of ochre to my cheeks, then worked the color into my skin.

Shimon had been hinting that the wife of a respected Pharisee should look more like a sophisticated lady and less like a rural Galilean, so I was attempting to do my best with what I had. Nazareth's marketplace did not offer a wide assortment of cosmetics, wigs, or fine tunics, but Shimon's father could procure whatever I needed—though he often had to pull it off a wagon bound for Jerusalem.

I checked my reflection one last time, then nodded my approval. As my maid moved toward the trunk holding himations and headscarves, I went to the window and peeked through the shutters. On the road beyond our gate, I spotted a familiar figure—Pheodora, walking toward our house. My heart leapt beneath my breastbone. What did she want? This was no casual visit or she would have brought her children. She must have something on her mind and had left her girls with one of the brothers so we could talk privately.

Anxiety crept into my mood like a wisp of smoke. I glanced at the himation the maid held toward me. "Too plain," I told her. "Something grander, please. There—the one with the gilded edge. I am about to have company."

"Ah." Yuta smiled. "Someone you wish to impress?"

"You could say that."

I stood with my arms outstretched as the girl expertly draped the fluid fabric across my body and fastened it at one shoulder, allowing the length to hang in gentle folds over the side of my tunic. The gilded edge sparkled in the slanting rays of sunlight, and the effect was most pleasing. Pheodora, bless her, would have nothing like this.

Why had she come? Was she going to make another plea for Shimon to pay Chiram's debt? Or had she realized she would have to take more drastic action if she wanted to free her husband? She could sell the house in Bethlehem, of course, but that might be a problem if Chiram wanted to return to his work as a shepherd. Pheodora and her children would have to live somewhere. Or she might be considering something else . . .

I looked at Yuta, still fussing with the folds of my garments. "Yuta, you are fourteen, correct?"

She looked up, startled. "Yes."

"How did you come to be a slave? You are not a foreigner, so you were not taken prisoner in war."

She lowered her gaze. "No, mistress."

228

"How, then, did you find yourself in the slave market?"

I was surprised to see tears spilling from the girl's long lashes.

"My mother and father died, mistress. I had no other relatives to support me, so I had no choice."

I nodded as the pieces fell into place. "You sold yourself into servitude. But the money—"

"Went to pay my parents' debts."

"Ah. Of course." I smiled and turned back to the mirror. "Do not be anxious, girl. You will always have a home here, and you will be freed in a few years—unless we can convince you to remain with us." I turned my most charming smile upon her, hoping she would commit to remaining my handmaid for life, but she did not meet my gaze.

"Anything else, mistress?"

"Some jewels, please, for my hair. And the scented slippers, with an ankle bracelet."

Yuta hurried to obey as I sat and tried to relax. Pheodora would be here before I was ready, yet she wouldn't mind waiting. Perhaps it would be good to have her wait. She would realize I had taken time to prepare for her, that I was not the sort of woman who greeted my guests in whatever I happened to be wearing.

"Ima?" Amarisa, my eldest, thrust her head through the door. "Should I stay with Sabba and Safta today?"

"Yes, and take your sisters with you," I said. At twelve, Amarisa was old enough for a betrothal, but we were waiting in hopes of making a match within Shimon's chaburah. "You look very nice, daughter."

Amarisa dimpled and disappeared. I smoothed my himation and exhaled in relief, grateful to know my girls would be occupied during the day. Shimon's mother loved having the girls around and was constantly reminding me they would not be underfoot forever.

A moment later, a servant knocked at my door. "Mistress, your sister is here to see you."

"Give her honey water," I said, "and tell her I will be down in a moment." I pressed my fingers to a stubborn curl that would not hang at the same angle as the others. When I was certain I looked presentable, I stood and went downstairs to greet Pheodora.

I found her sitting on a couch, a cup in her hand, her brow furrowed. She looked up when I called her name, but barely glanced at me before pointing to a thick scroll on the table. "What is that? I've never seen anything written in such small letters."

"Writings from Gamaliel," I replied, sinking onto the couch beside her. "Shimon is studying. Ever since he heard he would soon be admitted to the chaburah, he spends all his time studying."

"I did not know Shimon was such a scholar." Pheodora sipped from her cup. "What has he learned? Besides how to reinterpret Scripture through Gematria?"

I shrugged her question away. "Becoming a Pharisee is a serious and holy calling," I said, tugging at my tunic. "I know it is not the sort of calling a shepherd could consider—"

"*My* shepherd," Pheodora said, her tone cool, "has not been able to work for months. I'm sure you have not forgotten that men cannot work in prison."

I bit my lower lip, choking on the response I wanted to give. I felt compelled to apologize, to explain that my husband had good reasons for not paying her husband's debt, but why reopen a wound that would only drive us further apart?

"How *is* Chiram?" I asked, trying to keep my voice pleasant. "Jude said you went to visit him."

"He is alive, HaShem be praised. He is thin and covered in filth, but he has not yet developed a cough or a rash. If HaShem is willing, he will remain healthy until I am able to get him out of prison."

"Have you found someone willing to assume his debt?"

Pheodora lifted her chin in a gesture that swam up through the years, reminding me of our father. "We do not need a benefactor. We do not need charity or a loan from Shimon. Chiram will pay his debt himself."

"How is that possible?"

Pheodora folded her hands. "My husband bought two she-goats—*quality* goats—and bred them with a pure white he-goat. He had me fetch them from a breeder, and they have already given birth at home, where I am tending them. The kids are now weaned, and when they are yearlings, I will take them to Migdal-eder. From the beginning, Chiram planned to sell them as an identical pair for Yom Kippur."

I gasped in pleased surprise. "Wonderful! Chiram was clever to plan so far ahead. But you, sister—" I covered my mouth and fizzled with laughter—"you are raising *goats*? What do you know about goats?"

"Nothing." Pheodora laughed with me. "At least, I knew nothing in the beginning. But our brothers have helped, and Bethel, the woman next door, knows about goats and chickens and children and anything else you could name. I would not be the happy owner of four kids and a lovely she-goat if not for her."

I closed my eyes and struggled to remember. "I always forget about her and her husband. What was his name? Seth?"

"Yes, and Bethel has been taking care of our brothers since Ima left home. I think she enjoys being needed, and we seem to need her more every day. My daughters love her. With Ima away, Bethel has been like a grandmother."

"I am glad to hear all is well with you." I smiled and adjusted my himation. "Will you stay for dinner? I'm sure the servants have prepared something delicious. Shimon will be returning soon from the synagogue, and I know he'd love to hear all about Chiram's goats."

"I cannot stay." Pheodora inhaled a deep breath. "I came only because Jude said you had visited the house while I was gone. He thought you wanted to see me."

My mind went blank—what reason should I give for visiting my childhood home? I had gone because Shimon wanted me to be sure Pheodora had not offended Lavan by writing letters or begging him for her husband's release, but clearly Pheodora had not. She and Chiram were planning to pay his debt, and their plan seemed forthright and honorable. Shimon had nothing to fear from my sister.

I forced a smile. "Yes . . . I stopped by to say hello."

"You are a lady of leisure, then," Pheodora said, her face brightening. "Between caring for my girls, our brothers, and my animals, I have to rush through my daily prayers."

Not knowing how to respond, I laughed.

Pheodora stood and moved toward the door. "I left my children at home with Joses, and I still have to collect the eggs and feed the brothers—and you know how much they eat."

"I do," I said, standing. "I am glad you came. As sisters, we should be closer."

Her mouth twisted. "As close as we used to be?"

She held out her hands, so I stepped forward and caught them. "Come again when you can."

"I will," she said, pulling away. "But you should visit us, too. The brothers would like to see you."

I sent her out the door with a reluctant nod, knowing that once Shimon had been officially sworn into the chaburah, we would likely never visit my brothers' house again.

———•———

I listened halfheartedly as Shimon recited the latest lessons he had learned. He had read the writings of a rabbi from Alexandria and compared them with the writings of Gamaliel. The first rabbi believed one thing, Gamaliel another, and Shimon could not make up his mind about which man had found the true meaning.

"Perhaps they are both right?" I volunteered. "Or perhaps they are both wrong. What does the Scripture say about the matter?"

Shimon looked at me as if I had lost my head. "We must not think only of the Torah. There is so much more—the Halacha, containing the oral law, is not to be altered, but surrounds the Law of Moses with a hedge of protection. It is equal with the Pentateuch regarding the revelation of God to Moses, but it was handed down by word of mouth, not writing. Then there is the Haggadah, which covers the discussion, application, and exposition the great rabbis have developed—"

"Please!" I begged. "Your incessant talk of such things has left me with an aching head. Let us speak of something else."

Shimon sighed and crossed his arms on the table. "Sometimes I forget you are a woman. So what did you do today, wife?"

I stared at him, knowing anything I said would seem trivial in comparison with his religious study. "I got dressed, I visited with Pheodora, I told the servants what to prepare for dinner, I took a nap, and here we are, eating the dinner I planned."

"And the children? What did they do? I assume you lead them in their morning, midday, and evening prayers."

"Of course, and when we weren't praying, the girls spent time with your mother. She keeps reminding me of Amarisa's age—our daughter will soon begin her monthly cycles and will be ready for marriage."

Shimon dropped a chicken bone onto his plate, then wiped his fingers on a piece of linen. "What did your sister have to say? Her husband is still in prison?"

"He is—and she did not ask for money. Instead, she told me of Chiram's plan to be out of debt by the end of next year."

Shimon lifted both brows. "He will be free?"

"Apparently he had a plan to earn money even before he ran afoul of the lender. Pheodora expects to have more than enough to pay—"

"How is he to come by such a profit?"

I smiled, pleased I had piqued my husband's interest. "Goats."

He shot me a twisted smile. "Truly?"

"Why are you surprised? He is a shepherd, after all. Chiram has become interested in breeding goats, and he had two female goats bred to another goat. I don't know the details; I only know Pheodora has goats she plans to sell for the Yom Kippur sacrifices. She is confident that hers will be the most suitable goats in Israel."

Shimon calmly wiped his mouth. "So the shepherd will redeem himself."

"Is that not what I just said?"

"And Barauch the moneylender will receive the money owed him."

"Plus interest. So he should be happy, as well."

Shimon rested his head on his hand and tugged at his beard. "What if the moneylender does not want Chiram released?"

I stiffened. "Why wouldn't he?"

"Think, woman—if he only wanted money, he could have had it if we paid the shepherd's debt. But he did not want us to pay because he wants the shepherd in prison."

I frowned, trying to imagine a reason that made sense, but came up with nothing. "Surely you are mistaken. The moneylender wants to be repaid. That is why he makes loans. That is why he practices usury."

"I don't know his reasons," Shimon confessed, his expression tightening. "I only know he wants the shepherd to remain in prison."

"Forever?"

"I cannot say. And you must not repeat any of this conversation to your brothers or sister. I will report your news to Lavan, and whatever he does with it is up to him. As for you and me, we do not know what the moneylender is thinking, and we should not care. We offered to pay our relative's debt, and he refused our offer. That should be the end of our involvement."

But was it? He had forbidden me to say anything to Pheodora, and yet he was going to tell his Pharisee friend about Pheodora's plan. We were still involved, whether he wanted to admit it or not.

I swallowed hard, then finally nodded. Some men—including my own husband—would always be a mystery to me.

# CHAPTER TWENTY-SEVEN

# *Damaris*

With the wives of Nazareth's other Pharisees, I sat on a bench at the back of our synagogue and watched my husband become part of a select group of men who had sworn to devote themselves to purity and the utmost observance of the Law. The other members of Nazareth's chaburah sat up front, a living ribbon of white tunics and blue-banded prayer shawls.

Earlier that morning, Shimon had paused before my looking brass, peering at his image and fingering the bits of beard that sprouted near his ears. "Some members of my chaburah let the hair in front of their ears grow long." He frowned at his reflection. "I wonder if I should."

"Why?" I glanced up at him. "I know you are not to let a razor touch your beard like the heathens do, but you could still trim it with scissors."

"'You shall not destroy the corners of your beards,'" Shimon quoted. "And what is the portion in front of the ear, if not the corner?"

I lowered my comb to the dressing table, wondering if he was about to tell me how I should style my hair. Instead, he finished smoothing his beard and nodded at his reflection. "Some of the rabbis say the beard is holy," he said, resting his hand on my shoulder. "And one of the great rabbis refuses even to *touch* his beard lest he cause some hairs to fall out."

I shuddered. "Does he never wash it?"

Shimon did not answer, having shifted his attention to more urgent matters.

Now he stood before Lavan, his mentor, along with the assembled chaburah, wearing a white garment that covered him from shoulders to heels. To this, Lavan added a turban of what appeared to be expensive material. He wound the material around Shimon's head, then let the end hang gracefully over Shimon's back.

Next, Lavan placed the outer garment—of white wool with wide, blue edges—around my husband's shoulders. It would serve as protection and a prayer shawl, the blue reflecting the throne of the Glory.

Finally, Lavan presented Shimon with leather phylacteries, one for his head, another for his left arm. The ordinary Jew, one of the am ha'aretz (or, as Shimon referred to them, the ignorant people of the land), wore phylacteries only during prayer, while the Pharisees wore them all day long.

I watched, a lump rising in my throat, as Lavan fastened the first phylactery to Shimon's forehead. "These," Lavan intoned, his voice echoing in the nearly empty synagogue as he set the small black box at the top of Shimon's forehead, "are more sacred than the golden plate on the forehead of the high priest, since its inscription embodies the sacred name of Jehovah only once, but the writing inside contains it not less than twenty-three times."

He tied the leather straps at the back of Shimon's head and then picked up the second box, its leather strips more than twice as long as the first. "HaShem himself wears these," Lavan said, placing the second box of Scripture on the bulge of Shimon's upper arm. "Because in the Torah it is written, 'Then all the peoples of the earth will see that you are called by the name of Adonai and they will stand in awe of you.' *This* is what they will see—HaShem's name upon you."

He wrapped the leather strap around Shimon's arm seven times, then kept wrapping as he moved to Shimon's hand, where he wrapped it thrice more.

When Lavan had finished clothing Shimon in the garb of a Pharisee, both men turned to face the dozen or so observers who had assembled for the ceremony. "My fellow chabers," Lavan said, bringing his hands together, "I give you our new brother, who will now begin his first full year of study and learning. Welcome Shimon ben Jeremias to our fellowship."

We stood and moved into a smaller room, where we wives could mingle freely with our husbands. Nazareth was a fair-sized city, yet we had nowhere near the number of Pharisees as other cities in Judea. Shimon had told me that most Judeans considered Galileans ignorant and untutored, and perhaps we were. In Galilee, people worked for a living; they farmed, raised their children, fished, and produced goods for the marketplace. Judeans tended to be more urban, relying on sales, study, and synagogues for their livelihoods.

We ate honey cakes and drank wine, then Lavan led us in a benediction and sent us home. As we walked up the hill, I became aware that others on the street seemed to avoid us, even crossing to the other side at our approach. Was the offense in them or in us? I glanced up at Shimon and realized the truth at once—he had changed. Conscious of his new authority and aware that he walked with the sacred Name of God inscribed twenty-three times on his head and arm, he walked with stiff gravitas, his head high and his bearing regal. His white garments fairly shone in the fading light, and his gaze had gone soft with wonder.

I sighed and crossed my arms, wrapping myself in a dignity that seemed shabby next to Shimon's.

When we arrived home, even our daughters seemed daunted by their father's new regalia. The older girls hung back as if afraid they might soil his spotless garments by touching him, and the younger ones stared at the black boxes on his head and arm as though they were diseased growths. I was about to tell them they should not be afraid of objects they had seen before, but then I remembered—since men prayed at the front of the synagogue, my girls had only seen the devices from a distance. Shimon seemed to understand their reticence and bade them good-night without requesting his usual hug.

Once Shimon and I were alone in our room, I hoped he would set aside his new persona. I sat in bed, propped up on pillows, as he stepped out of his new tunic. He exhaled as the heavy fabric fell to his feet, the borders brushing the floor. "Some of the rabbis," he said, his voice heavy with awe, "say the blue border is to remind us of the way the Shekinah glory enwrapped itself in creation. They say the borders are our own *tzitzit*, so whenever we look at them, we will remember all the commands of Adonai and do them."

I had never heard this. Indeed, I had never heard many of the teachings Shimon had studied over the past few months. Many men of Israel wore tzitzit, or tassels, on the corners of their prayer shawls, but for the Pharisees, the blue borders served as personal reminders to obey Adonai's command-ments. Perhaps the borders were extra wide, I mused, because the Pharisees needed more reminders than ordinary men . . . Shimon removed his phylacteries and set them on the bed. I leaned forward, never having examined them up close—neither my father nor my brothers had worn them. They con-sisted of leather boxes, each containing rolled parchments covered in passages of Scripture. Whoever had inscribed the verses wrote with an exact and tiny hand.

"The importance of these," Shimon said, not looking at me, "cannot be exaggerated. They are reverenced as highly as the Scriptures, and, like the Scriptures, they can be rescued from the flames on Shabbat, though we do not wear them on the day of rest."

"Must you wear them every day?" I asked, running my fin-gertip over the odd appendages. "Do you wear them to bed?"

"Not to bed." Shimon scooped them up and set them on a table. "And not when I take my wife into my arms."

"Really?" I lifted a brow as he slid into bed beside me. "I would think a Pharisee would want to carry HaShem's name into all his undertakings."

Shimon did not answer, but put his arm on my waist and began to nuzzle my neck. I closed my eyes and inhaled a deep breath. We had just entered a new world. I could only hope it would bring all the blessings Shimon expected.

# CHAPTER TWENTY-EIGHT

# Pheodora

My daughters and I joined my brothers at synagogue on Shabbat. I sat with the women on the right side of the room, while my brothers filed into a bench on the left. We were early, so people were still entering, the room echoing with exchanged whispers and friendly greetings.

Without warning, silence fell over the gathering. I followed the direction of the stunned stares and saw Damaris and Shimon walk down the center aisle. She turned into the row ahead of mine, but Shimon walked directly to the front where he sat with Lavan and the other Pharisees of Nazareth.

I broke every rule of proper decorum and turned to gape at my brothers. Though we had known of Shimon's plan to join the Pharisees, something about seeing his white-and-blue robe, the haughty look in his eye, and the determined jut of his jaw . . .

I thought about the time James became angry because one of our Pharisees unseated an old man who sat on the front row. None of the old people sat there now because Pharisees filled the entire bench.

I focused on Damaris, sitting directly in front of me. I stared at the back of her neck—if my glare had been hot, it would have burned her skin—and when she squirmed, I knew she sensed my disapproval. Then, with the innocence of a child, Shiri spoke in a voice loud and high enough to echo through the building: "Why is Uncle Shimon acting like he doesn't know us?"

I pressed my hand over my mouth, wondering how to answer, as the back of Damaris's neck heated to red. She might have turned to say something, but James did not give her a chance. He stood, turned to Shiri, and said, "Because he no longer considers himself one of us, little niece. We are the am ha'aretz, the common and ignorant, while he fancies himself one of Adonai's elite."

Shiri's comment had been bold enough, but after James spoke, every head in the synagogue either stared or smiled in our direction. Lavan, the first Pharisee on the front row, hissed at James, and Shimon's eyes glowed with inner fire. Jude stood beside James in wordless support. Simeon leaned forward as if he would stand and fight anyone who challenged my brothers.

This was not the way to begin a Shabbat service.

I didn't know what to do. I held Shiri's hand, debating whether I should take her and leave or stay and pretend nothing had happened . . .

"Shalom." Lavan stood and turned to face the congregation, his expression as smooth as marble. Though I had never particularly liked the man, I had to admire his ability to recover and carry on.

Without another word, he opened the service with the

Shema. "'Hear O Israel, the Lord our God, the Lord is one. Love Adonai your God with all your heart and with all your soul and with all your strength. These words, which I am commanding you today, are to be on your heart. You are to teach them diligently to your children, and speak of them when you sit in your house, when you walk by the way, when you lie down and when you rise up. Bind them as a sign on your hand, they are to be as frontlets between your eyes, and write them on the doorposts of your house and on your gates.'"

Called to order by the words of Scripture, my brothers sat while the rest of us turned toward the front, corralling our wayward thoughts.

Throughout the service—the reading from the Law, the prophets, the sermon, and the pronouncing of the Aaronic blessing—my mind kept replaying Shiri's comment, James's response, and Shimon's burning eyes. He was angry with us, and from this point forward, nothing short of a miracle would convince my brothers to think of him as family.

# CHAPTER TWENTY-NINE

# *Pheodora*

Months passed, one after another. The month of Tishri brought the fall festivals—Rosh Hashanah, Yom Kippur, and Sukkot. And just as he had the previous two years, Yeshua went to the Holy City and stirred up trouble, though I do not believe he did it purposely.

From visitors at the well, James and I heard the details of an incident that took place in winter, at Hanukkah. Yeshua had been walking around Solomon's Colonnade at the Temple when a group of Judean leaders boldly asked if he was the Messiah. Yeshua replied, "I told you, but you don't believe! The works I do in my Father's name testify concerning me. But you don't believe because you are not my sheep. My Father, who has given them to me, is greater than all. And no one is able to snatch them out of the Father's hand. I and the Father are one."

According to the traveler who shared the story, at that point the Judean leaders picked up rocks to stone him. But

Yeshua said, "I've shown you many good works from the Father. For which of these are you going to stone me?"

The Judeans answered, "We aren't stoning you for a good work, but for blasphemy. Though you are a man, you make yourself God!"

Then Yeshua said, "Isn't it written in your writings, 'I have said you are gods'? If he called them 'gods,' to whom the Word of God came—and the Scripture cannot be broken—do you say I speak blasphemy because I said 'I am Ben-Elohim'? If I don't do the works of my Father, don't believe me! But if I do, even if you don't trust me, trust the deeds. Then you may come to know and understand that the Father is in me, and I am in the Father."

The visitor finished speaking and the group dispersed, but not before casting pointed looks at me and James. We endured these silently, filled our water jugs, and began the walk home.

Once we were away from the others, I looked at James. "I have never understood everything Yeshua said, but if what we just heard is true, Yeshua *is* claiming to be the Messiah."

James shook his head. "Yeshua is clever. He quoted the psalmist, who said, 'You are gods; you are all children of the Most High.' Yeshua meant he is *Elohim* in the sense that we are all sons of God—"

"I don't know what he meant," I said. "Sometimes I think he enjoys toying with those who want to kill him. But eventually they will grow weary of his games."

"I still cannot understand his reasons," James said, staring at the road ahead. "What is his purpose?"

"Whatever it is, I hope he settles down soon." I switched the heavy water jug from my right hand to my left. "We need him at home. Ima too; she has to be weary of traveling."

The coming weeks would bring the spring festivals—Passover, Unleavened Bread, Firstfruits, and Pentecost. I was not going to Jerusalem but would remain behind to care for my daughters and keep an eye on my goats. They were too precious and important to leave with anyone else. Though I loved Bethel and respected her knowledge of animals, her life did not depend on the goats' well-being. Chiram's did.

My girls loved playing with the goats, though Jordan and Shiri were a little intimidated by the animals' size. The kids were no longer little creatures who tumbled over each other in a joyous melee. Now they were solid, more sedate, and horned.

The goats were also noisy. The chickens rose with the sun, and within moments of hearing the chickens I would hear the goats bleating *maaa, maaa!* Tikvah and Simcha had deeper voices than Ora and Hupsah, but the four of them created quite a clamor in the early morning. I was afraid the neighbors would complain, but Bethel loved the sound, and I suspected she had ordered the other neighbors not to protest.

Once the kids began to grow, Bethel convinced me to sell Delilah. "You do not have enough room for five goats," she told me, trying to keep her balance as she dodged chickens in the courtyard. "Sell the mama goat. She will give milk and cheese to another family, and you will have more room for the chickens and the kids. And surely you could find a way to use a denarius?"

She was right about that. My girls were outgrowing their tunics, and though I could always pass worn tunics from older sister to younger, Judit did not have an older sister to give her outgrown garments.

So I sold Delilah to a family I met at the well, and Delilah passed out of our lives, having faithfully served us.

"Will Chiram mind that you sold his goat?" Joses asked as we watched Delilah leave town with her new family. "After all, didn't he choose her specially?"

"He did. But he is a practical man, and I think he would be pleased to know Delilah not only provided us with two kids, milk, and many rounds of cheese, but she also gave us a way to get new clothes for Judit."

Joses grinned and squeezed my shoulder. "Our mother would have answered the same way."

---

*Dear wife,*

*I pray you and the girls are well. Uriah has kindly brought me parchment and ink, so I am grateful for an opportunity to write my thoughts to you. Uriah has not been well for a month or so. He has developed a cough that will not go away. I have been praying for him, but the cough vexes him greatly.*

*As for me, I am as well as a man can expect to be in this place. I am learning to be patient. I have always thought of myself as a patient person—after all, when one watches sheep all day and night, one grows accustomed to stillness. But even in the fields around Migdal-eder, I could always get up and walk, climb a hill, or examine the sheep. A man does not have that simple freedom in prison. He has no sky to watch, no breeze to caress his cheek, no bird to sing him to sleep. He has only darkness, dirt, and companions as bereft and alone as he is.*

*But I do not want you to feel pity for me. Job was more miserable than I, for he had a wife who urged him to curse God and die, and you have never voiced such words. I still have four beautiful daughters and a semblance of health, so HaShem has showered me with great mercy.*

*Yet a man cannot help but wonder about many things. Why did Shimon not want to pay my debt? Why did the tax collector press me for payment when he had issued the loan only days before? And what good am I doing in this place when I could be caring for my daughters, providing for my family, and loving my beautiful wife?*

*But as the prophet Micah wrote, "But they do not know Adonai's thoughts, nor understand His plan." So I will trust that Adonai does have a plan for us.*

*I leave you with this blessing from our wedding:*

*"Blessed are You, Adonai our God, sovereign of the universe, who created joy and gladness, groom and bride, mirth, song, delight and rejoicing, love and harmony and peace and companionship. Quickly, Adonai our God, there should be heard in the cities of Judah and in the courtyards of Jerusalem the voice of joy and the voice of gladness, the voice of groom and the voice of bride, the jubilant voices of grooms from the bridal canopy, and of young people from the feast of their singing. Blessed are You, Adonai, Gladdener of the groom with his bride."*

*Chiram*

# CHAPTER THIRTY

# *Pheodora*

Days melted into weeks, weeks into months. At sunset I often stood in the courtyard and smiled at the hens marching to their roosts, following the God-given instinct to settle on their perches. I lingered in the twilight, watching the stars come out as HaShem gave us the blessing of a new day.

If my husband were with me, I might have said this was the happiest time in my life. But I could not be content as long as Chiram remained in prison.

In early autumn, we heard reports of a fever sweeping through the coastal cities, and Arimathea was not far from the coast. Dozens had died in Ashkelon, mainly children and old people, and of late the fever had spread to Joppa. If the sickness made its way to Arimathea, how could my husband and the other prisoners withstand it? They did not have proper food to maintain their strength, and they lived in dank air and filth.

Fired by urgency, every night I begged HaShem to show

me some faster way to redeem Chiram from prison. Did I have some distant relative who could die and leave me an inheritance? No, because the descendants of David were now as poor as David had been in his youth. Could I find a bag of coins by the side of the road? When I took the sheep out to graze the roadside, I searched the grasses, hoping to find some unclaimed treasure. Perhaps Shimon would reconsider his decision and come to tell me he had already sent money to Arimathea for Chiram . . . but no matter how I begged HaShem to send a persuasive vision to my brother-in-law, Shimon never came.

And so I stood outside at sunset, my face toward the western coast, and wondered if the breeze that lifted my hair carried the seeds of contagion. Was I already a widow? If Chiram died, how many days would pass before I heard the news?

My brothers continued their carpentry work and were gracious about helping me with my daughters. Every day, James or Jude or Joses or Simeon took a break from his regular labor and spent time with my girls—helping them graze the goats outside the city, shopping with them at the market, or standing in the city square and asking people to buy my eggs. James, the more serious of my brothers, enjoyed instructing my girls, helping them learn their alphabets and teaching them to read. Since most people spoke Hebrew, Aramaic, and at least a little Greek, James was convinced my daughters should be conversant in all three. "After they learn those tongues, we'll study Latin," he told me.

"Oh, no," I objected. "I don't want them ever going to Rome."

"They will not have to," he countered, "because from what I've been hearing, Rome may soon rule the world."

I did not believe him, but I did not argue because I did not have time to worry about politics. The Romans had ruled Galilee and Judea for as long as I had been alive, and as far as I could tell, they were not planning to leave. Who could stand against the Roman war machine? Certainly not any of our Judean zealots or would-be messiahs, including my eldest brother.

Our encounters with travelers in the city square brought more reports about Yeshua—stories of people he had healed, cunning traps he had evaded, and miracles he had performed. I heard he had enabled one of his disciples to walk on the Sea of Galilee for a brief time, and when I shared the story at dinner, my brothers howled with laughter.

"Couldn't we all walk on water for an instant?" Joses said. "If the man had walked all the way across the sea, now *that* would be a miracle!"

We were still hoping Yeshua would grow weary of his travels and come home. Jude frequently complained that Yeshua had left them sorely missing a skilled pair of hands, and we all knew why he felt Yeshua's absence so keenly—he was hoping to build a home for Tasmin. He wanted to be married, so he was eager for Yeshua to return. In some sense, I think we all were.

The cool days of winter were beautiful, but made all the more difficult when Chiram did not write as often as before. I would lie awake in bed, trying to imagine him in the darkness beside me, yet his image did not come as readily as it once had. I could no longer fill my mind with his scent or close my eyes and hear his voice.

Is this what happened after a death? Did we lose our loved ones in pieces, memory by memory? I wanted to think about Chiram always, but the routine of life in Nazareth numbed me to everything but an overwhelming fear that he would not live long enough for me to sell his goats.

As weeks passed with no word from him, I realized he might as well be in the grave. I would have been happy to receive even a secondhand greeting from Arimathea, but no travelers brought word of him or his health. I worried when I did not hear anything, yet what could I do? James would catch sight of my furrowed brow and point out that worry accomplished nothing, and Jude agreed.

"When Tasmin and I went to hear Yeshua speak, he taught about that very thing. He said, 'Therefore do not worry, saying, "What will we eat?" or "What will we drink?" or "What will we wear?" Your Father in heaven knows you need all these. But seek first the kingdom of God and His righteousness, and all these things shall be added to you. Therefore do not worry about tomorrow, for tomorrow will worry about itself. Each day has enough trouble of its own.'"

"I hardly think"—I lifted my chin—"that being concerned about Chiram is the same as fretting about what I will wear."

"Worry is worry." Jude shrugged. "Worry is taking a burden upon yourself when you are meant to trust HaShem."

I tried to trust HaShem with my husband's life, but it wasn't easy.

As the cool days of winter surrendered to the warmth of spring, I looked at my growing goats and smiled in relief. HaShem had not arranged for an alternate answer to Chiram's imprisonment, but if all went well, he would be restored to our lives in a few more months. He would come home, and I would keep him in Nazareth until he physically recovered from his confinement. The girls and I would spoil him and let him know how much we had missed him.

The passing months brought another change in our household, though I did not notice it at first. Shimon and Damaris had not appeared at our gate since Shimon joined the chaburah, and I did not expect them to attend our humble Shabbat dinner. But when they would not speak to us after synagogue or nod to us on the street, I realized they were avoiding us.

When I asked James about it, he gave me a look of exasperation. "I thought you understood."

"Understood what?"

"Shimon is no longer allowed to be near those who are ritually impure. He would not want to be made unclean by coming here, especially since there are animals about."

I blanched. "I am no more unclean than Damaris—"

"But you are am ha'aretz, ignorant and unaware of how impure you are. Did you walk on the street today? You might have walked through dust left by a dead animal."

"But I wash my feet when I enter the house."

"What about your garments—do you wash them every night? They might have encountered the same dust."

"But I shake—"

"It is useless to argue; you will never win a debate with a Pharisee."

Jude said Damaris would not visit as long as we kept animals in the courtyard. "And animals are not the only creatures that defile," he said. "Joses, James, Simeon, and I frequently work for Gentiles, and being in a Gentile's home makes us ritually impure. You can be sure Shimon will keep a safe distance from us."

"What about Yeshua?" I asked, thinking of our absent brother. "Would Shimon keep his distance from Yeshua?"

Jude chuckled. "*Especially* Yeshua. He mingles with Gentiles and *sinners*. Shimon would probably cross to the other side of the street lest Yeshua's shadow fall on him."

A few days before Passover, Tasmin appeared at our door in search of Jude. She had received a letter from her brother Thomas, one of Yeshua's disciples, in which he expressed his conviction that Yeshua would soon be arrested by the Temple authorities. After reading that Thomas was ready to die with his master, she came immediately to Nazareth.

I was not home when she arrived, and by the time I heard the details, Jude and Tasmin were already on their way to Jerusalem, where they would search for Yeshua and do what they could to avert disaster. James voiced the outlandish idea that Yeshua was trying to make a statement by dying with the Passover lambs—after all, John the Immerser had once called him the "Lamb of God."

A rise of panic threatened to choke me as I realized James was serious. "Is Jude sure Yeshua has gone to Jerusalem?" I asked. "Perhaps he will make the wise choice and avoid the crowds—"

"He won't," Simeon replied. "Where else would Yeshua be during Passover?"

I flinched at the sharp edge in James's voice, then told myself all would be well. Yeshua was strong, wise, and careful. For months the religious leaders had been trying to trap him, and he had outwitted them on every occasion. He would escape this time, too.

And then, perhaps, he would finally come home.

# CHAPTER THIRTY-ONE

# Damaris

To my surprise and delight, Lavan hired a closed conveyance for his annual pilgrimage to Jerusalem and invited Shimon and I to join him. The large wooden box, which he called a *coach*, was sturdily constructed and had shuttered windows and doors in the sides. Servants hoisted our trunks to the top of the box and tied them on with ropes. Another pair of servants rode at the front, on a sort of shelf, while they handled a team of two horses—strong beasts that, Shimon assured me, must have cost more than the coach.

I was thrilled when the coach pulled up at our house—so thrilled I nearly forgot to kiss our daughters good-bye. They would remain in Nazareth with their grandparents, and I gave them a cheerful smile as they stood at the top of the stairs and waved farewell. I caught a wistful look in Jeremias's eyes. I believe he was jealous of his son's opportunity to ride in the modern conveyance.

As for myself, I came close to giggling as I came down the

255

steps and waited for Shimon to help me into the coach. He opened the door, and I saw Lavan and Eritha already inside, seated together on a cushion-covered bench.

"Where on earth did you find this thing?" I asked, climbing in behind Shimon. "It is amazing!"

Lavan ignored my enthusiasm and said to my husband, "The Romans have been traveling in these conveyances for years. I have seen a few in Judea but never in Nazareth. We will travel in comfort and will reach the Holy City in half the time."

In two days, not four? Rather than interrupt the men's conversation, I shared a smile with Eritha. "So much better," I said quietly, arranging the folds of my tunic around me. "Such a wonderful thing."

Once we left Nazareth—and I admit, I peered through the window to see the reactions of our neighbors as we passed at a breathtaking speed—the only impediment to our swift progress was the overabundance of pilgrims on the road. I thought the sound of galloping hoofbeats would scatter the travelers, but time and again I felt the coach slow in order to avoid trampling people.

"The Romans built this road," Lavan groused every time we slowed to a walking pace, "and Roman vehicles should take precedence in using it. Why don't the people walk on the ground and reserve the pavement for vehicles?"

After an hour or two, I grew weary of the heat, for Lavan wanted the windows closed to keep out the dust. I fanned myself with a palm leaf for a while, then patted my chest with a linen cloth to absorb the perspiration. My opinion of the coach shifted over the hours we rode in it. Though we did not have to walk or feel the sun shining on our heads, the sun heated the conveyance greatly, until I thought I might be reduced to a puddle by the time we reached our destination.

By midday the road had cleared of the walking travelers, who stopped to eat and rest. I was ready to stop, too, but Lavan insisted we take advantage of the empty road and press on. The drivers snapped their whips, the horses broke into a run, and we swayed back and forth as the coach rolled over the paving stones, jarring our teeth and vibrating our voices when we tried to speak.

I closed my eyes, leaned my head against the wall, and hoped I would fall asleep. I was drifting into a light doze when the mention of my brother-in-law's name snapped me back to wakefulness.

"I have not heard much about Chiram," Shimon was saying. "I know he is still in prison or we would have heard something from Pheodora."

"Good."

I turned my head discreetly toward Lavan, not wanting to attract attention. He was sitting by a window, the shutters open just enough for him to look out at the passing scenery. His tight mouth was barely visible in his untrimmed beard.

"I do not know why," Shimon said, "Chiram must remain in prison. I understand it has something to do with your relationship with the moneylender, but—"

"The decision to hold the shepherd was not Barauch's," Lavan said, tilting one of the louvers of the shutter. "It was mine."

Shimon blinked. "Yours? But why would you—?"

"If you will hold your tongue, I will explain."

Lavan closed the louver and folded his hands. "More than a year ago, I traveled to Jerusalem with an esteemed group of Pharisees from Galilee. As we neared Jerusalem, we encountered the shepherds at Migdal-eder as they drove the flocks into the Holy City. Most of the men stopped and bowed as we passed . . . all but one. A thin fellow, and tall, a head taller than the rest. When we inquired as to who he was, we learned he was called Chiram, from Bethlehem."

Shock siphoned the blood from my head, leaving me dizzy. I stared at Lavan as the dark interior of the coach shuddered. Why would he care what a shepherd did or did not do?

"My brothers and I," Lavan went on, apparently unaware that both Shimon and I had frozen in astonishment, "decided we should make an example of the man. How could we not? Men who study Torah should be respected; to respect a scholar is to respect Adonai. So when he could not pay the taxes demanded by the tax collector, Barauch—a Greek moneylender employed by my Roman associate—loaned him the money. One of the other shepherds let us know his whereabouts so we could find him the next week. When he could not pay, Barauch had the shepherd imprisoned, and now he is no longer free to be a disgraceful example for others."

Shimon glanced at me, his eyes wide, then shifted his gaze to Lavan. "Surely he has already learned his lesson. Not bowing—perhaps he had other things on his mind. He was herding sheep, and while I've never done it, perhaps he was focused on them and didn't see—"

"If the Ark of the Covenant had been passing by, would he have been forgiven if he idly put out his hand to keep it from falling? Uzzah was struck down for his irreverence when he grasped the Ark of God." Lavan smiled without humor. "It gives me no pleasure to act as God's hand in a situation like this, but I am sure Adonai did not take pleasure in killing Uzzah. Regardless, holiness must be respected. People must be reverent."

Shimon crossed his arms and leaned back in his seat, his long face furrowed with sadness. My heart twisted—both for my husband, who had just learned a hard truth, and for my sister, who had married a man who might never enjoy freedom again.

# CHAPTER THIRTY-TWO

# *Pheodora*

The streets of Nazareth had an empty, almost haunted look as Passover drew near. Lifeless, unseasonably warm air hung over the city while melancholy clouds pressed on the upper elevations, shadowed and bruised. A great number of the city's residents had already left for Jerusalem, and many of those who remained had gone to visit friends and family in other cities.

Though Passover was to be a time of rejoicing, I had not been able to escape the cloud of concern that arrived with Tasmin and her dire message. All of us were affected by the news, and though we tried to pretend all was well, the air in the house had thickened with the dullness of despair.

What was Yeshua doing? Why didn't he and Ima come home? They had celebrated Pesach in Jerusalem for the past three years, so surely this year Yeshua could come to Nazareth and spend the festival with us.

James, Joses, Simeon, and I remained at home, content to share our Passover feast with my daughters and our neighbors, Bethel and Seth. I reminded myself to set two extra places at the table as I carried water to the house and so did not notice anything amiss when I approached the goat stalls. It was only when I lowered my buckets that the stench hit me, and a quick look in the enclosure revealed several piles of blood-streaked dung. The goats stood silently in their pens, their heads down, their voices silent.

I turned on the ball of my foot and raced to Bethel's house. "My goats," I said, struggling to catch my breath when she opened the door. "Something is wrong with my goats."

Bethel tied on her headscarf and hurried with me to the goat pens.

I cowered behind the railing, watching as my goats stood in a silent huddle. "Are they . . . ?" My voice cracked. "Are they dying?"

Bethel knelt in front of Hupsah, caught his collar, and peered into his eyes. With her other hand she pulled down the animal's lower eyelid. "The area around the eye is light in color. That does not bode well."

"What does it mean?"

"He's sick. Whatever the sickness is, they all have it."

I had been so worried about Chiram . . . I should have prayed for the goats' health, too.

I clung to the railing, my knees turning to water. "What should I do? They must not die. They *cannot*."

Bethel stood and wiped her hands on her tunic. "We will change their water morning, noon, and night. We must remove these piles and keep the stall clean. We will stop feeding grain because it is hard on the stomach. We will keep the animals quiet and warm—animals often get sick when the weather changes. Find some old blankets or clothing, and we will wrap them around the kids. We will make a soft stew . . .

if they don't eat it, we'll hand-feed them so we know food is getting into their bellies."

Her use of the word *we* fanned a flame of hope. "You will help me?"

She stepped forward and smiled. "Do you think I would desert you now?"

"But tonight is Passover, and you will want to enjoy the feast—"

"HaShem will understand. If the Law allows us to pull a lamb from a well on the Sabbath, I'm sure it allows us to save goats at Passover."

I blinked away tears, picked up the water buckets, and called up the stairs for Judit and Joses.

———•———

The goats got sicker before they got better. What had begun with diarrhea—*scours*, Bethel called it—progressed to fever, rapid breathing, coughing, and discharge from the nose and eyes. None of the goats wanted to eat and had to be persuaded even to drink. My brothers, Bethel, and Judit spent hours in the goat pen, trying to entice the kids with warm broth and buckets of fresh water.

My plans for our Passover feast evaporated. James led us in a quick prayer when we paused to eat, but I could think of nothing but saving the lives of my goats.

By the fourth day, Ora, the little female, and Hupsah were weaker than ever, while Tikvah and Simcha were lifting their heads and trying to eat. Bethel suggested we separate the two pairs, so I moved Ora and Hupsah into a separate stall. We allowed Judit and my brothers to tend the stronger kids while Bethel and I focused on the two who needed the most help.

On the fourth night, after sending Bethel home to rest, I

sat in the straw and pulled Ora's head into my lap. She had not risen all day, and something in her chest rattled with every breath. I stroked her forehead and ears, then ran my fingertips gently over her face and eyelids, encouraging her to close her eyes.

"I would not have you suffer, little one," I told her, my voice breaking. I hiccupped a laugh, knowing what Damaris would think if she looked into this stall and saw me comforting a goat. Most families considered lambs, goats, and chickens mere beasts, but did beasts not suffer when they were ill? I had watched these little ones dance and skip as they joyfully explored their new world, and I saw Delilah look on them with obvious fondness. I watched her determined efforts to wean the kids, and her exasperation had reminded me of my attempts to teach my babies to eat solid food.

Ora stirred in my lap, making a feeble attempt to straighten her bent leg. I ran my hand over it, stretching it out, then returned to rubbing the spot between her ears.

Why had I ever imagined I could succeed at raising goats? I had been foolishly confident. I, the shepherd's wife, supposed I could handle a shepherd's duties, but I let Chiram down. I failed my daughters, who loved these animals. Once again I proved myself to be the weak sibling, the one who dreamed big dreams and fell short.

The old feelings of inferiority surfaced, pulling me under like a powerful current. I struggled against the weight of dark and hurtful memories, the voices who praised my sister and my brothers and cut me with indifference.

The heavy sorrow seemed to spawn and spread until it mingled with the dread that had pervaded our house. We had heard no news from Jerusalem, nothing from Yeshua, Ima, or Jude. Were they on their way home? Were they still alive?

I looked at the dying goat in my lap and knew I was completely helpless. I wanted to pray—I wanted to believe HaShem would look down and answer my prayers, heal my goat, and ease our worries about Yeshua. But as I closed my eyes and searched my memory for comforting Scriptures, the only words that came to mind were from a song we always sang as we climbed the mountain road to Jerusalem:

"My help comes from Adonai,
Maker of heaven and earth.
He will not let your foot slip.
Your Keeper will not slumber.
Behold, the Keeper of Israel
neither slumbers nor sleeps."

Did Adonai, Keeper of Israel, care about a woman and her little goat? Was He awake, too, keeping watch over me and my family?

The rest of the psalm flooded my heart on a tide of memory:

"Adonai is your Keeper.
Adonai is your shadow at your right hand.
The sun will not strike you by day,
nor the moon by night.
Adonai will protect you from all evil.
He will guard your life.
Adonai will watch over your coming and your going
from this time forth and forevermore."

Exhaling in relief, I looked down at the goat in my lap. "Go on, sweet soul," I whispered, crooning to her as if to one of my daughters. "Go back to the Creator who made you. You were loved, and now you can rest."

I hesitated when she exhaled a long breath and shuddered. Then she was gone.

Tears rolled down my cheeks, drops of loss and defeat. Not only had I lost a beloved animal, but I had failed to protect the kids who would have brought much-needed income to our family.

Not far away, Hupsah bleated faintly. I wanted to comfort him, too, yet all I could do was reach over and stroke his side. I was too spent to hold another kid in my arms.

As dawn arrived, barely glowing through the cloud-covered sky, I covered my face with my hands and wept, then sat quietly until Hupsah breathed his last. Then, knowing my husband's life depended on the two remaining kids, I went upstairs to ask one of my brothers to help me burn the carcasses.

---

Simeon and I took the dead kids outside the city and burned them, then we walked home, defeated and covered with ashes. The clouds that had dulled the sunrise still sagged over the earth, heavy with unspent rain.

As we neared the house, I looked up and saw a group of people approaching our gate. My stomach clenched. "Are you expecting someone?" I asked.

Simeon grunted and shook his head, then gripped his staff and walked ahead, positioning himself between me and the crowd. The defensive gesture raised the hairs on the back of my neck. What sort of news was he expecting? Had Chiram died in prison?

I held my breath as a man strode toward us, an aura of grief radiating from his features. "Simeon." He stopped a few feet away and said in a firm voice, "We have received a message from Shimon, your brother-in-law. The scroll contained grave news about your family."

Shimon was in Jerusalem, not Arimathea. This news was not about Chiram. But Jude and Tasmin and Yeshua and Ima were in Jerusalem . . .

"What news?" Simeon asked.

"Your brother Yeshua . . . he died six days ago. The Romans crucified him."

I frowned and stared at the man, unable to hear him over an odd roar that filled my ears. I wanted him to be mistaken, but in my deepest heart I knew—Simeon and I both knew—Yeshua's teaching had troubled the Romans and the religious rulers. I did not want to believe the report from Jerusalem, but neither could I doubt it.

Simeon took an unsteady step back, then gripped a fence post. "Are you certain the dead man was my brother? Many have the same name, and so many pilgrims flood Jerusalem during Pesach . . ."

The man's mouth twisted. "The sign on the execution stake read, 'Yeshua of Nazareth, the King of the Jews'—was that not your brother?"

Simeon staggered. "I . . ."

Another man stepped forward and glared at Simeon. "You should have known this day was coming! When Yeshua spoke in our synagogue, did he not blaspheme? We should have stoned him that day, but we did not. Now the Romans have finished what we should have handled long ago."

Several men in the group nodded, their faces as hard and unyielding as stone.

My gentle brother lifted his head, and from the absent look in his eye I knew he was about to thank the messenger for bringing us word. But none of these people deserved our thanks, especially considering their heartless response to the terrible truth.

"Simeon. Brother." I gripped his arm and tugged him toward the house. "We must go. We must speak to James and Joses."

Simeon seemed to gather himself. Reflexively, he uttered the blessing for the dead. *"Barukh atah Adonai Eloheinu melekh ha'olam, dayan ha-emet."* *Blessed are You, Lord, our God, King of the universe, the Just Judge.*

Together we passed through the silent crowd, entered our courtyard, and closed the gate behind us.

James and Joses were not inside when Simeon and I entered the house. Simeon grabbed his staff and went in search of them while I peeked into the room where my daughters slept. They were still abed, sprawled over their mattress in the careless indifference of sleep. I walked away, determined that they should remain free from the truth for as long as possible.

I stepped into the hallway, exhausted and drained of will and conscious thought. My feet carried me to the stairs, which I followed until I reached the goat pens. Tikvah and Simcha stood in the corner, nibbling at the bottom of their empty trough. I nodded, telling myself to feed them later, then sank into the straw of the other pen. The enclosure stood empty, a painful reminder that Yeshua was gone and his place would never be filled again.

Why had he been so foolish? I slammed my fist against the railing, wishing my brother had paid attention to those who tried to advise him. Surely he knew he was treading the edge of danger. Jude had gone to warn him, Thomas had undoubtedly urged him to be cautious; only a fool would not have seen the imminent threat, and Yeshua was no fool. So why did he insist on remaining in Jerusalem? Why didn't he flee into the wilderness?

Yeshua had always been a trifle peculiar. We still talked about the time he stayed at the Temple long after the rest of the family had started traveling back to Nazareth. Though only a boy of twelve, he had known his own mind and delighted in debating the Torah teachers. James thought he was being prideful, showing off his considerable knowledge. But Ima squashed that notion, saying Yeshua did not have even a smattering of pride in him.

Why then had he stayed in the place where he was most vulnerable? Why hadn't he done the sensible thing and retreated to fight another day?

I felt a sharp stab of a memory and gasped a deep breath. I had been a young girl when I retreated to this same spot, only the goat belonged to my mother then. Damaris had been invited to a birthday celebration for the rabbi's daughter, but I was not. Jealous of my high-spirited sister's enthusiasm, I watched Damaris leave the house and then ran downstairs to weep in the shadows of the courtyard.

That was where Yeshua found me. Without a word of reprimand, he sat beside me and draped his arm around my skinny shoulders in brotherly companionship. After I finished crying all my angry tears, I began to weep out of loneliness, reminded once again that I was but an afterthought, the shadow of my older sister.

Yeshua raised my trembling chin and looked into my eyes. "Pheodora," he said, his voice brimming with love, "do the Scriptures not say 'Chazak! Be courageous! Do not be afraid or tremble before them. For Adonai your God,

He is the One who goes with you. He will not fail you or abandon you.'"

"But . . ." I struggled to speak through a tight throat. "But no one . . . no one loves me."

Yeshua chuckled softly and held me tighter. "Everyone loves you, little bird. Especially me."

I did not believe him in that moment, nor did I believe anything would change. I was right, and for the past three years, Yeshua's vacant seat at our table mocked us at Passover and Rosh Hashanah and every other feast. If he loved me—if he loved *us*—where was he when we needed him to come home? I understood he was a prophet, but he could have preached from Nazareth as easily as the mountains of Galilee. He could have healed the sick from our town center as easily as Capernaum's.

A tremor of guilt rose from the center of my chest—I should not be thinking ill of the dead. I should not be indulging my selfish desires when my brother was dead and my mother suffering the loss of her favorite son. But I could not escape the haunting question: why had he chosen to remain in Jerusalem when he could have come home?

———•———

I wept quietly as I prepared dinner and made no effort to hide my tears when Judit, Eden, and Jordan came upstairs from visiting the goats. Shiri had been quietly playing at the table for a while, oblivious to my dark mood.

My older girls were more perceptive, and more curious. "Ima . . ." Judit approached cautiously, as if I were a pot that might boil over. "Why are your eyes red?"

I inhaled a shaky breath, then sank onto a bench to address my daughters. "Come here," I said, gesturing for them to draw near. I pulled Shiri onto my lap and gathered Judit, Eden, and Jordan around me. "I am sad because your uncle Yeshua has died. I am especially sad because I did not get to see him before . . . I am sad because we will not see him ever again."

Judit frowned. "We have not seen him in a long time."

I stroked her hair. "He has been traveling and teaching people about HaShem. But now—his time with us is over, and we must go on without him."

"Isn't Uncle Jude with him? And Safta?"

I bit back fresh tears. "I don't know if they were with him, but they are also in Jerusalem, so I expect them to return home soon. When they do, they will also be sad. They loved Yeshua very much and will miss him." My voice wavered. "We will all miss him."

I looked up as James, Joses, and Simeon came through the front door. Joses took one look at me, then knelt and wrapped his arms around the girls as he wept. James did not weep but sat on our father's bench and stared at the floor. "This," he said, his voice breaking, "cannot be what HaShem intended."

Simeon came in last and broke the heavy silence with a question. "Do we know what happened to his body?"

James and Joses looked at each other, then at me, and none of us had an answer.

───────●───────

*My dearest husband,*
   *Shalom aleichem to you in your imprisonment. I write to you with a heavy heart.*
   *You may have already heard, but our brother Yeshua*

*has died in Jerusalem. I have not heard details, only that
the Romans nailed him to an execution stake. Ima was
with him, I am sure. She was utterly devoted to him,
so now we are hoping she will come home so we can
comfort her.*

*I have experienced another loss, that of two kids.
It feels wrong to mention the death of animals after
losing Yeshua in such a horrible manner, but my losses
have run together in a stream of grief. I feel as though
my hope—for freeing you, for seeing Yeshua again—
has shriveled into dust and blown away. Yes, I know I
will see Yeshua in the afterlife. Job spoke of seeing God
after death, and David spoke of seeing his dead son.
If they believed in an afterlife, how can we doubt it?*

*About the goats, James says HaShem was good to
send us four kids, but in His wisdom He has taken two,
the little female and one of the males. While I do not
understand why HaShem would send four and take
two, I will guard the remaining two with my life. I will
guard them for your sake, husband, and count the days
until you are home with us.*

*I would write more, but my mind is filled not with
words, but with ribbons of grief. I have not heard from
you in some time, though I understand you are not
always able to write. Does Uriah still visit you? Does
he bring parchment and pen?*

*I hope to hear from you soon. May Adonai keep
watch between you and me as we are out of each other's
sight.*

*Pheodora*

271

# CHAPTER THIRTY-THREE

# *Pheodora*

Two days after we received the news about Yeshua, the sun shook off its pallor and shone brightly as I led the remaining kids out of the courtyard and through our narrow street. I had decided to take them to graze, because a cloud of grief remained over our house. Even my daughters had been unusually subdued this morning. No one wanted to work. No one wanted to do anything.

We were in the first stage of mourning, *aninut*, which usually lasted until after the funeral. Damaris and Shimon, who should have been with us, were impossible to reach. Except for Bethel and Seth, no one in Nazareth wanted to join us in grieving Yeshua's death, so we mourned alone. No visitors came to sit shiva with us. Without a body, without a funeral, and without mourners, how could we measure our sorrow?

I had just passed through the city gates when I heard the clomping hooves of an approaching mule. I looked up, shading my eyes from the bright sun, and saw a stranger riding toward me.

"Shalom to you!" he called, his smile bright beneath his head covering. "Are you coming from Nazareth?"

I blinked, trying to place the man's face, but I did not recognize him. "I am."

"Good." The man reined in his mule and looked down at me, his smile broadening. "I have come from Jerusalem and am spreading the good news among the cities of Galilee. Yeshua has risen, just as he said he would."

I tightened my grip on the goats' leads, afraid the man might be a thief trying to distract me. "Are you mad?" I spat the words at him. "Be on your way."

He leaned toward me, dangerously close to falling off the mule. "Did he not say he would be three days and three nights in the belly of the earth? He fulfilled his own prophecy, and now he walks among men and eats with his disciples. He is alive! Spread the word to all his followers, for our Messiah lives."

Whether or not he spoke madness, his report was like a punch to my chest. I stood there, hunched forward, protecting that inner place that had been grievously wounded.

"So?" he said, straightening on the mule. "Will you help me spread the word?"

He sat there, waiting for an answer, and what could I do? I dipped my chin in a reluctant nod, terrified he would dismount and begin shrieking if I refused.

The crazy man grinned. "Shalom! Shalom to all men!" He kicked the mule, causing the animal to snort and lurch forward in an awkward trot.

I stood on the road and stared after the stranger. What if *he* wasn't crazy, but *I* was? He could be a vision, the product of my overwrought imagination.

Or . . . *could* Yeshua be alive? Impossible that we could mourn him one day and rejoice the next.

But Elijah had raised the widow's son from death. And some said Yeshua had raised a woman's son outside Nain, and the daughter of a synagogue's leader in Capernaum. I did not let the goats graze on the roadside because urgency had fired my blood. I had to find my brothers at once.

———•———

James, Joses, and Simeon stared at me when I told them what the rider had said. "Yeshua . . . alive," James repeated, his voice dull. "What evidence did the man present?"

"Who was he?" Simeon demanded. "Did you recognize him?"

"Had he come from Jerusalem?" Joses asked. "Perhaps he is a Galilean, intending to rouse Yeshua's followers to revolt."

I held up my hands, confused by their many questions. "I didn't know him. He said he had come from Jerusalem and wanted me to tell everyone Yeshua was alive—living, eating and drinking with his disciples."

"He died." Joses stared at the floor. "Six—no, seven days ago. So how could he now be alive?"

"The man said something else—apparently, Yeshua prophesied about being in the belly of the earth three days and three nights. If he died seven days ago, the day after three days and three nights would be—"

"The first day of the week," Simeon said. "And a rider would need four days to come from Jerusalem."

"Not if he rode a mule," James said.

"But more if he stopped in every city on his route," Joses added, his eyes sparkling. "The timing is possible. Unbelievable, but possible."

I sank to the bench and let my head fall back against the wall, reeling from such a rapid reversal of tragedy. This morning I had opened my eyes to a day darkened by grief; I could not accept joyous news so readily.

"Jude would know." Joses looked up, the grim line of his mouth relaxing. "Jude will be home soon, and he will know."

"And Ima," I added. "If Yeshua died, she will come home. Where else would she go to grieve?"

"And if Yeshua is alive?"

I lowered my head, reluctant to accept the inevitable consequence of this good news. "If Yeshua lives, we may not see her again for a long time."

CHAPTER THIRTY-FOUR

# Pheodora

During the next two weeks, rumors flew like sand in a windstorm. Each traveler who came into Nazareth seemed to bring—and believe—a different version of Yeshua's story.

Many claimed Yeshua had been crucified on Passover, but his disciples stole the body away in order to reveal an empty tomb the morning of the Feast of Firstfruits.

Others said Yeshua was crucified but did not die. After all, the Romans did not break his legs, and what appeared like death was only a deep, albeit temporary, sleep. The cool air of the tomb revived him, and with his disciples' help he walked out of the cemetery under cover of darkness and went into hiding.

Some reported that Yeshua was crucified and died, but he rose victorious over death on the first day of the week. Most of his disciples and several women saw him alive.

A few insisted an imposter was crucified and buried during Pesach while Yeshua slipped out of Jerusalem. "Wait a few weeks," they said. "When the Romans least expect it, he will reveal himself, claim to have defeated death, and lead an attack on the procurator's palace. Even now his followers are spreading the news throughout Judea and Galilee, preparing for an attack."

I did not know what to believe, and neither did my brothers. We hoped, of course, that our brother lived, yet how could we reconcile so many wildly differing stories? We waited to hear some word from Jude or Ima, but we heard nothing from them.

"Three facts are clear," James declared as we sat on the rooftop one afternoon in late spring. "Someone—either Yeshua or someone claiming to be him—was crucified outside Jerusalem on Passover. That man was buried in a tomb, and now the tomb is empty."

"I heard our mother stood at the foot of the cross throughout most of the execution," Joses said, fresh grief flickering over his face. "Surely she would know if the condemned man was not her son. I do not believe she would be a party to such a deception."

"I'm not certain she would know him," Simeon argued. "The prisoner had been flogged. I have seen flogged captives—afterward, it is often hard to tell who they are." When I groaned, he gave me an apologetic look. "I am sorry, but it is true. The Romans show no mercy to condemned men."

"I think Ima would know if the man was not our brother," Joses insisted. "The Romans are experts in death. How could they take a living man off the cross? Those soldiers would put their own lives at risk if they did not conduct the execution properly."

"What are you saying?" James looked up at Joses. "Are you saying Yeshua died?"

"That was the first report to reach us." Joses fingered his beard. "These other stories . . . feel like inventions. Explanations. People are trying to explain an impossibility."

"Honestly?" My voice cracked. "You believe our brother died and came back from the dead? How is that possible? Could *you* do it?"

"He resurrected a dead man in Bethany," Joses countered, the beginning of a smile playing at the corners of his mouth. "And that man had been dead four days."

I looked away and chewed on my thumbnail, grateful my girls were with Bethel and not listening. In truth, I had considered the possibility that Yeshua had arisen, for he was undoubtedly a prophet and had raised others. But never had a prophet of Israel raised *himself* from the dead.

The sound of voices floated up from the street, and I glanced at my brothers. James stood and moved toward the balustrade. "I think we may have visitors."

"I hope they have not come to stone us." Simeon rose to his full height. "By now those who spread rumors may be saying we were involved in a plot to counterfeit our brother's death."

We walked to the edge of the roof and looked down. A crowd had gathered at our gate, travelers, judging from the dusty look of them. Several led loaded donkeys, and more than a few women were part of the group. One of the women lifted her head and caught my eye . . .

"Ima!" My heart pounding, I flew down the stairs and met my mother in the road. Wrapping my arms around her, I breathed in the mingled aromas of sunlight and dust.

"Jude! Brother!" My brothers, who had come down behind me, were embracing Jude, who seemed to be in a merry mood. I released Ima and studied her face—I saw no grief there, though something had etched deep lines around her eyes and mouth. But her eyes sparkled with light, and her smile radiated joy.

"How are you?" she asked, squeezing my hands. "I have been praying for you and Chiram."

I blinked, unable to remember who had told her about our situation, then realized it didn't matter. "I am better, now that you are home." Enveloped by a cocoon of contentment, I hugged her again.

She kissed my cheek, released me and turned to my brothers, hugging each of them in turn. James's eyes filled with tears as he embraced her, and Simeon held her so tightly I thought he might break her ribs. Joses picked her up and spun her around, laughing as she clung to her headscarf and scolded him for being foolish.

"Is this your family?" A stranger came up beside Jude and nodded toward us.

"Yes." Jude grinned as he introduced us to his traveling companions. "Everyone, I want you to meet my brothers and sister. James, Joses, Simeon, and Pheodora. Family"—he pointed to the group—"meet some of the believers from Jerusalem. The twelve are here—minus the one who betrayed Yeshua—and of course you remember Tasmin. This is Manaen, who works for Antipas when he's not traveling with us. The tall woman is Miriam of Magdala, and you know Aunt Salome. With her are Susanna and Joanna, who also traveled with Yeshua."

Other men and women smiled at us and introduced themselves, so many I was confused and a little alarmed. I glanced at James, who wore a look of wariness.

Finally, James stepped forward and held up a hand. "Brother," he said, his face somber as he clasped Jude's shoulder. "Why have you brought all these people to us?"

Jude's smile deepened and he laughed. Behind him, Tasmin tipped her head back and laughed, too. Ima smiled as if she carried a secret.

"We are traveling to the place where Yeshua taught the crowds," Jude said, gripping James's elbow. "He is alive, brother! He was dead, but lives again, and he wants to meet us in Galilee. We are stopping in every town along the way, inviting people to join us." His gaze swept over us and stopped on me. "You should come," he said, his voice vibrating with tender concern. "Yeshua has much to tell us, and you will want to hear every word."

Horrified by the sudden fear that Jude had lost his mind, I took a step back. James must have had the same thought, because he did not accept Jude's invitation, but looked over the group and nodded as if all of them were in need of a physician. "You need a place to rest," he said. "We will host several of you, and so will some of our neighbors. If you wait here, I'm sure we can find places for all of you to spend the night—"

"We are not stopping here." Jude released James and gestured toward the sky. "The sun is still high. We will keep going until the day is spent. But we had to stop and see you. We could not invite all of Galilee to join us and forget our family."

James gave Jude a patronizing smile. "Surely Ima would like to—"

Our mother gripped James's arm. "I am continuing on, as well."

I gasped. I had not seen her in months, yet she would not stop to talk? She would not embrace her granddaughters? Had grief made her take leave of her senses?

"Wait." I stepped toward Ima. "The girls are at the market

with Bethel, so let me go get them. I know they will want to see you and spend some time—"

"Not today." Ima moved closer. "I have been praying for your daughters," she said, her voice low in my ear. "I have lifted you and your family in prayer every night. HaShem is faithful and will work His will. Do not be anxious, and do not be angry with your sister's husband."

I stared at her, my mind whirling. In that moment I didn't want HaShem to work His mysterious will; I wanted my husband restored to me. I wanted my girls to have a father. I wanted to live in my own home and have the means to clothe my children and put food on the table.

And why was Ima telling me not to be angry with Shimon?

I put up my hands and backed away, then turned and strode into the house.

---

"We might as well go after them," James said later, looking around the table. "At least we will be able to spend time with our mother."

"I don't know what happened, but Jude has certainly changed." Joses tugged on his beard. "Before he left for Jerusalem, he thought Yeshua was mad."

"We can talk to Jude while we travel," Simeon said, "but we'd better hurry if we want to catch them." He looked at me. "Can you pack a basket for us? Some boiled eggs, bread, cheese—whatever you have."

"You should come." Joses playfully nudged me with his elbow. "You probably miss Ima most, and I am sure she would like to talk to you. You could bring the girls."

"I cannot believe she didn't stay." I shook my head. "I suppose it's now obvious that she always loved Yeshua best."

James held up an admonishing finger. "She has always favored Yeshua, but she loves each of us. Abba did, too. I am sure Ima misses you."

"You go. I will stay here."

"Bring the girls," Joses urged again. "I will help you watch them."

"And who will care for my goats? I cannot leave them."

"Bethel—"

"Bethel is a good neighbor, but I will not forsake my responsibility to Chiram. I would never forgive myself if something happened to one of those goats while I was gone. If they are scarred or marked in any way, they will be worthless as a sacrifice, and my husband will remain in prison for life." I lifted my chin. "You go, all of you, and leave me with my daughters. And bring back a full report."

James looked at Joses and Simeon, and I knew they had made up their minds.

"We will not be away long," Joses promised, patting my arm. "When we return, we will bring you the truth. No more rumors."

"That," I said, "is what I am counting on."

# CHAPTER THIRTY-FIVE

# *Damaris*

The door creaked when I entered, and Pheodora looked up. I caught my breath, astounded at the change in her. She looked far older than her years—even older than me—and the eyes that rose to meet mine were shadowed with grief and loss. My eyes probably looked as red as hers.

"Little sister." I dropped my basket to the floor. "You are too thin."

Her daughters greeted me with shy smiles, but their eyes widened when I pushed the basket toward them and forced a smile. "Eat up, girls, take whatever you wish. I have brought bread, cheeses, and honey cakes, enough for all of you, even your uncles." I glanced around the quiet room. "Where *are* our brothers? I thought they would be here."

"They have gone to Galilee." Pheodora's voice was hoarse with weariness. "Yeshua said he would meet them there."

Her words sent a bead of perspiration racing from my armpit to my ribs. Had my little sister gone as mad as the rest of the world? "This is not a time for jesting, Pheodora Aiya. Why would you say such a horrible thing?"

Pheodora shrugged. "I am not jesting. We have heard so many conflicting stories, even from Ima, that our brothers decided to join Jude and the group traveling to Galilee."

Shock flew through me. "Ima was with them?"

The thin line of Pheodora's mouth tightened. "She was. And she did not remain long enough to even speak to my girls. I thought she would at least spend a day with us, but she was most anxious to reach the appointed place in Galilee."

"What appointed place?"

"How am I supposed to know?" Pheodora's gaze shifted and thawed slightly. "When it comes to Yeshua, I am as ignorant as you."

"Our mother has gone mad." I sank to the bench beside the table and pulled off my head covering. "Abba would be so upset if he were still with us. Ima has always been a gentle and loving woman, the most innocent and easily led—"

"Our brothers are with her," Pheodora interrupted. "So they will not allow her to entertain fantasies. And if Yeshua *does* meet them there . . ."

"Trust me, Pheodora—our brother is dead." I spoke in the firmest tone I could muster. "I was devastated when I saw him on the execution stake, but Shimon forbade me to mourn on Passover. Alone in my room, however, I wept bitterly for him. Others danced in the streets of Jerusalem, but when the sky went dark and the earth quaked, they stopped their dancing. It is never right to celebrate death, especially the death of a prophet."

Shock flickered over Pheodora's face like summer lightning. "I heard you were in Jerusalem, but you saw him?"

"Y-yes," I stammered, overcome by an inexplicable feeling

of guilt. "We were in the Temple, sacrificing our Passover lamb, when the sky went dark, the earth shook, and chaos fell over the city. We wandered around, lost in the confusion and darkness, and found ourselves on a road leading through one of the gates. That is when I saw the execution site. Shimon rushed me away. Later, when we arrived at Lavan's house, we heard the entire story. I wanted to go back to claim Yeshua's body, but Lavan assured me he had already been taken away for burial."

Pheodora sank to the bench across from me, her eyes lowered, her forehead creased in thought. She seemed to be pondering my words, then she looked up, her face rippling with anguish. "You were in Jerusalem and did not look for our mother?"

I met her accusing gaze without flinching. "How could I know where she was? How could I know our brother was on trial for his life? I spent all week with Lavan's wife, and we were busy with preparations for Pesach—"

"Many members of the Great Sanhedrin are Pharisees," Pheodora continued, spitting the words like stones. "Your husband is one of them. Surely he knew all that was happening in their chamber. He must have known. He could have told you—why, he could have defended our brother! Why did he not testify on Yeshua's behalf?"

I stared at her, my mouth going dry. Shimon was not a member of the Great Sanhedrin, but would he have known of their plans? Though acquainted with many who were part of the assembly, he was still a lower level chaber. Lavan, on the other hand, must have known about Yeshua's trial, and surely he could have said something to Shimon . . .

I drew a deep breath as my temple began to throb. "You forget, sister, that I am only a woman. Shimon is not a member of the Great Sanhedrin, and even if he were, he would be only one voice. Do not forget—Yeshua had been exhorted to stop teaching blasphemy. Even Pilate questioned him, and though he had opportunity, Yeshua did nothing to refute his words or defend his actions."

Pheodora stood and leaned over the table, her eyes burning. "You should leave, Damaris. I cannot look at you now."

I stood, too, and backed away from the table, though I could not believe she was angry with me. "What could I have done? Did Shimon not warn him? Didn't other Pharisees try to explain the error of his ways? They warned him time and again about consorting with sinners and publicans, working on the Sabbath, and violating the Law in myriad ways—"

Pheodora grabbed a loaf of bread and threw it at me, missing my head by inches. Stunned and insulted by the childish act, I turned and left the house, breathing hard as I hurried down the stairs.

My younger sister had lost her mind. She had to be mad with grief, so in time I would forgive her.

If she came back to ask my forgiveness. If any of them did.

# CHAPTER THIRTY-SIX

# Pheodora

The following week passed slowly, leaving me trapped in an endless cycle of menial tasks. The sun set, the stars rose, and I put the girls to bed and took to my mattress. I slept deeply until the sun rose again. Then I got up and did the same work I had done the day before: feed the goats, feed the chickens, gather the eggs and give them to Bethel, feed my daughters, graze the goats, feed my daughters again, watch the sun set, stare up at the stars, and go back to bed.

Like a woman who grinds grain, I turned on a wheel, doing the same things, uttering the same prayers, weeping the same tears of confusion and loss.

The house seemed empty without my brothers' robust voices, and, keenly aware of their absence, my daughters were quieter than usual. While we grazed the goats, I studied the greening wheat fields and watched workers prune the grapevines. Shavuot, the Feast of Pentecost, would soon be upon us. When the fields turned gold and the heads sagged with grain, the harvesters would begin their work, and afterward we would bake our loaves for HaShem. Shavuot was another pilgrimage festival, but my brothers had not mentioned whether or not they would observe the feast in Jerusalem.

I would stay home, because the arrival of Shavuot meant my goats had become yearlings. I would inspect their bodies to see if any dark hairs had sprouted among the white. The priests would—*must*—appreciate perfectly spotless goats.

Bethel kept me company during that time. She knew, of course, about Yeshua, and she had heard the conflicting rumors. She did not offer her opinion about the stories but studiously avoided any subject that hinted of death or dying. She kept our conversations focused on goats or chickens and helped me with the work my brothers usually did—cleaning out the stalls, carrying water, putting down fresh straw.

Mostly she was kind to me. In those days my nerves were tattered, and Bethel seemed to sense that my world and everything in it had been threatened by doubt and dismay. So she remained close, never intruding, never questioning, a steady and faithful friend.

On the first day of a new week, my heart lifted when I heard familiar voices in the distance. I ran out of the courtyard and stood at the gate, then saw James, Jude, Joses, Simeon, and Tasmin coming up the road. They were dusty and windblown, but their tanned faces were alive with broad smiles.

Could they have been with Yeshua?

Tasmin was the first to see me. She broke away from the men and ran forward, then wrapped me in an embrace. "We saw him!" she said, her eyes snapping with joy. "We saw him and heard Yeshua! He is as alive as you and me. He charged us with spreading the good news of his death and resurrection throughout Jerusalem and Judea."

Bewildered, I turned to Jude, who had reached Tasmin's side. "All true," he said, smiling. "Our brother was dead, but lives again by the power of HaShem. He *is* the promised Messiah. He died for the entire world, Jews and Gentiles, and spilled his blood to atone for our sins."

I backed away, trembling, and retreated to the safety of the goat pen. Yeshua wanted them to preach the good news of his death and resurrection? How could this be? Perhaps my brothers had been overcome by the heat, swept up in the madness of everything that happened in Jerusalem. If Yeshua was truly alive, why had they not brought him home? And where was our mother?

That last question propelled me back to the gate. "Where is Ima?" I called, looking up as my brothers climbed the stairs. "Why didn't she and Yeshua come home with you?"

Joses and Jude turned to James, who nodded at me. "Our mother is with the other women," he replied, his voice quiet. "They are traveling with the disciples to Jerusalem."

"Why didn't Yeshua come with you?"

Jude answered this time. "We cannot be greedy, Pheodora. For a time he was our brother, but now he is the Savior of the world. We cannot cling to him because he has other work to do."

"Come inside." James tilted his head toward the door. "We have much to tell you."

"About his birth," Simeon said.

"About his death," Jude added. "I saw him on the execution stake, but now I have seen him alive."

I stared at them through a haze of horror, then shook my head and hurried to find refuge with Bethel.

By the time I returned from Bethel's house, my brothers were preparing to leave again. They were going to Jerusalem, James told me, where many of Yeshua's followers were gathering. They would depart in the morning and welcome anyone who wanted to come with them. "Yeshua told us to tarry in Jerusalem until Pentecost," he said. "We would love to have you join us."

I crossed my arms, more determined than ever to remain where I was. In truth, I felt relieved to know they would soon be gone. Their madness, or whatever it was, made me uneasy and threatened to upset my plans.

If they were telling the truth about Yeshua's death and resurrection, what did this mean for Israel and the Temple? If Yeshua *had* personally atoned for our sins, why would we need a Day of Atonement? Why would we need the goats of Yom Kippur?

If everyone heard and believed my brothers' story, our system of worship, our entire *world*, would be turned upside down. I closed my eyes, trying to imagine what my father would say if he had lived through the last several days. Would he cling to the sacrificial system we had always known, or would he cast it all aside in favor of—what? What, exactly, were we supposed to do with Yeshua Messiah?

More important, if the Temple authorities no longer needed to offer sacrifices for the people, how was I supposed to free my husband?

I looked at my brothers' earnest faces and saw how desperately they wanted me to believe that Yeshua had given us a new way to interact with HaShem. They wanted me to go with them, to leave everything and go talk to Yeshua. But I couldn't. I had invested too much in the old ways.

I went to the animal pens where I could be alone with my thoughts. I found it easier to think when I wasn't hearing my brothers' joyous exclamations about Yeshua's victory over death. I believed them—only a fool would doubt the word of so many eyewitnesses, especially when they were friends and family—yet how could I embrace what had happened if Yeshua's victory meant my husband might die in prison? How could I neglect Chiram and go with my brothers, throwing all my energy into following the Messiah, when the man I loved languished in captivity?

I still had unanswered questions. If Yeshua was our Messiah, why had he cloaked his message in such mystery? Why did he not explain himself to his family before he set out to teach? Why did he leave us in the dark while he opened his heart to a dozen disciples, one of whom betrayed him?

Even more bewildering was the idea that HaShem, Creator of the universe, the One who had chosen Abraham to be the father of our nation, and Moses to deliver us from slavery— why did He choose Yeshua to be the Messiah? How could Yeshua be both the son of HaShem *and* the son of Joseph? How could he be the savior of the world and my older brother?

My brothers had clearly been convinced that Yeshua was meant to die in Jerusalem, but I did not know if Damaris had seen our resurrected brother. Would she and Shimon believe that he was meant to be the final remedy for our sins? How could he be when HaShem had appointed the Day of Atonement for that purpose?

I walked to the pen, where Tikvah and Simcha lay sleeping on a fresh layer of straw. We had named them for hope and joy, emotions that had filled my brothers and deserted me.

For over a year, I had struggled to protect these two goats contentedly sleeping in their pen, and I could not let anything upset my plans. In a little more than four months, I would take the goats to Migdal-eder, and I would begin the process that would end with Chiram's release.

Only four months—not such a long time. After the goats were sold, I would meet Yeshua anywhere, and Chiram could come with me. I would sit at my older brother's feet and let him answer my questions.

But until then, I could not afford to become distracted.

My brothers seemed reluctant to say farewell the morning they left for Jerusalem. I did not want them to think I was upset with them, so I filled a large basket with bread, cheese, figs, and dried fish, then stood back with my daughters and wished them a safe journey.

"Are you sure you will not come?" Jude asked, his eyes softening as he picked up the basket. "The world has changed, Pheodora. The salvation of Israel has come, and the kingdom of God awaits us."

"I have not seen much of a change in the world," I replied, struggling to keep my tumultuous feelings under control. "Life is still hard. It is still unfair. And my husband is still in prison."

Jude said good-bye, his faint smile tinged with regret. He motioned the others forward. Joses, James, Simeon, and Tasmin hugged me, then James helped Jude strap the basket to his back, and together they walked away.

Their departure left me with an inexplicable feeling of emptiness. I knew they wanted my support, but I had already given them all I had to give.

# CHAPTER THIRTY-SEVEN

# *Pheodora*

S ix weeks later, I sat in our synagogue, alone except for my daughters. My brothers had not returned from Jerusalem, and neither had Shimon and Damaris. I would not have been surprised to learn that Shimon had purchased a house in the Holy City, where he could be more involved with the Pharisees at the Temple.

Damaris had always been drawn to ambitious men.

Left alone at home, I had focused on caring for my daughters, my chickens, and the goats. The creatures under my care were doing well, and I could only hope they would remain healthy until Yom Kippur.

Though I felt cut off from everyone but Bethel, I still lived in a busy city and could not help but overhear the rumors about Yeshua and his followers.

A few days after my brothers departed, we heard that Yeshua's disciples watched him rise into heaven, *in the flesh*, from outside Bethany, a village on the Mount of Olives. "Before he left them," the storyteller reported, "he told them he had fulfilled the Scriptures. As our Messiah, he suffered and rose from the dead on the third day, and we are to proclaim repentance for the removal of sins in his name to all nations, beginning in Jerusalem. He said we are witnesses of those things, so he would send the promise of his Father to us."

"The promise of Yeshua's father?" Whispered questions buzzed around me as the crowd absorbed this report. "What promise did Joseph the carpenter give?"

Two weeks later, we heard another report—the disciples had caused a great commotion in Jerusalem. The eyewitness account came from a man who had been outside the building where Yeshua's followers gathered to pray in an upper room. After praying for hours, they spilled into the street, where they babbled in foreign tongues and caused a great deal of unrest. "They were clearly drunk," the eyewitness finished. "What a disgrace."

"Not true!" another visitor shouted. "They weren't drunk —they were touched by the power of God! Something that looked like the Shechinah glory alighted on their heads, man and woman alike. They began to speak in tongues they had never known and went into the street to tell the pilgrims about Yeshua's death and resurrection. Some say up to three thousand people stopped to listen to them, and everyone heard the story in their native languages."

"Many people can speak a foreign tongue," a listener objected.

"These were not the common tongues like Greek and Aramaic." The second man smiled. "These pilgrims were Parthians and Medes and Elamites and Mesopotamians. They came from Phrygia and Pamphylia and Egypt, many from the Jewish community in Rome. And all of them heard the disciples declare the mighty deeds of God. They have begun to meet daily at the Temple."

I did not understand what happened in Jerusalem, but these stories coming from the Holy City, as incredible as they were, had to be the result of exaggeration and misinterpretation. By the time such reports trickled over the highways to cities like Nazareth, I could not be certain what was truth and what was rumor—no one could.

A Pharisee moved to the front of the synagogue, snapping me back to the present. He opened our service with the Shema, and I bowed my head, wondering how HaShem intended to bring order in the midst of such confusion. I was fairly certain all of Judea and Galilee had heard about Yeshua, but how could my brother's work continue now that he had gone away?

"'You, O Lord,'" the Pharisee went on, reciting one of the traditional eulogies, "'are mighty forever; You, who quicken the dead, are mighty to save. In Your mercy You preserve the living; You quicken the dead. In Your abundant pity You support those who fall, heal those who are diseased, loose those who are bound, and fulfill Your faithful Word to those who sleep in the dust. Who is like You, Lord of strength, and who can be compared to You, Who kills and makes alive, and causes salvation to spring forth? Faithful are You to give life unto the dead. Blessed be You, Jehovah, Who quickens the dead.'"

I lifted my head as the words echoed in the synagogue. The eulogy was old and familiar, and James had told me Yeshua recited it when he spoke at this synagogue. Later he read a passage from Isaiah and told the congregation that the Scriptures had been fulfilled in their hearing. They were not happy to hear him imply that he was the Messiah, and yet we had just heard a eulogy about HaShem bringing salvation *by resurrecting the dead*. We had heard that passage *hundreds* of times, so often we refused to recognize the prophesied events when they occurred in our time, in our city . . .

A thrill of anticipation touched my spine as the Pharisee took his seat. Another man stood and walked to the stand holding the Torah scroll. Opening the scroll, he began to read, "'Then I will pour out on the house of David . . .'"

I recognized the words of the prophet Zechariah. My father had often read this passage, tears of sorrow and joy streaming down his face as he contemplated its meaning.

"'. . . and the inhabitants of Jerusalem a spirit of grace and supplication, when they will look toward Me whom they pierced. They will mourn for him as one mourns for an only son and grieves bitterly for him, as one grieves for a firstborn. In that day there will be a great mourning in Jerusalem, mourning like Hadad-rimmon in the Valley of Megiddo.

"'In that day a spring will be opened to the house of David and to the inhabitants of Jerusalem to cleanse them from sin and impurity. It will happen in that day'—it is a declaration of Adonai-Tzva'ot—'that I will erase the names of the idols from the land and they will no longer be remembered. Furthermore, I will remove the prophets and the unclean spirit from the land.'"

I sat frozen in the middle of the bench, flanked by my daughters, as the truth of the Scriptures swirled around me. The Temple authorities had implored Pilate to execute Yeshua . . . Nails had pierced his hands and feet, and the Romans had pierced his side to ensure he was dead. Few of the inhabitants of Jerusalem had mourned Yeshua, but one day they would realize whom they had killed. And on that day, those who refused to see, to understand, would be removed . . .

I looked up, and as the slanting sunbeams fell on the
Torah reader, I realized that Jude was right: everything *had*
changed. Inspired by the *Ruach HaKodesh*, Zachariah had
written about a future event, but he had written in the voice
of the man I knew as brother.

*"They will look toward Me whom they pierced . . ."*

After seeing Yeshua alive, Jude, James, Joses, and Simeon
understood. Ima had always understood. Abba, too. I had
come to understanding reluctantly, yet now comprehension
was spreading through my mind and heart.

The world had indeed shifted, moving into a new align-
ment with HaShem, though few people realized it. One day
the inhabitants of Jerusalem would receive a spirit of grace
and supplication. Until then they would continue in their
traditions.

They would continue to observe Yom Kippur, even though
the ritual was now unnecessary for atonement. And as long
as they continued in blindness, they would need goats.

In His mercy, HaShem had not removed my opportunity
to redeem Chiram.

# CHAPTER THIRTY-EIGHT

# Pheodora

The month of Sivan brought cooler weather and golden wheat fields. I watched the ripening crops with great anticipation, because as they matured and prepared for the harvest, so did my goats. We had spent a year in Nazareth, and I was more than ready to return to my own home.

Except for Bethel, who continued to be a good friend, no one visited. The townspeople, most of whom did not believe Yeshua had risen, wanted nothing to do with me and barely spoke at the well. Life had taken a hard turn since my brothers departed. If not for Bethel, my daughters, and my chickens, we would be desolate indeed.

One morning, I looked out to see Damaris approaching our gate. She wore a colorful tunic, probably of silk or some other expensive fabric, and her hair, piled high on her head, gleamed with pearls cunningly woven into coiled braids. I wore the unadorned tunic of a working woman, and my hair, in two braids, did not sparkle with jewels. Clearly, Damaris intended to impress me, though I was in no mood to be impressed.

Remembering the way we had parted after her last visit, I hesitated to welcome her. Yet I had not seen any family since my brothers left for Jerusalem and I was feeling a bit forlorn. So I went to the door and opened it, smiling as she walked through the gate.

Damaris climbed the stairs, then gasped as one of the hens flew past her.

"It's all right," I said, stepping forward to catch the chicken. "It's only a hen."

Damaris moved past me and peered into the house as if other animals might lurk in the living area. "Why don't you keep those creatures penned?"

I stroked the chicken as the bird kept straining and trying to reach Damaris. I frowned, then realized why—chickens liked shiny objects. My hen was trying to peck the pearls in my sister's hair.

I moved down the stairs and let the chicken go. When she had flapped her way to the ground, I turned and smiled. "I have to apologize to you, Damaris. The last time you were here, I should not have tried to hit you with a loaf of bread."

Her mouth curled in a lopsided grin. "You missed. Just as you did when we were children."

"I did not really want to hit you."

"I did not think you did." She looked around. "Where are your girls?"

"Next door, with Bethel. She is teaching them how to make cheese."

"Ah. A useful skill for a poor woman."

I gritted my teeth. "Why have you come, Damaris?"

She scrutinized a bench, probably searching for chicken

feathers, then sat down. "Shimon and I have been talking," she said, placing her hands in her lap. "We know the brothers have gone to Jerusalem, so they are no longer able to help you. We know you must be finding it difficult to provide for your children. So, Shimon and I have come up with a solution for your predicament."

I blew out a breath and sat at the table, warmed by Damaris's concern. She could be aggravating, but she had not forgotten me. And though Shimon might be a Pharisee, at least he had remembered that the Law commanded us to be considerate of the poor and needy.

I met my sister's gaze. "What did you have in mind?"

A blush deepened the color on Damaris's cheeks as she straightened her spine. "You should marry again. Divorce Chiram and allow Shimon to find a husband for you. His chaburah is filled with fine men, several of whom are widowers. They would welcome having a wife, even one with children. Most of them are wealthy and would be good fathers to your girls." She arched her manicured brows into triangles. "Think of it! Your daughters could marry the sons of esteemed Torah teachers. I must confess, that is one of the reasons I was thrilled to hear Shimon wanted to join the Pharisees. What could be better than knowing your daughter will marry a devout and respected man? If you follow our advice, you would never have to worry, and you would not look so tired and haggard. I say this out of love for you, so if you would only—"

"No." I had heard enough, so I flattened my hands on the table and gave her a weary smile. "I can tell you have placed a great deal of thought behind this, but no."

She drew back. "Why not? Surely you cannot object to marrying wealth—"

"I will not divorce my husband. Chiram has been imprisoned through no fault of his own, and I will not punish him further. I promised I would do everything I could to win his freedom, and I will keep my word."

Damaris pressed her hands together, but the tension in her fingers betrayed her frustration. "Your plan will not work. Two goats is not nearly enough to pay a debt that has accumulated for over a year."

I closed my eyes and wished she would go away. "Chiram believes these goats are special."

"Not *that* special, surely. Shimon says there are other options—you could sell your house or one of your daughters. But you don't want to do either of those things."

Sell one of my daughters? I snapped my mouth shut, stunned by the suggestion. How could Shimon even conceive of such a notion?

Damaris leaned closer. "Has your refusal anything to do with the madness that has infected our brothers? I hear they are in Jerusalem with others who followed Yeshua."

Somehow, I found my voice. "I have heard the same reports."

"Do you know what they're doing?"

"I do not. Waiting perhaps, or learning."

"Learning about what?"

"A new covenant?" I laughed to cover my ignorance. "Damaris, I am not privy to their plans. I have only one thing on my mind these days—I need to get my husband out of prison before he dies in that horrible place. So unless you and Shimon have a plan to help me free Chiram, I must say farewell because I have work to do."

She frowned, her eyes narrowing, then stood and turned toward the door. "He is not the man you think he is."

I stared, alarmed by her harsh tone. "Who?"

"Chiram. Do you think he is in prison by mere chance? There is a reason for his situation. There is a reason Shimon would not pay his debt."

Tension raced up the ladder of my spine as I stood, trembling at my core. "What reason?"

Damaris stepped toward me, her eyes blazing fire. "Do you think Shimon refused to pay Chiram's debt because he is heartless? He is not. But he has to obey his mentor."

"What is the reason?"

She lifted her chin. "Your husband is a proud man, much too haughty for his lowly estate. That is why Lavan would not allow Shimon to pay his debt. That is why your husband languishes in prison when he could be helping you."

I coughed, the result of inhaling too quickly. "You think Chiram *haughty?*"

Damaris dipped her head in a sharp nod. "Lavan told us of a time when he was going to Jerusalem, traveling with a group from his chaburah. They passed the shepherds, who were bringing in a group of lambs, and all the shepherds bowed, as was proper. All but one. Chiram."

I gaped at her, disbelieving. "Surely Lavan was mistaken."

"Not at all. He distinctly remembered Chiram's face, and that the prideful shepherd was taller than the rest. Your husband is far too proud, even arrogant, and you know there are seven things Adonai hates: haughty eyes, a lying tongue, hands that shed innocent blood . . ."

She had made her point, but I stuttered as the rest of the Scripture sprang to my tongue: "a heart that plots wicked schemes, feet that run to evil, a false witness who spouts lies, and one who stirs up strife among brothers." I paused, waiting for my words to take hold, then looked into my sister's eyes. "Can you not see that *Lavan* is the guilty one? Who else but a prideful man would care whether or not a shepherd bowed to him? Who has plotted a wicked scheme? Who has stirred up strife among brothers and sisters?"

Damaris stiffened as though I had struck her. "I only know what I have been told. I should not have told you—"

"That man has brought immeasurable grief to my family. My husband is in a loathsome place of pestilence, where even the strongest men weaken and die."

Her lips thinned with anger. "Then perhaps he should lower himself when a more righteous man approaches."

Something boiled over within me, something scalding and corrosive. I screamed in frustrated fury, and the sound was enough to smack the smug look off my sister's face. She stepped back, turned and hurried to the door, flying down the stairs and into the street before I could relax enough to unclench my hands and step forward.

I slammed the door behind her and pressed against it, my hot breaths misting the slab of wood that stood between us.

⬤

The information Damaris shared twisted and turned within me, poisoning every thought of my sister and her husband. How could they calmly accept Lavan's report, knowing what he had done to my family? How could she allow Chiram to sit in that foul prison when her husband was quickly becoming the personification of haughtiness and pride?

For two days I was so upset I could barely eat. Bethel knew something troubled me, yet I could not bring myself to tell her what I had learned. She had to live in the same city as Shimon and Damaris, and growing up in Nazareth had taught me that a word spoken against a neighbor could not be retracted. Abba used to say that anyone who tried to recall his words was like a man who plucked a chicken atop a windy mountain and then decided to recapture every feather.

All I knew—with deep certainty—was Yeshua had been right about the Pharisees. Most people considered them devoutly religious, set apart, and more spiritual than everyone else, but they were like old eggs, perfectly white and clean on the outside but filled with stinking rot within.

In order to keep myself from being eaten alive by resentment and anger, I focused on caring for my animals and my daughters. At night, I put the chickens in their henhouse and the goats in their pen, then went inside and led my girls in their evening prayers. Once they had fallen asleep, I walked through the house, wishing even one of my brothers would come home so I could spill the burden I carried.

A clenched ball of anger burned at my center—anger directed at my sister, her husband, and Lavan. When I could no longer stand the pressure, I went into my brothers' bedchamber and knelt beside a bed. "HaShem," I cried, still not certain He would take notice of me, "help me, please. Show me what to do with these awful feelings."

Though the feelings did not go away, they did ease a little as I rose and snuffed the lamp. At least, I consoled myself, my struggle would soon end. Yom Kippur was fast approaching, and I would take the goats to Migdal-eder a month before the festival. I would sell my yearlings and take the money to Arimathea, where I would free my husband. After that, we would travel together to Nazareth. We would gather the girls and the chickens and return home to Bethlehem.

I would not ask Chiram to live in Nazareth. I could not live in a city where men like Shimon and Lavan were respected. I could not shop or sell at a market where I might encounter Damaris.

Once Chiram and I collected our family, I would leave Nazareth behind me.

# CHAPTER THIRTY-NINE

# *Damaris*

I had not meant to divulge the reason behind Lavan's insistence that we leave Chiram in prison. Still, Pheodora was my sister, and I could no longer bear to see her suffer under the delusion that we did not care about her husband. The unspoken question hovered between us every time we met, and when she insisted her husband was innocent, I had to speak the truth. Shimon was *not* to blame for her husband's situation; the fault lay with Chiram. The shepherd did not know his place, and he did not respect those HaShem had elevated.

I expected her to be upset at the revelation, but the vehemence of her reaction surprised me. Truthfully, I did not think she was deeply in love with her husband. How could she be? He was a shepherd, which meant he spent more time away from home than in it, and he rarely went to Temple or synagogue due to near-constant ritual impurity. Despite our father's approval of the betrothal, Pheodora married a man beneath her station, and divorcing him would not be a sin.

Had he not abandoned her? Had he not failed to provide for his family?

Shimon and I had discussed the matter at great length, and we both agreed that divorce and remarriage was the only way for my sister to better her situation. When I worried aloud about a divorce in the family causing trouble for Shimon with the chaburah, he assured me the Pharisees saw nothing wrong with ending an unsuitable marriage. "Moses allowed a man to give his wife a certificate of divorce and send her away," he said, shrugging. "So it would not be a problem for us."

The relative ease with which he had uttered those words gave me pause. Would he find it easy to give *me* a certificate of divorce? What would I have to do to bring him to that point? Where was the line between acceptable and unacceptable behavior? I was about to ask him, but stopped, not wanting to plant the idea in his head.

When Shimon came in that night, I told him my visit with Pheodora had not gone well. "She did not throw anything at me," I said, settling onto the dining couch with him, "but she would have thrown me out of the house if I had not departed on my own. Our suggestion infuriated her."

His brows pulled into an affronted frown. "Why? It was the perfect solution."

"Because she loves her husband, she says. And because she would rather blame you and Lavan for the shepherd's situation."

Annoyance struggled with humor on his handsome face. "She would blame me? After all I've done to help her?"

I shrugged. "She is not thinking clearly. I think grief and hardship have clouded her mind."

He shook his head. "As the Talmud says, 'Who is the

wise person? The one who foresees the consequences.' If she would follow our advice, she would be a wealthy wife without care. If she follows her own way, she will grow poorer still, and her children will suffer." He tugged on his beard. "I am sorry, wife, that your visit did not go well."

I sighed and placed my hand on his arm. "You have to understand my relationship with Pheodora. Our emotions toward each other have always blown hot and cold. One day we are good friends, the next we struggle to be polite to each other. I don't know why, but it has always been that way with us."

"She is jealous of you." Shimon smiled. "Of your beauty, your charm. You must not let her attitude upset you."

I smiled and squeezed his arm, yet I could not get the image of Pheodora's flushed and angry face out of my mind.

# CHAPTER FORTY

# Pheodora

The month of Elul finally arrived, and with it my opportunity to end the most troubling chapter of my life. Bethel had agreed to take care of my children while I transported the goats to Jerusalem, so I looked forward to my departure day with mixed emotions.

As I counted the days, I watched my girls lovingly brush and feed Tikvah and Simcha and knew the goats would be missed. My daughters had always known we were raising the goats to sell, but I had not found the courage to tell them Tikvah and Simcha were intended for Temple sacrifice.

How could I let them know without breaking their hearts? My sensitive girls would not be able to look at the goats without weeping. Even now their eyes filled with tears when they walked past Ora's and Hupsah's collars, which Joses had hung on a nail by the pens. My daughters loved those goats and would not be able to bear such dire foreknowledge.

The day before I was to leave, we led the goats into the courtyard and bathed them with a paste made of goat fat and wood ash. Once their fur was perfectly white and the insides of their ears clean and pink, Jordan and Shiri hung flower wreaths around the goats' necks and kissed them good-bye.

"Will they miss us, Ima?" Eden asked, stroking Tikvah's side. "Do you think they will be happy in their new home?"

My throat tightened. "I am sure they will miss you on the journey." I struggled to smile at my daughter. "HaShem has a plan for them, so you need not worry."

"I wish I could go with you," Judit said. "I could make sure they stayed clean and pretty."

"Bethel would be heartbroken if you did not stay with her. She is looking forward to your visit."

"Will you be gone long, Ima?" Jordan looked up at me with her big brown eyes. "If you can't sell them, will you bring Tikvah and Simcha back with you?"

"I will bring someone better—your father. Imagine how happy he will be to see you!"

The next morning, I packed baskets with their clothes and favorite possessions, then walked my girls to Bethel's house. The girls were delighted by the idea of staying with Bethel and Seth. Though Shiri seemed a bit anxious, I assured her I would be back soon, bringing her father with me.

"And when he is ready, we will move back to our home in Bethlehem," I promised, kneeling to look directly in my daughters' eyes. "You will sleep in your old beds, and I will have my baking bowls and pots. And Abba will go back to work . . ." I halted, my voice clotting. I wasn't sure why my emotions kept veering out of control, but the sooner I finished my farewells, the better off we would be.

I hugged and kissed each of my daughters and hugged Bethel, as well. "Thank you again," I told her. "If you need anything from my brothers' house, please go over and take what you need. The chicken feed is in a stone pot, and the eggs are yours. Please take them."

I waved to the girls, who stood with Bethel in her doorway. Then Bethel closed the door, and I turned, determined to be under way. I walked quietly back to my childhood home to retrieve the basket I had packed. I would not carry water, for I had no donkey to carry water jugs. I would rely on the hospitality of strangers and frequent stops to water the goats. Wherever the animals quenched their thirst, so would I.

I also packed a small bag of coins in case we were stopped by a tax collector. I would not be caught empty-handed as Chiram had been. If some Pharisee had made up his mind to destroy *me*, I would not give him opportunity.

I slipped my arms through the basket straps, picked up the goats' leads, and attached each end to their collars. I would walk the animals slowly, lest they be worn out by the time we arrived at Migdal-eder.

My first task would be to find another traveling group and join their party. With the High Holy Days approaching, the task should not be difficult.

As I passed through the gates of Nazareth, the goats trotting behind me, I thought of all the things I was leaving behind: my childhood home, my older sister, and my conviction that Yeshua was nothing more than an older brother.

On this journey, I would undoubtedly hear conversations about him, and I was eager to discover how others had come to understand Yeshua in a way I had completely missed.

━━━━━━━◆━━━━━━━

Outside Japha, only a short distance from Nazareth, a group of travelers warmly welcomed me into their group. I'm sure many were curious about why a woman was traveling alone, and when questioned I answered briefly and truthfully. Yes, I was married, but my husband was away. Yes, I had raised the goats and was taking them to market. Yes, I had children, but they were with a friend of the family.

At Nain, a village near the border dividing Galilee and Samaria, we went immediately to the well. I was filling a trough for the goats when another woman, probably a resident, caught my eye. "Can I get you some water?" she asked. "You are certain to be as thirsty as your animals."

"Thank you," I said, my hand going to my parched throat. "Your kindness is appreciated."

As she drew water, she smiled. "Have you come far?"

"From Nazareth. I am going to a place near Bethlehem."

"I have heard many things about Nazareth of late. Everyone has been talking about Yeshua—did you know him?"

I looked up, torn between giving her the whole truth or only enough to satisfy. Finally, I nodded. "I knew him. Everyone in Nazareth knew him."

She laughed. "I went to hear him speak in Capernaum. He spoke unlike any teacher I have ever heard."

I gave her a polite smile. "They say he was a good teacher."

She dipped a cup into the water bucket and handed it to me, then she sat on the edge of the well. "He told a story I will never forget. He said the kingdom of heaven could be compared to a king who wanted to settle accounts with his slaves. When he began, a man who owed him ten thousand talents came before him. But since the man didn't have the money to repay the debt, his master ordered him to be sold, along with his wife and children and everything he had."

I glanced around, almost certain Damaris had sent this woman with a not-so-subtle message. But I did not see anyone I knew, and the woman spoke with complete detachment. This had to be a coincidence.

"When the slave heard the judgment, he fell on his knees," she continued, "and begged his master, saying, 'Be patient with me, and I will repay you everything.' And the master, filled with compassion, released him and forgave him the debt."

"Generous man," I murmured, wishing Chiram's creditor had possessed this same kind of mercy.

"That is not the end of the story," the woman said, smiling. "Then the slave went out and found a fellow slave who owed him a hundred denarii. He grabbed him and started choking him, saying, 'Pay back what you owe!' His fellow slave fell down and begged him, saying, 'Be patient with me, and I will pay you back.' But he was unwilling to be patient. Instead, he threw the man into prison until he could pay back all he owed."

I crossed my arms, grimly acknowledging the realistic turn her story had taken. Few masters were generous enough to forgive a great debt; most were like the miser in her story, the sort who counted every denarii and copper.

"And when his fellow slaves saw what had happened," the woman went on, her brows knitting in a frown, "they went to their master and reported all that had happened. Then, summoning the first man, the master said, 'You wicked slave! I forgave your debt because you pleaded with me. Should you not have shown mercy to your fellow slave, just as I showed mercy to you?' Enraged, the master handed him over to the torturers until he could pay back all he owed."

Which, of course, he would never be able to do.

The woman turned, probably expecting some kind of response, but my throat was so tight I could not speak. Finally,

I blurted out the first words that leapt onto my tongue: "Unfortunately, the story is all too realistic."

"But do you understand?" The woman looked at me with something fragile in her eyes. "The servants are men and women like you and me. The master is HaShem."

I frowned . . . until a spark of understanding flickered. HaShem was merciful; He forgave sins and debts. But to those who did not show mercy to their debtors, HaShem exacted justice.

"Yeshua told that story after a man asked how many times we should forgive someone who has wronged us," the woman explained, her voice low and tremulous. "It is not a story about money, but about forgiveness. When he finished telling it, Yeshua said, 'So also my heavenly Father will do to you, unless each of you, from your heart, forgives his brother.'"

*Or her sister . . .*

The woman's story—Yeshua's story—remained with me for the remaining days of my journey southward. I found it ironic that Yeshua could speak to me even though he no longer lived on earth. I wasn't exactly sure where he was living, but I did not doubt that he lived. I didn't understand who he was supposed to be—what was our Messiah to do?—but his story about forgiveness resonated in my heart.

I had thought my anger toward Damaris and Shimon stemmed from their treatment of Chiram, but as conflicting emotions warred in my heart, I realized I had been angry with Damaris for years. She had always been the pretty one, the vibrant one, the leader. Born after Yeshua and James, but before Jude, Simeon, Joses, and I, she was always the first girl in the family to do everything—the first to read and write, sew, cook, begin her monthly cycles, and become betrothed. No wonder I always felt inferior and slow. I had been behind her all my life.

I loved her as much as I loved my brothers, and yet I also resented her for being better than me at almost everything. Now that we were women, I resented her near-constant efforts to improve my lot in life . . . as if hers was so much better. She had been completely sincere when she suggested I would be better off married to a wealthy Pharisee, but she had never known the joy of lying in the arms of a man who had no ambition other than to love his God, his wife, and his children. She lived with a man who was always striving, while I loved a man who was content to be what HaShem had made him to be . . . and accepted me as a quiet, simple woman.

Realizing that, I could almost feel sorry for my sister.

---

As we neared Bethlehem, I steeled my resolve and girded my heart with courage. I had never bartered with such serious intentions, nor had I negotiated the sale of goats. Even so, I could not fail at this exchange.

In my last letter to Chiram, I asked if he knew the total amount of his debt. When his reply finally reached me, I learned he owed twenty denarii—the equivalent of twenty sheep or goats.

How was I supposed to get twenty denarii for two goats?

Yet Chiram had faith in these animals. He had chosen the sire and dam; he had bred them carefully. He had not planned, however, on needing twenty times what a typical goat was worth.

I could only hope the man I was to meet, Asher ben Yakov,

could see that these two identical white yearlings were worth far more than normal goats. They had been bred with care, handled with gentleness, and loved by ardent young hearts.

"Asher ben Yakov," I muttered as I walked, "I hope you can see beyond the ordinary."

We were nearing Bethlehem when we spotted a small family camped beside the road. They had no tent, only a tattered piece of fabric supported by an arrangement of sticks. I counted four people: a man lying on the ground, a thin-faced woman, and two children with eyes as large as their bloated bellies. The women with me murmured in sympathy and dropped food from their baskets onto a cloth the mother had spread on the ground. The children pounced on the food immediately, and I wondered aloud how long it had been since they had eaten.

"A good while, I suspect," one of my companions replied. "The man is lame—see how misshapen his legs are? With two children to watch over, the woman probably has little time to glean the fields."

My heart twisted in pity as we moved on. If not for my brothers and the strength of our bonds, I might well be that woman. I could be sitting by the roadside, my daughters around me, relying on the kindness and generosity of strangers.

At the village square in Bethlehem, I said farewell to my traveling companions and wished them Godspeed on their way to Jerusalem. After they had departed, I drew water to wash my face and hands, then filled a trough to water the goats. I quenched my thirst, stood back, and eyed the animals with a critical eye. They were no longer clean, having walked in the dust for several days, but they had eaten well and looked no worse for wear. They did not appear nervous

ANGELA HUNT

or stressed, so perhaps my presence comforted them. More-
over, no harm had befallen them, nothing to leave a scar or a
permanent discoloration. I could see no blemish that would
disqualify them for the Yom Kippur sacrifice.

I smoothed my disheveled hair, covered it with my headscarf, and picked up the goats' leads. "One more stop, my
little friends," I told them, "and then we must part ways."

The road to Migdal-eder led me past our house. I tried to
close my heart to the happy memories that lived within its
walls, but I was unsuccessful. As I turned a blind eye to the
beckoning gate, my mind flitted back to earlier, happier days:
the day I crossed the threshold as Chiram's bride, the days
each of my daughters was born, the way my heart used to lift
at the sound of Chiram's voice in the street. Those memories
now felt as if they belonged to someone else, someone who
had been young, naïve, and immune to sorrow.

Not long after leaving Bethlehem, I saw the watchtower
of the flock rising in the distance: Migdal-eder, the place
where an angel had appeared to Chiram's father and announced the birth of the Messiah. Where Chiram's father
and other shepherds had heard the news and hurried into
the village, where in a stable he met my parents and their
newborn son.

My brother.

A tide of gooseflesh rippled up my arms and collided at
the back of my neck as the pieces fitted together. Why had
I not seen the truth? Blindness. Stubbornness. Or perhaps
a simple unwillingness to believe that HaShem could work
miracles in the family of simple people like us.

I walked on, keeping the stone tower in sight. I passed
the monument Jacob had erected at Rachel's grave, and a
shiver went through me to think that an angel brushed by

this memorial on his way to share his news with humble shepherds on a hillside.

My goats lifted their heads and bleated as we drew near the tower, and I wondered if they could smell or hear the other livestock. I quickened my pace, eager to discharge my duty. "I will miss you," I told the goats, watching as they pulled ahead of me. "But you were conceived and birthed for a special duty."

Finally, I spotted an older man sitting on a rock and holding a staff as he looked out over the grazing livestock. He had spotted me, probably as soon as I reached the curve of the road, and he seemed to weigh my intent as I entered the grassy field and guided the goats toward him.

He had been chewing on a bit of grass, but spat it out and waited silently as I approached. I bowed my head in respect, then drew a deep breath. "Shalom. I am Pheodora, wife to Chiram, who shepherded in these fields."

The old man's eyes narrowed. "Shalom. I know Chiram, and I know what has happened to him."

I nodded, not wanting to get into a discussion about my husband's situation. "I am looking for Asher ben Yakov, who purchases livestock for the Temple."

The man's eyes crinkled at the corners as he smiled. "I am Asher ben Yakov. Why did Chiram send you to me?"

I stepped aside to allow him to better see the goats. "He has charged me with bringing you these yearlings for the Yom Kippur sacrifice. Chiram bred them to be spotless and white for Yom Kippur, and I have guarded them to ensure they remained without blemish or defect. He said you would pay a fair price for the pair."

The old man climbed down from his rocky perch and advanced toward the goats, quietly clucking between his teeth.

The goats, who had begun to browse the grass near my feet, retreated at first, then stood still long enough for him to run his hands over their chest, legs, and bodies. Finally the man straightened and looked at me.

"They are fine beasts, indeed, and I can find no blemish. Though the Law does not require the goats to be pure white, I know the High Priest will approve these animals. If he must make the sacrifice in spotless white linen, why not use white goats?"

He walked around the animals again, tugging on his beard. "I can give you four denarii for the pair. It is a generous offer."

My heart sank in my chest, and my countenance must have reflected my disappointment. "I was hoping . . . my husband owes twenty denarii to a moneylender—"

"Six, then. I cannot offer more."

Driven by desperation, I clasped my hands in a posture of entreaty. "Please. You know my husband. Out of regard for him, can you not be generous? Chiram bred these animals himself; he chose a fine buck and doe, he went all the way to Caesarea for the breeding—"

"I am sorry." Pity stirred in the man's dark eyes, and genuine regret filled his voice. "I would buy the goats for one hundred denarii, because if ever a man deserved mercy, Chiram does. But I have been warned not to spend over ten denarii for the Yom Kippur sacrifices, and I have yet to buy two bulls, two rams, and seven lambs. As it is, I do not know how I can offer you six denarii and still purchase the other beasts."

Too distraught to speak, I backed away, realizing the hopelessness of my quest. Only ten denarii for so many animals? The amount seemed paltry. Chiram might have been confident we would be able to raise the money we needed, yet he did not know he would need so much.

319

I looked up as a sudden thought reared its head. "Asher ben Yakov," I said, "have you always been allotted so little to buy for the Yom Kippur sacrifices?"

Snorting, Asher lifted his eyes to heaven. "Even this woman realizes how foolish they have become. Only ten denarii!" He lowered his gaze to mine. "I have never been restricted before this year. How can you put a limit on what is to be offered to HaShem? Especially at Yom Kippur when we are to atone for our sins? This year someone will need to atone for the sin of parsimony. One of the Sanhedrin no doubt—one of the tight-fisted Pharisees who control the Temple budget has imposed this limit on my spending."

He dropped his staff to the ground, then pulled a leather purse from a pocket inside his robe. "Here are the six denarii I promised," he said, counting out silver coins. "Go and be well. I wish I could do more."

He held out his hand, but I retreated again. "I cannot take your money. Since the amount is not enough, I will leave it all for you. But when you pray, ask HaShem to show me another way to redeem my husband. For this—clearly this is not the way."

The man watched me, confusion in his eyes, as he returned the coins to his purse. "Why do you not pray yourself? I am sure HaShem will hear the prayers of a woman."

"HaShem is busy caring for Israel," I called, turning away. "I will find an answer on my own."

# CHAPTER FORTY-ONE

# Pheodora

In a haze of confusion and disappointment, I retraced my steps and found myself back in Bethlehem, in front of my home. With its shutters lowered, the door closed, and a wisp of vine growing up the doorframe and over the lintel, the house looked as if it were asleep.

I glanced down the narrow street, where the setting sun had painted the houses in hues of orange and gold. Shabbat would soon begin. Bethlehem already wore the deserted look of a village in Sabbath stillness.

Tugging the goats forward, I opened the courtyard gate, released the goats' leads, and sank to the bench against the wall. Weeds had sprouted in the cracked earth, growth that would never have survived my chickens. I stared at the unexpected bursts of life, small miracles in a bleak landscape, and burst into tears.

Why had HaShem allowed me to invest so much in an endeavor that accomplished nothing? Why had all of us—myself, my daughters, my brothers, and Bethel—worked so hard to raise these goats if they were not able to help us free Chiram? What had been the point of all our labor? Why hadn't HaShem shown us a better way? So much energy, so much hope . . . wasted.

I swiped hot tears from my cheeks and stared at the animals, who watched me with impassive expressions. "Why?" I snapped, resisting a sudden urge to grab Simcha by the horns and shake him. "Why didn't HaShem open Asher ben Yakov's purse? Surely he could have supplied what we needed."

For every problem I had ever encountered, people urged me to pray. But amid the prescribed morning and evening prayers, the benedictions, the blessings for bread, fruit, wine, and mixed foods, I had never heard a prayer for coping with life's problems. Our relationship with HaShem was so regulated and meticulously ordered that I did not know how to approach HaShem on my own. I was no Torah scholar, no scribe, not even the wife of a Pharisee. I was a late arrival among seven children, the wife of a lowly shepherd who could not even attend the synagogue on most occasions. I could creep inside my small, abandoned house, lie on the earthen floor and never rise again, and few people would notice my absence. My daughters would, of course, but Bethel or Damaris would care for them . . .

That bleak thought brought another—what if I disappeared? Would anyone miss me? I had offered Chiram my life, my love, and my efforts. I gave him children because I loved him, and I did everything I could for those goats because they were supposed to buy his freedom. But our plan failed, and now I did not know what to do.

If I had been on better terms with Damaris, if I had been more lovable, more important to her, she would have found a way to pay Chiram's debt. Twenty denarii was nothing to her; she could have sent the coins to the moneylender and freed Chiram within days of his arrest.

But because the situation between us had always been difficult, she made only a perfunctory effort on Chiram's behalf. Caring more for her husband than her sister, she was content to let Chiram languish in prison, to let me struggle to feed my daughters. If my brothers had not been able to help put a roof over our heads, I might not have been able to keep my daughters alive. If Bethel had not been willing to offer her wisdom and support, I would have failed with the goats and the chickens . . .

I would be like that woman I saw by the side of the road outside Bethlehem. Like me, her husband had been incapacitated and was unable to work. Like me, she struggled to feed herself and her children. Unlike me, she had no family to offer a home and help with the little ones.

Now my family had done all they could or would do, and I had no one else to turn to.

A flood of pity threatened to engulf me, but I pushed it back. I could not afford to wallow in failure. Due to the kindness of others, I had survived thus far, but what of it? I had to come up with a new plan, something that would work. Something that would foil the machinations of the evil men who had consigned my husband to a fate he did not deserve.

Shimon would have me divorce my husband or sell one of my daughters . . . Thoughts swirled in my head, an endless repetition of words and blurred images. And then the image of my oldest brother's face pushed itself up from the fray and claimed my attention.

I would not have to divorce my husband or sell my daughter. Another option remained: Yeshua's choice.

He had lived with us, led us by example, and settled our

sibling spats. He left Nazareth to do the same for the world, and then he surrendered his life in the most painful way imaginable. He was our sacrifice, becoming our scapegoat for sin. Then he proved his claim of being one with HaShem by resurrecting himself from the dead and teaching us to live by a law of love and forgiveness, not legalities.

I loved my brother and I loved my husband. I thought I had given Chiram all I had to give, but I still had my freedom. Like Yeshua, I could prove my love by surrendering my life.

But first I had to finish what I had begun.

With great effort I pulled myself off the bench and went to the goats. I removed the leads from their collars, then pushed the lid off the small cistern that collected rainwater. I made a clucking sound and splashed, drawing the goats to the water. They drank deeply, which was good. I wanted them to be strong and healthy for their new family.

"You have been blessed," I told them. "Your future holds life, not death. You will thrive, my little friends."

I pressed my hands to the small of my back and looked around. Lamplight fringed the doorways of nearby homes as the women of Bethlehem lit the Shabbat candles and blessed their evening meal. I had no family to cook for, but I did not need one tonight.

I went to the gate, secured the latch, and walked back into the house. I sat at the table, propped my head on my hands, and contemplated the step I was about to take.

A slave was under the control of her master and therefore open to unimaginable risks, and I would never subject my daughters to such a situation. But I could, and would, sell myself.

The Law allowed a man or woman of Israel to sell themselves into slavery for a term of six years or until the next

Jubilee year. Since we had not observed a Jubilee year in my lifetime, I would submit to slavery for the allotted number of years. The mandated price of a mature female was thirty shekels, and one shekel equaled four denarii. Five shekels would pay off Chiram's debt, redeeming him from prison and leaving twenty-five shekels for my family.

I closed my eyes and considered possible complications. I would have to send the money with a trusted friend—one of my brothers, unless I could find another trustworthy person in Jerusalem. Since many people from Nazareth would be in Jerusalem for the High Holy Days, I should have no problem finding someone. Once Chiram was free, he could go to Nazareth, get our daughters, and return to Bethlehem, where all would be well. He would have chickens, and Judit knew how to care for the hens. She would be able to sell eggs at the market while Chiram shepherded the flocks.

Six years was not such a long time. Jacob had served Laban for fourteen years—seven for Rachel, seven for Leah. Once I finished my term, Judit would be sixteen and ready to be betrothed, and I would be home to support her. Eden would be fourteen, already a woman; Jordan thirteen, and Shiri twelve. Selling myself would not end my motherhood—I would return to my daughters before they began to leave home forever.

As for Chiram . . . I bit hard on my lip to tamp the rise of emotion that threatened my resolve. I had endured a year and a half without him; I could endure six years more. He had been careful to spare my feelings and not complain about our separation, so I would do the same. I would assure him of my return, and I would not speak of missing him and our daughters. When we corresponded, or if I happened to see him on a Jerusalem street, I would pretend to be perfectly content with my lot.

I smiled as one of the goats bleated outside. I had been tempted to leave the animals with Asher ben Yakov, but if Yeshua atoned for our sins, why did these goats have to die? Better that they live with people who would care for them, people who needed them more than I did.

I pressed my hands to the table and drew a deep breath. I would be well-suited for life as a servant. I was not overly proud and knew how to run a house. While I was not familiar with fashion, cosmetics, or hair styles, I could work with animals or in a kitchen. Perhaps someone would use me to sell items in the marketplace or care for children. I could handle those tasks easily, though caring for someone else's children would undoubtedly make me desperate to hold my own.

Still—I could do it. For the love of Chiram, I could do almost anything.

———◆———

I remained inside through Shabbat, observing it with fasting and prayer. As the sun set, I walked around the house, feeling as though the ghosts of my husband and daughters had joined me there. I was resolved to follow through with my decision, but one sight nearly stopped me. When I looked in the corner where my daughters slept, I saw their mattresses, with their gifts from Chiram waiting in the center of each bed: Judit's stylus and ink, Eden's pressed rose, Jordan's secret box, and Shiri's woolen lamb. Those gifts—and the taxes on them—had cost us far more than the pittance Chiram paid for them.

I ran my palm over our dusty table and wondered if Judit would remember to oil the wood frequently. My bowl and pestle stood on a stool near the window, my clay dishes stacked beneath the stool as if I had just put them away.

I wouldn't need those things for a while, but Chiram and the girls would use them. Judit could decide how she wanted to arrange the house.

I went to my bed and slept a deep, dreamless sleep, then I was awakened by the bleating of the goats. I gave them fresh water and scratched their foreheads, telling them we would soon be on our way.

I opened the trunk that held my clothing and pulled out a tunic I had not worn in years. I put it on, tied a girdle around my waist, and idly wondered what sort of clothing a slave wore in service. Damaris dressed her slaves in identical garments, so perhaps my new master would have a new tunic for me.

I combed my hair and braided it into a thick rope. Nothing ornate or fancy would be needed today.

I picked up my travel basket, found a stale crust at the bottom, and ate it to break my fast. My growling stomach brought a wry smile to my face—slaves usually enjoyed decent meals. The Torah commanded us to be kind to slaves, and a practical master wanted to keep his servants healthy. After today, finding food would not be a problem.

Before I could leave, I had to complete one other task. I searched through a cabinet and found a few sheets of parchment left over from Judit's studies. I picked up a stylus, and I was sure Judit would forgive me for opening her new bottle of ink. I sat at the table and wrote a letter to James, instructing him to take the money to Arimathea and pay the jailer.

*I don't know the process, but surely the jailer will. When Chiram is free, take him to Nazareth and have him fetch our daughters from Bethel and Seth. Keep as many chickens as you like and give the rest to Chiram. Tell him our home in*

*Bethlehem awaits, and I will count the days until we are all together again.*

I hesitated, considering whether or not to explain what happened when I tried to sell the goats, and decided not to dwell on that unhappy outcome. Chiram would hear the story from Asher ben Yakov soon enough, and then he would understand why I had gone to Jerusalem.

Finishing the letter, I folded it, placed it in my basket, and took a last look around our home.

Steeling my heart against memories that called irresistibly, I picked up my basket, stepped out of the house, and gathered the goats' leads. With a resolute step, I left the city and walked northward until I spotted the small family and their flimsy lean-to.

I approached the woman, knelt down, and pressed the leads into her hands. "Take these goats," I told her, smiling even as my eyes filled with tears. "They have been well bred and will bring a good price at the market. Do as you will with them, but I advise you to sell one and keep the other as a stud. He will be much in demand."

The woman blinked at the goats, then looked at me. "I have never had a goat."

"Neither had I," I told her, "but I learned how to care for them. These are sweet animals, and they will help you and your family prosper. Their names are Tikvah and Simcha."

"Joy . . . and hope." The man with the shriveled legs leaned forward and regarded me with an earnest expression. "Why would you do this for us?"

"Because . . . because my brother Yeshua gave up everything for me."

## CHAPTER FORTY-TWO

# *Pheodora*

Slaves, I soon learned, are not sold like jewelry or eggs. A seller of slaves does not set his wares out and wait for buyers to examine the merchandise. The foremost slave seller in Jerusalem, a Greek called Hector, held auctions only on the first day of the week, and only if he had enough slaves to draw a decent crowd. So when I arrived at his tent outside the city, I was told I would probably have to wait two weeks before I would stand on the block. In the meantime, I would be examined by a physician, given a new tunic and sandals, and put to work doing odd chores around the camp.

"One more thing," the slave seller told me, his mouth spreading into a thin-lipped smile, "you will not receive payment until you are purchased. At that point the payment will be given to whomever you wish, since you will not be able to take it with you."

I nodded; the arrangement suited me well.

"You will not receive your new tunic until auction day," he said, his gaze running over the garment I wore. "So do your best to keep your present clothing clean."

He asked my name, which I gave him, and then he made a notation on a parchment. "Age?"

"Twenty-seven—no, twenty-eight." A blush burned my cheek. "Time has passed quickly of late."

He grunted and looked me over again. "Married?"

"Yes, to a shepherd in Bethlehem."

"Does he approve of this? I can't have husbands claiming their wives from someone who has made a legitimate purchase."

"My husband . . . will not interfere."

"He had better not. Experience with children?"

"Yes. I have four." My voice, like my nerves, was ragged.

"Any useful skills?"

"I have raised chickens and goats." I turned the catch in my throat into a cough and pushed on. "And children."

"Do you braid hair?"

"Only very simply."

"Can you sew garments?"

"Only simple tunics."

"Can you cook for a crowd?"

"Only simple meals."

He lowered his stylus, then arched a brow. "You are a simple woman, no?"

I nodded.

"Can you sign your name?"

"I can."

He slid the parchment toward me, an agreement between Hector and me. I was offering myself for sale to anyone who would give Hector more than thirty shekels.

I took the pen he offered, signed my name, and set the pen down.

He gestured over his shoulder. "Go see my wife, Mira. You will find her in the back, behind the tent. She will put you to work."

"Hector?"

"Yes?"

"I will receive thirty shekels, correct? You will give that much to whomever I designate?"

He looked at me, a gleam of curiosity in his brown eyes. "That is the price, yes."

"Good. Thank you."

I walked away, relieved I had come to a bridge and crossed it. Chiram would be free. My family would survive. And if HaShem had mercy, I would see them in six years.

Only when I lifted my chin and walked away did I realize how light I felt without the burden I had carried for months.

I would have enjoyed being assigned more tasks as I waited for the auction, but Hector and Mira had little to do at this time of year. Every morning I helped Mira grind grain and bake bread; then I hauled water and washed the clay bowls and dishes. One day I met with the doctor, who examined my teeth and gums, looked at the roots of my hair, and smelled my breath. He turned to Mira, who witnessed the examination and pronounced me healthy.

Hector and Mira did not chain those of us who had willingly sold ourselves into slavery, and why would they? We would not receive payment unless we were sold, so desperation ensured our cooperation. One man, who arrived the day after I did, argued and railed against Hector and was immediately sent away, penniless and more hopeless than he had been when he arrived.

I watched the belligerent man go, then turned to Mira. "What will happen to him now?"

She shrugged. "He might go to another slave market. The Romans sell slaves, though they are more brutal and do little to consider a slave's welfare. Most of their slaves are prisoners of war, and they tend to treat everyone as an enemy who must be beaten into submission."

"And if he does not go to the Romans?"

She released a bitter laugh. "He will end up with the Romans anyway. If he does not sell himself as a slave, he will probably join the auxiliaries, where he will fight for the emperor. That is the hardest life of all, but a man who will not bend will ultimately be broken."

I pressed my lips together and went back to my dishwashing, realizing the option I had chosen was not the worst thing that could have happened to me. James would say HaShem had shown mercy to me, and I was beginning to think he would be right.

Though Hector and Mira were Greek, they allowed those of us who were Jews to observe Shabbat and Rosh Hashanah, which occurred five days after my arrival at the slave market. Though I understood we were not free to answer the call of the shofar and go to the Temple, we were allowed to do what Rosh Hashanah required: repent and prepare oneself to stand trial before HaShem, who would execute His judgment on the Day of Atonement. The ten days between Rosh Hashanah and Yom Kippur were supposed to be a time of personal reflection, a time to test our souls and weigh our motives in the light of HaShem's holiness.

With little else to do, I had plenty of time to think about

my shortcomings. My mind kept flitting back to that afternoon at the well, where the woman told me Yeshua's story about the man who owed a great debt. HaShem was the master, she said, and we were the debtors.

Did all of us owe Him a great debt? I had always thought HaShem took little notice of me, so I asked for little and expected even less. I was not like Shimon and Damaris, who prayed constantly in a bid for success and wealth and power.

"If I owe You a debt," I prayed as I scrubbed the pots, "open my eyes so I can see it. Then open my heart so I will know what to do about it."

On the ninth day of Tishri, only hours before the start of Yom Kippur, Hector decided to take advantage of the crowds and hold the auction. "We will be brief," he said after bringing all of us together beneath his tent. "Mira has your new clothing and sandals. Try to look humble and obedient, will you?"

"Will we have to leave today?" a young boy asked. My heart twisted every time I looked at him. Small and thin, he did not appear Jewish, so he must have been brought here by one of the foreigners who inhabited Jerusalem.

Hector's expression softened as he looked at the boy. "Perhaps not," he said. "If your new master is Jewish, he may wait and pick you up later, because tomorrow is a holy day for the Jews." He glanced around. "Any other questions? If not, when I call your name, step onto the platform and stand quietly while I describe your skills. When the auction is concluded, your new owner will meet with me and make arrangements for your transport."

I walked over to join four other women and attempted to

smile. One of them was Egyptian and had been a slave before her arrival. The other two were dark-skinned and spoke a language I did not understand.

Hector went outside and addressed the crowd of about thirty people, nearly all of whom were men. I peeked out from a crack in the tent flap, searching for a familiar face and finding none. Good. I did not want any of my friends or family to witness my humiliation. If I did not see anyone I knew, I would ask my new owner to deliver the money to one of Yeshua's followers, with instructions to give the coins to James.

Hector began with the men, calling them out individually and describing them by age, name, and skills. I had heard that some slave auctions were barbaric and pagan, but Hector seemed to sense that such a display would offend his primarily Jewish audience. The first slave sold to a man wearing a Roman toga; the second sold to a man dressed in the simple tunic of a tradesman. The third and fourth, a pair of brothers, sold together to a man in an expensive tunic. I heard him say he planned to use them as litter-bearers for his wife.

Without warning, Hector called my name. For a moment I thought he had made a mistake. Then I realized he had moved on to the women . . . and I was the first.

I stepped outside, felt the breeze lift the hair on my shoulders, and stood facing Hector. He looked at me, his eyes commanding *look pleasant*, then he made a gesture: *turn and face the crowd.*

Reluctantly, I obeyed.

"Pheodora," he said, his voice rising above the murmurs of the crowd. "Age twenty-eight years, in good health, and skilled with livestock. She has experience with children and would make an excellent nursemaid."

As he went on, exaggerating what few skills I had, I forced myself to look at the faces in the crowd, which had grown since the auction began. So many faces—young, old, bearded and smooth, round and square, heavy and bony, soft and hard. The men who watched and listened wore garments of every sort— the simple tunics of working men, the colorful garb of wealthy merchants, Roman togas, even—I stiffened in surprise—the blue-and-white garments of Pharisees. One of the Pharisees shifted and lifted his hand. "Thirty-two shekels," he called.

"Thirty-three," someone else countered.

The Pharisee lifted his hand again. "Thirty-four."

"Thirty-five."

The Pharisee sighed. "Forty shekels. Let that be the end of it."

"Sold!" Hector slammed his hand on his desk, and I squinted to better see the man beneath the blue-and-white prayer shawl. For a moment I hoped I would see Shimon, yet the face was unfamiliar, with hard eyes and deep lines beside the eyes and nose. This was a stranger.

Hector motioned for me to leave the stage so the next woman could come up. I moved away, walking on legs that felt like wooden stumps, and sank to a bench where I had been instructed to wait for my owner.

I sat for a long time. Hector finished with the other women, then he and Mira accepted coins from strangers and the other slaves were led away by their new masters.

About an hour before sunset, Hector walked over to the bench where I sat with the young boy. His name was Helios, I had learned, and he was seven years old.

"The same man has purchased both of you," Hector told us, "and he will not be able to meet you until tomorrow, after the Temple ceremony. You will remain with us tonight."

I looked at Helios, shivering in his loincloth. "Do you have a blanket?" I asked, gesturing to the child. "I will watch over him tonight."

Hector nodded. "Go inside and get some rest. Tomorrow will come soon enough."

A memory bubbled up as I led the boy back inside the tent: *"Do not worry about tomorrow, for tomorrow will worry about itself. Each day has enough trouble of its own."*

———◆———

"Pheodora."

The familiar voice called to me, dragging me from the depths of sleep, drawing me toward light. I swam up, struggling to free myself from the heaviness of exhaustion, and finally broke through to wakefulness.

I opened my eyes and saw Yeshua sitting in the goat pen, his back against a rail, his eyes bright as he smiled at me. I looked down, expecting to find myself a child again. Instead, I was a grown woman, not the girl who used to meet my oldest brother in the animal pens.

Was this only a dream? Something I had dredged up because I was anxious about the auction?

I looked at Yeshua, and in the light of his eyes I felt the truth. This was real. HaShem spoke to people in dreams, and my brother was now speaking to me.

And Yeshua had changed. His robe was brighter than the blinding sun, whiter than goat's milk. The air around him seemed to pulsate with gentle waves of glory, and, realizing who He really was, I fell to my knees in the straw.

"Yeshua." Slowly, I lifted my gaze. "I am sorry I never tried to see You before—sorry I was so slow to believe, to realize who You are."

He lifted his hand. "I saw you when you were yet un-formed, so do not worry if you cannot see Me. I had to leave you, dear one, so I could teach the brothers and sisters who have now taken their places in the family of God."

I bowed my head, understanding and yet not understanding. "You are Messiah," I whispered. "You are *ben Elohim*."

His smile deepened. "I am. As the Father is, so am I."

I pressed my lips together, realizing that once again I was the last to know. My brothers had already seen Him alive. I had not spoken to Damaris, but Yeshua had probably visited her, too . . ."

"Your sister," he said, "does not need to see me. When the time is right, she will believe."

I blinked in astonishment. Yeshua had come to see me before Damaris?

"You asked if you owed a debt." His voice was a low rumble, at once both powerful and gentle. "You wanted to know."

I looked up, filled with remembering. "Yes. If I owe you something, if I have transgressed—"

"Every man and woman falls short of the Father's perfect holiness," Yeshua said. "But I shed my blood so every sin would be forgiven and every shortcoming corrected. The atonement is complete for anyone who believes."

His voice passed over me like a wave, overflowing my head and heart, as my eyes filled with visions of how great a debt I owed. I saw my anger, my jealousy, my petty rivalry with Damaris, and even my brothers. I saw every unholy attitude, every moment of irritation, every time I believed God did not care, did not see me, did not answer my prayers . . .

Who had been indifferent? Not God, but me. I had never bothered to reach behind the ritual prayers; I never savored the Scriptures or probed the treasures contained within those inspired words.

I had been a spoiled child, overstuffed with knowledge of God and yet refusing to practice a single iota of the principles I had been privileged to receive.

I had lived with the *Son of God* . . . and refused to understand who He was. When my brothers realized the truth, I refused to see. What had I said? I did not want to be *distracted* . . .

"Yeshua, forgive me." Tears came in a rush, so strong my body trembled. "I have been so blind."

His mouth curved with tenderness. "You were not the only one." Then He laughed, and the sound was so warm, so human, so familiar that I smiled . . . and laughed with Him.

"Go, Pheodora," He said, wiping tears of mirth from his eyes. "Go with the man who comes for you tomorrow, and remember that I will always be with you. Always."

# CHAPTER FORTY-THREE

# *Damaris*

On the day of Yom Kippur, my heart bounded upward as Shimon led me across the Temple's Royal Porch, through the Court of the Gentiles, and into the Court of the Women. After completing a full year of study and taking a final vow, my husband became a fully professed member of the chaburah. I had never been prouder of him.

Shimon left me with the other women and walked with great dignity toward the steps that led to the Levite's court. He could not enter, not being a Levite, but from his position he would have the best view of the ceremonies.

We had never attended Yom Kippur services before, but since Shimon had joined the Pharisees, we were expected to take part in this most holy day of the year. Today, and today only, Caiaphas, our *cohen gadol* or high priest, would enter the Holy of Holies and not enter it again until next year. Because the ritual required complete purity, he would immerse himself in a mikvah five times.

Before we left our host's home, Shimon had explained that for a week Caiaphas had been sequestered in the Palhedrin chamber at the Temple, where he had been sprinkled with spring water containing the ashes of a pure red heifer. While sequestered, he had practiced the Yom Kippur service, for nothing could go amiss during this all-important ritual. Earlier this morning, the cohen gadol had immersed himself in a mikvah, then dressed in special golden garments to offer the regular morning sacrifices, usually performed by ordinary priests. "Afterward," Shimon said, "he immersed himself in the mikvah again and changed into linen garments, washing his hands and feet twice, in case any impurity from the courtyard landed on him and made him unclean."

Now our barefoot high priest stood before a bull, placing his hands on the animal's head, transmitting sins from himself and his household. He spoke the traditional words, and when he uttered the name of God, everyone from the lowliest servant to the highest-ranking Levite prostrated themselves on the floor. Then, like many others, I lifted my head in time to see the high priest draw a blade and slaughter the bull, holding a bowl below the severed neck to collect the blood.

When we stood again, Shimon and I followed the high priest, who had moved toward the Eastern Gate. Caiaphas positioned himself before two goats and drew lots from a box. I rose on tiptoes.

"What are you doing?" Shimon whispered.

"I want to see if the goats are Pheodora's," I answered, keeping my voice low.

Shimon groaned. "Impossible. The keeper of the flock was given a limited budget for the sacrificial beasts. Pheodora could not have sold them for as much as she wanted."

I blinked in stunned surprise. I had not seen my sister in

weeks, but I knew she had taken her goats to the place where the Temple flocks were kept. I assumed she had sold them and gone to Arimathea to free her husband—if she had not sold the goats, where was she?

I cast a sharp look at Shimon, but he was intent upon the lottery. "For centuries," Shimon said, glancing at me, "the *yes* lot has fallen to the goat on the right side, which means good fortune. Let us see if it happens again."

Caiaphas shook the box and pulled out the stones. I could not tell what they looked like, but when an audible gasp echoed over the crowd, I knew the lot had not fallen the way the priest expected.

Even Shimon looked upset by the revelation. A Levite tied a red cloth, representing the sins of the people around the horns of the first goat, then set it aside.

"The first goat is not for the Lord," Shimon said, his voice flat. "It will be for Azazel."

"Who?"

"The wilderness," he replied. "The second goat will be sacrificed on the altar."

I could not understand why the priests seemed to care so much about which goat went and which stayed, but Shimon would undoubtedly explain everything later.

We followed the crowd as it trailed behind Caiaphas, who went to the center of the Temple and ascended the steps of the altar of unhewn stones, freshly whitened for the occasion. There he picked up a small shovel filled with glowing embers while a group of Levites approached.

"This is the most difficult part of the ceremony," Shimon whispered. "He must keep the shovel balanced and use his teeth to prevent spilling its contents while the Levites fill his hands with incense."

I marveled and rose on tiptoes again, eager to see the balancing act. Finally, while holding the shovel and the incense, the high priest entered the Holy of Holies. "What will he do in there?" I asked.

Shimon glanced around to be sure no one was frowning at us, then whispered, "He will put the shovel where the Ark would be, if it were not missing. He will wait until the chamber fills with smoke, then he will leave."

A few moments later, the cohen gadol walked out of the Holy of Holies, his face flushed and streaked with perspiration. He took the bowl of bull's blood from an attendant and entered the Holy of Holies again.

"He is sprinkling the bull's blood with his finger," Shimon said, looking as though he envied the high priest this honor. "Eight times. He sprinkles the area where the Ark would have stood, and he is careful not to get blood on his garments."

Soon the high priest appeared again, the bowl in his hand. He placed it on a stand in front of the curtain separating the Holy Place from the Most Holy Place.

I nudged my husband. "I heard the curtain was torn on Passover. Yet now it is whole."

Shimon sighed. "The old curtain did tear, but weavers have since replaced it."

Caiaphas walked to the courtyard near the Eastern Gate and placed his hands on the goat that had been established as "for the Lord." As the animal looked up at him, I felt tears sting my eyes. Had that goat ever looked at my sister in that way? How foolish she had been to love a creature intended for sacrifice.

While I hung my head, weeping silently, the high priest pronounced confession of sin on behalf of the priests and all the people. Then he cut the goat and caught its blood in another bowl.

I could not watch. I did not want to embarrass Shimon, so I covered my eyes and tried to think of anything but the dying goat. Maybe Shimon was right and it *wasn't* Pheodora's pet, but how could he tell?

When I lifted my gaze, the high priest was coming out of the Holy of Holies, the bowl in his hand. He set it on another stand, then sprinkled bull's blood toward the curtain. He repeated this action with goat's blood, and by that time I felt faint and desperately nauseous.

"Shimon." I clutched at his arm.

"Shh." He threw me a stern glance.

I closed my eyes a few minutes more, but the odors of incense and blood and people assaulted my nostrils. The sounds flowing around me—whispers, prayers, quiet exclamations, and the soft rustling of the Levites' garments—seemed to increase in volume as my head began to pound.

I clung to Shimon's arm and prayed the ceremony would end.

# CHAPTER FORTY-FOUR

# Pheodora

I had just finished a bowl of stew when Hector rushed into the tent, his face flushed. "Pheodora!" His smile broadened when he spotted me with the boy. "Both of you, come at once. Your master is here."

I blinked, surprised by the early hour. Even here, outside the city, we were aware of what was happening at the Temple. We had heard the crowd, the shofar, and the stunning silence that resulted when the cohen gadol entered the Holy of Holies.

"Come." Hector motioned us forward. "Your master awaits."

I followed him out of the tent, my heart pounding, and stopped short when I saw the Pharisee. His appearance had not changed, but he was standing with my brother.

I gaped at him. "James?"

The Pharisee stepped forward and dipped his head in a polite bow. "Pheodora, I am Joseph, and we have much in common. I had a brother, he of blessed memory, who knew your husband."

I looked at James as my head filled with words and feelings, none of which made any sense.

"Chiram's friend," James said. "Uriah, who brought him parchment and ink."

I gasped when my confusion cleared. Chiram . . . who had not written in months because the man who provided the means had died. Uriah had suffered from a cough, which must have developed into something worse . . .

"I am so sorry." A wave of compassion flooded my heart. "Your brother was kind to my husband. That sort of kindness is rare."

A smile flashed in the man's graying beard. "Your brother James has been kind to me and some of my friends. But we will share that story later. Now we have business to arrange."

I looked at James, hoping he could enlighten me further, but he only crossed his arms and smiled.

"Yesterday, when I heard the slave seller give your name, I knew you had to be the sister James has so often mentioned," Joseph said. He suddenly looked at the boy, then held out a hand to him. "Come here, son, and do not fear. We have a plan for you, as well."

Helios walked over and stood next to Joseph, who nodded and continued with his explanation. "Last night I found James and told him where you were. This morning we arrived early and paid your slave price—that money is already on its way to Arimathea, where the jailer will free your husband and repay the moneylender."

Humbled beyond words, I pressed my hands to my chest and bowed before him. Was this the man I should go with? "I am your servant."

"Not exactly." The man smiled and gestured for me to stand erect. "You are free, Pheodora. James has agreed to escort you to Nazareth, where your husband will meet you. You may return to Bethlehem or remain in Nazareth, whatever you choose."

I looked at James, who was examining my face with considerable concentration. "Why would you do this?" he asked. "If Joseph had not seen you on that platform—"

"All things happened as HaShem wills," Joseph interrupted. "And let us not keep this young man waiting." He bent to look into Helios's eyes. "You are Greek, yes?"

Helios nodded.

"As it happens, Hector and Mira are Greek, too. We have learned that your parents died and you have no one to care for you. Your slave debt has been paid as well, so you are free. But if you would like a family, Hector and his wife have agreed to adopt you."

Helios glanced from me to Hector, a pair of dimples forming in his cheeks. "I would like that."

Hector picked the boy up, and Mira stepped forward to pat his back. I smiled at them, momentarily overcome by sheer joy, then felt James take my arm. "We will meet Joseph again," he promised, pulling me away, "but we need to prepare for our journey home."

I nodded and took a step toward him, then waited while James and Joseph embraced. "Grace and shalom be yours through Yeshua our Lord," Joseph said when they parted.

"The same to you," James replied. "Until He brings us together again!"

⸻

James held my hand, leading me through the crowded streets to the house where he had been staying. I barely had time to meet his hosts before my brother pulled me out again, a basket of provisions dangling from his arm.

"Hurry." His eyes sparked with excitement. "I want to see something."

"What?"

"Come, and you will find out."

What could I do but follow? I did, and before too long I realized James had not chosen a random road to take us out of Jerusalem. We walked out through the Eastern Gate, which led to the Mount of Olives. Crowds lined the road, people who jeered and shouted, "Let the sin-bearer be gone!" They looked toward the Temple, some of them waiting with uplifted fists, intent on . . .

"The goat." James uttered my unspoken question. "The goat will come this way, and they all want to see it."

I stumbled after him, distracted by so many angry faces. "Why are they intent on destroying it? I have read the Scripture, how the goat is to be abandoned in the wilderness—"

"Here it comes!"

James pulled me off the road as a man and a white goat appeared on the horizon. The man was clean-shaven, clearly a foreigner, and focused on his task. He stopped a few steps ahead of us, accepted water from an attendant, and willingly handed the rope to another man, who took the goat and jogged on.

I looked to James for an explanation. "There are ten stations," he said, leading me back into the street, "and none of the escorts travel more than a Sabbath-day's journey. It is the priests' way of making sure the goat does not come back into the city."

"And if it does?"

347

James shook his head. "It will not. When it reaches the wilderness, the last handler will push it off the cliff."

I turned away, dismayed to think of any goat dying such a horrible death—especially after Yeshua said the atonement was complete.

"What the priests have forgotten," James went on, guiding me through the crowd, "is that the goat sacrificed on the altar paid for our sins. His blood was spilled to atone for the sins we confessed."

I looked at the faces around me, faces that were now happy and alive with celebration. "Why do they kill the second goat?"

"Because the second goat does what the first goat could not do. The first goat could not give us permanent forgiveness; it could not make us holy. The second goat is to carry our sin into the wilderness and put it away until the perfect sacrifice becomes available."

I stopped in mid-step, gooseflesh pebbling my arms as James's words hung in the air. "The perfect sacrifice?"

"Only the sacrifice of one who had never sinned could make us holy before God. No goat or bull or ram could ever do that."

I lifted my face and felt the living sun warm my eyelids. "Yeshua was the perfect sacrifice," I whispered, the crowd's noise fading to a dull roar. "Because He was *ben Elohim.*"

"Yes," James said, grinning. "So let us see how the second goat fares today."

# CHAPTER FORTY-FIVE

# *Pheodora*

We did not arrive in time to see the second goat fall to its death, and I was glad for it. But what we *did* see affected us deeply.

James explained the ritual in detail as we followed the road, so I knew what would happen at the end. On the last leg of the journey, the crowds would stop, content to watch from a distance as the escort took the goat to a cliff at the edge of the wilderness. When he reached the appointed place, the man would take the scarlet cloth from the goat's horn and rip it in half, then tie one half onto the goat's horn and secure the first half to some nearby rocks. Then he would turn the goat away from the cliff—because no goat would willingly jump from such a height—and push it backward until it fell.

"At that point," James said, "he will take the cloth from the rocks and hold it up, using it as a flag to signal the previous way station. His response will be signaled to the station before that one, and so on, until word of the goat's demise is received at the Temple. Once that is assured, the cohen gadol will enter the Women's Courtyard and read the Torah descriptions of Yom Kippur and its sacrifices."

"There is more," he said, shrugging, "but perhaps none of it is necessary now."

We walked in relative quiet until we heard cheering, a wave of sound that swept over us and continued along the road to Jerusalem. "The goat is gone," James said, nodding. "Soon those at the Temple will know."

When we arrived at the last station, I thought we would discover more celebration. Instead, the quiet observers stood in small groups, their heads together, their faces somber. James gave me a puzzled look, then walked over to a man, who stood with his head bowed.

"What has happened?" James asked. "Why is everyone unsettled?"

The man looked up and drew a deep breath. "The scarlet cloth," he said, his voice cracking. "For hundreds of years it has turned white after the goat's death, but not this year. Not today."

I looked at James. Should I tell him what Yeshua told me? Or would he understand without my help?

James seemed preoccupied for a moment, then he smiled. "Perhaps, brother, there is no more need for a goat to set our sins aside. This year, atonement was made by the Lamb of God himself. Let me tell you about Yeshua, who was crucified and rose on the third day. God raised him to life, and I am a witness of that fact. Seeing this"—James pointed to the red cloth flapping at its place among the rocks—"let all Israel be assured that God has made Yeshua both Lord and Christ. Our atonement for sin is complete."

A crowd began to gather around us, men and women who

could not understand why the cloth had not changed color. I retreated, giving the others room to listen, and smiled as I lifted my eyes toward heaven.

*Yes, Yeshua. We may have been blind and hard of hearing, but we finally understand.*

# CHAPTER FORTY-SIX

# *Damaris*

T he day should have ended with feasting and celebration. Shimon had arranged a great banquet and had invited many of his friends from the chaburah, but once the rumors began to trickle our way, the festive atmosphere vanished.

Many of the Pharisees, particularly the venerable elders, said the omens meant nothing. What did it matter if the first goat had been chosen for the wilderness instead of the Lord? And what did it matter if the red cloth did not turn white? Perhaps in previous years the sun had bleached the cloth and this year it had been colored with a more resistant dye.

I found it odd that men who for hundreds of years had ascribed a spiritual significance to the cloth were now willing to reject that significance. I said as much to Shimon, thinking he would dismiss my comment with a flick of his fingers, yet he absorbed my words silently, staring into empty air.

Finally, he turned and looked at me. "Two members of the Great Sanhedrin would agree with you," he said, his voice rough with anxiety. "Nicodemus and Joseph of Arimathea. They have been shunned by some of the others because they did not vote to condemn Yeshua, but now they believe the final atonement was accomplished when Yeshua died. Nicodemus has even suggested that the veil in the Temple ripped during Yeshua's execution because anyone can now approach God because, through Yeshua, our sins have been set aside."

The thought of approaching God without a priest as intermediary was so inconceivable I laughed, though such a notion was anything but humorous. Men had been whipped for suggesting less outlandish ideas, and my own brother had been executed.

"Will we . . . ?" I floundered for words. "Will we stop observing Yom Kippur?"

Shimon guffawed. "Never. Caiaphas would never change one jot or tittle of the ritual."

"But you said others—"

"Not many." A tide of uncertainty washed through his eyes, and I knew he could see similar anxious currents in mine. "Most of the Pharisees will ignore these omens. A few will make note of them, but do nothing. Others . . ." He shrugged. "I do not know what Nicodemus and Joseph will do."

"And you? You have spent so much time studying the Law, so what will you do?"

A tremor touched his smooth lips. "I would like to find your brothers," he said, taking my hand. "I have heard they are changed men, and I would like to learn why."

I squeezed his fingers, grateful to know my husband had not forgotten how to reason for himself.

## CHAPTER FORTY-SEVEN

# *Pheodora*

Four days after leaving Jerusalem, James and I arrived in Nazareth. We did not go immediately to the house but knocked instead on Bethel's door, where I knelt and drew my daughters into my arms, weeping until my tears dampened their hair.

"Why are you sad?" Judit asked, and I could only shake my head. One day I would tell her about selling myself into slavery, but this was not the day. One day I would tell my daughters that only because of HaShem and a Pharisee was I free to resume my life as their mother. If Yeshua had not urged Uriah to visit Chiram in prison, if Chiram had not told him my name, and if Uriah and Joseph were not brothers, I would not be home with my girls, a free woman about to reunite with my husband.

After thanking Bethel and Seth, James and I walked home with the girls, then threw open the shutters to air out the house. Bethel had taken good care of my chickens. Our rooster seemed to understand that I had been away, because he strutted proudly between me and his flock, flapping his wings and crowing as if to say *Look how I kept them safe!* I laughed at his cocky attitude and threw him a handful of seed.

I went upstairs and started dinner, deciding to serve eggs, cheese, and bread, all of which we had on hand, thanks to Bethel. As we ate, the girls asked about the goats, and I smiled.

"Simcha and Tikvah are living with a new family," I said. "A family who needed them more than we did."

We were clearing the dishes away when I heard a call from the courtyard gate. Judit went to the door, and a moment later I heard her joyous cry: "Abba!"

I flew to the doorway and ran down the steps. A group of travelers had stopped at our gate, and on their wagon lay a thin, weak man I would have known anywhere. I threw open the gate, climbed onto the wagon, and wrapped Chiram in an embrace, patting his back as I murmured a thousand welcomes.

He put his arm around me and pulled me close, a ragged whimper escaping his lips.

"You are home, love," I whispered. "HaShem has brought us together again."

⸻

My husband had come home, but he was not well. In addition to being thin and weak, the result of eating nothing but bread, water, and the occasional offering from visitors, he had tripped over another prisoner and broken his left arm. The jailer had tended him as best he could, but the arm had not healed properly. It now had a decided bend and often ached, but he was grateful to be alive. Other men who had been imprisoned for the same length of time had not survived.

My family and I remained in Nazareth for the month of Tishri, giving Chiram time to eat and rest. With the extra money from the slave market, I was able to buy good food and hire a physician to look after my husband. The physician offered to re-break Chiram's arm and set it properly, but Chiram decided that a shepherd could manage well enough with a bent arm.

The months of imprisonment had changed my husband. Though he was still the kind and loving man I married, an air of isolation clung to him. He did not want to talk about prison, so when he sat with us at meals, I encouraged the girls not to question him but to tell him about their adventures with Bethel and the livestock. Judit made her father smile by describing her marketplace negotiating techniques, and Eden showed him her writing, which was remarkably elegant for a girl of eight years.

Shiri seemed to enjoy sitting on his lap, her head tucked against his chest as she played with her doll or stroked a baby chick. During those encounters, Chiram would hold Shiri with his good arm, close his eyes, and sigh. They did not talk, but sometimes I think being together was exactly what each of them needed.

Jordan did not seem to know how to interact with her father, so she usually remained with me, content to serve him by cooking, washing his feet, and trimming his beard.

James returned to Jerusalem soon after Chiram arrived. The number of Yeshua's followers was increasing every day, he told me, and he wanted to help the disciples as they cared for the new believers. "So many people have questions," he told me, a faraway look in his eye as he turned toward the road, "but we have the Spirit to teach us how to answer them." He cut me a swift glance and smiled. "This is an exciting time. Sometimes I cannot believe how blessed we were to know Yeshua before He began His ministry."

"Sometimes I cannot believe that our brother—"

James lifted his hand. "I will never speak of him as my brother again. Though it pleased God to bring him into our family, He will forever be my Lord and Savior, nothing less." His eyes softened. "I am glad you have come to see Him that way, as well."

A smile tugged at my lips. "I was blind for too long. I still have questions about how Yeshua's teachings correspond with the Law—we have been so accustomed to doing things as the Torah teachers taught us . . ."

"Yeshua came to fulfill the Law," James said. "Let His Spirit be your teacher now. You will find the truth and, in time, more believers will appear in Galilee and Judea. You can worship and learn with them, and the Spirit will guide you into all truth."

I was not so confident that believers would appear in Nazareth. Most of the locals still had trouble believing that one of their own could be the Son of God.

But one afternoon I looked up and gasped at what I saw: Damaris and Shimon striding down the road, coming directly toward our house.

# CHAPTER FORTY-EIGHT

# Pheodora

My husband and I went to the courtyard gate as Damaris and Shimon approached. I tilted my head, wondering why they had not arrived in a litter, then noticed that Damaris wore simple leather sandals, not perfumed slippers. Shimon wore his Pharisee garb, but his attitude had shifted since the last time I saw him in the synagogue. The haughtiness had disappeared, as had the straight back and uplifted chin. Now he walked like a man who had fought a hard battle and was ready to relax on a comfortable couch.

Damaris's eyes lit when she saw me. "Pheodora." She quickened her pace and hugged me, and then gently embraced Chiram as well. "Brother. It is good to see you."

I bit back the words I wanted to say: *You could have seen him sooner, before he became emaciated and sustained an injury.*

Shimon greeted Chiram with an embrace, then nodded at

me. I slipped my arm through Chiram's as opposing emotions swirled in my heart.

I had wondered what I would do when and if this moment occurred. I had hoped we would be back in Bethlehem before we saw Damaris and Shimon again, and yet avoidance was the coward's way out. After meeting Yeshua, I knew I needed to forgive my older sister, not only for the anger I harbored against her on Chiram's behalf, but also for the way I had resented her throughout my lifetime. But before I could speak of such things, another matter stood between us, and Shimon should be the one to address it . . .

I waited, looking pointedly at my brother-in-law, and he did not disappoint. After a moment of awkward silence, he looked down at the ground, cleared his throat, and pressed his hands together. "I have been in Jerusalem," he said, getting directly to the point, "talking to Jude, Joses, Joseph of Arimathea, and Nicodemus."

I looked at my husband. Shimon had just named four believers.

"I have come here to confess that I have wronged you, brother." He lifted his head and looked fully into Chiram's eyes. "I do not know how I could have placed my own welfare above yours, but I did, and I now confess it. I cared more about rising in power and stature than I did about you, and for that I am truly sorry. I disobeyed the first and greatest commandment, to love the Lord my God with all my heart, soul, and mind. If I had truly loved God, I would have obeyed the second greatest *mitzvot*—to love my neighbor as myself. I should have delivered you from prison, no matter the cost."

I looked up at my husband, not knowing what I would see—the hard glint of anger in his eyes? A stubborn jut of the chin? But instead I saw tears and a quivering lip, so I took his hand, entwining my fingers with his.

"Chiram. Pheodora." Shimon looked at both of us, misery darkening his face. "Can you forgive me? *Will* you forgive me?"

I wish I could say I forgave him easily . . . that I smiled and promised all would be forgiven and forgotten. But Shimon's ambition and pride had not come without a price, and my innocent husband had paid it.

But as my jaw tensed, another voice came whispering among my sharp-edged thoughts—the voice of the woman at the well, the one who told Yeshua's story about the hard-hearted slave: *"It is not a story about money but about forgiveness. When he finished telling it, Yeshua said, 'So also my heavenly Father will do to you, unless each of you, from your heart, forgives his brother.'"*

Shimon was not the only one who needed to confess. I had a confession of my own to make, and if I expected to be forgiven, I would have to forgive the man before me.

Chiram reached out and took Shimon's hand, then enclosed it with his own. I watched, my eyes filling, because I knew the gesture caused him physical pain. "All is forgiven, brother," Chiram said, his voice husky.

"I forgive you, too," I said. I shifted my gaze to Damaris. "As for you, sister, I find I must ask your forgiveness, as well. Throughout my life, I have resented you, though I took pains not to show it. I envied your beauty, your personality, and the place you occupied in the family. Since coming to Nazareth, I have treated you badly. I would have your forgiveness, if you can find it in your heart to love me."

Beneath the expression of surprise on my sister's face, I saw a hint of motion and swirling, as though a concealed stream were trying to break through. Then she cried out and drew me into her arms, her tears mingling with mine as our cheeks met. "I am so sorry," she said, weeping. "I have never stopped trying to remake you in my image. But you are beyond me in so many ways . . ."

We cried until we laughed, and then Chiram and I opened the gate and welcomed them into our house—but not only *our* house, for it belonged to the entire family.

# *Pheodora*

We renewed our relationships that day and began new lives the next. Shimon, who would be a Pharisee for life, decided to remain in his chaburah and speak the truth about Yeshua and the new covenant for as long as he lived. With Damaris and their daughters, he moved to Jerusalem where he became a leader among the believers who met in Jerusalem and were soon known as followers of the Way.

My brothers—James, Jude, Joses, and Simeon—planned to carry the good news about Yeshua throughout the land. James remained in Jerusalem, where he became the leader of the believers who met regularly at the Temple. The others wanted to go wherever the Spirit led them, telling everyone, Jew and Gentile, that Yeshua's blood had atoned for sin, once and for all.

Our mother remained in Jerusalem as well, though occasionally she traveled with my brothers. When she was not traveling, she lived in Jerusalem with Miriam of Magdala. Chiram and I visited her whenever we went to Jerusalem, so my girls were able to know and love her as they grew up.

Chiram loved caring for animals, but soon realized his days as a shepherd were finished. His crooked arm would have made it difficult to defend the animals and carry them when necessary, so we hired a wagon to fetch our few belongings.

Our family home in Nazareth became a way station for followers of Yeshua. As they passed by the city, they stopped at our house not only for refreshment but to see the place where Yeshua had slept, worked, and teased his sisters. Seeing our home, humble as it was, reminded our guests that Yeshua was as much man as He was God, and that he had come to save everyone . . . the poor as well as the powerful.

As for me, I have realized the truth of Yeshua's words about the last being first. Though I had always considered myself the least of our large family, I have learned that anyone who is willing to love will always be precious to our Yeshua.

# *Author's Note*

Thank you for joining me in this second book of the JERUSALEM ROAD series. I have enjoyed vicariously living through Pheodora's and Yeshua's siblings and hope you have enjoyed the experience, as well.

I'm always asked how much of my historical novels is historical and how much imagined, so I hope the following will satisfy your curiosity.

**Q. I've never heard of Migdal-eder—was this a real place?**

A. Absolutely! Also known as the "watchtower of the flock," it was a tower built expressly for the shepherds to watch over the flocks of animals intended for Temple sacrifice. It was also the place where the angels appeared to the shepherds when they announced the birth of Christ.

During the Second Temple period, it was prohibited to keep flocks in the land of Israel because of the negative effects on agriculture. The region around Jerusalem, as far out as Migdal-eder, was an exception in order to accommodate the need for sacrificial animals at the Temple. Sheep or goats within this area (of one year or more) were assumed to be for Temple service. Possibly as early as the prophet Micah (4:8), Migdal-eder has been associated with messianic expectations; and [a Jewish teaching, or *targum*] Gen. 35:21 states that Migdal-eder is the place where the Messiah will make himself manifest. Jerome, a fourth-century resident of Bethlehem, affirms the traditional identification and function of Migdal-eder and locates it by a road about one mile from Bethlehem.

**Q. Did Jesus really have two sisters?**

A. At least two. Scripture does not give us their names, but from this verse we know he had brothers (who *are* named) and sisters, plural:

> Now when Yeshua had finished these parables, He left that place. Coming into His hometown, He began to teach them in their synagogue so that they were amazed. "Where did this fellow get this wisdom and these mighty works?" they said. "Isn't this the carpenter's son? Isn't His mother called Miriam, and His brothers Jacob [James] and Joseph [Joses] and Simon [Simeon] and Judah [Jude]? And His sisters, aren't they all with us? (Matt. 13:53–56).

**Q. Regarding the goats of Yom Kippur—did you describe the Temple ritual accurately, and was there a cloth that stopped turning red after Christ's death?**

A. For the most part, I did give a full description of the Temple ritual, although I abbreviated it. And yes, the traditional cloth did stop turning red in A.D. 30. The Jews wrote about it, not understanding what it meant. Here's one report about the situation:

The rabbinic legend called the "Legend of Azazel, the Scapegoat" is based on Isaiah 1:18, where Isaiah stated: though your sins be as scarlet, they shall be as white as snow, it became a custom to tie a red ribbon on the horn of the scapegoat before it was sent out into the wilderness. Miraculously, year after year, the red ribbon always turned white, symbolizing that God had forgiven the sins of Israel for that year. This same legend points out that the red ribbon stopped turning white forty years before the Temple was destroyed in A.D. 70. Subtracting forty years brings one to A.D. 30, which was the year of the Crucifixion. Although the rabbis did not make the connection between the two, the connection is obvious. As of A.D. 30, the reason God was no longer forgiving the sins of Israel by means of these two goats was because of Hebrews 10:18, which states that there is no longer sacrifice for sin because He has sent His son. God is no longer forgiving sin through animal blood. Individuals must now come to the Messiah Jesus in order to receive forgiveness of sins.[1]

**Q. I never realized the Pharisees were such an organized group.**

A. I didn't either. Alfred Edersheim gives a full description of their organization in his book *Sketches of Jewish Social Life in the Days of Christ*. In some ways, his description of the chaburah reminds me of what a young man or woman went through when they wanted to become a priest or a nun. There was a probationary period, vows to be taken in the first year, more vows to be taken in later years, a "uniform" to wear, and strict guidelines for behavior. Unlike nuns and

1. Fruchtenbaum, Arnold G. *The Messianic Bible Study Collection*. Vol. 181. Tustin, CA: Ariel Ministries, 1983.

priests, Pharisees could be married, yet other similarities are striking.

**Q. Where is this series going next?**

A. In the third book in the series, I'll be writing from the point of view of a woman who has been much discussed in the first two books but rarely seen. I hope you will come back for her story.

# References

Balz, Horst Robert, and Gerhard Schneider. *Exegetical Dictionary of the New Testament*, 1990.

Edersheim, Alfred. *The Life and Times of Jesus the Messiah*. Vol. 1. New York: Longmans, Green, and Co., 1896.

————. *The Temple: Its Ministry and Services as they were at the Time of Jesus Christ*. Arcadia Press, 2017.

————. *Sketches of Jewish Social Life in the Days of Christ*, revised and illustrated. Hunt Haven Press, 2019.

Feinberg-Vamosh, Miriam. *Daily Life at the Time of Jesus*. Concordia Publishing House, 2007.

Fruchtenbaum, Arnold G. *Messianic Christology: A Study of Old Testament Prophecy Concerning the First Coming of the Messiah*. Tustin, CA: Ariel Ministries, 1998.

————. *The Messianic Bible Study Collection*. Vol. 119. Tustin, CA: Ariel Ministries, 1983.

Gower, Ralph, and Fred Wight. *The New Manners and Customs of Bible Times*. Chicago: Moody Press, 1987.

Jamieson, Robert, A. R. Fausset, and David Brown. *Commentary Critical and Explanatory on the Whole Bible*. Vol. 1. Oak Harbor, WA: Logos Research Systems, Inc., 1997.

Liid, Dale C. "Eder, Tower of (Place)." Ed. David Noel Freedman. *The Anchor Yale Bible Dictionary*. 1992.

Manser, Martin H., Natasha B. Fleming et al. *I Never Knew That Was in the Bible!* electronic ed. Nashville, TN: Thomas Nelson Publishers, 2000.

Negev, Avraham. *The Archaeological Encyclopedia of the Holy Land*, 1990.

Pfeiffer, Charles F., and Howard Frederic Vos. *The Wycliffe Historical Geography of Bible Lands*. Chicago: Moody Press, 1996.

Phillips, John. *Exploring the World of the Jew*. Chicago: Moody Press, 1988.

Pope, Charles. "Workers and Trades in Jesus' Time." http://blog.adw.org/2017/03/workers-trades-jesus-time/, accessed 1/31/2019.

Radmacher, Earl D., Ronald Barclay Allen, and H. Wayne House. *The Nelson Study Bible: New King James Version*. Nashville, TN: Thomas Nelson Publishers, 1997.

Rooker, Mark F. *Leviticus*. Vol. 3A. Nashville, TN: Broadman & Holman Publishers, 2000.

Saldarini, Anthony J. "Pharisees." Ed. David Noel Freedman. *The Anchor Yale Bible Dictionary*, 1992.

Stern, David H. *Jewish New Testament: A Translation of the New Testament that Expresses Its Jewishness*. 1st ed. Jerusalem, Israel; Clarksville, MD, USA: Jewish New Testament Publications, 1989.

Strange, James F. "Sepphoris." Ed. David Noel Freedman. *The Anchor Yale Bible Dictionary*, 1992.

Thomas, Robert L., The Lockman Foundation. *New American Standard Exhaustive Concordance of the Bible: Updated Edition*. Anaheim: Foundation Publications, Inc., 1998.

Youngblood, Ronald F., F. F. Bruce, and R. K. Harrison, eds. *Nelson's New Illustrated Bible Dictionary*. Nashville, TN: Thomas Nelson Publishers, 1995.

**Angela Hunt** has published more than 180 books, with sales exceeding five million copies worldwide. She's the *New York Times* bestselling author of *The Tale of Three Trees*, *The Note*, and *The Nativity Story*. Angela's novels have won or been nominated for several prestigious industry awards, such as the RITA Award, the Christy Award, the ECPA Christian Book Award, and the HOLT Medallion Award. Romantic Times Book Club presented her with a Lifetime Achievement Award in 2006. She holds both a doctorate in Biblical Studies and a Th.D. degree. Angela and her husband live in Florida, along with their mastiffs and chickens. For a complete list of the author's books, visit angelahuntbooks.com.

# Sign Up for Angela's Newsletter

Keep up to date with Angela's news on book releases and events by signing up for her email list at angelahuntbooks.com.

# More from Angela Hunt

When a wedding guest tells Tasmin to have the servants fill the pitchers with water, she reluctantly obeys and is amazed when it turns into the finest wine ever tasted in Cana. But when her twin brother, Thomas, impulsively chooses to follow the Teacher from Nazareth, she decides to follow the group and do whatever she must to bring her brother home.

*Daughter of Cana*
JERUSALEM ROAD #1

# ◊ BETHANYHOUSE

# You May Also Like . . .

Two women occupy a place in Herod's court: the king's only sister, Salome, a resentful woman who has been told she is from an inferior race, and her lowly handmaid, Zara, who sees the hurt in those around her. Both women struggle to reach their goals and survive in Herod the Great's tumultuous court, where no one is trustworthy and no one is safe.

*King's Shadow* by Angela Hunt
THE SILENT YEARS
angelahuntbooks.com

Determined to return the Ark of the Covenant to Shiloh, Levite musician Ronen never expected that Eliora, the Philistine girl he rescued years ago, would be part of the family he's tasked to deceive. As his attempts to charm her lead them in unexpected directions, they question their loyalties when their beliefs about the Ark and themselves are shaken.

*To Dwell among Cedars* by Connilyn Cossette
THE COVENANT HOUSE #1
connilyncossette.com

In her wildest dreams, Esther could never have imagined that she would end up as queen of Persia. But when she's caught in the middle of palace politics and finds herself in an impossible position while relying on a fragile trust in a silent God, can she pit her wisdom against a vicious enemy and win?

*Star of Persia* by Jill Eileen Smith
jilleileensmith.com

BETHANYHOUSE